Alex Gray is the *Sunday Times*-bestselling author of the Detective William Lorimer series. Born and raised in Glasgow, she has been awarded the Scottish Association of Writers' Constable and Pitlochry trophies for her crime writing and is the co-founder of the international Bloody Scotland Crime Writing Festival. To find exclusive articles, reviews and the latest news about Alex Gray and the DSI Lorimer series, visit www.alex-gray.com or follow Alex on Twitter @alexincrimeland.

Alex Gray

QUESTIONS FOR A DEAD MAN

SPHERE

SPHERE

First published in Great Britain in 2023 by Sphere

1 3 5 7 9 10 8 6 4 2

A CIP catalogue record for this book is available from the British Library.

ISBN 978-0-7515-8330-4

Typeset in Caslon by M Rules
Printed and bound in Great Britain by Clays Ltd, Elcograf S.p.A.

MIX
Paper from
responsible sources
FSC® C104740

Papers used by Sphere are from well-managed forests
and other responsible sources.

Sphere
An imprint of
Little, Brown Book Group
Carmelite House
50 Victoria Embankment
London
EC4Y 0DZ

An Hachette UK Company
www.hachette.co.uk

www.littlebrown.co.uk

This novel is dedicated to
all the officers of Police
Scotland, past and present.

Bi glic, bi glic (Gaelic)
Be wise, be wise

'Consistency is all I ask!'
'Give us this day our daily mask.'

> *Rosencrantz and Guildenstern are Dead*
> Tom Stoppard

When devils will the blackest sins put on,
They do suggest at first with
heavenly shows

> *Othello Act 2 Scene 3*
> Shakespeare

PROLOGUE

The dark-skinned man leaned forward and picked up the salt cellar then, without looking at his companion, sprinkled it liberally over the food on his plate. If he had been observed by other diners, which was not the case on this particular occasion (the dining room being furnished with a single table set for two), they might have noted him for his finely tailored suit and watered silk tie in shades of pink, matching handkerchief peeping modestly from his breast pocket. His face might also have given them pause for thought, the hooded eyes glancing up from time to time as if to capture an errant moment in another's life. It was a face not easily forgotten: downturned lips that looked incapable of smiling, firm jawline that hinted at more than mere strength; there was something dangerous about this man and he was not afraid who saw it.

His dining companion was a person who seemed far less significant by comparison, a man one might easily miss in a crowd. His tweed jacket had seen better days, though was admittedly clean and without any visible blemish, the tie, if he was wearing one, unseen beneath the linen napkin tucked into his shirt collar.

'We were so pleased to see you here again,' the tweed man said, his knife and fork momentarily held above his dinner plate. 'It has been good to ...' he paused as if searching for the right phrase, 'to understand one another's preferences.' He gave a slight laugh and looked at the man across the table whose jaws continued working, eyes never leaving the food on his plate.

Was that a tiny grunt in reply? Perhaps, but what did it signify; agreement with the words spoken by his dining companion?

For a few minutes neither man spoke, the business of eating taking precedence over conversation. It was only when the man with the pink tie laid down his knife and fork, askew on his plate (unlike the tweed man who had lined up his own with six o'clock precision) that he wiped his mouth with the napkin and began to speak.

'It was worth my while coming here, if that is what you mean,' he began. 'What you have outlined, I agree that it involves less risk, but it does seem to have given your people a lot to do.'

The tweed man smiled. 'Ah, just leave that to me. Yes, it would seem that simply eliminating a person is the easiest way to solve our particular problem. But sometimes it is better to look at the bigger picture.'

'Meaning?' The man with the pink tie narrowed his eyes as if he sensed some criticism in the fellow's words.

'Meaning you can only kill a man once.'

'But you said—'

'Ah, you were paying attention. Good. I like that. Yes,' the tweed man mused. 'Think of it like a game of chess. I hear you are rather good at that, incidentally,' he added. 'There is often a necessity to put some of our pieces back into the box, keep others for future moves. Sometimes sacrifices must be made in order to win the game.'

The man with the pink tie nodded, his lips parting in what might have passed for a grin but was more of a fleeting show of very white teeth.

'You see, to achieve our objective,' the tweed man continued, 'we must take pains to understand our opponents. See which of them is expendable, which can still be used to further our objectives.' He showed his teeth in a smile that did not reach his eyes. 'Of course, there are a few whose elimination would be desired sooner rather than later.'

The man with the pink tie sat back, setting his hands on the damask tablecloth, staring at his host.

There was silence between them for a moment, then, as if some unspoken agreement had been reached, his companion leaned across the table.

'Dessert?' he asked.

CHAPTER ONE

Sunlight filtered through the trees reminding him of early mornings out in the bush, impala grouped around the waterholes, tails swishing as the flies began to bite. African dawns could be colder than some mornings in Scotland before the sun had burned off the early mist. But today there were no watchful creatures ready to make a dash for cover, only rows of uniformed officers, with friends and family somewhere behind them.

There was a momentary hush in the parade ground, his fellow cadets standing motionless, arms folded behind backs, waiting as the top brass began to settle on the platform. There would be occasions in the future when they might have to endure this sort of thing, one of the lecturers had advised: standing firm against a tide of rabble-rousers or quietly guarding different individuals during important events, full kit weighing them down in all sorts of weather. From his current position Daniel caught sight of one familiar figure as she took her seat. He had met the chief constable during training: Caroline Flint was a no-nonsense sort, her firm handshake and concentrated look impressing him as much as the fact that she was a good friend of Lorimer's. She was there now, in the centre of the row, talking to a tall officer Daniel had never seen before today. One of the divisional commanders, perhaps, from the braid on his uniform cap?

A figure with a red sash across his uniform and matching cap band strode purposefully in front of them. A command to 'quick march' then the band struck up. It was a relief to begin their well-practised routine after standing so still. Once this part of the parade was over, some officers would be called forward to receive one of the shining cups displayed on a table draped in dark blue, emblazoned with Police Scotland's insignia, Daniel amongst them, receiving an award for top marks in First Aid. *It isn't fair*, one of the other cadets had complained. *You've been a cop before.* Daniel had shrugged that off with a smile and agreed that it ought to have been given to someone else but the superintendent had been adamant that PC Kohi deserved the recognition. After all, he wasn't the only trainee to have had experience in a different country, the senior officer had pointed out.

Daniel's thoughts flitted back to the previous time he had completed a training course, standing in a dusty parade ground in the sweltering noonday heat, his new uniform already damp with sweat. If he had known then what the future held ... He swallowed hard, banishing the vision of crackling flames and choking smoke.

A voice from the platform called him back to the present, the chief constable addressing them. He listened as first she thanked them for taking on the responsibility of serving their communities then continued to emphasise the importance of the values that had been instilled into them over the past few weeks. Daniel concentrated on her words, determined to lock them into his mind.

'A training, in my view, second to none ... maintain those standards when you go back into the community ... we are there to serve ... you will have multiple challenges ahead ... you are the custodians of this service ...'

His friends would be there, watching, listening to these words, and Daniel made a silent promise not to let them down. Later there would be goodbyes as the new officers, on the brink of their careers, made their way from this peaceful place with its swathes of green, far from the bustle of Scotland's largest city. He moved into line as the first name was called out, waiting his turn to march forward.

Lorimer felt his arm being squeezed as he looked out of the doorway at the scene beyond. He glanced down at the older woman and smiled as Netta nodded towards the crowded parade ground where the latest class of police cadets was assembled. They had watched the display of marching, listening to the piper to whose tune they had kept perfect time and heard the chief constable's wise words, but now all were still, eyes fixed on those about to go up to the rostrum to receive a special prize and commendation.

It was a perfect day, the sweet smell of newly mown grass, the cry of gulls as they swooped across pale blue skies and ripples of applause as each prize-winning officer held their trophy aloft. He could see their friend in the distance, waiting to be called forward, his dark face momentarily obscured by a shadow from the ancient birch trees that framed the grounds. How did Daniel Kohi feel right now? Proud of what he had achieved since his arrival in Scotland so many months ago? Or sad because none of his family could be here in Tulliallan to witness his success? *We're Daniel's family now*, Maggie had told Lorimer when he had expressed the same sentiment at breakfast that morning. And perhaps PC Daniel Kohi would find a new family within Police Scotland.

'Oh, if only his mum was here ...' Netta whispered, wiping away a tear with a lace-trimmed handkerchief that Lorimer guessed was kept for special occasions like weddings, funerals ... and the passing-out parade of a man she'd come to love like her own son.

'You can tell her all about it in your next letter,' Lorimer reassured her quietly. Back in Zimbabwe, Janette Kohi kept up the pretence that her son had perished in the house fire that had killed her grandson and daughter-in-law, fearful of any reprisals that might come from the murderous people who had driven Daniel away. She wrote regularly to her 'penfriend' Netta Gordon, knowing that all her news would be read by her dear son.

'Aye,' Netta replied, her eyes following a woman's progress as she marched back into formation, disappearing behind other lines of cadets. 'No' sure how often I'll get tae speak tae Daniel now, mind. A' thae long shifts, night times an' all.'

Lorimer nodded silently. Daniel Kohi was the old woman's neighbour in one of the city's high flats, her warm-hearted welcome to the refugee something that Lorimer knew Daniel greatly valued. Netta would have felt the loss keenly if Police Constable Kohi had been allocated to a division far from the city. But Govanhill near the national football stadium was where he would be posted, a short drive from his current home in the heart of the city.

Netta's grip tightened on his arm as Daniel strode up to receive his award. Then, as he turned and held it up to shouts of acclamation, Lorimer felt a shiver down his spine. There he was, a former inspector of the Zimbabwean Police, now a brand-new recruit in his adopted country. More than a friend, now; a fellow officer, comrade in arms, though it was unlikely that their professional paths would often cross.

As the head of the Major Incident Team based in Govan, Lorimer and his select team of officers could be required to attend serious crimes in any part of the country. Perhaps one day, if he delayed his retirement a few years, he might see Daniel join CID and even his own officers in the MIT. Lorimer shook his head and gave a rueful smile at the notion. Today was for celebrating, seeing his friend commit to a new life within Police Scotland, forging new friendships and perhaps finding a purpose that would help lessen the pain of what he had lost.

A piercing cry made him look up to see a flash of black and white. A pair of oystercatchers, the symbol of Tulliallan Police College. What did they see from their aerial vantage point? Lorimer mused. A mass of bodies, dark against the grey tarmac, then shades of green as they headed across the leafy grounds towards the river.

As the detective watched their flight, he could not have imagined the events that lay ahead, nor the twists and turns that were to blend his fate with that of PC Daniel Kohi.

CHAPTER TWO

It was the sort of night that Netta would have called *dreich*, the persistent drizzle and chill something that Daniel Kohi had come to associate with Scotland's west coast. Perhaps it was the weather, the fact that he was tired and hungry, no time for food during that late shift, so a takeaway had been an easy option. They'd been warned by their PE instructors up at Tulliallan to avoid too much fast food, reminded that lack of fitness came at a cost. Chasing criminals with fourteen pounds of kit strapped to your body was challenging enough without piling on any excess weight. Still, it was just this once, he told himself, the smell of vinegar from his pack of fish and chips hard to resist. And it was a comfort to have instant hot food straight after coming off his shift at Aikenhead Road police headquarters.

Daniel Kohi gave a sigh as he stepped out of the warmth of the chippie, fingers eagerly unwrapping his supper, paying little heed to the puddles beneath his thick-soled boots, the taste of hot, vinegary chips ridding him of any guilty feelings. He walked steadily from the brightness of the chip shop, stopping for a moment to savour the mouthwatering batter on a piece of fish before turning into a narrow lane that was a shortcut back to his car.

Then his attention was caught by something that made the hairs on his neck stand on end.

It was a familiar sound, that cry in the dark, causing Daniel to peer through the gloom and slanting drizzle, fists unconsciously crumpling the wrapper. He blinked once, wondering if it had been a cat. But no, that wasn't what he had heard, Daniel decided, his lips tightening.

Unless he was very much mistaken, that was a human cry.

Daniel's torch soon played along the cobbled lane, flicking this way and that as he stepped carefully now to avoid the puddles.

The place smelled bad, putrid food mingling with the stink of piss, making him wrinkle his nose in disgust. This hidden back lane was the rotten side of Glasgow, part of what he'd signed up for, Daniel reminded himself.

And then, under the torch beam, he saw what looked like a bundle of clothing tucked between two industrial-sized bins.

The noise began again, thin, mewling cries that tore at Daniel Kohi's heart. He'd heard such sounds night after night, so long ago . . .

Daniel was there in moments, fish supper cast aside as he crouched down, hands out to pull back the thick blanket.

A pair of tiny eyes squinted under the glare of the

12

torch and the infant's mouth opened, wails redoubling in protest.

'Oh, no!' he whispered, gazing down at what he had found.

The woman was lying on her back, one arm embracing the baby, the other tethered to a tight band, needle still fixed in place.

She might have been sleeping, her pale face serene, but as he knelt to touch her neck there was no pulse, Daniel's fingers meeting skin that was already cold.

His first instinct was to pull the dead woman's arm away and lift the screaming infant. The baby was wrapped in a blue hand-knitted shawl, its tiny fists raised in protest as raindrops splashed against his face. Daniel tucked in the edges of the shawl, cradling the infant in the crook of his left arm as he had done with his own son . . .

He swallowed down that sudden memory and stood up, ready to call it in, but for a moment Daniel Kohi could only stare at the body lying on the ground like so much discarded rubbish. This would be imprinted on his mind, something that was a curse at times, but useful to be taken out and examined once the initial shock had worn off.

He had a vision of Chipo cradling their baby, making the sort of soothing noises that came naturally to women. Then he became aware of his own voice shushing the tiny baby, feeling his body rocking back and forth.

'You'll be all right, little one,' he promised, watching the eyelids close and hearing the shuddering sigh that signified sleep. With his free hand, Daniel reached for his mobile, regretting that this discovery had been made so soon after he had packed his kit inside the lockers, his radio silent until the next day's shift. Now it was as if he was a mere civilian again, fingers tapping out 999.

He leaned against the rough stone of the wall, the slight overhang of the tenement roof their only shelter, and watched the entrance to the lane. Soon they'd be joined by the night shift, other officers taking over, dealing with whatever had happened here.

'Police and an ambulance, please,' Daniel told the operator, then gave brief but succinct details of the location and what he had found. It would not be long, he knew, till members of the emergency services turned up. Till then, he would look around to see what else he could see that might give a clue as to what had happened in this cold and dirty place, committing it to his memory.

Still clutching the baby, Daniel bent down gingerly to pick up his unfinished fish supper and tossed it into the nearest bin, then cursed himself as the lid's hollow clang reverberated in the damp air. The child gave a start, but thankfully did not awaken.

From the light of his torch, he could see a gentle mist slanting downwards, the rain easing now as he turned his attention back to the woman on the ground. For a moment it seemed as though tears glistened on her pale cheeks. Yet in all probability she had died in a moment of bliss, the drug filling her veins before casting her into oblivion. Once more he bent slowly forward, careful not to disturb the child tucked in his arm.

Heaving a sigh, he pulled the damp wool back over the dead woman's face, questions already in his mind.

How had she come to be in this filthy lane?

And whose hands had first covered mother and child with that blanket?

CHAPTER THREE

Maggie Lorimer heard the faint beat from the alarm on her husband's side of the bed and rolled closer, relishing the last few moments snuggled against his warm body.

She felt him stretch away then the sound stopped as he silenced the clock before turning back to her side. They would lie there slumbering, their dreams overshadowed by thoughts of the day ahead, until he sat up and kissed her cheek, a habitual gesture before throwing off the duvet and heading to the shower. Lorimer was always up first, his need to be at work early allowing Maggie a few minutes extra before padding downstairs.

She heaved a sigh as the sound of water cascaded from the bathroom next door, wriggling her toes in the cosy space he'd left. They'd breakfast together then Maggie would kiss him goodbye on the doorstep before heading back up to prepare for her own day. It wasn't always like this, however. *Crime never takes a holiday*, he'd once joked and that was true; long hours were common, particularly at the start of a difficult case, something that his wife had come to accept. Recently, life had been almost normal, Lorimer's days more regular, few major crimes intruding in their lives. *It's only a matter of time*, a small voice hinted in a cynical tone.

Tossing the cover aside, she stepped out of bed and grabbed her fleecy housecoat then drew open the curtains, shivering for a moment. Outside, a low mist had blotted out the end of their avenue, trees vague shadows behind a grey veil. The days were growing chillier now, the nights, too, autumn settling in around them, the first fallen leaves from their maple tree scattered in a blood-red trail across their lawn.

'Season of mists and mellow fruitfulness,' Maggie whispered, quoting the ode that she was going to teach a class this morning. Appropriate, she thought with a grin as she hastily tidied their bed then made her way downstairs.

Chancer, their old ginger cat, looked up at her from his warm bed by the radiator. Maggie glanced across the kitchen at his food dishes to see that yes, Bill had fed their pet, but only half of the food had been eaten. She gave a small frown. He was getting on in years, his days of wandering further than their garden and reappearing with some small rodent in his mouth long gone. The vet had given Chancer a clean bill of health on his last visit. Though nobody knew his true age for sure, the cat having been a stray who'd adopted them many years ago, the vet judged him to be around sixteen. Maggie sighed as she looked back at Chancer now curled asleep. It was a good age and she'd heard of other cats surviving into their twenties. Somehow the house would not be the same without the presence of their feline friend, the way he greeted her whenever she came home from work, his presence on her lap in the evenings, purrs reverberating through his furry body.

Everything changed, Maggie told herself briskly, thinking about their friend, Daniel, whose whole life had been turned upside down by the attack on his family back in Zimbabwe. He was making a new start here in Glasgow, though, his courage undaunted by the past. And what of their own future? Lately it had been more difficult to find time to write her children's books while holding down a full-time teaching job and her agent had suggested more than once the idea of cutting back her hours at school. Their mortgage had been paid off and each of them had good salaries with pensions attached. Perhaps it was time for a change in her own life, she thought, looking around the open-plan room that served as kitchen, dining room and study, her eyes falling once more on the marmalade-coloured cat. He'd welcome her company, Maggie thought, smiling, as she left the room and headed for the front door. And she'd be able to devote more time to her beloved garden.

As the garage door swung open, Maggie felt a sense of relief at a decision made. She would see the head teacher today and talk it through with him. Maybe suggest that after Christmas she could drop down to three days a week, giving an opportunity for a younger teacher to step in, someone who might be looking for a way of juggling work and family.

Detective Superintendent Lorimer flicked through a sheaf of crime reports, jaw hardening at the latest drug death in the city. A statistic. No name or identity, simply a life snuffed out. He glanced again, seeing that it had been over in Govanhill where Daniel was now a police officer beginning his two years' probation in the service. Scotland had an appalling record for the number of drug-related deaths, this latest adding to its tragic toll.

It wasn't as if they had been standing still, doing nothing, Lorimer told himself, his mouth a thin bitter line. The drugs strategy that had been launched at the start of 2020 had borne some fruit, a sizeable number of addicts able to receive help. To Greater Glasgow's shame, they'd had the highest average number of drug-related deaths in the country for the previous five years and, despite their best efforts, drugs were still pouring into the city. Those who enriched themselves at the expense of others had no conscience, Lorimer thought grimly, whether here or overseas. Much of this vicious cycle began with the farmers in Afghanistan whose poppy crops were harvested for drugs that could produce life-saving medicine but also be ensnared by others to feed an addiction that spread its menacing tentacles across the globe.

But the deaths were only one part of the story, babies born addicted to junkie mothers and left to the mercies of their always overstretched National Health Service. Neonatal abstinence syndrome was worst in NHS Lothian, figures three times higher than those in Greater Glasgow and Clyde. Did this mean more female addicts on that side of the country? Whatever way you looked at it, Scotland was suffering a national drugs emergency and Lorimer was well aware of the number of officers specifically deployed to deal with it.

He'd read his fellow superintendent's most recent report, nodding in agreement at the words, *Police Scotland can't completely solve the problem around drug-related deaths but it's about looking at what we can do to reduce stigma and understanding the trauma that is often behind addiction.* Every officer in the country had a duty of care to their fellow citizens, no matter what their situation. That was what was dinned into every recruit from the word go, Lorimer knew, thinking for a fleeting moment about that parade ground up in Tulliallan and his friend, Daniel. This particular report detailed a partnership between Police Scotland and Glasgow's Health and Social Care. But supporting addicts was not the only strategy, oh, no. Those who peddled drugs had to be weeded out, not just the dealers who ran around the housing schemes but also, crucially, those at the top of the chain and their suppliers overseas.

So many agencies were involved in a single operation, Lorimer knew; Customs and Excise officers, the current strategy group that included social work and NHS, as well as specialist agencies within Police Scotland. There was intelligence suggesting that a new conduit was finding a way to smuggle large quantities of hard drugs into Scotland, possibly via Ireland, rumours of money laundering linked to international drugs shipments from an organisation in South America. One recent haul on the west coast was 'just the tip of the iceberg', the Customs and Excise officer handling the case had declared to the press.

But it was neither the death of a young mother over on Glasgow's Southside nor the capture of a fishing vessel off the island of Jura that was about to trigger the involvement of the Major Incident Team.

The phone rang, breaking into his thoughts.

'Lorimer.'

The familiar voice of the chief constable came over loud and clear, her statement making the detective superintendent sit up a little straighter.

'Robert Truesdale has gone missing.'

'Truesdale? Has this come from the First Minister?' Lorimer asked, his thoughts immediately focusing on the Member of the Scottish Parliament who had been a thorn in the flesh of several government ministers. 'Does he think his MSP has come to harm?'

'You know it's been going on for months, Lorimer,' Caroline Flint continued. 'Truesdale was bombarded with death threats on social media, the coward's way of attacking anyone they regarded as fair game.'

'I knew it had been reported to police here in Govan in the beginning, when it was just the social media messages. Then it escalated into notes put through his letter box at home and at his constituency office,' Lorimer replied. 'Not a major incident; something that was being dealt with downstairs.' He was recalling a conversation with one of the CID officers who operated out of the same building that housed his own Major Incident Team.

'Don't forget the bricks thrown at his car. Unfortunately, very little CCTV footage was obtained and what the local police did have was too blurred to be of any use.'

Lorimer listened as the chief constable reminded him of Truesdale's campaign to legalise hard drugs, demanding change in the way the Scottish government approached the crisis, arguing that cutting out the illegal practices would eventually rid the country of the drug barons' stranglehold on the supply of dangerous drugs. Not everyone agreed, and it had even been suggested that the dealers themselves were behind many of the attacks on the MSP.

'That's a possibility, of course,' Lorimer conceded. 'How can the government be sure that he is missing?'

'He hasn't answered his mobile in days. Landline at his home address in Glasgow appears to have been disconnected and there is nobody at home. He was meant to be at Holyrood yesterday at an important meeting to discuss the new drugs bill.'

'And he didn't turn up?' Lorimer guessed.

'That set alarm bells ringing,' Flint agreed. 'Someone was dispatched to his address but there was no sign of life.'

'Neighbours?'

'There were none at home when the person they sent knocked on several doors.'

'Time to break in, I suppose. But isn't that a job for the cops downstairs?'

There was a moment's silence before the chief constable answered.

'It's more complicated than that,' she said slowly. 'I don't know why and the FM point-blank refuses to elaborate, but they want it kept as quiet as possible. No uniforms. No smashed glass.' She hesitated for a moment. 'Maybe something for one of your undercover people?'

Lorimer nodded to himself. DS Molly Newton had been an undercover police officer prior to joining his elite squad of officers and he was certain that she was the very person Caroline Flint had in mind.

'"Find him and find him quickly,"' Caroline Flint snapped. 'That's what the First Minister demanded of me less than fifteen minutes ago. I assured him that our Major Incident Team would be on top of it straight away,' she added, in a tone that brooked no argument.

'And we will,' he promised her, amazed how swiftly the FM's message had been passed down to Lorimer's office in Govan. Wasn't this a job for Special Branch? he wondered. Or was there some other reason behind the need to place this in the hands of the police? 'Complicated', the chief constable had said, and that could mean a lot of different things but hinted at secrecy as well as discretion.

'Leave it with me, ma'am,' Lorimer said. 'I'll begin with officers searching his home and constituency office.'

'Don't forget his office at Holyrood with the small private pod,' Flint reminded him. 'Never know what you might find there.'

Suddenly memories flooded back into Lorimer's mind from a case he'd been involved in a decade before when an MSP, Edward Pattison, had been found murdered. He'd spent considerable time travelling through to Edinburgh that winter, meetings with the previous First Minister and several of her colleagues giving him a glimpse behind the scenes of Holyrood. Unlike Pattison, Truesdale was a single man, said to have been devoted to his late mother and now living on his own in the big family house. No doubt his energies had been deployed in his mission to change the current legislation on class A drugs.

'We'll get the usual checks made to see if his passport's been used. See if he's still somewhere in the country,' Lorimer assured her.

'And it's imperative that the press does not get hold of the news,' Flint said crisply. 'Goodness knows what speculation might arise from *that*.'

CHAPTER FOUR

'He's moved,' Karen Douglas told the tall blonde who stood outside the large, detached villa on Glasgow's Southside. 'Didn't you know?' Her mouth twitched in a smile as if to mock the woman's questions about Robert Truesdale. 'Vans came last week and took all his furniture away.' She shrugged and looked harder at the smartly dressed lady with the silk scarf almost hiding a set of pearls. Her accent was strange, maybe Canadian? Had Robert actually got a lady friend after all these years? Naughty old dog, she thought, looking the woman up and down. 'No "for sale" notice so I expect he's done a private deal with someone. Can't blame him after all the stuff that's been going on.'

The blonde looked at Karen and gave an exaggerated sigh.

'Oh, dear. I guess it was a long shot. Robbie told me to call in when I came over. Tried his cell phone but couldn't get a signal. Do you happen to have a forwarding address for him, Mrs . . .?'

'It's Ms. Ms Douglas. Karen Douglas,' she added. 'And,

no, I don't. What are you wanting to see Robert about anyway?' she asked.

The stranger gave a girlish giggle. 'Oh, just catching up, you know how it is with old friends,' she said coyly. 'Did you see him the day he left? Was he looking well? Oh, gee, I wish I'd gotten a much earlier flight after all!'

Karen Douglas raised her eyebrows. An old flame come to see Robert. *Robbie*, she'd called him! That sounded as if they'd been more than just friends, somehow.

'He wasn't there when everything was moved out, as a matter of fact,' Karen said. 'Mr Truesdale is a very busy man, you know.' She tossed her head at this rather attractive woman who had appeared out of the blue. 'He even asked me to do a couple of favours for him just before he left.'

'Oh, that was kind of you,' the blonde gushed.

'Yes, just the sorts of things a good neighbour does, you know,' Karen added tartly. She wasn't going to give this stranger the satisfaction of knowing what her relationship had been with Robert, despite that curious expression on her pretty face.

'Oh well.' Her unexpected visitor turned to go, tucking the scarf into the collar of her camel coat. 'I guess I'll just text him. Let him know I came.' She stepped a little closer to Karen. 'Wanted this to be a surprise,' she smirked. 'Know what I mean?'

Karen straightened up. Yes, she did know what this person meant but was not at all sure that Robert Truesdale would have welcomed a long-lost lady friend after the amount of anguish he had suffered.

'Oh.' The woman turned back suddenly as though she

had remembered something. 'I don't suppose you remember the name of his removal company? They might be able to give me Robbie's new address.'

Karen frowned. She remembered all right, but a sudden thought had crossed her mind. What if this person was a nosy newspaper reporter trying to cause trouble for her former neighbour? She shook her head firmly then retreated back indoors, cross with herself for having been gulled into saying so much already.

Karen Douglas watched as the woman's hired car disappeared around a corner of the avenue. She'd stood at this same window only a few days before, noting the old, heavy furniture being lifted out of the house next door. She couldn't blame him, really. It had been hard enough keeping the old woman at home when everyone knew she'd be better off in care, but Robert had devoted himself to his mother, right to the end. Funny that he hadn't sold up straight after she'd died and moved to a smaller, more manageable place, Karen thought, but had waited till now. After all, with no partner or kids, why keep on the expense of that big house? MSPs didn't get paid *that* much, after all.

He'd not left a forwarding address, she'd told the blonde and now that she came to think of it, Karen realised that was probably quite deliberate. Robert wanted to rid himself of all the horrible people who had targeted his house and his car. Keeping a low profile during his house move was quite understandable under the circumstances. She bit her lip, still wondering about the mysterious blonde.

Tonight was bridge night, Karen reminded herself, and

this incident in an otherwise uneventful day would be a nice little snippet of news to share with the three neighbours who would call in at eight o'clock. *Sly old Robert*, she'd remark to them. *Where do you think he's gone?*

There had been sufficient time for the dark-clothed man to slip in the back door, unnoticed by Truesdale's neighbour, kept talking by DS Newton, the former undercover cop. What the neighbour had claimed was correct, however. The place looked totally empty, hardly a thing left behind. Only the window blinds remained, shutting out the daylight and convenient for his own secretive purpose. He reached up from where he sat astride the banister in the upper hallway and tugged at the thick cord dangling from the attic hatch. Slowly the door opened to reveal a set of metal steps. In one cat-like leap he grabbed the nearest tread and lowered them down.

Switching on his torch, the man saw that the attic was windowless, the roof space floored in dark timbers. A sweep of the area confirmed his worst fears. Empty. Not a single box left over from the man's hasty departure.

Sitting on his haunches, he thought hard about the MSP and where he might have gone. Wherever it was, it was clear that he had planned his disappearance carefully.

'There is only so much we can do with the resources we have,' the chief constable insisted.

'We've given you everything you asked for.'

'Saving a couple of billion pounds over the next three years is simply impossible,' she argued. 'Yes, we have the number of officers we were promised, but it's still not nearly enough, in my opinion.'

Chief Constable Caroline Flint glared at the man across the desk from her. A government official, formally in charge of the public purse, though with no real background in finance, Jerry McVeigh was a man whose rotund figure and chubby face made him appear much older than his thirty-one years. He had recently succeeded the former Scottish finance minister, a woman who had toiled in the role for so many years that she'd been almost gleeful about handing in her resignation. Caroline did not attempt to stifle her sigh as she looked up from the papers in front of her.

'Has the First Minister any notion of what is being asked here?' she demanded, tapping the folder with an insistent finger.

'Oh, indeed,' McVeigh replied. 'I'm sure—'

'The human face of the organisation . . .' Flint read off the page. 'Human, that's what we all are, young man, and if the First Minister saw fit to attend a few more of my meetings then perhaps we wouldn't be sitting here discussing more cuts to the service!'

'Pressure of time, you know.' McVeigh gave a half-hearted smile. 'So much to oversee, the new bill about legalising drugs . . .'

Caroline snorted. While her officers had been employed in a drugs raid on the north side of Scotland's largest city, the First Minister had been entertaining the good and the great from the film world, pictures in this morning's papers showing him glad-handing a famous star as she arrived at Edinburgh's Usher Hall. He had plenty of time for stuff like that, she told herself, furiously. Still, if drugs were to be legalised, as had been advocated by the missing MSP, that would certainly free up more time for officers to be deployed on other cases.

At least she'd been appointed under his predecessor, Caroline thought. The present incumbent at Holyrood was still finding it hard to acknowledge that CC Flint was the first woman chief constable to Police Scotland. And English, to boot.

It was not an easy ride, she'd told Lorimer at their last informal meeting, police were expected to do the job of social workers, and he'd nodded, before saying that was what his own wife often claimed about teachers. The public's expectations were understandable. But why could this silly man sitting in her office not see that more money needed to be given to social services and the NHS as well as to the police? That was his job, after all, not hers.

Later, after McVeigh had gobbled three of her Marks and Spencer chocolate biscuits with his coffee and made his farewell, Caroline sat looking over the grounds of Tulliallan, the sound of a motor mower in the distance. It had just been a few weeks since the last passing-out parade when she'd shaken Daniel Kohi's hand and wished him well. For a moment she had looked into those dark eyes and smiled, acknowledging with satisfaction that a man with his special abilities was now under her command. They had met briefly under strange circumstances, the Zimbabwean refugee helping to foil a terrorist plot in his adopted city. Lorimer had told her the man's story, of course, and she had felt a sense of pride that day, seeing him brave enough to begin all over again, a police inspector who'd been hounded out of his own country by forces that were meant to have had a duty of care.

Caroline sighed quietly. That was a phrase on the lips of all the best officers. A duty of care. For everyone, from finding wayward MSPs to giving a helping hand to the homeless addict on the street. But caring for them all came at a price and now she'd been tasked with finding just how to pay it.

CHAPTER FIVE

Other hands had taken the squalling child from Daniel eventually, first to hospital for a medical check and then later he'd go to some place of safety where his destiny would be decided. And that, Daniel admitted to himself, was something he ached to find out. Were there grandparents ready to care for the little mite? Siblings of the dead woman, perhaps? Even a father? He might ask his tutor, Police Sergeant Jacob Alexander, what he could find out. Alexander was a family type, his two kids at secondary school, nearing his thirty years' service as an officer in Govanhill.

Daniel drove his car across the city, trying to focus on the directions but finding it hard to banish that image of the woman lying under that sopping blanket, her face robbed of any colour under the light from his torch.

'Nearly there,' he murmured, stopping at a set of traffic lights, turning his mind to the day ahead.

*

'What happened to the baby?'

'Still in the sick kids',' Sergeant Alexander answered. 'Don't know the details but social services will have care of him until we can trace any relatives.'

'Do we know who she was?'

Alexander shook his head. 'Nothing on her person to identify her but maybe the PM will give us a clue.' The police sergeant threw Daniel a quizzical look.

'It's taking place during your shift,' he began. 'Wondered if it was too soon for you to pay your first visit to our mortuary?'

Daniel looked back steadily at his tutor. It would not do to show the emotions that accompanied that sudden sick feeling in his stomach. The last time he had been in any mortuary had been back in Zimbabwe ... flashes of a mutilated body came flooding back ...

'It has to happen sometime, Kohi, and, since you found the body, the SIO who's handling the case suggested this afternoon. How about it?'

Daniel affected a nonchalant shrug. 'Not a problem,' he replied.

Alexander threw him a sly smile. 'Doubt if it's the first time for you, eh?' he asked. 'Seeing how you were a police inspector in Zimbabwe a few years back?'

Glasgow City Mortuary lay between the High Court of Judiciary and Glasgow Green, juxtaposed between the confines of law and order and acres of freedom to breathe a fresher sort of air. *The dear green place*, Glasgow had been called, and certainly it deserved that accolade, its civic parks giving the city greater green space than any other in Europe. It was handy for the court, Rosie Fergusson told her students whenever they made their initial visit to the mortuary room, the back door facing the pillared portico of the High Court where the consultant pathologist had often been called as an expert witness.

Rosie pulled off her high-heeled shoes and flung them into the bottom of her locker. For a while she'd exchange her street clothes for scrubs and a waterproof apron, rubber boots covering her feet, a protective mask over her face. She had shown her first-year students the kit they would need, explaining that dangerous shards might fly into their faces once the high-powered saw began to cut through human bone.

This afternoon's post-mortem notes had been filed on a sheet of yellow paper to distinguish it as potentially hazardous, a drug-related death requiring special attention, HIV in the bloods a constant possibility. Rosie had heard about the child, her mouth twisting in pity, but now she was ready to carry out a professional examination of the dead mother, hoping to give the police officers in attendance some clue as to her identity.

Once in the mortuary room with her colleague, Aussie-born Dr Daisy Abercromby, Rosie looked towards the Perspex window that separated them from those who were here to view the proceedings. A familiar face made her raise her eyebrows in surprise, but she kept her hand from moving in an instinctive wave towards Daniel Kohi and his colleagues. The SIO, a DS from Govanhill that she had met before, stood between Daniel and Jacob Alexander, the stocky uniformed officer who was already looking down intently at the scene.

'It's probably not that officer's first PM,' Daisy whispered. 'He might be a rookie but the guy's been a cop before.'

Rosie nodded. She'd seen some cops crumple to the floor or rush away as they witnessed the sort of procedure that she undertook on an almost daily basis, the sight of human entrails too much for their sensibilities. Daniel would not be one of those, Rosie guessed.

The intercom system allowed the officers on the far side to hear every word as Rosie began describing the deceased, her pale body already showing lividity as gravity pulled the blood downwards.

'White female, wisdom teeth not yet showing. Possibly early twenties,' Rosie commented after examining the woman's mouth. She turned the woman's arm with a gloved hand.

'Several needle marks.' She glanced up at the window to ensure the officers could see what she was showing them. 'Toxicology will give us an idea of the type of drugs in her bloods at the time of death. But the syringe that was found in her arm gives a fairly clear idea of what we're looking at.'

She'd seen it too often, the results of drug overdose. Sometimes an addict cleaned up in jail, only to come out to their dealer, waiting to greet them outside the prison gates, that first lethal shot a dose their newly recovered body was unable to withstand. Often it was an accidental death and Rosie wondered if this was one such. For what mother would wish to depart the world leaving a tiny baby clinging to their breast?

The post-mortem continued, Rosie cutting through tissues, explaining the procedure as carefully as she would to every one of her newest students.

Daniel glanced across at his tutor who was standing stock-still as though riveted by what he was seeing down on that stainless-steel table. None of them uttered a word as the pathologist continued her work, mentioning the evidence that the woman had given birth recently, noting the breasts engorged with milk that would also contain traces of whatever drug had killed her. No wonder the infant was still in hospital, its tiny life in danger until detoxification could be ensured. But he must not think about the child or remember the plaintive cry that had sent him hurrying along that lane.

At last, the pathologist's assistant was stitching up the Y-shaped incision that had been necessary to remove and examine the vital organs. Daniel felt a trace of sweat across his forehead.

Okay? Alexander mouthed to Daniel and he nodded, turning back to watch the final stages of the procedure.

'Right, let's get out of here,' the SIO said as they walked out of the corridor at last. 'A fairly straightforward one today. Pity we can't put a name to her yet, but there might well be a match for her DNA on our database.' He stopped for a moment. 'That's something you might like to follow up, Kohi?' he asked and Daniel nodded, after glancing at Alexander who seemed to be in favour of the suggestion.

'Yes, sir. Shall I ask Dr Fergusson when the report is due back from the lab?'

The SIO chuckled. 'Have a word with the technician here. He'll be able to email it through to you, constable.'

Of course, Daniel thought. Things were done a bit differently here and he had better get used to that.

'All right, Kohi?' Sergeant Alexander clapped Daniel on the shoulder. 'Let's see what's waiting for us back at base.'

CHAPTER SIX

CCTV coverage in this city was always a good bet to trace any vehicles and now that they knew the date and time when Truesdale's Southside home had been emptied, it was easy enough to find the removal vans and follow their course across the city. It had troubled Lorimer to find that the removal service Truesdale had used was so reluctant to offer any help. Someone was off sick, he'd been told. Nobody in the office to look up the records. He knew an outright lie when he heard one and frowned when told bluntly that the van's destination could not be revealed.

Lorimer sat beside the traffic cop who was bringing the route to his attention, the red line showing the van's progress from the leafy avenues of Pollokshields to the edges of Glasgow and the villages beyond. He saw when the van stopped, the technician homing in on a street where several bungalows were strung out.

'There,' the man at his side declared at last. 'Fifty-four Strathmirren Gardens.'

Lorimer sat back, nodding his approval. It had been almost thirty years since he'd joined the force and he was still amazed at the progress that had been made in detection, features built into computers aiding the police in ways that had been unthought of back then. Now it was a matter of course to find what you wanted with a few clicks of a button, technology taking over from some aspects of the old-fashioned slog of policing. And yet, how much easier would it have been for the removal company to give out that address?

He gave a sigh of relief. It had been a simple enough matter, after all. Though, they still had to find Robert Truesdale.

'Thanks,' he said, giving a nod to the officer beside him then getting to his feet.

'A pleasure, sir,' the younger man replied with a grin.

He'd drive over there himself, Lorimer decided, talk to Truesdale and see if there was anything the man needed in the way of security. Perhaps all this cloak and dagger stuff was a sign that the events of recent months had got to the MSP.

Find him fast, he'd been told and, as he left the confines of the city, Lorimer resisted the temptation to accelerate, let the Lexus power along the country roads like a stallion being given its head after days confined to a stable. Leaving behind the suburbs of Bearsden and Milngavie, he headed past the new coffee stop that had long since replaced a country pub favoured by bikers. Drink-driving laws had changed many of these old establishments for ever, the old Carbeth Inn now a rubble of stones behind a wooden hoarding. He slowed down and turned right, passing the last of the popular wooden huts used mainly as weekend retreats by city dwellers, then drove more slowly along the narrow winding road.

Keeping a careful watch on the way ahead, Lorimer still managed to look around him for the tell-tale flash of white rump and was rewarded by the sight of a roe deer, its head buried deep in the long grasses. Further on, a glimmer of water brought a shadow to his face as he recalled a burned-out ambulance by the side of a small lochan and the case that had first brought him into contact with Professor Solomon Brightman. So many places were imbued with memories of cases from the past; he sighed as the road twisted again then fell down into a deep valley towards the village of Blanefield.

At the end of the Stockie Muir was a short drive left along to the famous Glengoyne distillery but Lorimer took the right fork that led into the village, past Netherblane and out towards his destination. Number fifty-four was one of several pre-war bungalows, many of their steep roofs displaying large dormer windows, extensions to different parts of the houses making the original buildings less uniform than they had been at one time. A few still had the tall chimneys that had been necessary for indoor fireplaces in several of the rooms, but most had moved with the times, solar panels often replacing these older structures. Robert Truesdale's new residence had not seen many improvements, Lorimer thought, as he sat in the car, looking at the old bungalow. Sure, there was a dormer to the front and a wooden garage to one side but the place looked as if it needed some attention, the front lawn sprouting long strands of grass and weeds. Still, it was impossible to tell much at first glance about the place the MSP had chosen to live except that it may have lain empty for some time before he had moved in.

There was a press button bell to one side, a security key case beneath making Lorimer guess that the previous occupant had been disabled or in need of care. That certainly explained the unkempt garden. The sound of the bell rang out, one long persistent note followed by footsteps hurrying towards the half-glazed door. He heard the rattle of a chain being drawn across the door then it opened sufficiently for him to see a small grey-haired woman looking up at him, a fluffy apricot and white moggy in her arms.

'Yes?' Her hazel eyes regarded him steadily.

'Hello, my name's Lorimer. I'm looking for Mr Truesdale,' he explained.

'Sorry, he's out shopping just now,' the woman replied. 'I'm his home help. Well, cleaner really. It's not like he needs much help. Not like some of my old dears,' she chattered. 'Seemed surprised to see me, so he did. Mind you, I like to turn up early first day, you know. Get a feel of a place, like.'

'Oh, can you ask him to give me a call when he gets in?' Lorimer smiled. 'Here's my number.' He took out a small notebook and pen then scribbled his name and mobile number rather than hand her one of his cards with the Police Scotland logo, sensing that to identify himself as a senior police officer might make the woman clam up.

'Do you know if he'll be back to work soon?' he asked, tearing the page out and handing it to her.

'Work?' The woman looked puzzled. 'Oh, I don't think

so. I was told he'd retired, you know.' She stroked the cat's long fur. 'Awfie young tae retire, mind you.'

Lorimer looked closely at the woman's face. Was it possible that she had no idea of Robert Truesdale's identity? Not everyone caught the latest stories about politics and no doubt some folk chose to avoid the politics pages of newspapers altogether.

'I'm just in today then back next week,' the woman offered. 'But I'll leave your note where he can see it.' She nodded up at the tall man.

'Thank you, Mrs . . .?'

'Jardine. Nancy Jardine. Careful Cleaners. I've got my own website,' she added, lifting her chin to throw him a keen look. 'If you need a cleaner . . .?'

'Thank you, I'll bear that in mind,' he said, smiling down at the woman then turning to leave.

Well, there was no real mystery about Robert Truesdale's whereabouts now, except that he had somehow failed to inform his colleagues at Holyrood that he would be absent for some time. Or retired, as his cleaning lady had said. Had he decided to quit, after all? But, why not put that in writing to the FM? Or at least tell his PR people of his intentions. It was puzzling, but perhaps an indication that the stress of recent months had finally got to Truesdale, making him sell up and move away to a quiet village where he might not be hounded by the media?

As Lorimer drove away, he had no idea just how much interest there was going to be in this sleepy little part of the world.

*

'But you didn't actually see him?' Flint said stiffly.

'No. His cleaning lady told me he was out shopping. Looks like he may have had it up to here,' Lorimer suggested, raising a hand above his head. 'Though, if he's trying to keep a low profile, why go *out* to the shops when he could purchase things over the internet instead?' he added thoughtfully.

Caroline Flint regarded the man across the table. She trusted his judgement, but in this case she was under direct instructions from the First Minister of Scotland to find their missing MSP, and hearsay on his whereabouts was simply not enough.

'We need to speak to him. I don't know why the FM is so adamant but there's more to Truesdale going AWOL than just absenting himself from Holyrood. They're in the middle of debating this drugs bill. And Truesdale was the most vocal supporter of the lobby to legalise.'

'If he doesn't call me . . .'

'If he doesn't call you in a couple of hours, I want someone back there. Discreetly, of course. No need to make a song and dance about it. He's moved away for some reason best known to himself, hasn't wanted his colleagues to know where he is.'

'Maybe he just needed a bit of space?'

'You think?' Flint tapped her fingers against the edge of the table.

'No, not really,' Lorimer sighed. 'It doesn't make sense for him to do this when all the interest in this bill is gathering pace. It would be more likely for him to have a continual presence at Holyrood, not go off. Unless . . .'

'Unless some of these threats against his life are actually more dangerous than we imagined,' Flint finished for him. 'My guess is he'll call you to explain himself. Then, if he's really being intimidated by some group or other, we can promise him security twenty-four seven.'

'Right,' Lorimer agreed. 'Soon as he calls me, I'll let you know.'

He didn't have long to wait.

'Robert Truesdale here. Am I speaking to Detective Superintendent William Lorimer, by any chance? I recognised the name though you didn't actually identify yourself to my cleaner.'

Lorimer heard the amusement in the man's voice as he spoke. He hadn't written his rank on the note but Truesdale evidently knew just who it was that had arrived at his front door.

'Yes, sir. Lorimer here.'

'You spoke to Mrs Jardine earlier on, I believe,' the man continued. 'Sorry I missed you, lots to do with the new house, you know.'

'Sir, your colleagues at Holyrood—'

'Can all go to hell as far as I'm concerned, Lorimer. I'm done with the lot of them. And if you want to pass that on to the FM, you can,' Truesdale replied testily, his voice trembling with emotion.

'We can offer you round-the-clock security, sir,' Lorimer offered.

'Well, that won't be necessary. I'm done with politics and when the FM reads my letter of resignation he'll know why.'

'Oh ...'

'But thank you for your concern. I've always had a high regard for Police Scotland. You do an awful lot to help addicts in so many ways. Not your fault that the whole drug scene has got out of hand. Anyway, not my business any more. Goodbye, Detective Superintendent.'

And, with that, Lorimer heard the final click as Truesdale ended the call.

Yes, it was Truesdale on that line, as he would affirm when he spoke to Caroline Flint, picking up the phone again to call her.

He recalled several debates on television, the MSP arguing for the legitimisation of drugs in the UK, his gravelly voice instantly recognisable.

But later, Lorimer was to replay that telephone conversation with Robert Truesdale in his mind, searching for clues that might dispel his own rising doubts.

CHAPTER SEVEN

The hospital reminded Daniel of the last time he had seen his grandmother in Harare, corridors leading off into different wards, a smell of something antiseptic wafting in the air. The old woman had seemed so much smaller, tiny fingers curled on top of the fresh white sheet, hair so thin that it seemed as though her whole head had shrunk.

He closed his eyes for a moment, remembering.

'Can I help you?' A voice broke into Daniel's reverie as he stood at the entrance to the ward.

'I came to see how the baby was,' he explained. 'My colleagues from Police Scotland brought him in the other night after I found him.'

'You're a police officer?' The woman looked at Daniel with a penetrating stare.

'Police Constable Kohi,' Daniel replied taking out his warrant card to show her, his chin tilting up as though to defy the nurse's expectations. Did the colour of his skin make it difficult for this nurse to see him as a cop? There were plenty of nurses and doctors from other countries, but perhaps black cops were unusual in Glasgow? 'The baby?' he ventured with a gracious smile.

'Oh, the nursery is along this way,' the nurse said, her face reddening. 'Come with me, please.'

It was strange, that sense of condescension suddenly changing to deference, the balance between them altered. He could see how some cops might get off on that sort of power, something else they'd been warned about during the weeks at Tulliallan. Theirs was a duty of care, not an abuse of the status that rank or uniform conferred.

The nursery was surprisingly quiet as Daniel was led along a row of clear plastic cots until they reached the far end.

'Here he is, poor wee mite.'

Daniel blinked, staring into the cot. He seemed different, less like the screaming child he'd held that night. His blond head lay to one side, the tiny rosebud mouth pursed as though dreaming of an imaginary nipple. He wanted to put his hand out, see if the baby would clutch a finger, but resisted the temptation. He was someone else's child, nothing to do with Daniel Kohi, an inner voice scolded.

'Will he recover?'

The nurse gave him a pitying look.

'We don't give up on these wee bairns easily,' she replied. 'Aye, he'll be okay once he's completely detoxed. It's not as rare as you might think.' She gave a heavy sigh. 'Mothers giving birth when they're full of drugs. And this one was breast-fed into the bargain. Filling his poor wee body with all her poison.'

'What will happen to him?'

'Depends on whether your lot find a relation for him. Meantime, he's under our care.'

'And if nobody claims him?'

'We turn him over to social services. But that doesn't often happen. Some family member normally turns up.'

The nurse gave him a curious look. 'You're new to this game, aren't you?'

Daniel felt his face warming under the woman's perceptive stare. Okay, nothing like this had happened to him before, but he wasn't about to protest that he'd risen to the rank of inspector elsewhere, so he merely nodded.

'Just beginning my probation,' he agreed.

'Well, good luck to you,' the nurse replied. 'It's a battlefield out there but we like to think we're all winning. And you've brought back one wee survivor.' She smiled, nodding at the baby.

Outside the hospital the wind was scattering leaves from half bare young maple trees as Daniel headed to the car park.

A survivor, the nurse had called him. Perhaps that was why Daniel felt a connection with the little baby. After all, wasn't he a survivor, too? He smiled to himself as he approached his car, nobody giving him a second glance. Sometimes it felt as if he already belonged here in this friendly city, though he was still receiving a few curious stares whilst in uniform. Would his trawl through missing persons unearth any clue as to the child's parentage? He hoped so, remembering the baby lying there in his cot, warm and safe for now but, oh so vulnerable to unseen forces once he was discharged from the hospital's care.

Daniel looked out of the window as he drove back into the city centre. Glasgow was fast becoming his home now, many of the landmarks like the university tower and the Finnieston crane familiar to him. He was on late shift tonight and faced his first two nightshifts on Friday and Saturday, followed by four rest days. It was still hard to adjust to any sort of pattern, he realised, and as winter approached with shorter days and darker nights there would be times when Daniel Kohi would see scarcely any daylight at all. Up till now he had been content to use his hours off helping his neighbour, Netta, seeing that his uniform was in perfect order and doing a bit of shopping. *Make sure you take your rests*, he remembered one instructor at Tulliallan telling them all. *Don't get sucked into ongoing cases.* Daniel blinked as he drove through the streets of Glasgow, tenement buildings flashing by on either side.

Was that a warning he should heed? Had he been wrong to visit the baby? He gave a sigh. No, he told himself, it had been a good impulse, something deep inside instinctively wanting to follow up that grisly discovery. After all, he knew what it was to be a father. There was nothing more he could do for the little child but hope he would be found by a family member. And that was something he could keep tabs on.

CHAPTER EIGHT

There was a pale milk-white streak, the promise of daylight, above the horizon as the man stepped out of number fifty-four Strathmirren Gardens. Night was still to be banished from the skies, lingering dark clouds not yet pierced by the sun. He locked the front door behind him and stood, one hand fingering the velvet lapel on his dark navy coat. It felt good. No, more than good, he thought, a smile playing about his lips. It felt *expensive*. Closing his eyes for a moment, he took a deep breath of the chilly air, savouring the moment. There was no sign of other residents up and about at this early hour, not even a dog walker to be seen, he realised, looking around him.

This was a good place to be. Peaceful. Quiet. And the man felt a sudden rush of gratitude for the quirks of fate that had led him here.

The Honda was parked in front of the garage, too many boxes inside from the recent removal that had taken place to accommodate the big CR-V. He straightened his shoulders at the thought of driving it through the nearby country lanes back towards the city centre, assured that there was still plenty of fuel in the tank. Pointing the key fob at the car, he stepped towards it and opened the driver's door. The briefcase was where it had been left the previous evening, on the floor below the passenger seat. He gave it a glance and chuckled as his hand reached out to start the Honda.

Who would have thought—

The explosion shook the nearby houses, shattering windows and blowing a nearby cherry sapling right out of the ground. A tower of flame engulfed the vehicle, stripping its paintwork, burning every fibre within. The man's clothes were gone in seconds, hair and skin torched.

Nearby, alarms were ringing, people dragged from their beds by the deafening boom. Pale faces looked out on the inferno till fear and thick black clouds of smoke forced them back from the broken windows.

Fingers pressed buttons, husky voices sobbed down the lines, seeking anyone who could deal with this terror.

For terror it must be, a bomb exploding right outside their front doors.

In number fifty-six, crying children were being comforted, wrapped in their duvets and cuddled in front of the television where other sounds might soothe and divert. Across the road an old man stood at his bedroom window, hand clasping his stick tightly with whitened knuckles, staring at the burning car and remembering someone else's war, in some other sleepy little village.

Then, like a counterpoint to the throbbing fire, the

double notes of a siren grew louder, blue flashing lights appearing over the brow of the hill.

'He's *dead*?'

The First Minister, Calum McKenzie, leaned back heavily into his chair, clutching the phone in one trembling hand as he listened to the chief constable's words.

'A bomb?' The man repeated Caroline Flint's words as she endeavoured to explain the fatal incident out in Strathblane.

'Detective Superintendent Lorimer spoke to him last night,' Flint continued. 'And, no, before you ask, there was no sign whatsoever that he had reason to be worried about an attack.'

'I see,' the FM replied, though in truth he did not see at all.

'According to Lorimer, Truesdale sounded quite calm,' Flint continued.

'What else did he say?'

The chief constable reiterated what she'd been told by the head of the Major Incident Team in Glasgow.

'I'm sorry, but it seems quite clear that Mr Truesdale had decided to quit the political life for good,' she concluded. She had tried to soften the blow, missing out the late MSP's apparent anger or frustration with his colleagues at Holyrood, but telling him the FM would know exactly what Truesdale felt once he'd read that letter of resignation.

'Could it be suicide?' McKenzie asked.

A small disapproving silence hung in the air between them.

'No, of course not, wh-what am I saying?' he stuttered. 'It's just such a shock.'

'We are investigating every aspect of the incident, sir, but it is doubtful that Mr Truesdale would have blown himself up,' Flint said, her polite words belied by an icy edge to her tone. A suicide would suit the Scottish Parliament just fine, sweeping everything under the carpet, but these politicians were going to have to deal with this horrific incident and its inevitable press coverage until the perpetrators were caught.

'Ah, yes ... sorry ... no ... you're right,' McKenzie stuttered.

'We'll keep you informed, sir, but I must warn you that there is no way this is going to be kept out of the media. Half of Strathblane is probably posting images on Facebook right now.'

'What happens next?'

'Forensics will recover what they can, the device will be examined so we can gauge where it might have come from, though that's probably not going to be much help. And, of course, there will be a post-mortem of the remains.'

'Tell Lorimer to call me. I'd like to know exactly what Truesdale said to him. Might have been the last person he spoke to,' he murmured thoughtfully, sighing.

Lorimer put down the telephone with a frown. He had given the FM as much information as he could remember. Yes, he had seemed adamant in his intention to resign from the Scottish Government and no, he hadn't actually said anything derogatory, Lorimer had assured him but, now he came to think of it, Robert Truesdale had uttered one phrase, hadn't he? *I'm done with the lot of them*, he'd told Lorimer. Still, the First Minister would be receiving his former colleague's letter of resignation and surely that would say all that the dead man had intended? A little niggle in his mind made him frown: why had the FM suggested suicide? The idea was frankly absurd. And yet ... was there something that the people in Holyrood weren't telling them?

One other thing made Lorimer pause for thought: surely, having refused his offer of round-the-clock security, Truesdale had had no inkling that this morning was to be the day his life was blown away?

He rose from behind his desk and grabbed the dark jacket hanging on his coat stand. It would take him a good half hour at this time of day to arrive at the scene, the morning traffic surging in and out of the city. By the time he arrived, there would be the inevitable pack of journos making their presence felt, something he could do without.

There was no detour to enjoy the countryside today, Lorimer choosing the route through Bearsden and Milngavie, past Mugdock Reservoir, his mood matching the sullen clouds that threatened overhead.

Why on earth had the man ducked out of his offer of help? It was obvious that First Minister Calum McKenzie had been concerned about Truesdale simply taking off like that, leaving no forwarding address. Moving house must have taken a lot of forethought and planning, not the impulse of a moment. Lorimer's frown deepened. If the man's mental health had suffered under the barrage of threatening messages, he could imagine the sudden need to get away, buy a ticket and jump on a plane. But this? No, Truesdale had known exactly what he was doing in buying the bungalow in this pretty little village. And, as he approached the road-block across the main street, William Lorimer wondered if they'd ever know what had been on the MSP's mind in recent weeks.

CHAPTER NINE

Daniel turned the television to mute as his doorbell rang out. He'd been sitting hunched in his chair, watching the lunchtime news for any sign of the discovery he had made. But the TV coverage had been dominated by an explosion in the village of Strathblane. The name of the victim had not yet been released but there were enough hints from the reporter on the ground to suggest that a bomb had been placed underneath a car.

'Netta, come on in.' Daniel grinned at the woman standing in his doorway carrying a bundle of something wrapped up in a tea towel. 'Scones?' he guessed, ushering his elderly neighbour inside and closing the front door.

'Thought ye might like a few afore ye go off on yer shift,' she said, walking towards Daniel's kitchen and reaching for a clean plate from a rack on the wall. 'It's a really late yin this wan, eh? Nae clockin' off at midnight?'

'Yes,' Daniel agreed, surprised that his elderly friend had kept up with his shift patterns. 'Night shift tonight and tomorrow,' he murmured, half reminding himself of the undoubted challenges of Friday and Saturday nights in Glasgow. 'Then four days off,' he added with a grin.

'Here, stick oan the kettle and we'll have a cuppa. You're no' off fur a wee while yet, eh no?'

Daniel shook his head. Night shifts began at ten o'clock but he'd leave here a good hour or more before that, leaving plenty of time to change into his uniform ready to accompany Jacob Alexander, his tutor cop, on whatever tonight might bring.

'Here, seize a haud o' them and dinna spare the butter,' Netta chuckled. 'Noo that ye're earning, ye'll be able tae buy fancy jam an' a', I reckon,' she teased.

'Aye. Right,' Daniel replied, his speech now tinged with a proper Glasgow accent. 'Netta, you're too good to me.' He sighed, shaking his head in mock despair. Daniel had been grateful but a bit embarrassed by Netta's generosity when his resources had been constrained, knowing how she existed on a frugal widow's pension. A handsome salary had been paid into his bank account ever since his first day at Tulliallan and the former refugee was insistent on returning every favour the old lady had shown him, something that Netta brushed off with a *tsk tsk* each time the subject arose.

'Terrible thing that, eh?' Netta remarked, turning from the kitchen to stare at the television screen. 'IRA, no doubt. Ma mammy aye said they were a bad lot.'

Daniel suppressed a smile. Netta's Irish mammy came up often in her conversation, a mixture of forthright, politically incorrect statements and myths that never ceased to make him wonder about the personality of the lady who had brought his friend into the world more than seventy years ago.

'You involved in that, son?' she asked, pointing a finger towards the screen.

'No,' he answered, picking up the remote and turning on the sound.

They stared at the screen together, listening as the newscaster, his voice modulated to a suitably sombre note, related the story of the explosion.

'Defin-*ately* IRA.' Netta nodded. 'Car bombs. Famous for them, so they are.'

Daniel did not reply, knowing that once Netta had made up her mind on something it was not useful to argue. Perhaps this was a good time to bring up another subject, however, one that had been on his mind a lot.

'Netta,' he began, then cleared his throat. 'I've been thinking about finding another flat.'

'See they yins ... ye *whit*?' Netta's mouth opened wide, her diatribe against the terrorist element across the Irish Sea suddenly forgotten.

'The Housing Association need this flat for another refugee family,' he said softly. 'They gave me notice a few weeks ago.'

'Oh.' She turned her face back to the TV screen, trying to hide the emotion he could see in that trembling lip, eyes blinking back some sudden tears.

'No worries, son,' she said at last, patting the back of his hand. 'I guess ye need tae move on, right enough.'

Daniel looked at his friend's profile, the tilt of her head as she tried to be brave despite the wobbling chin.

'I wondered ...' he began, then stopped, chewing his lower lip anxiously, seeking the right words.

'Aye?' She turned to face him, her mouth a firm line as she sought to regain her composure.

'Would you like to come with me? Flat share? I mean, the view up here is fantastic, but isn't it a bit too hard for you being so high up? Eleventh floor ...'

'Och, no, ah'm fine here, son. Cannae complain,' she said with a smile that he could see was somewhat forced. 'Jist you get oan and find a nice wee place fur yersel. Ah'll come an visit ye on yer days off. Bring ye scones,' she laughed.

Daniel nodded, a lump forming in his throat. They'd both known that this day might come, the flat Daniel currently lived in earmarked for refugees, his current tenancy extended for a few months till he had enough money for a decent deposit on another property. He'd enquired about renting this one indefinitely but that had not been possible, the lady at the Housing Association had told him.

'Ach, never you mind,' Netta said, giving his arm a squeeze. 'Ah'll help ye tae find anither place. Naebody kens auld Glesca like me!'

Lorimer sat in his car, jacket collar turned up as he watched the reporters and cameramen and -women flooding past. At least here he was safe from prying eyes, the scene of crime tape separating the police vehicles from those of civilians. Their own scene of crime officers had erected a large waterproof tent over the burned-out vehicle and what remained of the timber garage and he could see their white-suited figures entering and leaving, some with their own photographic equipment to hand. The smell of burning permeated the whole area, impossible to keep out even with the car windows closed. The fire officers had been quick on the scene, the fireball extinguished long before Lorimer's arrival. Sadly, it was not difficult to imagine the flames licking at the car's paintwork, roaring as they took hold.

He'd seen other horrific fires in his time and it was not so very far from where he'd stood twenty years or more ago, facing another burned-out vehicle. That death had been worse, though, the victim left to die in the inferno. Truesdale wouldn't have known a thing about it, Lorimer reckoned, the explosion killing him instantly. He'd wait a while longer then pull on his own forensic suit and see for himself.

A knock on the passenger window made him look up.

'Bill.'

'Rosie!' Lorimer's face creased into a grin as he saw the woman bending towards the car. Consultant pathologist Dr Rosie Fergusson had been with him in innumerable cases over the years, their shared experiences giving them a unique bond of friendship. It had been on the very same homicide case that they had both first encountered Solomon Brightman, now Professor of Psychology at Glasgow University and Rosie's husband.

He stepped out of the car, searching her face to see how she was taking this latest death. 'A bad one, eh?' he murmured.

'Seen worse,' Rosie replied, pulling down her hood with one gloved hand. 'But that's not to belittle the poor sod who copped it.' She turned to look back at the forensic tent. 'Know who he is?'

Lorimer nodded, gazing past her as one of the SOCOs emerged from the tent. 'I think we do. But for now, we're keeping it from them,' he replied in a whisper, nodding towards the crowd of reporters who were straining to hear anything that was being said.

'Okay. We'll be getting the remains back to the mortuary as soon as they're finished in there,' she told him. 'Nothing much I can do till then.'

'Just one thing,' Lorimer asked, guiding the pathologist further away from any listening ears. 'Any sign of a pugilistic attitude?'

His question was relevant, of course. If a man had died from the hell of being burned alive, his arms and fists might show that particular shape.

'None,' Rosie replied. 'Explosion must have killed him in a split second. Doubt if he even saw the flash.'

Lorimer breathed out a sigh of relief. It was a thought that might keep him awake at nights, thinking of the victim dying in a blazing fire. Like the deaths of PC Daniel Kohi's wife and son, the tragedy that had forced the former police inspector to flee his home in Zimbabwe. God alone knew how Daniel coped with the lingering nightmares, the man's capacity for visual recall far more acute than that of most mortals.

It didn't take long for Lorimer to suit up and soon the pair of them were heading towards the tent, ignoring the shouts from reporters ringing in their ears.

Lorimer swore under his breath. What was left of the

Honda had been reduced to a frame of twisted metal, ashes thick on the ground. There was no longer any roof, the blackened vehicle showing hardly any sign of its original shape.

The remains of the victim were in a seated posture, and, like the car, simply an outline of what he had once been, a skeletal frame diminished in the explosion. He would look at all of the photographs taken by the scene of crime officers but right now there was a need to be here, see it for himself, smell the stink of burned flesh and leather.

Why didn't you let us protect you? Lorimer asked silently of the charred shape. Could this have been avoided? He swallowed hard as he fixed his eyes on the sight, vowing to find whoever had committed this evil deed.

'We need to lift him as carefully as we can,' he heard Rosie saying. But she was speaking to someone outside the forensic tent, not to Lorimer.

'Done?' she asked and he nodded, knowing that she was really asking him to leave now and let others do their work.

Voices rose once more as he retreated to the safety of his own car, clamouring for answers to their questions.

'Who was it, Lorimer? Anyone we know?'

Despite himself, he turned at the sound of his name to see a slim red-haired woman in a beige raincoat. He'd recognised that voice a second too late. There was no love lost between Lorimer and the reporter from the *Gazette* who could always be guaranteed to stir up trouble.

'Well? What brings the head of the MIT out to a burned-out car?' she persisted, defiant chin in the air.

For a moment they stared at one another, each knowing that there would be no answer given to that question right now. Then Lorimer walked away.

CHAPTER TEN

Nights could be longer than any other shift, they'd been told, the hours dragging by as fewer calls came through to the police switchboard, the good citizens of Glasgow slumbering innocently, for the most part.

But darkness covered many things and once the city was asleep that was the time for some to creep out from hidden places, intent on harm.

Daniel's first shift in the early hours of that cold October night was one that he would always remember. The call had come from a telephone box, the caller leaving no name, just a frantic demand that someone come to a place where there appeared to be a body caught under branches on the edge of the River Cart. He'd sounded foreign, Daniel and his fellow officer had been told, Eastern European. That in itself was not unusual, the tenements of Govanhill home to many immigrants from that part of the world.

Now they stood beside the flowing river, its current illuminated by nearby streetlamps, gazing down at what might have been a bundle of rubbish caught in the detritus beside the flowing waters. Recent storms had blown pieces of trees and branches down to the banks, plastic bags caught on their twigs like pale membranes of ghostly fingers.

'Second one this year,' Daniel's neighbour snorted, the tone of disgust evident in his voice.

'Suicide?'

'Nah. Bet you anything it's a drug death,' the older man replied. 'See up there?' He turned to point at a space by the railings. 'Lots of them shoot up just where they can't be seen. No CCTV. Place can be littered with needles and stuff. Blooming health hazard.' He tutted. 'One of them overdoses and falls in, more than likely. Probably his mate that called it in. Then ran off before we got here.'

'We secure the scene?' Daniel suggested.

'Nah. No point,' the officer told him. 'Weight of the body under that branch will keep it safe till plain clothes arrive, mark my words. And if any of them grumble about disturbing the locus, well,' he shrugged, 'our hands are clean.'

Daniel bit back his response. Weren't they supposed to be first responders? Didn't he have a duty of care for whoever was lying sodden in that icy cold water? A sudden gust of wind blew the rain into his face, making Daniel shiver.

'Here,' his senior officer patted PC Kohi's shoulder, 'I can see you're freezing, son. You away and get some hot drinks. Coffees with sugar and maybe a few sticky buns. CID will be here by the time you get back. There's that all-night caff just along the road. You know it?'

Daniel nodded, half annoyed at being dismissed as the

tea boy but also relieved to be on the move, his limbs beginning to ache with the cold.

By the time he'd returned and clambered down to the bank, balancing a cardboard tray of drinks in one hand, there were several more figures by the fast-flowing river. The body had been pulled from its place beneath the tree branch and was lying on a plastic sheet, face turned upwards.

Daniel handed out the drinks, silently watching the detectives at work, wondering if they would follow the same lines of investigation that he himself had carried out when presented with a dead body, back in the days when he'd been an inspector.

The corpse was that of a man, his face deathly white under the light from several torches. If his neighbour really had put a bet on this being death from an overdose, he'd have lost, Daniel thought grimly. The slashes across his cheek and neck looked black in this light but come day and under the pathologist's lamps they would be a different colour altogether. The water must have washed away most of the blood, he realised. He saw one of the plain clothes officers turning his way.

'PC Kohi? Begin a search along this side. See if there's any sign of a weapon,' the woman's voice called out. 'You're looking for something a fair size. Wasn't a penknife that did this,' she commented drily.

'Yes, ma'am,' he murmured, unsure whether she was his superior or not. Might be a detective constable, same rank as himself, just a sideways move after sufficient experience in uniform. He slipped on a pair of protective gloves to prevent his fingers making contact with the weapon, should he find it.

Taking care where he stepped lest he slip into the stream, Daniel walked slowly, eyes to the ground, his torch beam playing this way and that. There was a narrow bank of grass along this side of the river and it was possible that the perpetrator had flung a weapon away, missing the deeper waters in their haste to escape. Above him he could hear voices relaying information on their radios, no doubt summoning the unmarked van that would be needed to take the poor man's body to the city mortuary.

Daniel felt his feet slip for a moment and threw out a hand, clutching some shrubbery growing from the wall, a tangle of ivy left to thicken over the years. Steadying himself, he cast the torch beam along the edges of the bank, the water shallower here, moss-covered stones emerging from the riverbed.

It was then that he saw it. One small glint of metal against a swirl of waterweeds. Daniel stopped and stared then dropped to his knees, inching forward. One swift lunge was all it took for him to scoop up the long-bladed weapon, a heavy machete not far beneath the surface.

Had the person wielding this thing panicked? Or, confused by the darkness, did they assume the river was deep enough for it never to be found?

Daniel got to his feet and then stopped, looking at the ground. There had been a struggle here, he told himself, seeing clumps of flattened grass and slicks of mud. Had the victim staggered back a few yards then tottered into the River Cart, his body catching on that tree branch? Then flung out a hand, hoping to save himself? So many questions that deserved answers. This was a story that others must interpret, he thought, turning to see the figures further along the bank of the river.

'Over here!' Daniel called. 'I've found it.'

'Bring the damned thing along!' a male voice commanded.

But Daniel shook his head stubbornly, refusing to move. 'There's something you need to see!' he shouted. 'I think there are signs of a fight.'

Later, back in Govanhill police station, Daniel sat next to the woman who had introduced herself as Detective Sergeant Miller, each of them holding a restorative mug of tea in their hands.

'Good work, Kohi,' she said, nodding to Daniel. 'You're a new trainee, I gather?'

'Yes, ma'am, but I was a serving police officer before I moved to the UK,' he replied quietly. 'Inspector Kohi, in those days,' he added with an ironic smile.

'Ah, that explains it,' DS Miller said, smiling. 'I did wonder how a rookie could spot things like that in the dark.'

'I often worked in the dark,' Daniel explained. 'African nights can be far darker than here, especially out in the bush where there are no streetlights.'

'Well, we're glad that you did. Who knows how long it might have taken us to find that particular spot, not to mention the weapon.'

Daniel regarded her thoughtfully. She looked like an intelligent young woman, possibly about his own age.

'What happens now?' he asked.

'Body's off to the mortuary, but you know that. And we'll need a police presence at the scene till daylight when the SOCOs can do a more thorough search of the area. Establish what might have happened.' She tilted her head as Daniel nodded. 'You'll be there till the end of your shift now, with a couple of other uniforms for back-up, but how would it be if I asked for you to come in on our next briefing? I think we owe you that at least, former Inspector Kohi,' she said, grinning.

The prospect of being invited onto the investigation team, even in some small way, kept Daniel a little bit warmer as he stood guard by the River Cart. There was not a lot to do but walk up and down, eyes mostly on the scene of crime below and the pavement nearby where pedestrians could not cross the swathes of tape.

But that was not all that he watched, his dark eyes drawn to the sky as it changed from ebony to inky blue and burning scarlet, reminding him of the twin colours of a paradise flycatcher. Morning was coming and with it a new day when many questions would be asked.

CHAPTER ELEVEN

It was a typical day for autumn to begin, sudden gusts of wind stripping leaves from trees that were already turning scarlet and bronze. The traffic was flowing again, no cordons barring the road that had been blocked the previous day. The police had taken away everything they felt was required and now only a huge dark stain remained where a ferocious fire had burned out the car, its occupant killed by the blast, his dead body now just burned and charred remains. Rain swept across the tarmac, obliterating the place where it had happened, water streaming into culverts either side of the street.

The BMW slowed down, its driver giving a hard stare at the mark on the road as he drove around the bend, the merest trace of a smile on his lips.

He'd had it coming, he told himself, heaving a sigh of satisfaction. Messing with the grown-ups always ends up with someone getting hurt. This job was done. And now it was time to focus on the next one. He tapped his fingers on the steering wheel in time to the beat from his radio, concentrating on the junction up ahead.

He turned the big car along the twisting country road that led out of the village, feeling the wind rock the car slightly as he passed an open space next to a small loch. Let the cops do their bit, rooting around on the ground, trying to find what had caused the explosion. His smile broadened as he drove through puddles, watching the arc of spray smash across his windscreen. The device used had been made from standard stuff, the sort of thing anybody could access. Nothing to give a clue as to who had placed it beneath the car or, indeed, why.

He listened as jingles from adverts gave way to the news. Today it was full of hints speculating that paramilitary activity was once more active in Northern Ireland. So what? Nobody was going to find out the truth, and meantime they could make all the claims they liked.

As he left the narrow country road, he turned up the radio as if to deliberately block out any thoughts of what he'd left behind. His head moved in time to the rapper's repetitive tone, lyrics meaningless, a sonorous beat drowning out the car's swishing wipers, the image of that explosion already forgotten.

CHAPTER TWELVE

I t was one of those post-mortems that everyone dreaded, second worst only to that of a child. Burned bodies seemed so alien, like creatures from another planet or those mummified figures that archaeologists find buried deep beneath the desert sands. Rosie studied the man's remains carefully as she walked around the stainless-steel table. She had to remind herself that this had been a living, breathing human being not so long ago. Someone who'd been dispatched to an early grave.

How old had Truesdale been? Sixty-four? The thought brought to mind lyrics of the Beatles' 'When I'm Sixty-Four', written from the perspective of young men who possibly imagined that such a number meant decrepitude at the very least. Truesdale had insisted to Lorimer that he was done with politics, but it looked very much as if someone else had made that a certainty.

Rosie had dealt with car bomb victims before, some of them blown clear of the vehicle, but this one had been in much the same position as the moment the explosion had happened. She walked around the corpse, one of the pathology assistants photographing it from different angles, her eyes coming back repeatedly to the chain around its neck.

She lifted it up slightly with the edge of a scalpel, the small silver cross coming to rest against the blade. Had Truesdale been a religious man, then? Rosie wondered. She hadn't paid much attention to anything about the MSP except for his crusade in trying to legalise drugs. Now she began to wonder about the person behind all of the media storm.

Carefully, she unclasped the chain and set it aside, to be bagged and tagged.

Now the actual work would begin, cutting into what remained of his flesh, obtaining the usual samples for toxicology and DNA, procedures that might occur in any sudden death.

Yet it was not just any death, was it? This one felt like the result of a terrorist act and when she had completed her examination, Rosie might have sufficient evidence to make some sort of statement in a court of law one day.

'A crucifix?' Lorimer sat back, surprised.

'No, not that sort. No figure of Jesus hanging there.'

'Ah, just a plain cross? Send me some images over, would you, thanks.'

'D'you think he was a devout Christian? I hadn't seen anything like that about him on social media.'

'I've no idea if he was a religious man, Rosie. But thanks for that. Always something to look into.'

He put down the phone, nodding to himself. That was an interesting snippet of information from the initial findings of the PM. Yes, death had been caused by an exploding device, the burns coming post-mortem, something that might be a relief to those who had been close to Robert Truesdale. Rosie had been good enough to prioritise this above some of the other work that she was carrying out, on a Saturday, too, the pressure from both the chief constable and First Minister sufficient to overrule any objection from the Crown Office, had there been any.

And Robert Truesdale had worn a small silver cross around his neck. Lorimer thought about that for a moment. The irony was, of course, that such a talisman had not guarded him against the dreadful ending of his life. But had he been a man of faith? Believing that his soul would be dispatched to the Great Hereafter? These were questions for philosophers, Lorimer reminded himself. Right now, he was tasked with finding who had murdered this man, and why. First, though, he had to delegate the unpleasant task of arranging for the victim to be officially identified, if that was at all possible.

It was well into her day when DS Molly Newton sat back from her laptop rubbing her eyes. In normal circumstances a corpse would be identified by a next-of-kin, but not only was this a very unusual circumstance, it now appeared that Truesdale had no near relatives living in Scotland. She'd managed to trace a cousin in Christchurch, New Zealand, calling the fellow at what was for them one a.m. on a Sunday morning. She winced even now at his string of expletives as he'd objected to being woken in the middle of the night by a police officer from Scotland. Molly had to use all her charm and persuasion to stop him cutting her off, the mention of a bomb making him change his belligerent tone a little.

However, it transpired that this cousin had not been aware of his relative's profession in politics, let alone the sudden horror of his death. Truesdale was not a common name but this cousin had been related through Truesdale's late mother's side of the family, the Kings.

Lorimer had then suggested that Molly contact Holyrood to see if anyone there might volunteer to help. Several phone calls later, after the detective sergeant had been passed from one official to the next, Molly had a result.

The finance minister and Truesdale's parliamentary secretary were due to arrive off the train from Edinburgh this afternoon, each having told the officer from the MIT that they'd been friendly enough with Truesdale, but that nobody in Holyrood had been really close to the man. That was sad, Molly thought now as she flexed her shoulders.

A quick glance at the wall clock in their office showed Molly that there was just enough time to grab a quick sandwich before heading to Queen's Street station to meet them.

The stout figure of Jerry McVeigh was hard to miss as he waddled down the platform from the first-class section of the Edinburgh to Glasgow train, Truesdale's secretary by his side. Molly had positioned herself a good distance from the barriers, her black coat merging with the commuters crowding the concourse on this cold Saturday afternoon. It was only when McVeigh had regained his ticket and stuffed it into his overcoat pocket that she sidled up to them both.

'DS Newton,' she said, catching both men's attention as she stepped in front of them. 'I have a car waiting, gentlemen.'

'Jerry McVeigh,' the finance minister replied, taking Molly's hand in a sweaty grasp. 'And this is Malcolm Hinchliffe,' he added, introducing a tall, slim man who shook her hand.

'How do you do.' Hinchliffe nodded gravely. 'Dreadful business, altogether. I'm still shocked by it.'

McVeigh was the chatty one, Molly found as they travelled the short distance through the city to the old mortuary, rattling on about how dreadfully inconvenient it was having to come all the way through from the capital, as if he'd trekked overland to some foreign outpost of civilisation. Molly nodded politely, gritting her teeth through his stream of put-down remarks about Glasgow. Her city. She loved going to visit Edinburgh, recognising its glorious architecture and history, but Glasgow was home. Her fellow citizens' pawky humour and friendliness were what made this city 'miles better', as one old slogan had it. Glasgow folk sometimes scoffed at the good citizens of Edinburgh: 'fur coat and nae knickers,' they'd laugh, in their good-natured banter.

She turned back as the car pulled in at the rear of the mortuary, her mouth stiff from the effort of smiling.

'This is your mortuary?' McVeigh looked at the old Victorian building with disdain.

Molly risked a swift glance at Malcolm Hinchliffe who

raised his eyebrows just a fraction, the gesture letting her know his opinion of the finance minister's lack of courtesy.

'Dr Fergusson will be waiting for us,' Molly said, leading the way to the front of the building that faced Glasgow Green.

'Big park,' McVeigh remarked grudgingly.

'Glasgow has the highest amount of green space of any European city,' Molly replied sweetly. 'I had such fun over there during the Commonwealth Games,' she added, dropping a wink to Hinchliffe who grinned back at her.

Once inside there was no place for levity, the business of identifying a corpse silencing even McVeigh.

'DS Newton, hello.' A small blonde woman in a grey trouser suit approached the trio, glancing at the men from Edinburgh in turn. 'I'm Dr Fergusson,' Rosie said, introducing herself, not waiting for handshakes but turning on her heel and beckoning them to follow her along a corridor.

Molly breathed a sigh of relief. The sooner this was over, the sooner she could escort the two men to Queen Street for their train back to Edinburgh.

It was not like the television dramas where one entered a room and someone lifted a white sheet off the body, to gasps of horror from the nearest and dearest. Instead, Malcolm Hinchliffe stood at a large window, gazing down at the charred remains of the man who had been killed in that car bomb. He heard a noise by his side and looked to see McVeigh gagging into his cupped hand before stumbling away from the sight.

'Can you say if there is anything at all that you would

recognise?' the blonde detective whispered. 'I know he's badly burned ...'

He looked at it for a moment, then back to the figure, astonished that it was still recognisably human. Though much of it was black, some reddened flesh could be seen. For a moment it reminded Malcolm of the prosthetics and technical expertise in films such as *The Lord of the Rings*, the hideous twisted figures of orcs only faintly resembling those of people.

'Did he burn to death?' he asked, swallowing hard.

'No, the explosion killed him instantly,' the pathologist confirmed in a tone that Malcolm recognised as the truth. This was a scientist he was dealing with, he reminded himself, not someone trying to sugar a bitter pill.

'Sorry,' he said at last. 'This could be anyone. I couldn't honestly say I would recognise this as Robert Truesdale.'

'We found this around his neck,' the pathologist told him, holding out a plastic bag on the palm of her hand. 'Would that help?'

'A cross?' Malcolm frowned, looking at the pathologist. 'He was wearing this round his neck, you say?'

Rosie nodded, her eyes on his own.

'I'm sorry, but this is just absurd,' Malcolm said. 'Robert was never a man of faith as far as I know, at least not in the time he was my boss.'

'Why "absurd"?' the detective called Newton asked him, picking up on his choice of word.

Malcolm spread his hands helplessly. 'This is all a bit mad,' he explained, glancing back at the burned body then to the cross nestling in the pathologist's hand. 'The Robert

Truesdale I knew was a confirmed atheist. Despised any-thing to do with organised religion. "Opium of the people" and all that,' he concluded, quoting Karl Marx.

'What was he like?' the detective asked him, evidently curious to know more about his former boss.

'He was good to work for,' Malcolm admitted. 'But he didn't socialise much with us after hours.' He made a face. 'Fact is, and I hate to speak ill of the dead, but Robert had a reputation as a bit of a skinflint. I wasn't in the least sur-prised he'd sold his family home and bought a smaller one out in the country.'

He watched as DS Newton nodded, her eyes fixed on his as if she were filing this away for future reference, which he supposed she was, given her job. Was she trying to make him think uncomfortable thoughts? Biting his lip, Malcolm Hinchliffe gave a huge sigh.

'You know, it makes me wonder if this man who crusaded long and hard to legalise drugs might actually have led a completely different life away from politics. I mean, isn't this a terrorist act? And . . . well, what would you have to do to be killed in this horrible way?' He gave a visible shudder.

'His previous car had been vandalised, I believe?'

'That's correct. But Robert was scrupulous about purchas-ing second-hand. Used to say the moment you drove out of the showroom the value of a new car plummeted. Yet, you say he was in a brand-new car?'

'Well, perhaps this was his retirement treat?' the DS sug-gested. 'Anything else you can tell us?'

Malcolm shook his head. 'I'm sorry, we haven't been much help, have we?' He sighed then gazed back at the wreck of the body beyond the viewing window. 'From what you've shown me . . . that cross . . . and, well, everything . . .' He gave another huge sigh then turned to face the pathologist again.

'It's making me wonder if I really knew Robert at all.'

It was a relief to be back in the office at Govan, the day waning into dusk as Molly sat once more at her desk. Truesdale's previous vehicle had been traced to a scrapyard, no further details about who had delivered it there were available. A dead end, she told herself, but they still had plenty other matters to investigate. The toxicology report would be back as soon as they could manage, Rosie had assured her, and now it fell to them to arrange a DNA match for the MSP's remains. Something in his home, a few hairs from his pillow, saliva from an unwashed teacup, any object that would provide the other side of this equation. For there was none of the man's DNA on any database. Still, it was a routine matter, surely? Molly yawned, thinking about the journey back to Strathblane. Dental records might also need to be checked. There would be statements in Holyrood, a funeral in St Giles or somewhere. There was nobody to give instruction on his funeral, she realised, and it fell to the Scottish Parliament to do the necessary. Somehow, she felt that Truesdale would be given the sort of lavish send-off he'd have hated, if his secretary was to be believed, the government ensuring they were seen to do their duty to a fallen comrade.

Ah well, the poor man wasn't here to object, so why did she have this niggling feeling that something wasn't right?

'How did it go?'

A voice from the doorway made Molly turn around.

'Oh, you're still here, sir,' she remarked, seeing the tall figure of Lorimer leaning against the door frame.

'Wanted to see you,' he said simply. 'Was it horrible?'

'Ach, seeing something like that could give you nightmares, if you let it.' She shrugged.

As she told him all about the visit, Molly sensed a growing interest, particularly when she recounted Hinchliffe's words about Truesdale's parsimonious habits as well as what the secretary had told her concerning the silver cross.

'Aye, that is strange, right enough. We need to see if there are any of his old neighbours who could confirm if he attended a local church,' Lorimer said at last. 'Tomorrow's Sunday. I know you're coming over to us for dinner later. Daniel, too, you know.' He paused and gave her a meaningful grin. 'However, think you might be able to put on that Canadian accent again?'

CHAPTER THIRTEEN

The villagers of Strathblane were becoming accustomed to uniformed police officers walking around their quiet streets. There was no doubt that the police were doing a thorough job of house-to-house interviews, neighbours in Strathmirren Gardens and adjoining streets questioned to see if they had noticed anything out of the ordinary in the days preceding the car bomb. Few would admit to it, but there was a sense of excitement at having one's door knocked and being asked questions, something to share with friends and neighbours in this close-knit community. It was the first topic of conversation on everyone's lips, details of visits compared over teacups, older heads shaking at the terrible way the world was going.

Evan listened to the voices from downstairs from the sanctuary of his room. She'd be loving this, he thought, imagining his mother, Dr Williams, talking about the old woman who had lived in the next street as if she was still there, her bungalow bought by that politician. The old lady had been one of his mother's patients before she'd ended up in that care home. *God's Waiting Room*, his father had called it. She'd be regaling that police officer with stories, probably nothing at all to do with that horrible morning when he'd leapt out of bed with a cry, thinking the house was under attack.

Nobody on this street had security cameras, he'd heard his dad sigh as they'd discussed installing one. Just that guy near to where it had happened. So, it stood to reason that the police were depending on the people who lived around here and what they remembered, didn't it?

Evan stood at the window in the landing and looked down at the street. There was a police car parked along the road but no sign of any officers. Were there two of them downstairs right now? They did go about in pairs, didn't they?

The boy crept to the top of the stairs, listening once more. Yes, he could make out a man and a woman, neither of whose voices he recognised. Mum had told him to get on with his homework, but Evan really knew she'd been telling him to stay upstairs out of the way of the grown-ups.

His mouth twisted in a moue of discontent as he thought about the open Chromebook on his desk. More maths, he thought, sullenly. That could have waited, surely? And why not be part of whatever was being said downstairs? He was twelve now, at high school, not some wee kid who didn't have a clue about anything. He had his opinion about the explosion – well, everyone at Balfron High did, to be fair; theories ranging from foreign terrorists to aliens in spaceships, the dafter ideas causing giggles in the playground. But nobody had asked him *proper* questions, had they?

Like, what he'd seen on the three consecutive nights before it had happened.

Evan drew in a deep breath, thinking about his mum's dismissive reaction, belittling him when he'd tried to tell her. *You've an overactive imagination, Evan*, she'd tutted, as if that was a fault.

But, looking out from his bedroom window on these dark nights, Evan Williams knew what he had seen.

CHAPTER FOURTEEN

'Good news,' Sergeant Alexander said as Daniel arrived to begin his night shift. 'We've managed to identify your dead woman.'

'Oh, tell me.'

'She's from the Romanian community in Govanhill. Angelika Mahbed. She shared a room with a few other women who are known street workers,' Alexander said with a twist to his mouth. 'Sad story. Got hooked on heroin like far too many of these poor women, then of course she was in thrall to her pimp. It's an old story, Kohi. They're brought over here with dreams of earning money but pretty soon find themselves on the game.' He shrugged. 'The kind man gives them something to make their sex work palatable then before they know it the vicious circle begins.'

'They need heroin to do the work but need the money from the work to buy drugs,' Daniel said sadly.

'Exactly. You know the score, right? Their dealer is

often the same guy who sets them up with sex work in the first place.'

'What about the baby?'

'We've spoken to the other women and it seems that Angelika kept on working right up till she gave birth.'

Daniel's mouth tightened at the thought, remembering the last weeks of Chipo's pregnancy. How desperate had the woman been?

'Anyway, there's some progress now and we're trying to find a next-of-kin back in Romania.'

'What about the baby's father?'

'Hm, that's a strange one,' Alexander continued. 'We hoped his DNA would be on our database, one of the low-lifes in the same area, but apparently it isn't there.'

'Who do you think he might be, then?'

'Someone who's been sneaky enough to evade the system,' Alexander said. 'Anyway, poor wee mite will be in hospital for a good while yet, needing to be detoxed very carefully.'

Daniel bit his lip, reluctant to tell the police sergeant of his visit to the Queen Elizabeth University Hospital. That might be seen as a mark against him and there was no way he wanted a reprimand this early in his probationary period.

'Right, let's see what tonight has in store for us,' Alexander said, walking along the corridor, with Daniel close behind. 'You're to attend a CID briefing, that right?'

'Yes,' Daniel replied, moving aside as another uniformed cop swept past.

It was a split second, a moment that might have been missed altogether had it not been for the hushed whisper as he passed him. A burly-looking cop, his small mean eyes glinting at Daniel, that racist word unmistakable.

Daniel clenched his jaw and strode past, determined to conceal his anger. It was an offence, he knew, a slur against him by a fellow officer. Racism still existed here in the very place he had hoped might be safe from such matters. Nobody but Daniel had heard that vile whisper and, he decided right there, nobody would. His word against a more experienced cop? It was foolish even to contemplate it. Still, he'd keep a lookout for this older man in future, steer clear of any occasion when he might find him alone. As he drew level with Jacob Alexander, he shivered, the sudden realisation that being a uniformed cop was no protection against the sort of discrimination he had been warned about back in his training days.

Although the CID room was full of unfamiliar faces, Daniel was pleased to be indoors, after his experience by the riverside the previous night. A few heads had turned when he slipped into a seat at the back. If he had expected the SIO to introduce him then he was disappointed. The woman simply launched into an update on the body hauled from the riverside with no mention of PC Kohi finding the murder weapon.

'White man in his forties, dark hair, some tattoos on his upper arms, no ID but sufficient marks on his clothing to show that the garments he was wearing at the time of death had been purchased in the UK.' She pointed to these different objects as they were shown on the whiteboard. 'Early signs are that he could be part of a drug gang. We've had a bit of trouble from these people lately,' she added, and now she gave a small nod towards Daniel as if to bring him up to speed.

Once again heads turned and there were one or two officers who smiled at the uniformed cop and one who even gave him a thumbs up. Did that mean that his part in this investigation was known to the team of detectives? Or was this simply a kind, inclusive gesture of welcome?

One man kept his eyes on Daniel for a little longer than the others, looking him up and down with no expression on his face at all. As the officer turned back to attend to the SIO's words, Daniel felt a shiver of disquiet down his spine. Was it the colour of his skin that had caused that stare? Or had the recent incident in the corridor heightened his imagination?

'Right, here's a list of actions for tonight,' the SIO said, then proceeded to allot different actions to the officers on her team who immediately disappeared into different cor- ners of the room, leaving Daniel sitting alone, wondering what was now expected of him.

'Thanks for attending,' DS Miller told him as she walked him to the door. 'Hope you got some sort of insight into the ways CID works on a case here.'

And with that, Daniel was dismissed, his walk back through the police station to his own area making him feel a longing for his former status. The next two years were going to be a struggle if he didn't accept that he was at the bottom of the ladder once again. It would take a long time to achieve the rank of inspector, an ambition that Daniel Kohi was determined to fulfil one day.

*

'How was your shift?' Netta asked as they sat together, Daniel nursing his second cup of tea. He had confided some of what he'd experienced to his elderly friend, knowing that anything he told her would not be repeated.

'They've identified that woman I found,' Daniel told her. 'She's called Angelika Mahbed. She was a sex worker. Romanian.'

'Aye, that figures,' Netta nodded. 'I mind there was a raid a few years back in that same area. Romany women. Gypsies for the most part.'

'Sergeant Alexander, Jacob, my tutor, said there had been discussions with some of the other women she lived with and now they're trying to find her family back in Romania.'

'Good luck wi' that,' Netta sighed. 'If she was brought over here as a youngster, it could be that she's from a poor Roma family. Disgusting, so it is, selling your ain bairns intae slavery like that!'

'Something else, though,' Daniel continued and then told Netta about the search for the baby's father.

'One thing that's interesting is that so far there is no sign of paternal DNA on any database. So, he could be one of her punters. In which case he'll never be found.'

'And never know he has a son,' Netta said sadly.

Daniel suppressed a sigh.

'No casual punter would want to acknowledge an illegit-imate child, especially one born to a heroin addict.'

'Aye, richt enough,' Netta agreed, picking up her empty teacup and walking back into her kitchenette.

It was a thought that saddened Daniel but he was realistic enough to see the truth of that. No questions were being asked now about why the young mother had been covered in that blanket and left to die. An overdose was explanation enough. But there was still something about it that troubled Daniel Kohi.

He looked around the comfortable lounge full of Netta's knick-knacks; china figurines and colourful postcards on the mantelpiece, their edges curled with age. He'd become so used to dropping in on his neighbour, he knew how much he was going to miss her.

'Thanks for the tea,' he said. 'Better get along to my place.'

'Aye, away and get some kip. See ye soon, son,' Netta answered, turning and giving him her usual grin.

His tenancy there would not continue for much longer, he realised with a pang as he turned the key to his own front door. It was surprising how easily he'd developed the routine of driving back from his shifts then calling in to see Netta.

There had been such changes in his life, Daniel realised, fatigue settling on his shoulders like a heavy cloak. Torn away from the land of his birth, forced to become a refugee in this cold country and losing . . . well, everything.

Once indoors, he turned on the radio, hoping for something to banish these dark thoughts.

'News has just come in that the victim of the Strathblane car bomb was MSP Robert Truesdale,' a male voice told him.

Daniel listened intently, imagining the scene, his fists clenched tightly, and, as the reporter continued, he slumped onto his bed. Closing his eyes for a moment, he saw again the flames and the plumes of dark smoke as his home had burned, his beloved Chipo and Johannes inside.

A tear threatened to spill but he dashed it away with an angry hand. Self-pity was not in his nature, Daniel scolded himself, pressing the off button on his radio and silencing the reporter's voice. He'd been lucky to have a second chance at being a police officer, fortunate to have found good friends, especially the tall detective with whom he had forged a special bond.

He hadn't managed to meet up with Lorimer recently, each of them immersed in the work of Police Scotland. Today was Sunday, the first of four rest days, and he'd been invited over to the Lorimers' home in Giffnock for dinner after he'd caught up with some sleep. The thought cheered him. Time spent with the Lorimers was guaranteed to lift his spirits. And Molly Newton would be there, a little voice reminded him, a voice that seemed to soothe Daniel Kohi as he turned on his side and fell into a dreamless sleep.

'What time will you be home from church?'

'Oh, about twelve-thirty, why?'

'Mind if I'm a bit late back for lunch?'

'Are you working? I thought this was a day off?' Maggie asked, rolling onto her side and cuddling closer to her husband.

Lorimer took her hand and gave it a squeeze. 'I want to spend a bit of time over in Robert Truesdale's new house. SOCOs have been in and out but I'd like to see it for myself.'

'Won't it be a mess after that explosion?'

'Not too bad, apparently,' he replied. 'Garage went up. A

wooden affair, full of boxes of his stuff that were burned. Front windows blew out but I'm told the interior is basically okay.'

'They'll have boarded up all the windows, I suppose.'

'Yes. I think the local joiners had a field day in that street,' Lorimer sighed. 'Quite a few families were affected by the blast and there was a lot of clearing up to be done.'

'Okay. See you when you get back. And don't forget Daniel and Molly are coming for dinner,' Maggie said, easing herself out of his grasp and pulling a face. 'I'm on duty this morning, greeting our parishioners at the door, so I'd better think about getting up.'

'Five more minutes,' Lorimer teased, pulling her back down and nuzzling her neck. 'You can't be in that much of a hurry.'

The journey to Strathblane was slower than he'd expected, a tractor on the narrower road holding up the line of traffic, Sunday drivers apparently content to follow in its wake. Rain was blotting out any view of the surrounding hills and Lorimer had to avoid several potholes full of muddy water. At last, he drew up near the house where Robert Truesdale had died, parking the Lexus a little way around a corner to avoid any prying eyes. He hurried to the front door, unlocked it and slipped inside, hoping that he'd avoided detection from any of the neighbours.

The smell would take a long time to fade, especially now that the house was securely locked up, no fresh air to disperse the smokiness. Lorimer was accustomed to foul smells, finding a body that had badly decayed the worst of all, and the aftermath of this fire was mild in comparison. He walked from the hallway towards the back of the bungalow and into the kitchen. It had been thoroughly examined and samples had been taken from several items to determine DNA. He looked at the Formica tabletop, seeing a layer of toast crumbs. Had Truesdale sat here eating his breakfast that morning, drinking a mug of his favourite tea? There were several mugs stacked on a shelf, identical to the one that had been bagged and taken away, bone china with a floral pattern that Lorimer guessed had belonged to Truesdale's late mother. Was that a sign of sentimentality? Maggie's old mother had always maintained that tea tasted better from a china cup, something the late MSP might have acknowledged. Beneath the kitchen table lay a pet bed furred around the edges where the cat had slept, its empty food bowl on the floor near the sink. There was no sign now of Truesdale's pet, no doubt rescued by the cops and being cared for in an animal shelter.

What else could he find out about the man who had so recently moved into this house? Lorimer wondered, gazing out of the window above the kitchen sink at a very over-grown back garden. There were four clothes poles painted a dark shade of green, a few mildewed pegs still clipped onto a sagging washing line. A hawthorn hedge straggled upwards, screening the garden from the house further up the hill that backed onto the property. Had that been a factor in the MSP's choice of residence, providing a mod-icum of privacy? It was a very modest property compared with the big family home. And somehow at odds with the new car that had gone up in smoke. An inconsistency that Lorimer felt like an uncomfortable itch.

He turned back to the kitchen, taking a long look at the layout. It was quite modern with off-white units and wood-effect worktops though the laminate flooring was chipped in places. He opened a few cupboards with gloved hands, noting the neatly stacked rows of tins and bottles, smaller jars of spices to the front.

The fridge was full, as if someone had done a recent shop, Lorimer thought, kneeling down and examining the fresh fruit, vegetables, and packs of butcher meat, all with Waitrose labels, that would never now be made into meals. *Waitrose, not Aldi*, a small voice pointed out. Was this yet another inconsistency in a man who'd been known to watch his pennies? He stood up again, thinking hard, then bent down once more. The butter had only recently been opened, two small slicks across its creamy yellow surface where a knife had been drawn. Lorimer frowned. That was a bit odd, surely? Hadn't Truesdale been in his new home for several days before the incident? Enough time to have used up more of the butter but not long enough to finish an entire pack.

It was little things like that which stuck in his mind as Lorimer moved around the house, opening the back bedroom door. The previous owner had favoured Laura Ashley wallpaper, a pussywillow pattern in grey, toning with a silver-grey carpet that was badly stained in places. Why hadn't the MSP replaced that prior to moving in? Lorimer frowned. Questions for the dead were frustrating at times, especially when there appeared to be so few people in Truesdale's life who might now supply answers.

The man's bed was neatly made, the corners of the sheet

tucked in the way Lorimer had seen in hospitals, the duvet smoothed down, pillows tilted at an angle against the headboard. Mr Neat and Tidy, he decided. A single man with his own particular little ways of doing things? Or someone who'd been trained well? A quick look in the wardrobe showed several suits plus a full kilt outfit zipped into their dress bags, a raincoat and a couple of rain jackets pushed to one side. Several pairs of shoes were scattered beneath, not lined up in pairs which Lorimer found at odds with the rest of the man's possessions. Had he rummaged for a favourite pair, intending to return and tidy these up later, a task he would now never fulfil?

Something wasn't quite right, he thought, leaving the bedroom and heading for the lounge at the front of the house. A man who appeared to be against organised religion yet wore a cross around his neck? Someone who appeared to be set in his ways, taking time to fold the corners of his bedding yet leaving his footwear in a shambles. Where had he intended to go as he sat in that expensive car? And more to the point, who had wanted to stop him?

Molly didn't mind giving up a few hours of her Sunday to don her good clothes and brush up her Canadian accent. Her time in undercover had been a contrast of boredom and adrenalin rush, the results satisfying enough to have kept her in that role for several years until she had almost come to grief. The move to the MIT had been welcome but there were times that DS Newton missed the chance to change, chameleon-like, into a different persona.

Sunday lunchtime seemed like the right time to go calling

on the neighbour again. If Karen Douglas was a churchgoer she would be home by now, Molly had decided. The media had got wind of the explosion and Truesdale's new address and this morning's front pages were full of the story. Molly must act as if she was a grieving friend while taking a hard look at how Truesdale's old neighbour responded. She parked the car outside the villa and took a long look around. This was a well-established neighbourhood, she guessed, large gardens with mature trees and shrubs, neatly tended. Truesdale would have made a nice profit from the sale of the old family home in Newton Mearns, an affluent suburb on Glasgow's Southside, now that he had no one else with whom to share it. Molly had looked up recent property valuations and had been surprised that similar villas in this area had sold for over a million pounds. The purchase of that small bungalow out in Strathblane must have left Truesdale with a very substantial profit.

Shrouds have no pockets, a small voice reminded Molly. Robert Truesdale may have had plans for retirement but that was something he had never lived long enough to enjoy.

Her high heels clip-clopped up the garden path as Molly approached the entrance to Karen Douglas's home. The storm doors were pushed back, suggesting that someone had been up and doing, at least, and, as she rang the bell, she could see movement behind a patterned glazed front door.

'Act two, Scene one,' Molly murmured under her breath, staring as a figure came into sight.

'Oh, it's you again.' Karen Douglas stood in the hallway, a frown on her face. 'Well, given what's happened you'd better come in,' she said, closing her mouth tightly as if Molly's arrival had caught the woman at a bad moment. 'Best go into the lounge.' Karen led Molly along a corridor, turning into a spacious room with French windows that looked out onto a manicured lawn.

'I'm so sorry to bother you. It's just that poor Robert . . . Oh, my!' Molly pulled out a handkerchief from her coat pocket and dabbed her eyes.

'I was just preparing lunch, but the soup's made and, well, it can wait, I suppose. Sit down, won't you?' she said, giving Molly a more sympathetic look. 'You must have had a terrible shock.' Karen Douglas glanced towards the coffee table where a copy of *The Sunday Times* lay, the picture on the front a head and shoulders photo of the late MSP.

'I can't believe it,' Molly said huskily. 'Who does evil things like that?'

'Just the very words our minister used at this morning's service,' Karen told her.

'Oh, was Robert one of his flock?' Molly whispered.

'Goodness, no,' Karen retorted. 'I don't think he ever set foot inside the kirk unless it was for a funeral. And even then, he insisted that his own mother was cremated. No Christian burial, no nice church service with all the proper hymns. A *funeral celebrant*, if you please! And poor Mrs Truesdale a regular attender at St Andrew's till she couldn't get out of that house! She'll be birling in her grave, most likely.'

'I think I remember Robert showing me a picture of his mom.' Molly sat back, a dreamy look in her eyes as though she were trying to bring it to mind, though each word was being made up on the spot. 'Didn't she used to wear a little silver cross around her neck?'

'A cross!' Karen Douglas exclaimed. 'Good Lord, no! Jenny Truesdale wouldn't be seen out in anything but her good pearls. Besides, she held that wearing crosses was rather ... *Popish*, if you know what I mean. Not that I'm against the Catholic Church, myself,' she added hurriedly. 'But Jenny did hold some very firm views about religion.'

'Which put Robert off for life,' Molly murmured, as if she had been party to the MSP's inner thoughts and beliefs.

'Well, you'd know that, being an old friend,' Karen agreed, leaning forward and looking steadily at the well-dressed blonde woman sitting opposite. 'Though I must say you look a lot younger than Robert. How did you two meet?'

'Oh, through work,' Molly replied, ready to trot out her cover story. 'I represent a charity back in Quebec that was linked to work the Scottish government was doing a few years ago. We ...' She looked down shyly then back at Karen. 'Well, we found we had a lot in common. But we lost touch after a while,' she added with an exaggerated sigh, pulling out the handkerchief once more. 'I'm sorry, I just wanted to give you my condolences and ask if you knew anything about a funeral? I have to return home in a few days but if it was happening soon ...?'

'Oh, I doubt it, my dear,' Karen Douglas replied, rising to her feet as Molly stood up, ready to leave. 'The police won't release his ... well, it will take quite a while, you understand.'

'Thank you,' Molly said, sniffing back unshed tears. 'You've been so kind. Robert will be such a loss.'

'Well, yes,' Karen Douglas agreed as she led Molly back to the front door. 'I'll ...' She stopped for a moment and Molly saw her biting her lower lip as though to cut off whatever she'd been going to say.

The woman swallowed hard before continuing. ' I ... I suppose he'll be missed by all of those people that wanted to legalise drugs.'

Molly turned, her eyes widening for a moment. 'You didn't agree with him on that?'

'No indeed I did not,' Karen Douglas declared. 'But people can express an opinion without resorting to mindless violence.'

Well, she'd got what she'd come for, Molly thought as she drove away from the leafy avenue. Robert Truesdale did not have any truck with organised religion and, what was more, he had no apparent sentimental reason for wearing that small silver cross around his neck. As she headed back home to Glasgow's West End, Molly pondered the thought of what the late Mrs Truesdale might have made of her son's crusade and his determination to rob her of a Christian burial.

She grinned to herself, thinking of the reaction of Daniel and the Lorimers if she were to discuss this morning's visit with them over dinner this evening. For a moment Molly imagined the Zimbabwean's face, his gentle smile, and the way he sometimes looked at her. There was something about this man that had awoken a longing in Molly Newton's heart, feelings she had never truly experienced before. But, she warned herself, if Daniel Kohi did not feel the same way, then perhaps she was heading for the biggest disappointment of her life.

CHAPTER FIFTEEN

It was well into the afternoon before Daniel surfaced from a dreamless sleep.

He gave a long sigh, curling himself more tightly into the duvet. Four whole days off, he thought, snuggling into the warmth of the bed. The long shifts had taken their toll since Daniel had begun his probation, something the trainee cops had been warned about. Keep up your level of fitness, their PE trainer at Tulliallan had urged, prompting several of them to chat about their memberships of different gyms. There was a fitness studio near Hampden, his tutor at Govanhill police station had told them, and Daniel made a mental note to seek it out soon.

However, he needed to use his off-duty time wisely and perhaps he could begin looking for a new flat. Netta might know of places that were not too far from here; after all, he didn't want to lose touch with his old friend. A two-bedroom place, he told himself. Just in case he could persuade the old lady to join him.

Today was for rest and recreation, though, and Daniel's smile broadened as he thought of his visit across the city to the Lorimers' home. And seeing a certain blonde detective sergeant. He had a bit of catching up to do and was keen to tell them all about the events of the last few days.

The rain had eased off as Daniel turned into the cul-de-sac where Maggie and Lorimer lived. He spotted the new dark blue Lexus in the driveway, a different beast from the old silver car that the detective superintendent had driven for many years. He raised his eyebrows at the Lexus ES300, noting its registration plate, not brand new but expensive enough to turn heads in the police car park. Once, Daniel had remarked on Lorimer's big car. Would people not wonder at a police officer driving such a vehicle? He'd seen a few of his former colleagues in Zimbabwe driving souped-up Mercs, the spoils of corrupt dealing. Lorimer had laughed quietly. *No mortgage and no kids, Daniel*, he'd replied. *We're lucky to be comfortably off and the car's my one big indulgence.* Happily, Lorimer had told him, most of his fellow officers were aware of this and didn't cast envious eyes at the car.

Daniel's finger was hardly off the bell when the door opened.

'Daniel! At last, come in. We haven't seen you for ages.' Maggie Lorimer beamed, ushering him into the warmth of the house. 'Look, here's Chancer come to greet you,' she added with a chuckle and Daniel looked down to see the old ginger cat rubbing himself against his trouser leg.

The cat was duly patted on his furry head then Daniel

followed Maggie into the large open-plan room. Lorimer was at the far end, behind the breakfast bar that separated the kitchen from the main living-dining room, Maggie's desk tucked under the bay window to the front.

'A small one before dinner?' Lorimer asked, holding up a bottle of malt whisky. 'Molly shouldn't be long,' he added.

'Just one. I'm driving,' Daniel reminded him.

'A three-course dinner tonight in your honour, PC Kohi,' Lorimer laughed. 'That's plenty of time to soak up a wee dram before you go back home. Maggie's made your favourite apple pie.'

'Apples from our own tree,' Maggie said. 'Do you think Netta would like some?'

'I'm sure she would,' Daniel replied. It would give him a reason to visit his neighbour tomorrow, not that any excuse was needed, Netta always happy to see him.

At that minute the doorbell rang and Daniel turned to see Maggie striding across the room, a small flutter of excitement in his stomach. Then the female voices as Maggie greeted the detective sergeant and Daniel felt his face broaden in a smile as he heard Molly's familiar laugh.

'Right, sit yourself down and tell us what you've been doing.' Lorimer brought two crystal glasses over to comfortable chairs that were positioned next to the fireplace. 'Ah, Molly, just in time,' he added as the tall blonde entered the room. 'What'll you have?'

'Oh, just a glass of water, thanks,' she replied. 'Hi, Daniel.' She came towards both men, raising a hand in greeting.

'Okay. Make yourselves comfortable. We were just about to hear how this fellow's been doing over at Govanhill,'

Lorimer said, loping across to the kitchen area to fetch her drink.

While Maggie busied herself in the kitchen, looking up now and then to listen to their friends, Daniel told them all about finding the dead woman in that filthy lane and then the discovery of a body in the River Cart.

'And they took you to the city mortuary?' Molly asked.

'Yes. It's an interesting place. Back home ours is part of a big modern hospital,' Daniel remarked. 'But there's something about the Glasgow mortuary … a sort of atmosphere …'

'It's so close to the High Court on one side and the wide-open expanse of Glasgow Green on the other,' Lorimer agreed. 'Life and death,' he murmured. 'And the choice between freedom and incarceration. I've often thought about the juxtaposition of those particular places.'

Daniel nodded and went on to tell his friends about the latest developments in both cases.

'I still do wonder if she simply lay down on the ground, wrapping herself in that blanket. Or if there had been some-body with her who had covered her over after she died. Not that knowing will make any difference now. Poor woman must have had a dreadful sort of existence.'

'Drugs and sexual enslavement, twin evils that go hand-in-hand.' Lorimer sighed. 'I wonder what difference it might make if drugs were to be completely legalised.'

'Are you working on a case to do with that?' Daniel asked.

'You'll know about the car bomb? Robert Truesdale, the MSP? He was spearheading a campaign to legalise drugs. It's all over the news today.'

Daniel nodded. 'I heard it on the radio on my way back home this morning.'

'Bill's been asked to do an investigation on behalf of the Scottish government,' Maggie chipped in. 'Molly, you must be busy with that too?'

'A bit.' The detective sergeant smiled but did not give any details of her involvement.

Daniel was not surprised by this news. William Lorimer was well respected in the higher echelons of Police Scotland and, though he might never aspire to one of the top jobs, being a detective superintendent and head of the Major Incident Team seemed to satisfy his friend. It was not that he lacked ambition, Daniel knew, more that Lorimer had found the right fit in his current place within the force and his easy relationship with the chief constable occasionally made for more interesting cases, like this one.

'Can't say too much.' Lorimer smiled, glancing approvingly at Molly. 'Politics is a strange business and the newspapers are always one small step behind each move that government figures make.'

'Did you ever meet him? Truesdale, I mean?' Daniel asked.

Lorimer sat back, a frown appearing between his eyes as he turned the glass in his hand thoughtfully.

'Sadly, no. I spoke to him on the phone the night before it happened, however. Tried to persuade him to accept some police security, but he was having none of it.'

'I wonder why?' Maggie asked as she set down a plate of nibbles and dips.

'Why he couldn't be persuaded? I suppose he felt a bit

more removed from the political scene since his resignation,' Lorimer replied.

'What did the First Minister make of that?' she asked, sitting down beside them.

Lorimer shook his head. 'I don't know,' he answered. 'I can imagine what he must have thought when he read the letter of resignation, though. I got the feeling that Truesdale wasn't one to mince his words.'

'He'd had a rotten time on social media,' Maggie murmured. 'It can be such a blight on some folks' lives.'

Daniel nodded. 'I have absolutely no social media footprint,' he told them. 'Of course, as far as most people in Zimbabwe are concerned, I'm supposed to be dead.'

'This poor wee baby you told us about,' Maggie began, changing the subject as her husband's frown deepened. 'What will happen to him?'

'Well, we are still trying to locate the father and the mother's family so he remains in hospital for now and then he'll be found a foster home by social services,' Daniel told her.

'And, if you do find the father . . .?' Molly asked.

Daniel shrugged. 'I don't really know what happens then,' he said. 'So far we haven't traced a familial match on any database and nobody has come forward to claim the child.' He made a face. 'It's what you might expect if he was just one of the woman's clients.' He stopped to take a swig from his glass, the memory of that pallid face and the syringe hanging from her arm still clear in his mind.

There was silence amongst them for a few moments as Daniel reflected on the unfairness of it all; his own child burned to death, Maggie and Lorimer unable to have kids and this poor baby abandoned in a filthy Glasgow alley, no one to care for him except the nursing staff in the QEUH.

'Right, time for dinner.' Maggie sprang to her feet and walked briskly to the kitchen where appetising smells wafted across the room.

The rest of the evening passed without further comments on either of their ongoing cases, Maggie making them laugh about some of the amusing moments she'd experienced during her book talks to young children. By the end of the meal the candles on the table were burned halfway down, their long yellow flames flickering. Daniel glanced across at Molly several times, meeting her eyes and wondering what thoughts were going through the woman's mind. Once he caught Lorimer gazing their way, the blue eyes crinkling at the corners as though he had seen something to make him smile.

It was as he was taking his leave of them that Daniel brought up the subject of cars once more. Molly had left already, giving his arm a little squeeze as she made her goodbyes. She'd have the usual morning start to her day, Daniel free to enjoy his rest period.

'I like the new Lexus,' he remarked as he stood outside with Lorimer. 'What sort of car was it that the MSP owned? The one that was blown up?'

'Funny you should ask,' Lorimer replied drily. 'That's been on my mind, too. It was a brand-new Honda CR-V. Worth quite a bit of money.' He stopped and frowned. 'Yet, if you were going to spend a fair sum on a new car, why not buy a hybrid? All our politicians seem to wave the flag for a greener environment.'

'Had he bought it for his retirement? After years on the political stage?' Daniel looked puzzled. 'But a single man with a big family-sized car? That doesn't sound right. Most people in his position would buy a smaller car, surely? And if he was retiring, wouldn't he be watching his spending? I mean, even with a decent pension, the cost of living has rocketed in recent times.'

'I agree,' Lorimer said. 'Though he probably made a good profit on selling the family home.' He shrugged, sighing. 'Just one more question I'd like to ask a dead man.'

CHAPTER SIXTEEN

'It could have been done by anyone,' the man in the lab coat told Lorimer, peering over his half-moon spectacles at the detective superintendent. 'Planting a car bomb such as this one and detonating it isn't rocket science these days, I'm afraid. Everything you might need can be all too easily accessed on the internet.'

Lorimer heard the man's sigh. 'Standard sort of stuff,' he continued. 'Detonator set to explode the device as soon as the engine was switched on. All the perpetrator required was access to the boot. There's a switch inside that was attached to the device beneath the car. I can draw a diagram to show you if you like?'

Lorimer nodded. Anything that would help explain exactly how this bomb went off would give him an insight into who had done this terrible thing. But the man's words had not filled him with much hope. *Standard sort of stuff. Not rocket science.* He stifled a sigh. Any expectations that examination of the wreckage might have shown something significant were gone, it seemed.

'It was deliberately nasty, in my humble opinion,' the scientist went on. 'The bomb was placed directly beneath the petrol tank so that the explosion caused the petrol to ignite and ... well ...'

'The driver was incinerated, not just blown up,' Lorimer finished for him.

'Mmm, and of course that would only have happened with a petrol-driven car, not a diesel model.'

'Almost as though it were designed to make life difficult for forensic scientists.'

'Exactly. Not much left to work with, as you can see.'

Lorimer did see as he looked at the wreckage. It was a miracle there was anything left for this man to have worked on at all. But every bit of evidence might help, no matter how small.

'A bloody good job it happened when it did. Goodness knows who else might have been affected if it had happened a couple of hours later when there were more people about.'

'I'm told the village is usually quiet that early in the morning.' Lorimer's mind harked back to the CCTV film from one of Truesdale's neighbours he had watched repeatedly.

'Would they be aware their victim was in the habit of leaving early, perhaps? Making sure their target didn't interfere with any other civilians?'

'Are you suggesting we're looking for someone with a conscience?' Lorimer asked, his tone tinged with deliberate sarcasm.

'Hm,' the scientist nodded, eyebrows raised in agreement, 'I dare say not. Someone wanted to dispatch this vehicle and its occupant, all right, though. And now we know whose car it was. Yes?' he asked, looking up at Lorimer.

'Yes,' he replied with a sigh. 'You'll have heard the latest reports, I suppose? Media are having a field day about Robert Truesdale. He left the car in his driveway probably because he'd just moved in and the garage was full of stuff. And somebody knew that.' It was inevitable that this information was now public knowledge although the police press office had tried their best to keep a lid on it as long as they could.

'I read that he'd been targeted by the IRA. Any truth in that?' the scientist asked, his bushy grey eyebrows raised expectantly.

'Not able to say, not yet. But nobody that side of the water has claimed responsibility,' Lorimer replied drily.

'Sad to see a brand-new job like this go up with a bang,' the man continued, pointing a gloved finger at the chassis of the Honda. 'Poor chap didn't get much joy of it, did he?'

Lorimer shook his head. 'No. Though I wonder why he wanted a car like this? Not a family man and it was the top of the range, all the bells and whistles you could wish for. Plus, he seems to have been known as a thrifty sort of chap.'

'Curiouser and curiouser, Superintendent,' came the reply. 'Well, good luck with your investigation,' he added with the hint of a smile.

As he drove back from Gartcosh, past the sleepy villages of Moodiesburn and Chryston, Lorimer wondered about the man who'd been blown up by what might have been a terrorist bomb. Robert Truesdale was becoming something of an enigma, he realised. A man not given to spending pots of money yet forking out tens of thousands on a nice new

Honda CR-V. An avowed atheist who wore a silver cross around his neck. No, it didn't add up one bit and William Lorimer knew he would not rest until he had satisfied himself with knowing much, much more about the late MSP. He had instructed one of the team to do a thorough search of Truesdale's financial affairs and he hoped that a report about that would be waiting when he returned to Govan.

First, however, came a development that he had not been expecting, the phone suddenly interrupting his thoughts. He put out a finger to receive the call.

'Lorimer, it's Caroline Flint.'

'Ma'am, I'm just on my way back from Gartcosh,' he replied.

'I've just had the FM on,' Flint said without any preamble. 'No letter of resignation has turned up on his desk this morning. And he wants to know why.'

Lorimer drew into the side of the road, close to a row of shops so he could better concentrate on the call.

'All I can say, ma'am, is what the late Mr Truesdale told me on that telephone call. He had sent his letter of resignation. It was Thursday he spoke about that. If he'd posted his letter first class it would have arrived by now.'

'Sent? Or merely written?' Flint asked.

Lorimer struggled with the memory of the man's words. 'Hard to say, ma'am. He did say that once the First Minister read his letter of resignation, he would know why it had been written. I can't say with any certainty that it had been posted, of course.'

He heard the chief constable swear softly under her breath.

'It might even have been burned to a crisp in the car,' she seethed. 'Oh, very well, then. I will have to tell him that.'

'Does it make that much of a difference?' Lorimer asked. 'The man's dead, after all.'

'It matters to the bean counters, apparently,' Flint growled. 'Truesdale's salary and severance pay will be paid into his estate. And they want to know who's paying for the funeral.'

The costs of his funeral would certainly not come from the dead man's bank account, Lorimer told himself as he read the pages of the report, eyes widening in astonishment.

There were several pages fastened with a paperclip that gave evidence of Truesdale's banking activities over the past year, something that one of his diligent DCs had ferreted out. Twelve months of bank statements gave some insight into the late MSP's spending habits and Lorimer noted from his credit card activity that he had always paid his monthly bill in full.

Careful with money? He flicked through the pages, shaking his head. But *what* money?

For it was clear to see that Truesdale had made several large withdrawals shortly before his death, leaving his accounts almost depleted.

Had he been under pressure from someone? The word *blackmail* had sprung to mind almost immediately but there were no matching sums withdrawn at regular intervals, the usual sign that one person had a hold over another.

Or could he have been a secret philanthropist?

Was this yet another dichotomy in his understanding of

the dead man? Had Truesdale given away his small fortune, deciding to retire from the dirty world of politics and live quietly in that sleepy little village? Yet, if that were so, why purchase that huge car? A one-off purchase, perhaps, bought to last?

Follow the money was the mantra of the forensic account-ant but that only made sense in the context of some crime having been committed and there was none that Lorimer could see, except the demise of the man whose money had been taken out of these bank accounts by his very own hand.

He pressed a hand to his forehead, acknowledging the ache that was beginning. Perhaps it was time to cast his net a bit further, see if another mind could fathom the depths of this mystery.

Professor Solomon Brightman took time to rub the blue cloth around the lenses of his tortoiseshell spectacles, then, after holding them up to the light and giving a faint smile of satisfaction, he put them on again, blinking owlishly at the sun streaming through the stained-glass windows of his room. Solly sat back in the ancient leather chair, contemplat-ing the arrival of his visitor. Lorimer had sat in this room at University Gardens many times as the pair discussed some of the detective's more difficult cases. As a psychologist who had specialised in the study of the criminal mind, Solly took a perennial interest in Lorimer's work and had occasionally been asked by Police Scotland to join their investigation team. Often, such a request was preceded by a visit just like this and so he sat pondering the commitments he had as a university professor and how much time he might need to relinquish should the police need his services.

Solly had been aware of the bomb, of course, and shuddered as he thought about the sort of nameless person who had left that destructive device. A mind closed to the awfulness of the bomb's consequences, removed from the scene, leaving no obvious trace of his presence. It was like the work of a poisoner, drawing apart from the scene of death, only profiting from it afterwards. A cowardly act, in some respects. Was this the work of a psychopath, someone devoid of much imagination? A cold creature, unable to empathise with his fellow humans? Perhaps. And yet it was from a passionate fervour on the part of terrorists in several of the world's trouble spots that similar deadly acts took place. Some of them would imagine the results of their acts only too well, glorying in the fall of whoever had been targeted.

The sound of a knock on his door broke the professor's reverie and he rose from his chair.

'Lorimer, come in.' He beamed, looking intently at the tall figure entering the room. He was tired, Solly decided, noting the dark circles beneath the blue eyes and the deepening lines around his mouth. Each new case brought its own difficulties, heaping long hours upon the shoulders of this man, an officer who cared about bringing justice to the victims of crime. Being head of the Major Incident Team involved a lot of administrative duties, too, and these could be just as wearing for a man like Lorimer, whose preference was to be out and about.

'Tea? The kettle's not long boiled.'

'Aye, something strong, though, none of your herbal stuff,'

Lorimer laughed, sinking down into an adjacent chair, his long limbs stretched out in front of him.

Solly fussed around, selecting the cleanest mugs he could find, listening as the detective gave a long sigh as if he were glad to be in a place where he could finally relax.

'How's Maggie?' Solly asked, when the tea was in front of them both, deliberately putting off the moment when more serious business would be discussed.

'Fine,' came the reply, a trifle too quick to be a considered response. 'Working on her next story. Can't tell you how proud I am of her success,' he added.

'She did well,' Solly continued, eyeing his friend. 'Being shortlisted for that children's book prize, I mean.'

'Yes.' Lorimer ran a tired hand through his dark hair, letting it flop across his forehead. 'Pity she didn't win it, but she seemed thrilled to have got that far.'

'That was a big achievement in itself,' Solly went on. 'We're all very proud of her. And Abby loves her books.'

He watched as Lorimer closed his eyes and took a deep breath.

'Ah, she has a nice life,' he sighed quietly. 'All these long hours of me being at work have been put to good use. Four books now, in her series.' He nodded. 'And the publishers are clamouring for more.'

'That's good. Isn't it?'

Lorimer opened his eyes and turned to the psychologist. 'She's thinking of cutting back at school, as it happens. The writing isn't just what takes up her time nowadays, you see, there are lots of events in the evenings and weekend book festivals too.'

'Changes,' Solly murmured. 'We have to adapt as human beings to the things we sometimes cannot control.'

'Aye, well, that poor guy who got himself blown up didn't change his views on the legalising of drugs. And to be honest, that's the only thing we have that seems to give a reason for his murder.'

'Drug barons stopping one crusader won't make that much of a difference to new legislation, surely?' Solly asked.

'Who knows? Maybe it was a message. Don't mess with the system or we'll deal with you like this?'

'If you really think that is the line of investigation to follow,' Solly began slowly, 'why did you want to see me? There was something you "wanted to run past me", as you put it.'

The detective sat up straighter in his chair and gulped down the last of his tea.

'Yes, there are several inconsistencies that bother me,' he began. 'Let me describe the late Robert Truesdale as best I can. Here is a member of the Scottish Parliament, well known for his drive to legalise drugs. Single man, lived with his elderly mother until her death last year. Sells the big family home and decides to relocate to a small bungalow in Strathblane. So far, so reasonable.'

'But ...?'

Lorimer leaned forward, catching Solly's eye. 'But he does not let his colleagues at Holyrood know a thing about his change of address, making them alert Police Scotland to a missing person.' He lifted his hands wide. 'I mean, it's absurd. Coupled with that, he seems to have decided to hand in his resignation, something he was adamant about when I spoke to him once we'd finally located his whereabouts. Yet nobody at Holyrood had an inkling about that, including the First Minister.'

'That is odd,' Solly agreed.

'And that's not the half of it, Solly,' Lorimer went on. 'The man was known for being extremely careful with money, and yet he appears to have bought an expensive new car.'

'The one that was blown up?'

'Exactly. And there's more.'

Solly waited, curious to build up a picture of the victim.

'When your Rosie examined him, she found a silver cross on a chain around his neck. No big deal. Until, that is, we found out that the man was a committed atheist who had a real grudge against the Christian Church. Now,' he said, staring hard at Solly. 'Wouldn't you say that was odd?'

'Inconsistencies,' Solly said thoughtfully. 'Hm.'

There was silence between the two men as Solly looked into the distance, Lorimer waiting for a response. These lengthy pauses were not infrequent during their discussions about human behaviour and Lorimer had learned long since to be patient.

At last, the psychologist seemed to wake from his reverie and, stroking his beard thoughtfully, he turned back to Lorimer.

'I suppose there's no doubt that the body in that car was Robert Truesdale's? Rosie did tell me one thing after the post-mortem. She said that it was practically impossible for his secretary to identify him.'

He watched as Lorimer blinked. That very thought had been pushed to the furthest recesses of his mind for some time now, he realised. And it had taken this conversation with the psychologist to bring it out into the open.

'We have had DNA samples taken from the body and they're being cross-checked against certain items in the man's home,' Lorimer replied with a frown. 'Plus, it was definitely Truesdale I spoke to the night before ...'

'But did anyone actually see him there?' Solly persisted. 'And do you know if the man was talking to you from his home?'

He looked at the detective who was now sitting hunched in the chair, the airing of this idea taking shape.

'If it wasn't Truesdale, then who was it?' Lorimer said softly. He looked up at Solly, his blue eyes brightening. 'And if it was someone else, then where is Robert Truesdale now?'

It was imperative to establish that the DNA of that burned man in the morgue matched whatever traces their forensic officers could find, Lorimer told himself as he drove down Byres Road and headed towards the Clyde tunnel. Ask them to double-check dental records. If Professor Brightman's theory was correct, then this case was suddenly taking a new and unexpected twist.

'Are you sure?' Rosie's brow creased in a frown of annoyance. 'Never?'

'Sorry,' the voice on the telephone line replied. 'I think he may have had a bad experience as a kid. Anyway, according to our records, he never saw a dentist in all his adult life.'

Rosie thought about what the receptionist at Truesdale's medical practice had said as she ground her own teeth in frustration. There would be no dental records with which to compare those of the body in the mortuary. Lorimer wouldn't be happy with this snippet of news.

CHAPTER SEVENTEEN

There seemed to be some more activity back at that house, she thought, catching the net curtain and twitching it aside for a better look. Nancy could hear the television downstairs, the old man engrossed in the afternoon's horse racing. They'd had a chat about the explosion, of course, that topic of conversation on everybody's lips, and Nancy had trotted out all the usual platitudes about *poor Mr Truesdale,* as if she'd been cleaning for him for years instead of the single day she'd spent across the road. The police had sent a squad of folk to clean up the mess after that tent thing had been dismantled and a pickup truck had loaded the wreck of his car and towed it away. Nancy had watched every news item on the telly, with the morbid curiosity of someone who'd been close to the victim, thrilled in spite of herself. Strange how she had never known who he was, an MSP, too. The woman who had called to engage her services had asked if she knew him and Nancy had said, no, never heard of him. Then she'd put it out of her mind. Till now.

Somewhere the faint jingle of music rang out, barely discernible above the voice of the racing commentator, and Nancy dropped the curtain, recognising the ring tone of her mobile.

Could it be her Emily gone into labour? But she had nearly three weeks to go, *if* her calculations were correct, the woman told herself, hurrying down the stairs and into the kitchen where her handbag lay open.

'Hello?' The cleaner gasped a little, out of breath in her haste to answer the phone.

It was not the voice of her heavily pregnant daughter but a man who was asking if he was speaking to Mrs Nancy Jardine.

'This is Detective Superintendent Lorimer,' the man went on. 'We met recently in Mr Truesdale's house.'

'Oh yes, such a dreadful thing . . .' Nancy began, her mind spinning with the realisation that the tall man who'd visited number fifty-four had actually been a policeman. But before she could continue, her words were cut short.

'I would very much like to ask you some things about Mr Truesdale,' the voice continued. 'And today, if it's not inconvenient.'

'Oh, well,' Nancy gasped, taken by surprise. 'I'm across the road right now at one of my client's . . . but after that . . .?'

'Would it be possible to meet you at Mr Truesdale's house or would you prefer to come into the city?'

'I don't think I want to come into Glasgow,' Nancy said quickly. 'I live in Blanefield, as it happens, not very far from Strathmirren Gardens. Could you come to the flat?'

'What time would suit, Mrs Jardine?'

She gave a swift look at her wristwatch. 'Would two-thirty be okay? And it's number forty-six Netherblane. You'll see the name on the entry pad.' Nancy swallowed hard and wondered if she'd left her own home as tidy as the one she was currently cleaning.

Well, she thought, standing in a daze, the phone in her hand. Wait till she told Emily about this. A policeman coming to visit her!

Lorimer and DS David Giles turned into the winding drive that took him down to rows of modern flats that looked as if they had been built on the acreage of an old country estate, the mature trees showing vibrant autumn tints. He peered through the rain-splattered windscreen for the number Truesdale's cleaner had given him. Mrs Jardine's flat was about halfway along on the left-hand side and Lorimer was relieved to see several empty parking bays close by, a brisk wind blowing heavy rain down from the Campsies.

They hurried up the steps and pressed the buzzer opposite the name JARDINE. Almost immediately there was a click and he pushed open the security door and entered a carpeted hallway with stairs leading up to the flat.

By the time he had reached the front door, there she was, smaller than he remembered. She was not wearing her dark overalls but had evidently taken pains to change them for a smart jersey and pair of tailored trousers. Appearances were important to Mrs Nancy Jardine, Lorimer realised as he looked down at the woman.

'Detective Superintendent?'

'Mrs Jardine.' Lorimer smiled. 'This is my colleague, Detective Sergeant Giles.'

'Come in,' she said, stepping back and closing the door behind them. 'Best go through to the sitting room,' she added, pointing to a door a little further along the corridor to their left.

'Oh, look at that,' Lorimer said as he stood in the centre of a well-lit room. Glass doors to a balcony outside gave onto a panorama of lake and trees, a few geese waddling along the grass. 'Canada geese,' he murmured.

'They come every year,' the woman told him. 'Make a terrible mess, right enough, but they're nice to look at. Aye, we were lucky to buy a flat on this side of the place,' she added, biting the edge of her fingernail.

'Great view,' Giles murmured.

For a few minutes Lorimer and Giles listened as Nancy Jardine regaled them with the history of Netherblane, how it was (as he had guessed) the site of a former estate, now enjoyed by scores of residents, mainly retired, but a few, including herself, still working.

'Though, it's just pin money, really,' she confided, blushing. 'My full-time job was in the local primary school, cleaned that place for years, so I did. But sitting in all day on my lonesome after Archie passed away wasn't my cup of tea,' she rattled on, 'so I put this advert in the local library and bingo! Lots of oldies replied wanting an hour or so every week to tidy up their homes.'

Lorimer had been content to let the woman chatter, identifying signs of stress beneath her torrent of words. It would allow her to settle any nerves before he came to the reason for his visit.

124

'How did Mr Truesdale find out about your cleaning services?' he asked.

She turned to him with a frown. 'Well, I don't know,' she began. 'This lady calls me up one day and asks if I can do for a single man who's moving into Strathblane village. Didn't ask what my rates are so I assumed she'd seen the advert somewhere. Like I told you, it's on the local Facebook page now too,' she said, tilting her chin up proudly.

Giles caught his glance, one eyebrow raised questioningly.

'Tell me about the lady.' Lorimer smiled, moving across to seat himself on a comfortable leather sofa, beckoning his detective sergeant to join him. You didn't have to be a psychologist to understand that towering over the cleaner like this was not conducive to an easy conversation and a less dominant stance would make her feel a lot more comfortable.

Nancy Jardine gave a deep sigh as she settled into a high-backed easy chair opposite, resting her feet on a small, upholstered footstool.

'She was a *lady*,' she began thoughtfully. 'Spoke really nicely, like most of them around here. No accent, I mean she wasn't English or very Glasgow ... just a strong voice ... like a teacher or something ...'

'Did she give her name?'

The cleaner pursed her lips and looked to one side as though trying to think back to the conversation.

'No,' she said at last, turning to look back at Lorimer. 'She didn't, now you mention it. Just asked if I could clean for a Mr Truesdale. Gave me the address and the times he would need me. Agreed the rates.' She coloured up once more at this and Lorimer guessed that the woman's business was strictly cash in hand with no recourse to letting the tax man see her annual income from the business. Pin money, she'd told him. Topping up her pension, no doubt, and that was no business of his right now.

Nancy Jardine frowned a little then added, 'Thought it was funny at the time, y'know, sending me a key through the post, writing down all the *do*s and *don't*s. I was just to go in and clean, the note said. Mr Truesdale would not be at home much during the day so my money was to be left in an envelope in the hall.'

'She sent you a house key?'

Nancy nodded. 'Aye, a Yale. It was in one of these padded envelopes. Along with a typed note about when to arrive and so on.'

'Do you still have this note?' Lorimer asked.

'Sorry, binned it. And I used the envelope to post a present to my niece in South Africa. Why? It was just a short note, asking me to turn up at two o'clock till three-thirty each week.'

'And was that the time you arrived, about an hour before I talked to you?' Lorimer asked.

'Well, now you mention it, no. That was my first day there, see, and I like to have a look around at a place before I begin. Get an idea of what needs done, where things are, you know? So, I turned up a bit earlier.'

'And you met Mr Truesdale when you went to clean for him?'

'Oh, yes, I did. Ever such a nice gentleman, he was.' She looked down at her hands and fidgeted, rolling a pair of sparkling rings round her finger. 'Funny name that, Truesdale. Irish, isn't it?'

'Is it?' Giles asked. 'Could be. Certainly never came across another Truesdale, have you, sir?'

Lorimer shook his head. 'No, can't say I have.'

'Well, like I was saying, he was ever so nice, even if he did seem surprised that I'd come early. Made me a cup of tea, showed me where the biscuits were kept. Not posh at all, like the lady was. I mean, I didn't even know he was an MSP, did I? Thought he was going to be one of my oldies, though he wasn't old at all, was he?'

'Do you have the lady's number?' Giles asked.

'No, she didn't leave me her number.'

'But it will be on your phone, won't it?'

'Oh, aye, of course.' Nancy Jardine's cheeks coloured a little, betraying her lack of technological awareness.

'Perhaps we might have a look . . .?' Lorimer asked with a kindly smile.

It did not take long for him to take a screen shot of the date and time of the woman's call, and her number. Easy enough to trace, he guessed.

She looked at Lorimer nervously then straightened her back. 'Can I ask you something, Mr Lorimer?'

'Of course.' Lorimer smiled encouragingly.

'The cat. What happened to her?'

Lorimer paused for a moment but it was Giles who answered.

'Oh, she was taken away to a rescue shelter. If there isn't anyone in Mr Truesdale's family who step up to take her she'll be rehomed.'

They could both see the relief in the woman's face as she relaxed.

127

'Oh, thank goodness. I was worried she might have strayed. New to the district, like she was. You're supposed to butter a cat's paws when they move house. I told him that but he just laughed.'

'I take it you've watched all the news items about the car bomb?' Lorimer asked her.

Some vigorous nodding from the woman gave him the answer he had expected.

'They didn't do him justice, though,' she said firmly. 'I mean, using a terrible photo like that!'

Lorimer stopped for a moment, staring at her intently. 'What do you mean?'

He could see her nervous swallow as she fiddled with the rings, clearly upset about something.

'Well, he was much better-looking in real life,' she whispered. 'And that photo they kept using made him look a lot older.'

Solly's words came back to him suddenly. What if . . .

'Mrs Jardine, would you be kind enough to let me show you more photographs of Mr Truesdale?' he asked gently, taking out his phone and clicking onto a search engine.

He beckoned her over to sit beside him, Giles moving to make way for the woman, and together they looked at the small screen as Lorimer scrolled down a page full of images of the late Robert Truesdale.

There was silence for a moment.

'There's a vague resemblance,' she sighed.

Then, she turned towards Lorimer and shook her head.

'They say he was burned to death in that car of his,' she whispered, one hand flying to her mouth. 'But . . .' She looked back again at the phone then up into Lorimer's blue gaze, colour fading from her cheeks. 'If I was to swear it in a court of law . . .' She hesitated then looked up at Lorimer then towards Giles.

He saw the way she chewed her bottom lip, then, shaking her head, the woman looked back at the photograph.

'I don't honestly think I could say that's the man I met at number fifty-four Strathmirren Gardens.'

CHAPTER EIGHTEEN

'There's a match between the victim and several items in the house,' Giles told him. 'The forensic report shows that whoever drank tea from the cup left on the kitchen table and brushed his teeth in the bathroom was the man who went into that car a short time later.'

'So, was it Truesdale?' Lorimer asked.

'Ah, now we come to the interesting bit.' Giles grinned. 'There are several different fingerprints in that house as well as traces that have been tested for DNA. You'd expect that after furniture removers had been in and out, of course, plus those of the previous owner, a Mrs Edna Adamson. None of them on any fingerprint database, sadly.'

'Let's think about who had been in that bungalow most recently,' Lorimer began, counting on his fingers. 'The cleaning lady for one, Truesdale we can assume, the person whom she met that she thought was Truesdale, and possibly the lady who made the arrangement with Mrs Jardine.'

'Any luck with finding out who she is, sir?'

'Yes, as it happens. Truesdale's neighbour, Karen Douglas. Interestingly enough, she did let slip to our DS Newton that she'd done Truesdale a couple of favours. And now we can guess that was one of them. I'll be very interested to see what Ms Douglas has to tell us about that.'

'We've also asked Holyrood for any help they might be able to give us,' Giles said. 'Forensics are there in Truesdale's office now, picking up what traces they can find to test for DNA. That would have been done earlier if we'd had any doubts, of course.'

Lorimer ran a hand through his hair. 'It's almost a week since that bomb killed him,' he sighed. 'And, despite every procedure being followed to the letter, we may be no further forward in knowing who he is. Dr Fergusson has advised us that Truesdale never visited a dentist.'

'Oh well. So, we're dependent on DNA, then,' Giles concluded. 'If there's a match from traces in his office with the body then we'll know for certain that it's Robert Truesdale.'

'And if not?'

Giles's grin widened. 'Well, sir, then the plot really thickens, doesn't it?'

'And we're back to the original problem of a missing MSP,' Lorimer sighed. 'As well as the murder of a someone who vaguely resembles him.'

The white-suited figures caused a small stir amongst the members of the Scottish Parliament and their staff as they moved about inside Robert Truesdale's office. Calum McKenzie was grim-faced as he overheard their whispered comments in the corridor outside. Before the day was done, word would have spread and speculation run rife, he thought, grinding his teeth in a moment of frustrated fury. Damn Truesdale! Not content with trying to thwart the current legislation governing hard drugs, he'd only gone and made headlines for a very different reason. And now there was some doubt as to whether the burned body in that car was actually his! McKenzie had been asked politely but firmly to keep all staff out of the man's office, though who had already been in since that bomb exploded was anyone's guess.

As if to answer that unspoken thought, Malcolm Hinchliffe appeared by his side, a worried expression on his face.

'Malcolm, what d'you make of this?' McKenzie hissed, walking the man away from the closed door and striding towards his own much larger office.

He saw Truesdale's secretary turn and give him a pitying look. *What?* McKenzie frowned.

'In here,' he ordered the taller man and shut his office door hard behind them.

'Right, Malcolm, sit down and start by telling me everything,' McKenzie demanded, glaring at the secretary.

He watched as Malcolm Hinchliffe calmly hitched his trousers a fraction before settling himself on the other side of the First Minister's capacious desk.

'They have every reason to be cautious,' Hinchliffe began. 'Neither Mr McVeigh nor I could adequately identify that ... those ... remains as Robert Truesdale.' He stifled a sigh. 'It was quite impossible to see anything that would have given us a clue,' he concluded.

'You told me all that already,' McKenzie fumed, banging a fist on the table. 'What I want to know is what you *think*, Malcolm. After all, you were the person who saw him day in, day out. You must have known all his little foibles, yes?'

'Apparently not, First Minister,' Hinchliffe drawled, his smooth tone reminding McKenzie that this well-dressed man had been educated at Fettes, along with a few MPs who now sat in the House of Commons. Why had Hinchliffe not shown more ambition, he wondered for a moment, tried to make his own mark in politics? After all, he'd gained a double first at Cambridge, rowed for their bally team against the darker blues. But then he remembered that sprawling estate near Peebles. No doubt Hinchliffe was just marking time here at Holyrood until the time came for him to inherit it.

'There seems to be some question about the identity of the deceased,' Hinchliffe continued, breaking into McKenzie's thoughts. 'There's the problem of that silver chain with the cross. Everybody who knew Robert was aware of his feelings about the Church.' A faint deprecatory smile spread across his face.

'Well, of course we did!' McKenzie snapped. 'Only attended funerals, and I remember one in particular when he couldn't get out of St Giles fast enough.'

'If it turns out that the victim of the bombing is not who we thought it to be ...' Hinchliffe left the sentence unfinished, his fair eyebrows raised.

'It makes for an unholy mess!' McKenzie exclaimed, unaware of the aptness of his words.

'And if Robert has gone walkabout? Do we have any notion why he would want to do that?'

McKenzie removed his glasses and rubbed his eyes. 'God knows,' he replied with a shake of the head. 'There's been no letter of resignation so we still have a duty towards a sitting member. Then there's all that stuff about him being a major shareholder in the pharmaceutical business that sponsored the drug rehab programme. I don't like it, Malcolm,' he sighed.

'Back to square one, then,' Hinchliffe said thoughtfully. 'Asking the police to find him.'

It would take time to see if the samples taken from the MSP's office matched those obtained from the victim. Meantime, certain members of the press were baying for more information, asking about funeral arrangements, and Lorimer could only keep them dangling for so long. He sat back and thought hard. The next few days would be crucial. If the DNA samples proved to be those of Truesdale then there would be a collective sigh of relief. But, if not, then he was going to be left with the problem of identifying a mystery man and of finding the whereabouts of Truesdale.

Once again, he closed his eyes and recalled that gravelly voice, assuring himself that yes, it had been the MSP who had spoken to him the previous week. And yet Nancy Jardine had seen a different person that same day. It didn't make sense.

Why would someone impersonate the man like that? Had he been a friend, covering up for Truesdale so that the MSP might slip somewhere far away from the avalanche of threats on social media? But the threats had been real, the bomb had happened. Was it someone unaware of the reality of such death threats or so loyal to Truesdale that they would do his bidding unquestioningly? And who, amongst his circle could that person be?

And, if they did identify that the victim was not Robert Truesdale, would either of these questions ever be answered?

Daniel sat in the canteen nursing a mug of tea in his hands. He'd seen a few familiar faces pass him by during his break, most of the other officers giving him a smile or a nod but there was one particular chap who had not only given him a different sort of look but had whispered that derogatory word. It had made him feel hot, that expression of disgust on the man's curled lip as if to express contempt for having a black man in their midst.

But it was not the first time that sort of thing had occurred; it had happened up at Tulliallan, near the beginning of the training course.

'Who the hell do you think you are? Taking up a place that white guys could use?' the young man had sneered in a moment when Daniel was alone with him in the changing room after a run outside.

It had to happen sometime, Daniel had realised that day and he had replied politely, looking the man straight in the eyes as he did so.

'Who am I? Well, you know that,' he began. 'But perhaps a better answer to your question is to say who I was.'

'Oh, and what's that?' the fellow had sneered. 'Some native king or other in a tiger skin?'

'I was Inspector Kohi in the Zimbabwean police,' Daniel

had replied mildly, gratified to see the man's jaw drop. 'Oh, and there are no tigers in Africa, you only find them in Asia,' he had added, a smile on his face as he'd gripped his sports bag and walked out of the locker room.

He'd hoped that such an attitude would not follow him to his current police office but the racist slur and that look of disdain showed Daniel that prejudice might still exist, even here.

'Hi, you on your own? Can I join you?'

Daniel looked up to see one of the CID team who had been at the riverside on the night when he had assisted them.

'Kohi, isn't it?'

'Yes, Daniel Kohi,' he replied, smiling as the man laid down his tray on the table. 'Any more news about the man they found in the river?' he asked, eager to find out what was happening in the case.

'Aye, as it happens. Dead man's been identified as Kenny Ritchie, one of Frankie Fleming's lot. Fleming's a known drug dealer,' he explained.

'Hard drugs?' Daniel asked.

'Aye.' The officer nodded. 'Got form for assault as well as other things,' he told Daniel. 'Nasty wee character. Ritchie had already spent time in more than one Scottish prison.' He bit into a salad roll and chewed hard.

'Did he live near there?'

'Aye. He'd been seen around that area in the days before his murder. We made enquiries about Fleming and that led us to some rumours about a feud between rival drug gangs in Govanhill, some of the locals vying for ascendancy with Romanians who've settled here,' he said, rolling his eyes. 'Might have been a fight that went too far.'

Daniel glanced up at the clock. His break time was over. 'Have to go, thanks for filling me in on the case,' he added.

'Oh, no offence or anything, but you should know there's another gang peddling some dodgy heroin in our area. Mostly Colombians,' the cop said. 'But we think at least one of them is from your neck of the woods. A Zimbabwean.'

It was good to have caught up with that CID officer, Daniel thought, particularly as the SIO in the case had not called him to attend any further briefings. His duties lay elsewhere today and he'd have to put thoughts of that cold night on hold for now. But it was the idea that some of his fellow countrymen had crossed thousands of miles to carry out their deadly business that caused Daniel Kohi some real disquiet.

CHAPTER NINETEEN

Netta turned a corner of the stairs and stopped, gasping for breath. It was becoming a more frequent occurrence, the lift out of order, causing the old lady to struggle up and down the eleven flights of stairs if she wanted to go out into the city. She was only at the fourth floor now, she realised, leaning against the wall, one gnarled hand clutching the banister. She swallowed hard, looking upwards at the grey-painted walls and the lift doors still firmly shut.

Daniel's words came back to her. *Flat share*, he'd said. But just what would that mean? Certainly no climbing laboriously up so many flights of stairs, not if she had anything to do with it.

Her breath came in ragged bursts as Netta resumed her ascent, stopping at every landing, a renewed determination on her face. It was force of habit to keep going like this. Hadn't she always done just that? Kept house for a man who'd been in and out of the jail, raised her kids on a shoestring and now managed on her own. Folk like her were survivors, her GP had told her last time she'd been to the surgery for a check-up, cautioning her against trying to do so much on her own. A home help had been suggested last time she'd complained of breathlessness; Netta had listened and smiled but ignored her advice. Nobody was going to come in and do her wee house! Not so long as she was fit . . .

Four more flights to go, she thought, steadying herself as her head swam in a moment of dizziness.

She closed her eyes. 'Just need to sit down a wee minute,' she gasped, slumping onto the cold stair, one hand grasping her shopping bag, head bowed as the pain began.

Then a ringing sounded in her ears as darkness flooded her mind.

CHAPTER TWENTY

'Hampden Park is our national football stadium,' Police Sergeant Jacob Alexander told Daniel. 'But perhaps you've been in Glasgow long enough to know that?'

'Aye,' Daniel agreed as the two men walked steadily towards the famous landmark.

The police sergeant hid a smile. His newest recruit actually sounded as though he had been brought up in the city, his Glasgow accent somewhat at odds with his real heritage. Alexander was aware that Daniel had been a senior officer back in Zimbabwe and had decided that he could allow the man a bit of leeway when it came to giving him different tasks. He'd hinted as much to the SIO in the drug death, particularly after hearing Kohi's own account of finding the woman and her child. She'd nodded and raised one eyebrow speculatively, as if she already had something particular in mind.

'We normally drive round the back and make our way straight into the grounds, but I thought you might as well see the whole place,' Alexander told him as they stood at the foot of a massive set of stairs that led to the front entrance of Hampden.

Daniel took in everything from the bank of reception desks, the various function suites on the upper levels, to the physiotherapy clinic with its hydrotherapy pool in the depths of the building. He passed black and white pictures of footballing heroes from the past, names that meant nothing to him, though filing them away in his photographic memory would allow him to discuss them with Netta later on. He was happy to be on an early shift for a couple of days and he might even suggest taking the old lady out for dinner. She'd been so good to him, he thought, as he followed the other officer through a dim tunnel.

The actual grounds came as a pleasant surprise, the noise of a greenkeeper's mower reverberating around the huge stadium, a fresh scent in the air. He closed his eyes and remembered the sensation of walking out on the pitches back home, shouts from the crowds at the sides welcoming him as he led his team out. His reverie was short-lived, however, as his tutor's words broke in.

'A pre-match inspection has to take place in every stadium,' Alexander explained. 'We're looking for anything that might constitute the possibility of a criminal act. The Old Firm's the worst for that, sadly. I mind seeing a goalkeeper once picking up bits of a broken bottle out of his area. Anyone on either team could've been hurt. Just plain stupid. But of course, it's not just objects like that we look for that could disrupt a game.'

'Maybe things like a bomb?' Daniel suggested, grimly, the recent car explosion still on everybody's mind.

Alexander gave him a keen look. 'It wouldn't be the first time we'd found explosives hidden down the back of a seat. Fireworks mostly,' he added, 'though I can recall a game over in Firhill when someone discharged a shotgun just before half-time.'

'How did they get in ...?'

'Ach, that was back in the seventies,' Alexander laughed. 'I was just a wee boy with my dad that day. We supported the Jags ...'

'The ...'

'Partick Thistle,' Alexander grinned. 'Lots of clubs have their nicknames. St Mirren are the Buddies, Dunfermline are the Pars ... Och, you'll get to know it all in time, Kohi.'

Daniel's mouth twitched in a smile. Apparently, there was a lot more to policing this city than simply knowing the facts of law and order, and that might include learning about Scottish football divisions.

'Anyhow, it gave me the fright of my life. They were playing Raith Rovers that day. Cannae remember the score but I never forgot the sound of that gun going off.'

They had climbed to the very top tier of the stand and now Daniel had a view of the entire stadium as well as the buildings of nearby Mount Florida that looked into these hallowed grounds. A sniper could fire a gun from one of those tenement windows, he thought, pausing for a moment.

'Great view if you have the right binoculars,' Alexander chuckled, following Daniel's gaze. 'Anyway, it'll be packed in here tomorrow for the International between Iceland and us. You're off at four and the kick-off isn't till seven-forty-five. You should try to come along, just to see the numbers of officers deployed plus our mounted division. That's another area you've still to see, of course.'

Daniel nodded. It was a sensible suggestion but his late afternoon off was already planned out, making a start on a list of rented flats to see, all of them containing two bedrooms, just in case he could persuade Netta Gordon to come and stay with him. Was he being selfish, reluctant to leave the first person who had made him so welcome here in Glasgow? Her link with his mother back in Zimbabwe was another feature of their friendship, Netta's willingness at being a penfriend to Janette Kohi enabling the correspondence between mother and son to flourish, hidden from anyone who might suspect that Daniel had survived that fatal fire.

Although it had been a long day, Daniel was whistling as he drove back through the city. As he reached Byres Road he smiled. At this time on a Thursday evening, Glasgow still had on its happy face, full of people out for late shopping milling around the streets, offices long closed, pubs packed with punters gearing up for the following evening's football match. By closing time tomorrow, it might well be a different scene as drunken behaviour spilled out into the streets, especially if Iceland beat the home side. He'd seen some of that on his late shifts, not just guys but young women staggering barefoot, their high-heeled shoes dangling in one hand, the inevitable bottle clutched in the other, hair and make-up that had probably taken hours of preparation now dishevelled and smeared. But Daniel was content to watch as people strolled along, laughter echoing from the lanes that bisected the street, rows of gaudy lights swinging in the breeze.

He parked the car outside the high flats, making a mental note to transfer the lease hire agreement from William Lorimer to himself. The detective superintendent's generosity was typical of the man but now that he was earning decent money, Daniel was determined to make his own way and eventually pay him back. It was easy to save money, having been a refugee for so many months here in the UK, living on very straitened means, his police officer's salary a fortune by comparison. As he locked the car and headed to the secure entrance, Daniel felt a frisson of excitement at the prospect of renting a place of his own.

His mood changed as soon as he saw the notice still hanging on the front of the lifts. With a small groan, he began to ascend the stairs, telling himself that this was perhaps good exercise, though the inspection at Hampden had tested his legs a bit earlier in the day, walking up and down the steep stands.

At last, he reached the eleventh floor, his pace slower now than at first, and headed for his flat, shuffling in his coat pocket for his keys.

It was just a folded piece of paper, stuck halfway through his letterbox, probably a flyer, Daniel decided, ready to crush it in his fist. Pity whoever had to climb all these stairs to deliver them, he chuckled.

His smile changed as soon as he read the note.

Mrs Gordon is in the Queen Elizabeth hospital. Thought you should know.
Janice McLeish, flat 7/10.

There was constant noise in the hospital, trolleys rattling along the nearby corridor as well as voices coming from the nurses' station nearby. The windows near Netta's bed were shut fast but even so, she could hear a hum of distant traffic as she lay in her narrow bed. All night long there had been moans and cries from across the way, some poor soul struggling to leave the safety of her bed, nurses running to stop her falling. Dementia, Netta had decided when it first began, the woman too weak to stand without help, too far gone to realise the extent of her injuries. Netta had seen the metal walker parked beside the patient's bed, noticed the dark patches of bruising down one arm and the thick surgical collar around her neck. An accident, perhaps?

Netta shifted and tried to turn onto her side but immediately the cannula fixed to the back of her hand stopped her. What had happened? Why was she here? A vague memory filtered through of a nice young male nurse bringing apple juice and a sandwich at midnight. She'd left most of it, the nausea making her slump back onto the pillows.

The sound of a trolley bumping across the floor came closer and then the blue curtains were whisked back and she heard a man's cheerful voice.

'Come to take you to theatre, Mrs Gordon. Just relax, hen, you'll do fine,' the porter assured her as Netta began to sit up.

'Here we go,' another voice proclaimed and then, in one swift movement, Netta felt herself being hoisted off the bed and laid onto the trolley. She'd felt no pain on the transfer, she realised, a memory of kind hands bringing little phials full of pills.

In minutes she'd been wheeled through two sets of double doors and into a lift where bright overhead lights made her close her eyes.

There were so many people, all masked, in blue V-neck tops and matching trousers, both men and women wearing tight-fitting caps on their heads that reminded Netta of the packs of J-cloths she bought at the corner shop.

'Hello, I'm just going to administer your anaesthetic.'

Netta saw a pair of kind brown eyes above a mask, the man's voice soothing and reassuring as her body stiffened.

'Think of something really nice,' he suggested, his gloved hands holding something that she could not quite see. But before Netta could gather her thoughts to reply, the anaesthetist was counting down from ten . . .

The first thing Netta Gordon saw when she awoke was a man sitting by her bedside, a newspaper hiding his face. Her eyes flickered for a moment before she recognised Daniel's black fingers.

Perhaps she groaned, Netta wasn't sure, but the paper was cast onto the floor and Daniel was there by her side, gently holding her hand, careful not to disturb the tubing attached to her frail skin.

'Netta,' she heard him gasp. 'You're awake.' There was relief in his voice.

She blinked a little, wondering where she was and why Daniel was in her room. Then she noticed the fabric screen and the cannula in the back of her hand. And the cotton gown that was standard issue in places like this.

Hospital.

'What happened?' she whispered. 'What am I doing here?'

'You collapsed on the seventh floor,' he told her. 'A lady found you and called for the ambulance.'

'A lady?'

'Mrs McLeish. She lives on that floor. You've been here since yesterday, Netta dear.'

Netta frowned. That couldn't be right. She closed her eyes and tried to think. But her last memory had been of stuffing a cut-price bag of satsumas into her shopping bag, a wee treat for Daniel when he came round after work.

'Did you get the oranges?' she asked at last.

Daniel stood listening as the charge nurse explained that Mrs Gordon would be kept in for observation for three more nights at least following her cardiac surgery.

'And is there any relative who could take her when she's discharged?'

'She has family but I've only seen them visit on Christmas Day,' Daniel replied, remembering the noisy tribe who had descended on their elderly relative for the traditional Christmas pudding and bundles of carefully wrapped gifts, items that Daniel guessed his neighbour could ill afford. *Christmas is Christmas*, she'd told him sternly when he'd warned her not to spend her pension on him. Yet there had been no sign of family since that dark December day, another spring and summer giving way to autumn.

The nurse nodded but passed no comment. She'll have seen all sorts, Daniel told himself, knowing how both police officers and health staff were exposed to the vagaries of humanity.

'It's certainly not ideal, her living on the eleventh floor of a high rise,' the woman sniffed. 'I think perhaps social work might become involved if she can't return to her own home.'

'I want her to live with me when I find a rented flat of my own,' Daniel said suddenly. 'I've asked her and asked her but she's a proud old lady.'

'Who no doubt values her independence. Oh, we know the type,' the nurse sighed.

'I'm a police officer,' Daniel told her. 'I earn enough to keep us both, but she won't hear of it.'

'Well, maybe this accident might help Mrs Gordon to change her mind?' the woman said, with a twinkle in her eye.

The grey sandstone building was on a quiet street, opposite a car showroom, tiny fenced-in strips of garden bordering the ground-floor flats. Daniel looked up from his car to see the smartly dressed woman from the letting agency who had agreed to meet him there.

'Hello, Mr Kohi? Fiona MacBride. We spoke earlier,' she said, tossing back her long shiny hair then teetering down from the single step in impossibly high heels to shake his hand. 'Right, let's go inside,' she said, unlocking the big front door and turning immediately to the left where Daniel saw a black-painted door, its well-polished brass letter box and doorknob giving a good first impression. Netta would approve, he thought, mobile in his hand ready to take a few pictures.

'It's a roomy flat,' Ms MacBride stated, waving a hand around the large reception hall before walking into the airy lounge that overlooked the street.

'It's already furnished?'

'Yes, but you can bring your own bits and bobs, of course. The owner is good about replacing any items that he considers past their sell-by date,' she gushed.

It was a lovely room by anybody's standards, but for Daniel, used to the small one-bedroom flat across the city, it felt perfect.

'You said you worked on this side of town?'

'Yes. Govanhill police station,' Daniel replied, eyeing up the tall bay windows and the radiators beneath.

'Oh, you're a cop?' The woman seemed surprised.

Daniel gave a smile and a nod. She didn't need to know any details, but perhaps his profession would stand him in good stead with the landlord as a safe bet against any rowdy parties?

He followed as she led him back through the hallway into a kitchen that might have been bigger than his entire flat, pale wooden cupboards surrounding an oak table with four matching chairs, colourful blinds pulled up on a window over the kitchen sink that looked out to the back of the property.

'There's a drying green plus a basement cellar belonging to the flat, but the owner uses that for his personal storage,' she told him. 'However ...' She led him out of the kitchen and, with a flourish, opened a door in the hall, revealing a huge walk-in cupboard with shelving at the back. There was a vacuum cleaner and other gadgets but Daniel had little time to examine them as the letting agent drew his attention to the two main bedrooms, one at the front and the other at the back of the property, a long bathroom with a bath and shower, the porcelainware finished in pale cream. Everything gleamed, Daniel realised. Either the previous tenants had left this place in an immaculate condition or else the agency had taken pains to show it off for viewing.

'Well, what do you think?' she asked, glancing at her wristwatch. 'I do have other viewings booked in for tomorrow.'

'I'll take it,' Daniel told her with a grin. 'I'm afraid you are going to have to disappoint them.'

He sat for a while in the car, glancing at the exterior of the flat, trying to remember everything Ms MacBride had told him about taking a turn to clean the common stair and when the rubbish bins needed to be left on the pavement for weekly collections. It would all be on an email, she had promised him, along with a contract to be signed.

'You just need the guarantee of someone reliable to give a character reference, but I suppose that won't be hard in your line of work,' she had giggled, flirting with him under her long fake eyelashes. 'And the deposit, of course.'

He could move in almost immediately, once the letting agency had received his payment, a deposit plus one month's rent. Daniel glanced at the big window with its gauzy curtain hiding the interior from prying eyes. Netta would love it, he assured himself.

'You did *whit?*' Her shriek made the other patients in the ward turn towards Netta's bed, one of them clearly tutting and raising her eyebrows.

'It's either that or you need to move in with your own family,' Daniel told her.

He could see the old lady purse her mouth as she savoured that particular idea.

'The hospital won't discharge you permanently to your current home, Netta,' Daniel explained gently. 'You need someone to look after you. The stents they put in will solve a lot of problems but you need to be very careful, for a while. Let me take care of you.'

'And how're you going tae do that on ten-hour shifts, eh?'

'We'll find a way,' Daniel assured her. 'The hospital can liaise with social services to make sure someone comes in to help you when I'm at work.'

'Never needed any help afore,' she grumbled, turning away from him, but not before he saw tears glistening in her eyes.

'It's nice, Netta,' Daniel continued. 'See, I've even got a few photos to show you.'

'That's the kitchen?' Netta gasped, one trembling hand on her chin.

Daniel grinned. 'It's a nice big flat, Netta. A lot older than ours,' he added.

'A gen-ui-ine tenement,' the old lady whispered. 'I wis

brought up in one,' she said softly. 'Before they pulled it down and sent us all away from the city.'

Daniel watched as she blinked back tears, wondering what Netta Gordon's life had been like all these years ago.

'Is it dear?' she asked, a sharper tone in her voice.

'I can afford it on my salary,' Daniel said. 'And I wouldn't want any money from you.'

'Well, that settles it, then,' Netta said, folding her arms across her thin nightdress and scowling at him. 'Never took charity and never will!' she exclaimed.

'Ah, well, I had an idea about how you might pay rent,' Daniel chuckled.

'Oh?' Netta's brows were drawn down in a frown.

'How would it be if you became my housekeeper?'

'Whit?'

'Hear me out, Netta, dear. It's hard having these long shifts and finding time to keep a home clean and tidy plus cooking and doing my laundry,' he said, hoping his tone sounded sufficiently persuasive. 'If you could take all that on, well . . . that would equal any share of the rent.'

'And how about bills? Let's hae anither look at thon kitchen. Is it a gas cooker?'

Daniel smiled as she examined the photos he had taken of the kitchen, the pale oak units housing a double electric oven beside a stainless-steel gas hob.

'Michty! There's a microwave an' all! And whit's that?' she asked, pointing to the American-style fridge freezer. 'Never seen onything like that.' She sighed, her voice betraying a tone of longing.

'I'll take care of utility bills if you help out with some

of the groceries,' Daniel assured her, crossing his fingers behind his back.

'Och, son, I don't know what to say,' she cried, pulling out a crumpled hanky from under her pillow and dabbing her eyes.

'Just say yes,' Daniel pleaded.

And, though his friend did not utter a word, her nodding head as she blew her nose told him everything he wanted to know.

CHAPTER TWENTY-ONE

Anybody entering the Scottish Crime Campus for the first time might be impressed by the grey walls towering into the skies, the long lines of their design reflecting chromosome biology, a hint of just one of the many agencies that worked inside the building. Standing between the main security gate and the front entrance and surrounded by green hills and fields, one could be forgiven for thinking how far removed this place was from the city of Glasgow, the pathologist thought. That was how Rosie had felt when she had first visited here so many years before. Now, with her mind full of the high-profile case that had brought her to the campus at Gartcosh, she only gave the exterior of the building a cursory nod, as if to acknowledge its purpose.

The forensic scientist who had called her wanted to have Rosie here in person before she made her official report. That was unusual now that a flick of a key could transmit information back to her own office and Rosie was curious to find out what the woman had to show her.

Inside, having been passed through reception and given her identity lanyard, Rosie gazed up at the atrium, light flooding the different levels. It never failed to make her feel a sense of pride that here, close to the city of her birth, was the biggest and best centre for the purposes of criminal investigation, a place that was the envy of every force in Europe. She headed to the lifts and pressed the button, already imagining the place where she was heading.

Before entering the main laboratory, Rosie was given a dark navy lab coat by the receptionist and asked to put on mask and gloves, precautions in a highly sensitive area where any contamination might blight precious samples.

She found the woman who had called her earlier that day sitting at a lab table, dark hair pulled back in a ponytail, peering intently through the lens of a powerful microscope. For a moment Rosie waited, loath to disturb the scientist's concentration but eager to know why her presence had been requested. Several white-coated figures sat around the lab, each of them wearing masks and protective gloves as they examined specimens.

At last, she looked up and saw Rosie standing nearby.

'Dr Fergusson! Thanks so much for coming out to see me.'

'That's all right, Jennifer.' Rosie smiled. She'd known this woman for several years now, each of them working cases in their separate ways, Dr Jennifer Strang often providing some feature of DNA identification that helped in a difficult case.

The woman stood up and clasped Rosie's arm for a moment. 'Sorry for all the cloak and dagger stuff,' she whispered, making a face, 'but we had instructions from on high to keep this quiet. No passing info along the internet lest someone sneak a peek.' She shook her head as if to say what a fuss it all was.

'It is a pretty high-profile matter,' Rosie agreed, keeping her own voice down.

'Come with me,' Jennifer said, leading Rosie from the lab towards a door at the far end that bore her name. 'We won't be disturbed in here.'

Once she had closed the door behind them, she began. 'Now, I want to show you something rather odd. Sit over here.' She ushered Rosie to a chair behind her desk.

Rosie felt a shiver running down her spine. Something rather odd? And she had to be here face to face with the scientist to see what that was?

'We found a relation of the bomb victim,' Jennifer told her, pointing to a printout that showed matching examples of DNA.

'Is it Truesdale?' Rosie asked immediately. 'Can we identify him now?'

The scientist gave a lopsided smile. 'Wait and see. Look, here's the DNA from the victim and here,' she pointed to another row of lines, 'is DNA taken from a living relative.'

Rosie gasped. 'But how? We didn't find any match at all after the post-mortem.'

'Ah, but this sample doesn't come from your path lab,' she grinned. 'It is on a database in the Queen Elizabeth hospital.'

'So, why hasn't it come up till now?' Rosie wanted to know. 'And who's this relative?'

Jennifer's face softened for a moment. 'He might not

have a name yet,' she said. 'But we can be certain that the victim of that car bomb was the father of a baby born with neonatal abstinence syndrome. You did the mother's PM yourself,' she added.

'My goodness!' Rosie exclaimed. 'So, Robert Truesdale was a father?'

There was silence for a moment as the two women regarded one another. Then Jennifer Strang shook her head.

'No, we think not,' she sighed. 'So far, we have no idea who this man was. But one thing we can now tell for sure.'

Rosie waited, holding her breath before heaving a huge sigh.

'That's what you wanted to tell me.'

'Yes,' the woman agreed, glancing back at the printouts. 'The man in that car was definitely not Robert Truesdale.'

There had been so many samples, Dr Strang had told Rosie, all carefully checked, but their main concern had been those obtained from the MSP's office in Holyrood, none of which had matched the profile of the dead man. No wonder she'd been asked to call in person, Rosie thought, heading from the north of the city to the headquarters of the Major Incident Team, her heart still racing. This was something that had to be kept as secret as possible, for now, the chief constable had demanded after Dr Strang had met with her earlier in the day. The First Minister would be told in time, but first it fell to Detective Superintendent Lorimer to be told of these astonishing results.

Rosie cast her mind back to the post-mortem of that undernourished young mother, her life ruined by hard drugs, the baby lucky to be alive. Could this be a small breakthrough in finding out who that bomb victim really was? And would Lorimer's team manage to track down the missing MSP?

William Lorimer sat silently as Rosie talked him through the results from the Gartcosh lab. Her psychologist husband had been right, he thought; Solly's inclination was to look at different aspects of human behaviour in order to pinpoint a person's profile. Someone who wore a cross around their neck was more than likely to have been a person of faith. And that did not fit Robert Truesdale's profile. Not one of the samples from his Holyrood office had matched the body of the deceased, though most of the clothes and shoes in his bedroom showed that they had been worn by the MSP.

'Butter in the fridge,' Lorimer murmured.

'What?' He saw Rosie's mouth open in astonishment. 'Did I hear you say butter?'

Lorimer gave a sniff. 'Aye, I know it sounds odd. Well, everything about this case is beginning to feel strange, but I checked the butter in the fridge.' He gave her a self-deprecating smile. 'An old trick that I remembered seeing at a scene of crime conference one time. See how much butter has been used to calculate how long a person's been in the house. Doesn't always work, of course, especially if there are several occupants. But here . . .'

'Where Truesdale was a single man . . .'

'It did show me something,' Lorimer agreed. 'Two tiny slicks off a new pack of butter. No empty butter cartons in the rubbish. Plenty of frozen meals for one plus unopened packs of fresh vegetables. Looked like someone had just moved in. And I am willing to bet that someone was not Robert Truesdale.'

'The man that the cleaner had met?'

'Exactly. In fact,' he drew a deep breath before continuing, 'I wonder if Truesdale had simply moved his belongings to that bungalow then left.'

'Letting another man stay there in his stead?'

Lorimer nodded. 'I think that's possible. Unless Truesdale has been abducted, of course. Whoever it was had the run of his house. We saw that from the traces of DNA on the bedclothes and that toothbrush. Plus, Mrs Jardine had assumed he was the new owner.'

'How long would he have got away with masquerading as the MSP?' Rosie wondered aloud.

Lorimer gave her a long and penetrating look. 'Perhaps he wasn't meant to stay that long,' he said grimly.

'You mean Truesdale knew he was going to be blown up? Surely not?'

Lorimer raised his eyebrows. 'I wonder if Truesdale guessed exactly what sort of threats there had been to his life,' he said slowly. 'And had put someone else into his shoes.'

STRICTLY CONFIDENTIAL, the report was marked, for a few eyes only. However, there was someone that Lorimer knew he could trust and, as Rosie had filled him in about the DNA results, Lorimer's mind had strayed to Daniel. There were so many things now to put into place, actions handed out to members of his team, and for a moment Lorimer wished that the Zimbabwean was one of their number.

He texted his friend, keeping the wording neutral but intriguing enough to make the police constable aware that he wanted to see him. Perhaps once Daniel Kohi arrived, he might find a way to seek his assistance. Tackling the problem of the dead man's identity might best be done from different angles, the Govanhill cops working to establish who he was.

There had been leaks from certain quarters within the police in previous cases and Lorimer was reluctant to make an official request to the divisional commander over on the Southside until Holyrood had stopped being so jittery. Was there some intelligence about Truesdale that the First Minister was keeping from them? He frowned as the thought crossed his mind. Caroline Flint had not hinted at anything like that but then politicians were wary creatures, not always given to sharing information unless it suited their own purposes.

As if some thought had made her materialise, Lorimer rose to his feet as the chief constable walked through the door of his room.

'Ma'am,' he said, striding forward and clasping the woman's cold hand.

The CC swept off her hat and sat down heavily.

'You've heard,' she said. It was not a question but Lorimer still nodded as he pulled a chair around to sit closer to his colleague.

'What a situation!' Flint seethed. 'We've got a dead man who shouldn't have been in that car, a missing member of the Scottish Parliament and a bomber on the loose. Not to mention that poor little scrap suffering from his late mother's drug problem.'

Lorimer clenched his teeth. That about summed it up and they were no further forward on any of these fronts than they had been when Robert Truesdale had first been reported missing by his parliamentary colleagues.

'Just humour me for a few minutes, Lorimer,' Flint continued. 'What is your own take on this?'

'What do I think happened?' Lorimer's dark eyebrows rose speculatively. 'Well, I do think Truesdale was organised. It looks to me that he'd planned his disappearance months ago, possibly when he first put his house on the market.'

'When was that, exactly?'

'End of June this year,' Lorimer told her. 'He had said absolutely nothing to anyone in Holyrood and nobody there picked up on it. I mean, why would they? It's a busy time in the housing market and, unless any of them had been studying house prices in that area, it was easy enough to slip it under the radar.'

'That was a risk Truesdale had to take, though,' Flint put in.

'Yes, but not much of one, especially as he had instructed his solicitor to do the deal in his name.'

'Oh, you found that out, did you?'

Lorimer nodded. 'That didn't seem to be all that significant at the time. A hard-working MSP leading a well-publicised crusade handing the work over to his solicitor . . .' He shrugged. 'It made sense for him to keep his head down if he was intending to make his new home hard for other people to find.'

'There's still no sign of that letter of resignation,' Flint reminded him.

'I think that might have been a bluff,' Lorimer said slowly. 'What if . . .' he stared over the chief constable's head as she listened intently, 'what if Truesdale meant all along to disappear from the political scene? He'd cleared out all his bank accounts, for one thing. And he also came off every one of his social media platforms . . .' He paused and chewed his lower lip for a moment. Hadn't Daniel said something like that? *I no longer have an online footprint and they all think I'm dead?* 'It is entirely possible that someone else put pressure on him to disappear. Someone who was determined to put a stop to his involvement in changing the law on drugs.'

He looked at the chief constable whose eyes did not flinch under his gaze.

'We must find him, Lorimer,' she said at last. 'Especially if you think he may still be in some danger.'

Lorimer shook his head. 'If that genuinely was Robert Truesdale I spoke to on the phone, and I am ninety-nine per cent sure that it was, there was nothing in his manner to suggest that he was afraid in the least. On the contrary, he seemed bullish.'

'Determined to resign?'

'Absolutely determined. But,' he paused again, 'what if that *was* a bluff? What if he wanted us to think that he was finished with politics? Nothing in his recent past suggested that he was cooling off from his campaign. The very opposite, in fact.'

'Which would give credence to your theory that someone else wanted him to stop.'

'If that is the case then whoever planted that car bomb thought that he really was blowing up Truesdale, not someone he'd arranged to live in his place.'

'And the bomber must have known Truesdale's new location in Strathblane,' Flint agreed.

'Not only that,' Lorimer added, 'they must have seen Truesdale at least once to confirm that he had moved into that bungalow. But here's the thing,' he leaned forward, eyes shining, 'I don't think that Truesdale spent much time at all in that house. The cleaner didn't recognise the occupant as Robert Truesdale and there were signs that whoever that person was he'd been there less than twenty-four hours. Mrs Jardine left a note from me after my visit and someone passed the information to Truesdale,' he said at last. 'And I am betting that person was the bomb victim.'

Lorimer went on to relate the contents of the fridge and freezer, so many unopened food items plus these two small slicks on the surface of the butter.

'I think whoever had been persuaded to stay in his stead was expecting to be there for much longer,' he concluded.

'And did Truesdale think that too?'

Lorimer heaved a sigh. 'I'm not certain. He possibly wanted time to put a distance between himself and whoever was threatening him though I cannot imagine he had any inkling of what was going to happen the very next morning. As you know, there was no further activity on his mobile phone so we have no way of finding out where he might have gone after he left Strathblane.'

'Who was the person he'd persuaded to stay there in his place?' Flint murmured.

'The father of that poor unfortunate infant,' Lorimer agreed.

'Find out who that is and we will have a clue about just where Truesdale might be and who has a hold over him.'

Lorimer nodded. Then, in a moment of decision, he began to remind Caroline Flint about the recent recruit to Police Scotland who had found the dead mother and her baby in that back lane.

'You think Kohi will want to be involved?' Flint mused. Then a faint smile played around her mouth. 'Why not? He's always struck me as a highly intelligent man. Might even rise to play a part in your own operations here,' she added, her smile broadening at the prospect.

CHAPTER TWENTY-TWO

Daniel's lips curved into a smile as he closed the car door, a feeling of lightness in his heart. Netta would be safe in hospital for the next few days and meantime it was up to him to prepare their new home. There were things to see to, the old lady had reminded him, like informing the Housing Association of her notice to relocate. And packing, he'd added, but that notion appeared to have worn her out, remembering how Netta had laid her head on the bank of pillows with a sigh. It wasn't so much the thought of actual moving that had made her exhausted, Daniel had realised, but all of the things she was unable to do for the next few months as she recovered.

His visit to the hospital had been a success, he thought, fastening his seat belt before setting off for home. There was a ping from his mobile so he picked it up to see who was trying to reach him. It was Lorimer. Daniel scrolled down to read the message and then sat for a moment, wondering what was on the detective superintendent's mind and why he wanted Daniel to come across town to see him. Luckily the Queen Elizabeth hospital was close to the MIT in Govan so he sent a quick text of his own: *On my way.*

It was dusk as Daniel made his way there, streetlights glimmering along the road that bordered Bellahouston Park, its grassy banks and trees now shadowy shapes beyond the metal railings. Out of the gloom came the now familiar chequered emblem of Police Scotland and Daniel turned into the car park, casting around for Lorimer's new Lexus. It was still there, a space beside it, as if inviting him to park.

A quick nod to the officer on reception and a flash of his warrant card were sufficient for him to enter the main building and head upstairs.

A knock on the door and a voice calling 'come in' were all Daniel needed before slipping into the detective superintendent's office and settling into a chair opposite Lorimer.

'You wanted to see me?'

Lorimer nodded then rose from behind his desk, drawing another chair closer to his friend. 'I've been speaking to the chief constable today,' he began, fixing Daniel with his blue gaze. 'And I think you will be interested to hear what we discussed.'

Much later, when Daniel finally turned the key in his front door, Lorimer's words were still ringing in his ears. Once before, he had taken on a clandestine assignment for the man, risking his time as a refugee hoping to gain settled status. That had worked out, however, and gained him the respect of the senior officer who was now head of Police

Scotland. This would present him with equal difficulties but he had Caroline Flint's guarantee that his probationary period would not be jeopardised. He would not be working alone, of course, several officers from the MIT also investigating what lay behind the death of Angelika Mahbed. But being part of the case already gave Daniel a unique advantage. However, he would arrive at the Calder Street flat in his ordinary clothes, uniformed cops possibly scaring off some of the locals who were more reluctant to talk.

So, the baby had a father, Daniel thought as he filled a kettle full of water. Or at least, he'd had a father before the man had been murdered by that car bomb. Begin with the mother, Lorimer had suggested, knowing that some investigating had been done so far. It would be Daniel Kohi's remit to find out what he could about the men who had frequented Angelika's flat, should he be able to ask the right people.

Many of these people were outsiders, those who had escaped lives of poverty in eastern Europe and he could identify with that at least. Being a refugee had been a great leveller, bringing Daniel a keener awareness of the plight faced by so many after their descent from a decent standard of living to utter penury in a strange country. And being a black man in Glasgow had elicited stares and sometimes comments, something that might well be to his advantage as he sought the help of some of the folk from the Romanian community, especially anyone who had known Angelika.

Ask for Miranda, Lorimer had told him. The dead woman's flatmates had not given the police much information apart from Angelika's address in Romania, most of them putting on a pretence at having no understanding of English. That particular name had come up a few times, the other girls claiming that she knew more about Angelika than they did, though, whoever she was, Miranda had proved elusive so far. That was odd since she lived in that flat and the police had made several visits there already. Perhaps Daniel Kohi might have better luck.

Tomorrow began the first of two late shifts, beginning at two in the afternoon, so, if he rose before dawn, he could be across on the Southside asking questions before he had to be at Aikenhead Road.

His hand shook with excitement as he poured boiling water into a mug, spilling a few drops onto the work surface. It would mean an early night but Daniel Kohi was not at all sure if he'd be able to sleep for all the thoughts that were burning in his mind.

CHAPTER TWENTY-THREE

It was still dark when he drove out of the car park next morning, few lights showing in the windows of the high flats. Daniel had become familiar with the streets around Govanhill, from Hampden all the way to the different districts like Mount Florida, Langside and Cathcart so he knew exactly where he was heading. Memories of standing by the swiftly flowing River Cart still caused him a shiver, not least because of the hours he had spent guarding the scene of crime. He'd heard no more about the dead man nor whether the CID team had found any link to the ongoing feud between the different dealers. Certainly, no arrests had been made and so he would have to tread carefully when he made enquiries of his own this morning.

There was a strong wind blowing when he left the car parked on a side street, leaves whirling through the damp air and sweeping into the gutters. Autumn was a season he remembered from his time down south before he had arrived in Glasgow, the change from warm evenings to frosty mornings something that had fascinated the man from Zimbabwe. Now, however, he was accustomed to the different cycles in this northern land, though whether he'd ever get used to the changes of weather was another matter, rain, hail and sunshine in a single day something of which Glaswegians seemed almost proud.

Angelika Mahbed's former home had been a shared flat on the top floor of an old tenement building in Calder Street, between the main arteries of Pollokshaws Road on one side and Victoria Road on the other. Daniel took the steps up to a red door that showed scuff marks around the base as if it had received a regular kicking from somebody's size tens. The security buttons on the left were mostly without a name, apart from L/1 which bore a handwritten scrawl. Angelika Mahbed had lived in L/4, Daniel had found out, a flat shared with other, mostly Romanian, women, some of whom were known addicts like her.

He pressed the buzzer opposite and was surprised when the door simply opened at his touch. No security? Or an open invitation to visit these ladies of the night on the top floor?

Inside, it was like most Victorian-era tenements that Daniel had seen in this city, the walls tiled ('a wally close,' Netta had informed him); a stone staircase leading upwards, its treads badly worn from centuries of weary feet. He followed them upwards, taking note of the doors of each flat.

The top floor landing was a mess, old magazines piled in one corner, their torn pages rustling in a draught rising up the stairwell. Empty bottles lay discarded in plastic carrier bags, waiting for someone to take them downstairs for recycling, and a blue plastic basin with dirty towels inside had been chucked out into the middle of the floor, a strong smell of disinfectant making Daniel wrinkle his nose.

He rapped on the door, noticing that there was no bell. If punters had come a-visiting here then perhaps, as downstairs, it was simply left open for them?

There was no sound from within so he rapped again, lifting the metal letter box and letting it fall again loudly several times.

At last, he heard a faint sound of footsteps then the rattle of a chain.

The door opened and Daniel saw a young girl of about fourteen standing there barefoot and bleary-eyed as if she had just awoken from sleep.

'I'm looking for Miranda,' Daniel said. 'May I come in please, miss ...?'

The girl looked at him for a moment through long hair that straggled across her face then, without demur, took off the chain and opened the door wide to let Daniel enter, walking back along the hall, leaving Daniel to close it behind him.

'Were you a friend of Angelika?' Daniel asked her, catching the girl up before she tried to go back to what he guessed was her own bedroom.

The girl started at the name, a frightened look in her eyes. 'No Eenglish,' she said, glancing over her shoulder at Daniel. Then, hooking a thumb towards a door on the opposite side of the corridor, she stopped.

'Angelika?' Daniel asked again, to see if that elicited any further response.

But the girl merely shook her head and pushed open her door, disappearing inside.

There was a faint sound of snoring behind the door that the girl had indicated and so Daniel gave it a quick rat-tat before pushing down the handle.

Inside it was dark, rust-coloured curtains sealing off the burgeoning daylight. He was aware of a female form under the bedclothes, dark hair spread on a pillow, the woman's face hidden.

'Hello,' Daniel called out and immediately the woman rolled over with a groan.

'Whoissit?' she mumbled.

'My name's Daniel,' he said, coming towards the bed.

'Who the . . .?' She sat up suddenly, clutching the bed-clothes to her chest, dark eyes staring at this stranger.

'I heard that Angelika lived here,' he said softly. 'I've come to talk to you about the baby.'

'Effing social workers,' the woman grumbled in an accent that was distinctly Glaswegian. 'What the hell time is this to come and see us anyway?'

Daniel let that pass. If she had taken him for a social worker, that was fine by him. The young girl might choose not to say very much to any other visitor but one thing was certain, they would both remember a black man and it would probably not be long before he'd be asked some awkward questions back at the station.

'We wanted to ask you about the baby's father,' Daniel said gently.

'Poor Angelika loved that kid,' the woman sighed. 'Look, mister, we cannae talk in here so why don't you shove off

172

into the kitchen and make us a pot of tea, eh? Let me get dressed.' She looked down pointedly at her bare shoulders. 'Unless you fancy a quickie? Never had a darkie before,' she laughed. 'They say you lot are ...' She raised a lascivious eyebrow and patted the bed invitingly.

Daniel shook his head and left the room, noticing the way she smiled slyly at him. Had that been a genuine come-on? Or was she simply trying to discomfit him?

For a moment he wondered what it would be like to be held in the warmth of a woman's arms once again. But he was startled to find that it was not his late wife Chipo that came to mind but a certain blonde detective sergeant in Lorimer's team. Molly, he thought with stab of guilt. Daniel had not made anything of their burgeoning friendship so far and it dawned on him now that he may have left that too late. Surely the tall detective sergeant would have her pick of the men in her own circle? And yet ... hadn't she sometimes looked at Daniel Kohi, the refugee from Zimbabwe, with an expression in her eyes that ought to have encouraged him to ask her out?

He swallowed hard, shaking these thoughts from his mind, telling himself to concentrate on the here and now. *Make tea for Miranda*, he scolded. *Find out more about Angelika.*

It was just a few minutes later that the woman crept into the kitchen, a grey towelling bathrobe tied tightly round her waist, and perched on a bar stool next to a small wooden table.

'Feart of Miranda, ur ye?' she laughed, tossing her long dark hair over one shoulder.

'That's your name? Miranda?' Daniel asked, though he'd already guessed who she was.

'Aye. Well, that's the name you can call me.' She grinned.

'Angelika. Was that her real name?'

'Oh, aye. Wee Angelika Mahbed.'

He saw her smile fade as she laid hold of an empty mug, turning it round and round as if to avoid looking in Daniel's direction.

'Do you know who the baby's father was?'

She shrugged, clearly bored by the turn of the conversation.

'You got any fags?'

Daniel shook his head. 'Sorry, I don't smoke.'

'Whit dae ye do fur fun, then, black man?' she asked, crossing her legs so that the dressing gown fell away to reveal a pair of pale thighs.

Daniel gave her a sad smile. 'I like walking. Climbed a mountain with my friend a few months ago. Scotland is a beautiful country. But sometimes bad things happen here too.'

'Aye.' She looked down at her hands, all attempts at flirtation suddenly gone as if the thought of her flatmate's death had cast a shadow over them.

'I don't know who it was that got her pregnant,' Miranda told him. 'Cops came and asked that too, y'know. But the lassies here telt them nuthin'.' She jutted her chin in the air defiantly.

'If we can trace the baby's family . . .' Daniel left the rest of his words hanging in the air. 'Surely Angelika would have wanted that?'

'Aye, well, mibbe. Social services wumman wasnae that nice tae us when she barged in here. Threatened tae have us all evicted so she did, rotten cow!'

'I won't do that,' Daniel told her.

'Naw.' She looked up into his soft brown eyes. 'You dinna look that type,' she said. 'Sure ye dinna fancy . . .' She jerked her head in the direction of the bedroom.

'Thank you for the offer, but no,' Daniel replied.

'Oh, well, God loves a trier.' She gave a throaty chuckle.

'Angelika had several clients coming here, I gather?'

'Oh, aye. Popular lassie, so she wis. Careful, an' all. How she got in the family way, Gawd alone knows,' she said, shrugging. 'There were a few regulars, mind you. One of them came every Sunday night, stayed over sometimes too. That wasn't usual.' She shook her head. 'Get 'em in, grab the cash, kick 'em out, I used to tell her.'

'And this man. Did he have a name?'

The woman seemed to think for a moment then shook her head. 'Sorry, cannae mind if we ever knew his proper name. He jist always asked fur Angelika, naebody else. But we all called him Paddy.'

'Paddy?'

'Aye.' She looked at Daniel pityingly. 'How long've ye been in Glesca, mister? Dae ye no' get called names? Some folk dinna care if it's racist or no'.'

Daniel winced as she cackled mirthlessly.

'Here, nae offence. The English ca' us Jocks an' Paddy's whit we call an Irishman.'

'Paddy?' Daniel repeated, ashamed of his own ignorance.

'He wis Irish, right? But whether or no' that particular

punter wis the wan that got her up the duff is onybody's guess. Poor lassie wis that far gone on the heroin back then she didnae know the time o' day, nivver mind who wis banging her.'

'Can you tell me anything else about him, Miranda? What he looked like?'

'Sure you dinna have ony fags, mister?' she wheedled. 'And ahm that strapped fur cash the now ...' She gave him a lopsided smile.

Daniel took out his wallet and produced a twenty-pound note, holding it up between them and looking into her eyes. 'Would this jog your memory?'

She smiled and laid a finger on her dimpled chin, pretending to think. 'Well now, let me see. Oh, aye, I do remember something. That wee cross he wore round his neck ...'

Daniel felt something cold slide down his spine, then, before he could blink, she'd snatched the money from his fingers.

'I see you know somethin' about that, eh?' she asked, wagging a finger at him and sliding off the stool. She came closer to Daniel. 'Will that help find the wee guy's faither?'

He nodded, sensing the change in the woman's tone.

'The baby ... did he have a name?'

Miranda shook her head. 'Angelika hadnae decided. He wis that wee ... will he be all right?'

'Yes, he'll be taken care of,' Daniel told her. 'Thank you, Miss ...?'

'Miranda. Jist Miranda. Randy fur short,' she snorted in a self-deprecating laugh.

'Well, that was very helpful.' He turned and gave her

a long stare. 'You really ought to tell the police over at Govanhill.'

'Naw, you dae it, mister. Then come 'n' see us again, eh?' She smiled widely and tossed back her head, laughing once again as Daniel made his way along the hallway towards the front door.

CHAPTER TWENTY-FOUR

An Irishman who frequented the Calder Street flat, staying over on Sunday nights. Lorimer thought hard. There must be some CCTV footage in the nearby shops, a row of grocers, tobacconists, and several takeaway establishments. One place in particular caught his attention as he and Molly Newton pored over a street view of the area.

'This one,' he said, pointing at a blue and white sign saying *Lorenzo's Fish and Chips*. 'I know this place. Guy's sons were done for dealing.'

'Lorenzo's sons?' Molly asked.

'Lorenzo's not his real name. Oh, there probably was an Italian called Lorenzo that owned it back in the day but not now. Chap who runs it is called Morrison, Des Morrison. Used to run with Gallagher's gang for a while but money came his way and he bought this place.'

'Known dealer?'

Lorimer shook his head. 'We've nothing on Morrison apart from knowing he was one of Gallagher's hard men and he's kept his nose clean since he took over the chippie. His two boys are a different story, however. Desmond junior is currently serving time in Saughton for attempted murder and the younger one was put away for dealing drugs. What was his name?' Lorimer made a tsk-ing sound. 'Zander!' he exclaimed. 'That was it. Alexander Morrison. Good Scottish name but he was known as Zander.'

'You think there might be a link between the addicts and the chip shop?'

Lorimer gave her an appraising look. 'Well, they'll have security cameras,' he said. 'Even if it's just to warn off their backroom lads when the cops are arriving.'

'You want Kohi to visit them? Ask questions?'

Lorimer paused for a moment, considering. 'They'll remember a black cop easily enough,' he began, 'and Daniel will begin his shift in another hour or so. No,' he decided. 'I think you and DS Giles must just treat yourself to a couple of fish suppers for lunch today, DS Newton.'

He saw the slow smile appear on the former undercover officer's face. Molly was not yet well known amongst the low-life on Glasgow's Southside and so perhaps she might have the advantage of surprise, ask if they knew this Irishman that the street women called Paddy before demanding to see the establishment's CCTV tapes. Davie Giles would be in the queue, apparently just another solitary customer, but actually there to corroborate everything that was said.

And, elsewhere on the Southside of the city, questions would be asked of Karen Douglas, the woman who had lived for so long next door to Robert Truesdale.

*

179

It was a bright day but there was still a chill wind from the east as Molly walked into the chip shop, its bell pinging loudly to alert the staff, Davie still a few yards behind. Two men in work clothes stood waiting for their orders, watching as a balding man in a greasy white apron behind the counter shovelled chips out of the fryer and into polystyrene containers. The smell of hot fat and vinegar made Molly's mouth water in spite of herself, remembering the paper bags of chips that had been their chittery bites after the swimming baths when she and her brothers were kids.

Molly looked at the noticeboard on the right-hand wall, as if reading the menu. Yes, there was the telltale camera, its swivel head showing it to be a fairly expensive piece of kit. Molly smoothed her hair with one hand as if to repair the damage from the wind, but what she was really doing was posting that particular gesture in order to check its placement on the camera footage later.

'Here ye are.' The man handed over two thick bundles for the workmen who turned to go back into the street, the doorbell pinging once more.

'Right, what'll it be?' the bald man asked, rubbing his hands and looking up at Molly who, in her high-heeled boots, stood several inches taller than the fish fryer.

'A single fish please,' she asked, coming closer to lean against the counter. 'I was told this was the best place round here.' She shot the man a dazzling smile. *Flattery gets you everywhere*, she thought as the wee man seemed to preen himself like a cock sparrow.

'Oh, aye, naebody does chips like we do.' He beamed proudly. 'A' the punters come here after the games over at

180

Hampden,' he added, evidently keen to show off despite his place being a bit of a trek from the national stadium.

'That right? You'll be famous then?' she teased, ignoring the next customer who entered, DS Giles pretending to look at the menu as if it was far more interesting than what the tall blonde woman was saying.

'Aw, we get all the big names in here, so we do. Ally McCoist, Giovanni van Bronckhorst. Aye, wan time we even had Rod Stewart in fur an order,' he boasted.

Molly's eyes flicked around the walls of the shop, bare of even a single football poster. If the man's claims were true then he'd have a signed photo of these men at the very least. She guessed this was all a lot of tosh as there were plenty more chippies between Hampden Park and Calder Street but decided to humour him as much as she could.

'If you know everyone, maybe you know a guy I'm looking for?' she asked innocently.

'Who's that?' the bald man asked, sliding out a couple of pieces of fish from the shelf above the fryer.

'The girls along the road call him Paddy,' Molly replied. 'Used to visit Angelika Mahbed.'

Desmond Morrison stopped suddenly, the hand holding the fish slice frozen in mid-air, and stared at Molly.

'Who's asking?' he growled, lowering the fish onto a clean piece of white paper.

'Detective Sergeant Newton,' Molly replied sweetly, her warrant card suddenly appearing like a magician's sleight of hand, her colleague suddenly by her side. 'And we would just love to see your recent CCTV tapes while I enjoy that delicious-looking fish, Mr Morrison.'

181

Desmond Morrison scowled at her then turned and called out, 'Jessie! Come and mind the shop!'

A stout woman in a floral apron appeared and bustled towards them, eyeing Molly and Davie with a frank stare while he escorted the detectives through a hatch in the counter and into the back of the premises.

'Polis,' he growled at the woman, drawing down his brows in disapproval.

'CCTV for the past few weeks. Or however long you've got them on record,' Molly demanded, fixing Morrison with a glare every bit as steely as the one her boss sometimes used.

Molly and Davie sat beside the man as he flicked through the tapes, checking dates.

'It'll take hours tae get through this lot,' he grumbled.

'That's all right, Mr Morrison,' Molly told him sweetly. 'I'll let you know if we're still hungry before we go.'

Morrison was cooperative to a point, Molly realised soon enough as he left them to trawl through three weeks of tapes (*they're a' scrubbed once a month*, he'd told her) which might or might not give her some inkling into the Romanian woman's life.

'You weren't wrong when you mentioned that the girls from the nearby flat were in the habit of coming into the chip shop,' said Giles, grinning. 'Intelligence has it that fish suppers were not the only thing they'd left with on several occasions.'

'Bet Morrison's frantic right now,' she replied.

'Aye, probably on the phone to his dealers warning them

off,' agreed Giles. 'Lorenzo's might well be a conduit for shifting heroin, given the Morrison boys' past reputation.'

'Not to mention their father's previous association with one of Glasgow's most notorious gangsters, Jack Gallagher.'

'And it was Lorimer himself who put *him* away,' said Giles reminding her of the once-affluent drug baron who would never see the outside of any prison walls.

Undercover operations had schooled DS Newton to long stretches of boredom, surveillance duties demanding a clear head and a readiness to move at any moment despite hours of watching and waiting. Looking through the tapes, Molly found, was equally mind-numbing and she kept her focus on each person coming and going in the chip shop, their movements becoming almost rhythmic at times. Hours passed with only a few halts on the tapes to scrutinise the girls whose photos she'd taken from Angelika's case file. So far, so innocent, she thought until . . .

Gotcha! Molly grinned as she watched the handover, not just a bulky pack of pie and chips, but something else that had caught her eye.

'Look at this,' she told Giles.

There were two of them, Angelika and another girl who looked like a half-starved teenager, the latter constantly turning her head nervously to look towards the door.

Molly sat up, excitedly, staring at the date and time on the footage. It was just a few hours before Daniel had finished his shift and found the woman's dead body.

It was over in one swift movement but, as Molly stopped the tape once more, she could see the roll of notes being passed from Angelika's fist to a dark-haired man standing close beside her.

'Is that the elusive Paddy?' Giles asked.

'I doubt it,' Molly answered. 'Surely the man sleeping with Angelika on Sunday nights could have managed a handover within the safety of the girls' flat? This was the middle of a Monday evening when most good folk could be watching *University Challenge* on TV.'

'Mr Morrison, a moment, please,' she called out and saw the bald man spin round at the sound of her voice.

'Who is that man?' Molly asked, keeping her eyes fixed on Morrison, who looked at the screen where she had frozen the image. He was licking his lips anxiously, flicking his glance from Molly and Giles to the man on the screen who was quite obviously conducting some transaction with the drug addict.

'Never seen him in my—'

'Oh, come on, Des,' Molly said wearily. 'Sooner you tell us, sooner we'll be out of here.'

'Some wee lowlife,' Morrison began. 'Don't know his name—'

'Aye, you do,' Molly laughed. 'I can see fine you know exactly who that is. Now, either you give me a name or you waste police time. Or perhaps you'd rather come back to Govan with me? See some more of Detective Superintendent Lorimer's colleagues?'

'Aye, well, mibbe ...' Morrison made a great show of peering closer at the screen, uhm-ing and ah-ing as he shook his head.

'Think it might be a lad called Frankie Fleming,' he said

at last. 'Bad wee toerag, so he is. Won't let him back in here again, I can tell you,' he added, putting on a tone of righteous indignation that made Molly want to laugh out loud. Morrison had avoided jail himself, bobbing and weaving his way through life, always letting the other guy take the fall. He might be an insignificant figure of a man, wee and bald, but he reminded Molly of T.S. Eliot's mystery cat, Macavity, who had the habit of disappearing whenever the going got too hot.

'Not an Irishman, then?' Giles asked.

'Naw, Frankie's frae Castlemilk,' Morrison told them, mentioning a housing estate on the outskirts of the city.

'Okay, thanks.' Molly nodded and, as Morrison prepared to leave, added, 'A pot of tea for two wouldn't go amiss, Des. Just milk, no sugar.'

Morrison turned and opened his mouth as if to say something then closed it again as she smiled at him.

'Good of you, Des,' she said. 'Thank you.'

'Oh, and there's this wan. Sorry, it wis under a pile of papers,' he apologised, handing her another tape.

Molly rubbed her neck. She was tired now and it was hard to keep her focus on the footage. There were several more sightings of the girls from the flat and Molly was about to give up and take the lot back to Govan with her when she spotted it. The date on this tape was the Sunday before Daniel had found Angelika's body in that dismal lane, shortly before eleven o'clock. She saw the woman entering the chip shop then stopping to turn and speak to someone behind her.

'Wait a minute,' she said, making Davie look closer.

Molly froze the image then ran it back a little. Beyond the plate-glass window, she could see them arriving, the man's arm around Angelika's shoulder, the woman smiling up into his eyes.

Molly let the tape run on again and gave a gasp as she saw exactly what was happening. Angelika wasn't just turning to say something to the man but was handing him a bundle that could only be her little baby. The man remained outside the shop and Molly slowed down the tape until she could zoom in, hoping to catch a glimpse of his face.

It was dark outside but there was a streetlight close by. However, the man was turned away from the window, moving in a way that suggested he was rocking the infant in his arms.

'Turn round,' Molly hissed at the shadowy figure as the tape ran on again.

Then, as if he had heard her, the man did just that.

Molly stopped the tape at once, catching the stranger's face. Was this the mysterious Irishman? The baby's father who, days later, would be blown up in that deadly car bomb?

'Morrison. Here. Now!'

CHAPTER TWENTY-FIVE

'Your dead guy was no loss to society.' The woman nodded to Daniel. She picked up her cigarette and inhaled then blew the smoke across her shoulder. 'Kenny Ritchie, one of Frankie Fleming's lot.'

Daniel had finished his cup of coffee, but still clutched the mug to warm his hands. They were sitting outside a small café in Victoria Road, the place chosen by the SIO for meeting with Police Constable Kohi, a request he had accepted, though he was a little unsure why she had insisted on meeting so far from the divisional HQ.

Daniel wanted to say something about each person being special, one of God's children, but he was no longer as sure of his faith as he used to be. Instead, he remembered what the chief constable had said in her speech at the passing-out parade, how every officer owed a duty of care to each member of the public.

'You think I'm being cynical, Kohi?' DS Diana Miller asked, her smile challenging him.

'I suppose after a few years we all become hardened in this job,' he replied at last. 'I know it happened to me a bit. But not enough to lose sight of why I wanted to be a cop.' He shrugged. 'It's why I'm back doing it all over again.'

'Well, good for you.' Miller gave a mirthless laugh. 'And maybe you're right. I often ask myself why I wanted to do this in the first place. Fish dead bodies out of a filthy river, see pitiable women crawling back to their abusive husbands, changing their minds about how they got their broken teeth ... Ach, cynicism keeps some of us going, Kohi. Anyway, your dead guy. Drug deal gone wrong, apparently.' She frowned, pausing to flick ash onto the pavement. 'Blows from a weapon that could be a machete, according to the post-mortem. And I wondered if you would like to see the updated report into his death?'

Daniel laid down his mug as Miller reached into a slim briefcase that she had laid against the legs of her chair and brought out a buff-coloured file.

'Even printed off a hard copy for you. Homework, if you like,' she said, tossing the paperwork onto the table.

Daniel eyed her curiously. 'Why?' he asked, no longer able to suppress his curiosity about this woman's motives.

'Why am I giving you this? Or why did I single you out for a date?' She burst out laughing at the pained expression on Daniel's face.

'Don't worry, Kohi, I'm joking. My wife would have a fit,' she said with a chortle. 'No, it's really your face we're after.'

He gave her a questioning look. 'My face? Why me?'

'Let's just say I was advised to include you in this matter. See, I have a different reason for bringing you all the way along to my favourite café. We know you visited a young lady in Calder Street recently ... No don't deny it, and you're not going to be hauled up about that.' She raised an admonishing finger as Daniel opened his mouth to speak. 'It's like this. We happen to need a person of colour to push this case along,' she said quietly, leaning her elbows on the table and coming closer to Daniel. 'How would you feel about going undercover?'

DS Miller had outlined the current situation concerning the different drug gangs in Glasgow, the Southside groups split between foreign nationals and home-grown Glasgow neds. But there was a new element that had crept in, one that the drug squad had alerted them about quite recently. *Colombians*, Miller had told Daniel eventually, although one of their number was a Zimbabwean national with a shady past. And word had filtered down from someone well above Miller's pay grade, as she'd put it, that PC Kohi had fled Zimbabwe for his new life here in Scotland. He ought to be flattered, Miller had told him, but right now all that Daniel could think of was the level of secrecy he would have to maintain during the next few weeks. And how he might keep the knowledge of what he was doing from Netta.

'He's in.'

Jacob Alexander nodded, hearing the woman's voice. It had been the chief constable's suggestion that Daniel be seconded to the Govanhill drugs murder cases. *We need a black man to infiltrate the Colombian gang*, she'd insisted. And who better than former Inspector Kohi?

'Can we keep an eye on him?'

'Only from a discreet distance,' Diana Miller chuckled. 'Don't worry, I'm sure Kohi is more than capable of looking after himself.'

Alexander stifled a sigh. As his tutor cop it was impossible not to feel concern for his newest probationer. And besides, he'd truly warmed to the guy.

'You'll keep me posted about everything that happens, though?'

There was a short silence as he imagined his colleague in CID digesting this idea.

'All right, but the fewer who know what is going on with Kohi, the better,' she replied. 'And stop worrying, Jacob. I can hear it in your voice!'

CHAPTER TWENTY-SIX

Karen Douglas was passing through the hall as she saw the dark shadow of a man behind the frosted glass of her front door. Then the bell rang. Who on earth was calling at this hour? she thought crossly, ready to give this stranger a piece of her mind. Could they not read the prominent NO COLD CALLERS sign? She approached the door, aware of a second shape, smaller and slimmer. A woman? A natural caution made her fix the security chain and yet still be curious enough to open the door to see who was there.

'Yes?' Her tart question that had cowed many a child in the classroom did not have the desired effect on the tall man standing there on her step.

'Detective Superintendent Lorimer, DC Singh,' the man said, presenting his warrant card at eye level where she had no trouble reading it. 'May we come in, Miss Douglas?'

Karen swallowed hard. This was completely unexpected, two police officers entering her home, one a huge chap well over six foot, the other, not female after all but a slightly built figure, a young man of Asian origin who instantly reminded her of one of the clever children she had taught during her career.

'Is this about Robert?'

Lorimer took in the woman's appearance, the mid-calf suede skirt, mint-coloured cashmere polo neck sweater with a knotted silk scarf in shades of green, sensible flat shoes, expensive but well worn. She looked like a woman who knew what she suited and stuck to it. Outside he had noted a well-tended front garden, the lawn smooth and free of autumn leaves, privet hedges clipped, signalling a determination to keep on top of things. Did Karen Douglas spend hours busy in her garden, watching the world going by? Or was there a paid gardener to do the work?

'Yes, we have come to ask you about Mr Truesdale,' Lorimer agreed at last. 'It is important to find out everything we can about his movements prior to the explosion.' He got straight to the point. 'You had been neighbours for many years, I believe?'

She gave him a stare as if surprised that a stranger should know this, then, as if she suddenly remembered that it was a senior police officer asking that question, she inclined her head a little.

'We moved in about a year before the Truesdales,' she said. 'I was five, just starting school when they came to live next door. Robert and I were in the same class all through primary.'

'A local school?'

'Hutchie,' she replied stiffly, not bothering to give the

famous establishment its full title: Hutchesons' Grammar School. 'We travelled into Kingarth Street together and later on to Beaton Road when we began big school.'

Lorimer refrained from smiling. *Big school* was no doubt what this former school mistress referred to when she had been speaking to her primary charges. 'So, you must have known him very well.'

He saw the flare of nostrils and that sharp intake of breath. Did that indicate something?

'I thought I did,' she answered quietly, looking down at the wrinkled hands clasped together on her lap.

'You were good friends, had known one another since childhood,' Lorimer suggested. 'You must have known more about Robert Truesdale than most people of his acquaintance.'

'I wouldn't have called us good friends,' she replied slowly. 'We did certain things together, going to school, attending church, till Robert began university then refused point-blank to go.'

'Did you see a lot of him outside these areas?'

Karen Douglas did not meet his eyes, looking away as she answered. 'No. We were simply companions. None of that boy-and-girl-next-door nonsense,' she insisted, pursing her lips, her eyes sliding away.

Somehow, her words did not strike Lorimer as completely true and he might have hazarded a guess that the teenage Karen Douglas had held a candle for her neighbour at one time. Or, if he was right, had that been a feeling persisting over the years? Neither had ever married, so had she ever held out hopes for some sort of a relationship?

'I believe you arranged a cleaning lady for his new home. Can you tell us about that?'

Her mouth fell open in surprise. 'How did you . . .?' Then her expression changed, the jaw hardening. 'That Canadian woman . . .'

'Please tell us exactly what favours you did for your former neighbour.'

'Oh, well . . .' she began, a pink flush spreading across her cheeks. 'Just what any neighbour would do.'

'But Robert Truesdale wasn't just any neighbour, Miss Douglas, was he? A well-known member of the Scottish Parliament, harassed by the media and by those who wanted to stop his campaign to legalise drugs. Plus, he was a man you'd known for most of your lives. Tell us, what was it he wanted you to do?'

'It wasn't anything untoward,' the woman insisted. 'Just helping him out a bit. I don't really know in retrospect why he insisted on all that cloak-and-dagger stuff but at the time it seemed fairly reasonable. After all, he was trying to get away from all the furore, settle down in a new village where people didn't know him.'

'And . . .?'

'Well, he gave me a door key for the new house. Asked me to post it to the cleaning lady after I'd spoken to her on the telephone to make arrangements. I thought perhaps he was just busy or was delegating a task like that to a woman who could do a better job of sorting out a cleaner than he could. My own lady comes in twice a week and did for old Mrs Truesdale before she passed on.'

'Mr Truesdale did not keep her on after his mother died?'

She shook her head. 'No. Perhaps he wanted to do things his own way.' She shrugged. 'Anyway, there were always people coming in for meetings later in the evenings. I suppose a politician has to spend more hours at work than most of us, though goodness knows, teachers take plenty of work home with them.'

Lorimer gave a faint grin, knowing first-hand how hard Maggie worked in the evenings.

'And what exactly were the arrangements with the cleaner?' he asked. Even though Nancy Jardine had already given him these details he wanted to see if they tallied with this woman's account.

'She was to come in at two p.m. each week and stay till three-thirty. Let herself in with that Yale key and lock up afterwards. All the cleaning things were supplied by Mrs Jardine and money would be left in an envelope to pay her each week.'

'Let's get back to the day of the actual removal. Did you see him on the day he moved away?'

He saw her glance uneasily between Singh and himself, before replying.

'Actually, I never saw Robert again,' she whispered. 'Not after he'd asked me to post that key. The removal van came as I was out in the garden, weeding the path.'

Lorimer could imagine that scene, the woman's curiosity needing to be satisfied. Or had she hoped to make some sort of farewell to the man who'd grown up next door?

'He wasn't there with them?'

'No. And his car had gone, too. An old Toyota Avensis. Hatchback, you know, the sort you could pack masses of things in. I thought maybe I'd missed him and he'd gone on ahead.'

'Who locked up the house next door after the removal people left?' DC Singh enquired.

'Oh, well, that was me,' she said, her face redder than ever.

'Another favour?' Lorimer asked.

The woman nodded miserably. 'Robert asked me to hold on to the key till his solicitor came to collect it later that day.'

'And he did?'

'Yes. I'd met him a couple of times when he had visited Robert in the past. I just handed it over and, well, that was that.'

Lorimer felt sudden pity for this woman. Had she been used by Truesdale, become an unwitting pawn in whatever little game he had been playing? And he had never even had the grace to say thank you or goodbye.

'Was Robert Truesdale a likeable man?' he asked.

'What do you mean?'

'Did he have the sort of charm that makes it hard for anybody to refuse a request by him?'

'Oh, no, he was far from being a charmer, Superintendent. Robert was more of a . . . how can I describe him? Sometimes he could appear to be a bit contained in his own world, so busy with important matters that small things like keys and cleaners were just too much for him. Some men are just like that,' she added, raising her chin, and fixing them both with a defiant stare.

As they made their way back to Govan, Lorimer wondered about Karen Douglas's final words. Had Truesdale managed to convince other people of his helplessness over domestic matters? In particular, the man who had been in his brand-new car that fatal morning?

Soon he would find out how Newton and Giles had fared across in Calder Street, the fish and chip shop a short walk away from where Karen Douglas and Robert Truesdale had gone to primary school. And, he thought to himself, Truesdale would be familiar with that area.

'Are you sure? Des Morrison is a slippery wee customer. He'd sell his granny to keep himself out of our hands,' Lorimer told her.

'That's what he said,' Molly replied. 'An Irish fellow called James. Or Seamus. Didn't have a second name but when we pressed him, Morrison did say he thought the guy might be the baby's father. He'd seen him with Angelika and the baby since the kid was born.'

'If Morrison knew that, then the other women in her flat knew him too,' Lorimer fumed. 'Why didn't they just come clean and tell us?'

'Good question, sir.' Molly yawned, rubbing the back of her neck that was strained from hours of sitting staring at the CCTV screen. She'd insisted that Giles went home, their shift long ended, her younger colleague happy to let her report back on her own. 'Could be they're afraid of something?'

Lorimer heaved a sigh. 'Daniel reckons most of them genuinely don't have good English. That was the feedback he got from the officers who'd already visited the flat.'

'All except for that woman, Miranda,' Molly added.

Lorimer tried to hide a smile. Daniel's report of the woman's come-on had shown a more vulnerable side to his friend. He hadn't missed out anything, even the hint of racial slur against him, but had told Lorimer word for word what the prostitute had said.

'Well. We have an image of the man the girls called Paddy but whose real name was possibly James. Or Seamus, in Ireland. Get that circulated. See if there's any intelligence on the fellow. If that was the bairn's father then his DNA isn't on any of our systems prior to the man's death. Not a wrong 'un.'

'Desmond Morrison isn't on our system either, sir,' Molly remarked.

Lorimer gave her a tired smile. 'Point taken, DS Newton. Now, I think it's time we both pushed off home.' He looked out of the window at the night sky. 'You've done your bit for today. Maybe tomorrow we'll find out a little more about this,' he added, then yawned. 'Right. Let's call it a night.'

'Whisky?' Maggie lifted the bottle and gave her husband a smile. 'Looks as if you could do with a nightcap.'

Lorimer nodded as he sat slumped on his favourite chair by the fireplace. The wind had grown stronger and Maggie could hear it howling down the chimney, flames from the gas fire flickering in the draught. Chancer lifted his head from where he'd been asleep on the rug, giving an inquiring miaow before closing his eyes and curling himself into a tighter ball of ginger fur. Autumn was bringing the first cold reminders that snow was blowing off the mountain tops further north and Lorimer reached out his hand, smiling up in gratitude to her for the whisky.

'Thanks, love,' he sighed, taking a sip of the amber liquid. 'Needed that.'

'Tough day?'

'Aye, but we made a bit of progress,' he replied, turning the glass around, catching the glowing colour of the whisky in the firelight.

'Any idea about the man who was killed?'

Lorimer smiled and shook his head. 'No. Well, that's not strictly true. I've plenty of ideas . . .'

'Go on.'

'He might be Irish,' he told her. 'We have an image of an Irishman, possibly named James. Looks as if he had been the baby's father from the CCTV footage we discovered. But there are still other sources to check. And we will be bringing Morrison in to answer further questions.'

'Do you think he knows more than he's letting on?'

She saw him nodding slowly, his eyes turned away from hers as he looked into the whisky glass. 'Could be. We still have to check other CCTV footage from around that neighbourhood but we might just have struck gold with Morrison's fish and chip shop. Here. Have a look at this.' As he leaned forward Maggie saw her husband pull a folded piece of paper from his pocket. 'That's all we have so far,' he said, handing her a grainy picture of a man's face.

'Could this be the man who was killed in that bomb?'

'Aye, we think so.'

'Well, that sounds more promising,' Maggie told him. But her husband was gazing absently into the fire.

'James, the Irishman,' he murmured. 'Who were you?

And what were you doing risking your life, leaving that wee baby on his own?'

'Wouldn't he have come forward after the Romanian woman had overdosed?' Maggie asked. 'Surely, if he was the father . . .?'

Lorimer nodded. 'Well, you would think so but perhaps nobody told him about Angelika. After all, she wasn't identified for several days.'

'The other women in her flat? Wouldn't they have called him?'

Lorimer shook his head and sighed. 'They didn't even know his full name. Or so they say. It wasn't the sort of place where the girls kept their clients' phone numbers.'

'So, what next? Look for a missing person called James, the Irishman?'

'Aye, something like that,' Lorimer replied, closing his eyes and yawning widely.

Maggie looked at her husband, seeing the dark smudges under his eyes that were more to do with exhaustion than the shadows cast by the firelight. This job was taking its toll. There were so many demands being made on him, from politicians as well as his most senior-in-command, a woman who knew all about the strains on an officer like William Lorimer. If only . . . She bit her lip as the idea of retirement came into her mind, and not for the first time Maggie wished that her husband would contemplate a life beyond his career.

But, she thought sadly, it was his career as a dedicated senior police officer that seemed to define him. Yes, she was proud of all he'd achieved but more and more recently she'd felt a yearning that it might come to a satisfactory end, giving him a chance to enjoy other things; climb more hills while he was still fit.

Meantime she would continue to provide the comfort and support he needed after a long day like this. A shiver ran down her spine. That poor little baby, first losing his mother to those deadly drugs and then the father he would never know being murdered in such a dramatic fashion. She closed her eyes then, sending up a small prayer for the child's future safety, assured that a greater presence would be listening.

'Come on, bedtime,' she said, taking the glass out of Lorimer's hand and kissing him gently on the cheek.

CHAPTER TWENTY-SEVEN

'Thanks,' Maggie said, taking the pile of mail from the postman as she left the house next morning. It was still secured by an elastic band and Maggie tucked it into the side of her bag, something to look at during the morning interval if she didn't have any interruptions from pupils. It had rained all night and she could hear the swish of her car's tyres driving through puddles that had gathered along the roadside. Now, however, the wind had died down and the morning sun was blinding her vision as Maggie made her way across the city to her school in the West End.

The two-note sound and blue flashing lights made motorists veer into the inside lane, letting a couple of police cars whizz past. An accident, Maggie supposed, as an ambulance followed in their wake, its siren screaming loudly.

The traffic slowed down to a halt and Maggie drummed her fingers on the steering wheel, resigned to being late for her first class. They were at a point in the city where several lanes intersected, pedestrian footpaths parallel to the particular place where Maggie had stopped. Something made her glance out of the window to her left and she saw a young woman standing at the side of the road, white hands clutching the metal barrier.

For a moment Maggie blinked, shocked by what she was seeing. The girl might have been the same age as one of her own pupils, but was dressed in a skimpy pink dress, her bare legs white against the dirty black ankle boots. But it was her face that drew Maggie's attention, the haggard look of a junkie, cheekbones jutting out, eyes hollow and expressionless. What was her story? And why was she clinging onto that rail so tightly? Maggie held her breath as the girl moved along to a space ... surely she wasn't preparing to fling herself into the line of traffic?

Just then the car in front began to move and Maggie had to follow, casting a glance in her rear-view mirror as the girl turned and walked away. She blew out a sigh of relief, concentrating once more on the traffic ahead. But the image of the desolate girl remained with her, a sharp reminder of the young mother who had overdosed in that back lane, where Daniel had heard her baby's cry. Would that be the fate of the girl she had just seen? So many poor souls in this city, she thought forlornly.

She gave herself a mental shake. It wasn't all bad, of course, and she was thankful for those whose determination to help had turned some tragic lives around. Like Glasgow City Mission, a place of refuge and relief that she and Bill were pleased to support.

Now the traffic was flowing again and soon she would turn off this main road and head towards the school gates, hopefully in time to park and rush upstairs to her classroom before the first bell of the day.

Lorimer's day had begun much earlier, his presence at the Govan office necessary to activate several of his officers.

'No phone records since the bombing,' Davie Giles was explaining to him as they sat together after the morning briefing. 'The landline hadn't been used since the previous resident lived there and Truesdale's mobile phone seems to have been lost in the blaze.'

There was something nagging him about that phone, Karen Douglas, the woman with a posh voice who had called the cleaning service. Had Truesdale been standing beside her, listening, directing her, using his neighbour's goodwill (and her own mobile) so he could not be traced? Or had she simply 'done him a favour'?

'What were the last calls made?'

Giles gave a lopsided smile. 'Yours, sir,' he said. 'After that there were no calls made from that mobile number. So . . .'

'Either, Truesdale had a second mobile phone . . . a burner? Or he'd given it to the man who was blown up in his Honda.'

'James, the Irishman?'

'Well, we're calling him that for now,' Lorimer agreed, recalling the intense discussion that had preceded this conversation between himself and his younger colleague. 'Perhaps by the time the day's out we'll have more than just his first name.'

The appearance of the man's face on CCTV had given rise to a plea to every force in the country to try to identify him as a matter of urgency. But several hours had already passed with no response from any quarter.

'You said to keep it from the press meantime, sir,' Giles remarked, harking back to Lorimer's instructions to the team at the earlier briefing.

'We may need to release that photo eventually but for now we've been told by the powers that be to let the general public assume that the dead man is Robert Truesdale.' He turned to Giles. 'If Truesdale is in any real danger, then having another man's face out there will tell the bombers they made a grave mistake,' he said.

'You think Truesdale deliberately switched places with that man?'

Lorimer frowned. 'It sounds cold-blooded, put like that. I doubt if Truesdale had any idea that someone planned to blow him up, but he must have had some inkling that his life was in danger.'

'And he asked another man to stay in his place?'

'Or perhaps James the Irishman volunteered? Och, questions like that . . .' Lorimer gave an exasperated sigh. 'If only he was here to answer them. I mean, what motivates a man to stand in for a well-known MSP when he surely knew there was a risk of some sort?'

'What motivates anyone, sir?' Giles shrugged. 'Money?'

Lorimer tapped his teeth for a moment, thoughtfully. 'Truesdale had cleaned out his account, right enough. And Mrs Jardine was to be paid cash on the day she came. So, maybe this fellow was tempted by the promise of a lot of money?'

'He consorted with a known prostitute,' Giles reasoned. 'Was the father of her child.'

'Hm. Perhaps we ought to send Daniel back to talk to that woman, Miranda. See if Angelika and James the Irishman had any plans. How was he to know she'd end up overdosing?'

'Maybe he was a drug user too, sir?'

'And a friend of Truesdale? A man wanting to clamp down on drug abuse by stopping it being illegal?' He sighed heavily. 'No, I don't think our Irishman was a user. What I reckon is that either she'd got hold of more heroin than she knew what to do with or it was a more powerful grade than she was used to injecting.'

'She got the drugs from Frankie Fleming,' Giles reminded him. 'She handed over a fair roll of money that Sunday night.'

'And where did she get that from? A few punters?' Lorimer shook his head. 'No, my guess is that money came from the father of her baby.'

'So, first we find Frankie Fleming, then we see what he has to say about using Morrison's place as a handover to the Romanian woman and other customers.'

'Exactly.' Lorimer managed the semblance of a smile. 'I'll see our friend Morrison first, though. Might put the frighteners on him seeing a more senior officer. See what else I can squeeze out of him.'

'And right now, sir?'

Lorimer smiled. 'I'd like you to accompany DS Newton on a visit to Mrs Jardine. She's met you before so won't be too intimidated by another senior officer there.'

'He's evaded us for so long,' Molly Newton remarked as they walked along the corridor together. 'Just like Macavity, the mystery cat,' she added.

Lorimer laughed, knowing what she meant. The poem was one of Maggie's favourites that she often taught to her juniors.

'Aye, his nine lives might just be used up by now,' he agreed as they approached the place where Morrison and his solicitor were waiting.

Lorimer could see a sheen of sweat gathered on the man's bald head as he walked into the interview room with DS Newton by his side. Desmond Morrison had avoided confrontation with the detective superintendent so far in his nefarious career but today it looked as if his luck had run out.

'Mr Morrison, so good of you to come in to see us.' Lorimer grinned as Des Morrison wiped his brow with a handkerchief.

The glower and grunt he received in reply showed that the slight sarcasm in his words was not lost on the man. From the moment DS Newton had held up her warrant card, Morrison must have guessed he was fated to attend an interview such as this.

'Now, let's see what you can help us with, Mr Morrison. Or would you prefer me to call you Des?'

He heard the man clear his throat and then Morrison seemed to find his voice.

'All one with me,' he mumbled.

'Grand, that's what we like, eh, DS Newton?' Lorimer turned to Molly. 'Cooperation from a stalwart member of the community.'

Des Morrison's face darkened as his eyes flicked between the blonde detective sergeant and her boss.

'We have CCTV footage of a transaction between a man identified as Frankie Fleming and a woman who died recently of a drug overdose, name of Angelika Mahbed,' Lorimer began, his tone changing to one of formality. 'Thank you for identifying this man.' He handed pictures from the CCTV cameras across the table for both Morrison and his lawyer to see. 'Footage dated Monday the eleventh of October, eight-thirty p.m. Busy night, I suppose? Week of the school half-term holiday,' he reminded Morrison.

The man did not reply, but sat back, arms folded, staring at Lorimer.

'It would appear that your premises were being used for purposes other than those advertised on your walls, Des,' Lorimer continued. 'See, your friend Frankie—'

'Not my friend, Mr Lorimer,' Morrison whined, unclasping his arms and laying his hands on the edge of the table. 'How wis I tae know what he wis doin'?'

'I am guessing that the parcel handed to the late Ms Mahbed did not just contain a fish supper,' Lorimer suggested.

'Cannae prove it wis mair than that!' Morrison declared, glancing at his solicitor who nodded his approval.

Lorimer smiled back at him. He'd let that one pass. For now. 'Well, there is the matter of Ms Mahbed's death some hours after this,' he said quietly, fixing Morrison with a stare.

'Nothin' to dae wi' me,' Morrison said, licking his lips nervously.

'Perhaps, but toxicology reports from the woman's

post-mortem suggest that the quantity of heroin and its strength indicate a source that the drug user was unfamiliar with. Care to explain that?'

Morrison shifted uncomfortably in his seat. 'Like I said, nothin' to dae wi' me. Whit Frankie Fleming gets up to is his business.'

'So, you admit to knowing that Fleming is a drug dealer?'

Morrison ducked his head, muttering, 'Aye.'

'Please speak up for the tape, Mr Morrison.'

'He's a bad man, that one,' Morrison replied, a tone of self-righteousness creeping into his gravelly voice. 'A drug dealer.'

'Let's see if I can jolt your memory a little more,' Lorimer continued smoothly, producing another photograph, this time of Angelika Mahbed carrying her tiny infant son. 'Do you recognise this woman?'

Morrison made a show of turning the picture this way and that before he nodded. 'Aye, that's her, wee Romanian lassie ca'd Angelika. Had the bairn no' long afore that,' he said, his expression softening.

'And this man? Who is he, Des?'

Lorimer put down the image of the man they currently referred to as James the Irishman.

'Already telt her.' Morrison jerked his thumb at Molly Newton. 'Lassies ca'd him Paddy but ah heard wee Angelika ca' him James.' He rubbed a sweaty hand across his head. 'Came in a coupla times with her. Saw him haudin' the bairn an' all,' he said.

'Did you ever see him with Fleming?'

'Naw.' Morrison shook his head. 'He wisnae fae roon here.'

'How do you know that?' Molly interjected suddenly.

Morrison's mouth hung open as he let the question hang in the air.

'Well, he wis Irish, wasn't he?' he gabbled.

'You had a conversation with him? Heard his accent?' Lorimer insisted.

Morrison licked his lips and glanced nervously from Molly back to the tall detective superintendent as if he felt a trap closing in on him.

'Aye, mibbe,' he said at last, a catch in his voice.

'Did you or did you not speak to the man you thought was the father of that child?' Lorimer demanded.

'Aye, jist the wance,' Morrison muttered. 'Fellow asked me tae keep an eye on Angelika. Said he was goin' away somewhere.'

'When was this?'

'Same night they were both in fur fish 'n' chips. A Sunday it wis. Come tae think of it, he only turned up on Sundays. I wis outside having a fag and he stopped me as the lassie walked back tae her flat.'

'He didn't follow her home?'

'Naw, no' then he jist ...' Morrison squirmed under Lorimer's penetrating blue gaze.

'Just what?'

'Ach, he jist asked me tae keep an eye on her. He seemed, I dunno ... kind of anxious but excited as well.'

Morrison put a hand up to his face and Lorimer was surprised to see him wipe away a tear.

'Ah'm sorry, really ah am. Didnae know the lassie wis that bad. Thought she'd given up afore the bairn came alang.

This James fellow seemed to be tryin' tae sort her out, know whit ah mean?'

Lorimer remained silent, stunned by this revelation as much as by this man's apparent sorrow for the dead Romanian woman.

'That it then?' Morrison began to stand up, a hopeful expression on his face.

Lorimer thought hard for a moment. It would not do any good to detain this man, despite the possibility that Lorenzo's was being used as a howf for drug dealing. Keeping Morrison onside was a much better ploy right now.

'Thank you, Mr Morrison,' Lorimer said, stretching his hand across the table.

He felt the clammy fist clasped in his grasp as the two men regarded each other, then Lorimer gave a slight nod as if to reassure the man that he was free to go.

'We may need to talk to you again sometime, though,' he remarked, as he gathered up the papers from the table. 'It might be helpful to find out a bit more about Fleming. Where he lives, for example.'

'Oh, nowhere near me, Mr Lorimer. He's ower at Castlemilk,' Morrison declared. 'And I didnae tell ye that,' he added with a nervous laugh. 'A'body knows where wee Frankie lives.'

Lorimer managed a thin smile. Having been on Gallagher's payroll back in the day, Morrison would know all about the repercussions of grassing someone up.

'I hear you, Des,' Lorimer said. 'Maybe I'll call in for a fish supper some evening, hm? Just to make sure you're still managing that *legitimate* business.'

'Any time, any time. Oan the house,' Morrison gabbled, as he headed towards the door.

Lorimer and Molly watched as the man and his solicitor walked swiftly away from the interview room, Morrison wiping the sweat from his bald head.

'You're just letting him go?' Molly ventured.

'Aye, for now. Suits us better to keep him sweet than to kick up a hornets' nest. I reckon Frankie Fleming will get short shrift if he comes back to use Lorenzo's. Morrison's not stupid. And our priority right now is to find out what we can about this man, James. And hope that it might lead us to Robert Truesdale.'

'And whoever it was that thought they'd killed him,' Molly added.

Nancy Jardine was not unhappy to be sitting in the café of the local garden shop opposite a tall, blonde woman and the same nice-looking young sergeant she'd met before. Detective Sergeant David Giles had assured her that Lorimer was grateful that she had taken the time to see them. Then he introduced her to the other officer, Detective Sergeant Molly Newton.

'Pleased to meet you,' Molly told her.

At that moment a slim, dark-haired waitress came to take their order. 'What'll you all be wanting this morning?' she asked in her sing-song voice.

'You're not from around here, are you?' Nancy asked, her curiosity demanding satisfaction.

'You're right.' The girl smiled. 'I'm from the Isle of Lewis.'

'Ah, that's where they all speak the Gaelic, isn't it?'

'It is,' the girl agreed. 'We are bilingual for the most part. Gaelic is our native tongue and we all learn English at school.'

'I sometimes watch BBC Alba,' Nancy remarked. 'But I need the subtitles.'

'May we have three coffees, please,' Molly asked, picking up her briefcase and setting it on the table.

Once the waitress had left them, Molly produced a file. 'I wonder if you might take a look at a photograph, Mrs Jardine,' she said, pulling out a sheet of paper and sliding it across the table.

Nancy fussed a little, rummaging in a capacious handbag for her glasses.

'Now then,' she said, peering at the photograph that was currently circulating throughout the UK police network.

'Oh, yes, I know the man,' she gasped. 'It's him, isn't it?' Her voice fell in a whisper then she looked up at the detectives. 'The one who was in Mr Truesdale's house when I went to see about cleaning it?'

'You told Detective Superintendent Lorimer that you had taken this man for the owner, is that correct?'

'Yes.' Nancy was nodding vigorously. 'Never knew what the poor man looked like before that explosion,' she said. 'They say now that he was in the Scottish government, right? Even though he was Irish?'

'What did you say?' Giles looked startled. 'Irish?'

Nancy Jardine gave him an odd look. 'I told you that last time when you came to the house. Truesdale. Irish name, I says to you and Mr Lorimer.' She looked from one of them to the other. 'You can't mistake an Irish accent, after all,' she went on. 'Just like you can always tell when someone's from

213

Lewis, like thon lassie. And he spoke to me that morning. Lovely voice . . . poor man.' She broke off with a sniff, groping for a handkerchief.

Giles swallowed hard, kicking himself that they had missed this vital piece of information. Truesdale's had been a strong voice within the parliament, particularly with his crusade for legalising drugs. Not an Irish voice, but apparently his cleaner had never heard of him before she had begun work in his bungalow.

'So, you can positively identify this man as the one you met in Mr Truesdale's property?' Giles asked.

'Oh, yes, Defin-*ately*,' Nancy assured them. 'Was that who done him in? Planted that bomb under his car? Was it the IRA?' Her voice dropped to a hushed whisper.

Molly shook her head and gave the cleaner a rueful look. 'Sorry, we can't comment on that at this stage and we'd be very grateful if you can keep our meeting here this morning as confidential as possible,' she told her gravely.

'You can count on me,' Nancy Jardine told them firmly. 'Our family know how to keep secrets. My granny was in Bletchley Park during the war, you know. We never found out about it till just before she passed away.'

'Thank you,' Giles said, then pointed at the table. 'Another cup of coffee? A cake to go with it?'

Nancy smiled and shook her head. 'Thanks. I'm all right. One coffee a day is all I can take. More makes me jittery.' She paused then picked up the laminated menu from the table. 'Wouldn't mind a flies' cemetery to take away, though. They do really good ones in here,' she said with a coy smile.

*

'Mrs Jardine has positively identified this man as the one who was staying in Truesdale's house. She took him for the MSP, which is interesting,' Giles told Lorimer. 'Although he seems much younger, there is a likeness, don't you think?'

His DCI had already spoken about Nancy Jardine's insistence that the man she had met was Irish, her throwaway remark about Truesdale being an Irish name not pursued by Lorimer and Giles on their own visit. That was something they might come to regret, the chance to identify the man sooner being missed.

They were standing in front of a board that had already several photos pinned with captions written beneath.

It was true, Lorimer thought. James the Irishman definitely possessed some of the older man's characteristics, his dark hair, the shape of his jawline and eyes of similar colour. The post-mortem of the Irishman's remains had thrown up very little, of course, but now, with these stills taken from the CCTV footage, there was much more to go on.

'Anything yet from within our own divisions?' Cameron asked.

'No.' Lorimer shook his head. 'And I am reluctant to post this as a missing person just yet. The longer we can keep the real victim's identity under wraps the better chance we have of finding Truesdale alive.'

CHAPTER TWENTY-EIGHT

Maggie slung her bag onto the carpet and trudged across to the kitchen. A cup of tea and a bit of her own shortbread, she thought. The house was chilly, the heating not due to click on for another hour, so she'd light the fire, sit on the rocking chair that had been her mum's favourite and have a bit of time to herself. Chancer followed her into the kitchen and sat beside the cupboard where his food was kept, looking up hopefully, green eyes fixed on his mistress.

Soon Maggie was settled by the fire, draining the cup of Earl Grey, and giving a satisfied sigh. She closed her eyes and thought about the day she'd had, two unexpected 'please takes' in the English and Modern Languages departments to cover for members of staff who'd succumbed to the first wave of the winter vomiting bug. Both the non-teaching slots in today's timetable had been used up and so marking and preparation would have to be done this evening. She smiled as she remembered the friendly greetings some kids had given her as they'd entered the classroom, evidently pleased to see that it was a familiar teacher waiting for them. It had been hectic but fun, too, since Mrs Lorimer taught most of them in her own English classes. Knowing the kids made all the difference; the ones who might disrupt a lesson as well as the ones that needed a bit more drawing out. The afternoon bell had come as a relief, though, and Maggie Lorimer was glad to be in the comfort of her own home.

She stretched a hand down to the bag she'd left beside the chair, fingers grasping the bundle of mail she'd left there that morning. It would be the usual stuff, she thought, slipping off the elastic band and laying it aside; a white envelope that was probably her Mastercard bill, a couple of flyers for the local pizzeria and money-off vouchers for a nearby Spar. Oh, and a small booklet called *Connect* that came every so often, and which Maggie put to the top, deciding to have a quick read before she began her work. Both she and Bill supported Glasgow City Mission but it was Maggie who kept up to date with the news from the Christian organisation in the *Connect* magazine. There was something uplifting about reading the stories where different people had turned their lives around for the better and Maggie opened the latest newsletter anticipating a good read.

There were pictures of families enjoying the summer activities a few weeks previously, then a couple of updates about the ongoing work and the numbers of homeless people who had found help in the premises in Crimea Street. There were always stories, too, of men or women who had come to a belief in Jesus, their spiritual lives as well as their physical well-being improved significantly. Maggie didn't pay much attention to the black and white photo of a smiling man but instead read all about how he had overcome drug addiction and was now helping others to do the same. A long sigh escaped her. There was so much bad news on the media day after day that it was good to read a positive story like this. Finishing the article, Maggie glanced back at the man's face and the words beneath: *James O'Hare, from addict to activist*. It was a pithy caption, the man not only succeeding in kicking his deadly habit but actually being chosen to assist in the Scottish government's latest initiative to help addicts.

She was about to turn the page when something stopped her.

Hadn't she seen that face before?

Maggie swallowed, a strange sensation thrilling through her. It couldn't be? But something told her that the man smiling out from *Connect* magazine was the same person that her husband had shown her the previous evening.

Her hand trembled as she pressed her husband's direct number then waited.

'Maggie, is anything wrong?'

She could almost imagine his frown as he heard her voice. Calling him at work was highly unusual and she could hear a catch in his breath as if he was expecting some bad news.

'It's that man you showed me,' she told him. 'I think I know who he is.'

The next hour passed in a whirl of activity as an officer was dispatched to Lorimer's home in Giffnock to pick up the magazine and Lorimer was soon in possession of more background information, though he was still to talk to the man who currently ran the Glasgow Mission. James O'Hare had been one of several people giving their time and efforts to help addicts recover from the grip of drugs just as they themselves had done. Custody peer mentors, they'd been termed, those who had experienced addiction themselves and who wanted to lift others out of that pit of despair after a spell in prison. And now he was gone, burned to a crisp in a deliberate act of evil. It could be seen, Lorimer thought, as an act of terrorism, a warning sounded by the drug lords to stop interfering in their nefarious business, if O'Hare had been their target. *If* that was what it really was, of course. Had they known the identity of their victim? Or had that bomb been intended for Robert Truesdale? Perhaps he'd find some answers once he'd visited the Crimea Street mission.

'I'll be going there myself, along with DS Giles,' Lorimer told the members of his team as he briefed them on this latest development. 'Given the nature of this inquiry we need to keep a lid on anything to do with the man's identity.'

'Can you trust them not to blab?' someone ventured to ask.

'Ah, they're a good bunch,' Lorimer replied. 'And I think they'll see it as part of their Christian as well as their civic duty to be fully cooperative.'

He looked at them all in turn. These were hand-picked officers who took their work very seriously and deserved to question his moves sometimes. For now, he had to give them as much information concerning the car bomb victim as he could before handing out various actions.

'We know quite a bit about O'Hare from the magazine article. He was a former drug addict and until his death he appeared to be working on the rehabilitation programme set up by the government. One more money pit for our resources, some might think,' Lorimer said, unconsciously echoing the chief constable's own recent thoughts. 'Not that I think there's anything wrong with the joint strategy,' he added. 'Such a programme was badly needed. But it took some good officers away from front-line duties. That was why men like these were invaluable, working with others to assist addicts who wanted to kick their habit.'

He turned to the whiteboard behind him where photos of the victim were displayed.

'James O'Hare.'

Several pairs of eyes stared at the pictures of the man whose life had ended with that car bomb.

'As a former addict, O'Hare worked initially with the Rehab Pathways team at Glasgow City Mission.' He turned to point at the man, a dark-haired fellow with a full beard and a small hoop earring in one ear that gave him a piratical look. 'That's an old photo we found in a back issue of their magazine. He actually looked much more like Truesdale in this one.' He pointed to the clean-shaven image Maggie had found.

'O'Hare was originally from Belfast and so if the news-hounds get hold of this, they are going to be making whatever they can of that. Linking it to IRA activities, no doubt.'

'Could that be possible?' a voice asked.

'We certainly hope not,' Lorimer replied. 'Intelligence is

still to come in to confirm that O'Hare had nothing in his background that would suggest any paramilitary activities but so far all we know about him is that he came over to Glasgow as a teenager to work, fell in with a bad crowd but was never arrested, hence the lack of DNA or fingerprints on any database. Joined the navy but was medically discharged after just a few years' service.'

There was a murmur from the officers in the team, some of whom were now reading the initial background information about the bomb victim.

'Glasgow City Mission took O'Hare in four years ago and that was where he was counselled. Rehabilitation, ladies and gentlemen, is one way forward, remember.' It did not pay to forget that they had to treat each and every individual citizen with the same sense of compassion. 'Aye, we can't yet rule out anything from across the water but we'll not have anything to back up such a theory until forensics are finished examining the wreckage and the remains of the explosive device.'

'What about his family?' DS Molly Newton asked.

'In that recent article he claims to have been estranged from his family, not an uncommon thing to happen after years of drug abuse. However, we're hoping that family liaison will manage to locate some of them in Ireland and we could be interviewing them over the next few days.' He turned back from the board to face the officers seated in front of him.

'We need to find out why this bomb was targeting Truesdale. Was it something to do with his campaign? Could it have been meant for O'Hare himself? A dreadful warning? Something to hamper the man's work with the Joint Drug Strategy? Or something more sinister, say, if he'd maintained links to one of the big dealers? Or was it personal? At this stage it is unwise to speculate about any of these possibilities. You all know the score. We find as much evidence as we can, seek out everything we can lay our hands on about James O'Hare and his life before that bomb exploded.'

Later, once each member of the Major Incident Team had been given their particular actions, Lorimer sat in his office, staring at the images of the Northern Irishman, O'Hare, taken almost a decade before his death.

A born-again Christian, was how O'Hare had been described by the good folks at Glasgow City Mission, proud to include the former addict's testimony in their *Connect* magazine. Lorimer had visited their premises in the city centre several times over the years, marvelling at the work done there for those who'd reached rock bottom in their lives. Further investigation now revealed why O'Hare had been medically discharged from the navy years before, a knee injury making him seek out whatever pain relief he could find, first prescription drugs, then, on the advice of a so-called friend, something different that would lead him down the path of addiction and near death. He had been hauled out of the River Clyde by the riverman, George Parsonage, one dark winter's night and then taken to hospital where a nurse had suggested the mission as a place of refuge. Reading the man's own reflections of that bad time, Lorimer felt a wave of shame. How could a man who'd served his country end up like that? Police officers did their best, helping addicts every day to find a place of safety away from the streets, but there were always stories about the ones that slipped through the cracks. His mind flicked back to the bedroom in Strathblane with its neatly made bed – a habit picked up during O'Hare's years at sea, perhaps?

His hand rested on the file containing the preliminary background reports about the victim. The number of drug deaths was escalating in his city, poor souls chained to those whose aim was to exploit them in order to gain those twin ambitions, wealth and power; things that might corrupt a person, robbing them of any moral conscience. He paused for a moment, thinking of that other death across the Southside, Angelika Mahbed, found in a filthy back lane, her baby still clinging to her. More than a mere statistic, he sighed, wondering how fate had brought that young mother so low. And what her relationship had been to the man blown up in that car bomb. James O'Hare might have turned his life around but his new path had not prevented him fathering a child with a known prostitute.

CHAPTER TWENTY-NINE

The dog handler had been somewhat protective of the big long-haired Alsatian, though Daniel assured him he would take the greatest care of the animal. It was only at a certain time that Cody would be needed to walk through the park, an unmarked van and driver ready to return the dog to his kennels. It was a bright and breezy morning when they set off from Pollok Park where PC Kohi had glimpsed a little more behind the scenes of Police Scotland. It was his first time there and he kept staring from the window as the van slowly drove over one speed bump after the other. How strange to find a place like this almost in the heart of the city! Lush green fields and well-established trees made him imagine for a few minutes that he was actually in the countryside, a fantasy made all the more real when Daniel spotted a small herd of Highland cows, their shaggy coats and long horns reminding him of cattle he had seen on the journey with Lorimer to Lochaber. He had told the handler about his own experience of being out with the SARDA dogs on the hunt for a missing teenager, a story that seemed to satisfy the man who had taken Cody from his kennel and let him jump into the back of the white van.

'So, you're well used to animals?' the driver ventured.

Daniel grinned. 'I wouldn't say that. We always had dogs at home in Zimbabwe when I was a kid, but not recently.' He fell silent for a moment, remembering the days since he and Chipo had married, their plans for the future crowned with the birth of a son.

'I've got a couple of these fellows at home. Retired now,' the driver told him. 'Great dogs, so they are, especially with kids.'

'Tell me more about Cody,' Daniel answered, swallowing down the lump in his throat. 'Does he fraternise with other dogs?'

The conversation turned to the police dog behind them, his breath soft against Daniel's neck. All through the city, he was regaled with stories of canine heroism and by the time they had reached the edges of Kelvingrove Park, Daniel felt far more confident about taking Cody for a walk.

'There you go, then. See you back here whenever you're done,' the driver said, handing the lead to Daniel.

Cody looked up at the handler, an intelligent expression in his tawny eyes.

'Go on, boy,' he was told. Then, with one last backward look at his handler, the dog began to lope along the path at Daniel's side.

If anybody had told him that his probationary years might include being undercover and walking a police dog, Daniel might have raised a sceptical eyebrow. Yet, here he was, off for what looked like a stroll in the park but was in fact a deliberate attempt to make contact with one of the gang members that the security services had been following.

'He takes his dog through the park same time each morning,' Daniel had been informed. 'Regular as clockwork, hail, rain or shine.'

Glancing up to his right, Daniel could see the curved terrace of luxury flats where Professor Brightman and his family lived. Somehow, just knowing that they were not far off gave Daniel a good feeling.

Cody was a strong dog, but did not pull on the lead, content to walk at Daniel's own pace. There were not many folk about at this time of the morning, too early for school kids to be up and about, though there were other dog walkers in the distance, one woman with her curly-haired animal off the leash, running across the grassy hillside, chasing a ball. He glanced down at Cody, but the big Alsatian made no attempt to run off the path. They passed a large fountain, its water dried up, then proceeded along towards the duckpond where, Daniel had been told, his target always stopped for a smoke.

He heard the other dog before he saw it, a frenzied barking then the sound of flapping wings as a flock of pigeons wheeled skywards. Rounding the corner, Daniel saw the Alsatian, tongue lolling out of its mouth, ears pricked, as it scattered the birds.

It was not the first time that Daniel Kohi had met a fellow countryman, other refugees from Zimbabwe meeting in a charity in Paisley. But none of them had looked quite like this man.

He was wearing a black padded jacket over jeans and running shoes, his hands clad in leather gloves, the dog's leash slung around his neck. He was older than Daniel, in his fifties, perhaps, his once curly hair cropped short across his head, chin sporting a three-day-old beard that was peppered with grey. But it was the face that made this man memorable, that livid slash beneath his left eye and down his cheek.

What sort of weapon had made that injury? Daniel wondered, even as he stepped forward with Cody, the other Alsatian wagging its tail and running towards them excitedly.

'Good morning.' Daniel smiled. 'Nice dog you've got there.'

'You think so?' The man gave a scornful laugh. 'Big beasts. Take a lot of feeding, yes?' But, despite his words, his hand had reached out to pat his own animal who was now sniffing Cody with interest.

'Oh, they sure do,' Daniel replied. 'Come on, Cody. See you around,' he added, giving the man a nod and preparing to walk away. It would not do to engage the man in conversation on their first meeting, he'd been advised. Let him get used to the morning walks, the dogs establishing a routine.

'Good to see you,' the other man replied, taking a pack of cigarettes from his jacket pocket. 'We seem to share the same liking for big animals.'

Daniel smiled and gave him a cursory wave, Cody trotting obediently beside him. It was a start, he thought, and a good one, having exchanged pleasantries and moving along as if he was on a tight schedule. If the man had lit up

227

his cigarette and was looking back at Daniel with any kind of interest, he could not tell, instructed not to turn around and stare. But PC Kohi knew that other eyes were watching and that a report would be sent to those who wanted this particular ploy to succeed.

Indeed, other eyes had seen Daniel Kohi. It had been a long night, the last of her punters was gone, and the Romanian man by her side was tugging her sleeve to lead her back to his car.

The girl had paused to stare at the two men with their dogs, her eyes widening. She would say nothing now, too fearful to draw their attention.

But her heart thudded with the knowledge that these men were together. And that she must tell Miranda.

It was strange to have the rest of the day to himself, Daniel thought, his current instructions simply to appear in the park every morning until he might engage in a proper conversation with the Zimbabwean. Any hastiness on his part might be regarded as suspicious and so he might very well be in for several days of this particular mission. It would give him time to spend with Netta, he decided, once Cody and his handler had driven back to the kennels. Tucking his scarf closer around his neck, he set off back through the park at a steady pace to retrieve his own car, the morning breeze freshening.

Somewhere in the shrubbery a blackbird sang out, its liquid note making Daniel stop and listen. A feeling of gratitude filled his heart in that moment. It was a perfect morning. He had a job that was giving him a new purpose in life, friends who cared about him, and hope for a better future. Taking a deep breath, Daniel Kohi sent up a small prayer of thanks to the God he thought had forsaken him. That, too, was a blessing; to have found a glimmer of his old faith. Life, with all its twists and turns, he was discovering, could still surprise him with small moments of joy like these.

CHAPTER THIRTY

'I would have called James a friend,' Mark Granger told Lorimer and Giles as they walked upstairs to his office on the first floor of Glasgow City Mission. 'I hadn't known him back when he was an addict.' He ushered Lorimer into a small bright room that overlooked the street. 'I only took up my post here as manager two years ago,' he explained, an apologetic tone to his voice.

'What else can you tell us about him?'

'Well, hard to know where to start,' Granger began, signalling for the officers to take one of several high-backed chairs that were angled next to a low coffee table covered in brightly coloured pamphlets. 'As I told you on the phone, James was our poster boy for the rehabilitation programme before being invited to work on the joint strategy.'

'Was he paid?'

'Oh, not by us, Superintendent,' Granger laughed. 'We operate on a shoestring here, sometimes more by faith than anything else. But, yes, he was remunerated by the finance team behind the joint strategy. They'd recently found sponsorship with a big firm of pharmaceuticals. It seems fair, don't you think? He was being asked to do an important job in assisting rehabilitation of addicts alongside health professionals and police officers. *They* all took home decent pay packets, after all,' he added pointedly.

Lorimer had known this, but his question had been asked simply to see if the former addict had shown any mercenary tendencies in his association with the mission, secretly funding an ongoing but hidden habit of his own. That seemed unlikely now, from Granger's reaction.

Sometimes Lorimer wished he could share the Christian beliefs of his wife along with the unswerving faith that the folk in this Mission seemed to display. He'd seen so much of the darker side of humanity in his career, once so overwhelmed that it had taken its toll on his own mental health. Yet there had been instances of a few who'd made seriously bad choices suddenly seeing the light and turning their lives around. Was this bomb victim a case in point, perhaps?

'How did he die, Superintendent? You didn't make that clear on the phone.'

'I'm afraid we cannot give you any details at present, Mr Granger. Ongoing enquiries are being made and I'd actually appreciate if you did not share this information with any of your colleagues. Or with anyone at all, for that matter.'

'Oh, I see,' Granger replied, looking puzzled. 'Well, of course, that isn't true. I don't see at all, but I suppose I just have to accept what you're telling me.' He hesitated then looked at both officers. 'I may be making an assumption here, but I guess James's death is being regarded as suspicious?'

Neither Lorimer nor Giles replied and so Granger continued, 'Please tell me he didn't die of a drug overdose? We were so sure he'd stayed away from that world . . .'

Lorimer cleared his throat and nodded. 'You are safe to know that drugs were not the cause of death but truly I cannot say any more at this point.'

'Oh, well, that's something of a relief.' Granger sighed. 'What else can I tell you?'

'At the time of his death he wasn't short of money?'

'I wouldn't think so,' Granger replied slowly, pondering the question. 'James lived in a flat near Battlefield. Not an expensive place to rent, he told me.' He heaved another sigh. 'Oh, it's really sad. He'd spoken to me only recently about a lady he'd met.' A faint smile of satisfaction crossed his face. 'Told me she was also a recovered addict. Oh, dear, now, what was her name?'

'You don't happen to know if she was Romanian?' Giles asked.

Granger shook his head. 'I don't know. I never met her,' he said.

Lorimer let that pass for now. By virtue of the way she'd died, poor Angelika Mahbed could never have been described as a recovered addict. And yet, hadn't she tried to give up before her child had been born?

'Angelika?' he asked softly.

Granger nodded. 'It was a name like that, yes. Does she know about this?'

Lorimer shook his head. One tragic death was enough for this man to know right now though perhaps in time the entire sad story would be related. It was quite evident that

O'Hare had not confided the details of his lover's pregnancy or her background to this good man.

'O'Hare's name won't be released at the moment,' Lorimer told him. 'In any case, apart from the present need for confidentiality, we would not normally make the victim's name public until next-of-kin have been notified.'

Granger leaned forward. 'You've traced his family?' His voice betrayed genuine excitement.

'Well, not yet, but we hope to,' Lorimer replied, mentally crossing his fingers. There was no way they were going to mention that tiny baby in the Queen Elizabeth.

Then, open-mouthed, Granger slumped back. 'Oh, dear. If only he'd been in touch with them . . .'

Lorimer saw the young man bite his lip. 'Now, it's too late,' he finished quietly, a rush of sympathy for the manager.

'You said James O'Hare was your friend,' he continued. 'Did you notice anything different about him recently?'

'What sort of thing?' Granger frowned.

'Was he depressed? Anxious? Or did he seem fearful in any way?'

Granger thought about that for a minute then shook his head. 'As I said, James was really happy. Excited, even, I think. About this new lady in his life.'

Giles and Lorimer exchanged a swift glance. A new lady and a baby son. There was something achingly sad about what had happened to both parents of this orphaned child.

'Is there anything else you can tell us about Mr O'Hare? Anything that might give us an insight about his character?' Lorimer asked at last.

'Oh, he was a great guy, really. Some people may have

thought his only weakness was having his soft spot for lame ducks, y'know. He was always the first to speak up for those that other folk may have regarded as lost causes. But in our world that isn't a weakness at all,' Granger said softly, smiling at both of the detectives.

Lorimer knew that Maggie would understand this completely and he found himself wishing for a moment that he'd met O'Hare, spoken to him about his life.

'So, was he under any sort of stress that you know of?' Lorimer continued, picking up the thread of his earlier question.

'We saw him regularly at Bible study nights and so I think I'd have noticed if anything had been bothering him.'

'He attended meetings here a lot?'

'Well . . .' Granger paused for a moment, running a hand across his fair hair. 'Not so much recently. I guess he was pretty caught up in his new role with the joint strategy and . . . right enough . . .' He stopped, his frown deepening. 'James was supposed to be leading the study one Sunday . . .' Granger bit his lip. 'He never showed up. I rang his mobile but it was switched off.' He looked anxiously from one officer to the other. 'Is that significant, after whatever happened to him . . .?'

Lorimer stared at the man but did not answer.

'What did you do when he didn't turn up?' Giles asked.

'Well, we waited for a bit but I took the session myself in the end,' he said.

'Was that unusual?' Giles continued.

Granger shook his head. 'Not really. So many of the folk who come here lead pretty chaotic lives so we are glad when a few of them show up, the regulars as well as friends they bring along. Actually, now I come to think of it, I hadn't seen James for about a week or more. And, like I said, he'd seemed happy enough then.'

'And,' Lorimer looked at the man carefully, 'that's the last time you saw him?'

Mark Granger blinked back tears as he nodded, evidently too full to speak, the realisation that the man he'd known was gone for good now lying heavily upon him.

Downstairs, they shook the man's hand and turned to go.

'Oh, there is one thing I'll always remember,' Granger said as they turned to walk away.

'Yes?' Lorimer asked.

'It was what James said a couple of times when he was concluding his testimony. He said, "If I should die tomorrow, I know my life's been worthwhile."'

He was grateful that Granger had made no glib remarks about O'Hare now safely in heaven, Lorimer told himself as they left the mission, gusts of autumn wind blowing empty crisp packets and discarded newspapers along the street.

Perhaps the good he'd done for others had earned him a place in a better hereafter? But what about the dead woman in that filthy lane and the child he had left behind? Who could tell what O'Hare's intentions had been for them before it all went so horrifically wrong?

Someone had decided to dispatch either Truesdale or O'Hare to an early grave. And it was their job now to seek them out.

'It was a ruthless and deliberate act but was O'Hare its

intended target?' Lorimer murmured to Davie Giles as they set off from Crimea Street.

'Well, the Irishman had a history of drug abuse but his life had been turned around,' Giles insisted.

'Apparently,' Lorimer said, the cynicism in his voice quite deliberate. 'Things are often different from what they seem at first glance,' he reminded the younger man. It was something they'd both learned in their years as detectives. It made some men and women in the police force bitter and hardened, their outlook on life jaded by the things they came across in serious cases, the people they encountered who seemed to have been born with no conscience. Happily, his DS still had a positive enough view of humanity. There was a lightness of spirit about the young man sitting in the passenger seat that Lorimer suddenly envied, wishing that the dark clouds that sometimes settled on his own mind might be dispelled more easily.

Was that his fate? To be so immersed in his work that he became a sombre companion, too caught up in his work to see the good side of life any longer?

Then, as if a breeze had come to disperse the clouds, a woman's smiling face appeared in his mind. He had his beloved Maggie and she had kept him anchored all through the years.

Who had loved O'Hare? Lorimer's thoughts turned to Angelika Mahbed, the woman who seemed to have made him happy. It sounded as if O'Hare had been smitten with the Romanian addict, maybe even helped to wean her off drugs, for a while at least. He'd certainly spent regular Sunday nights with her, often enough to have made her pregnant. He thought hard about the dead Irishman. So many questions and so few answers, he thought, wishing not for the first time that James O'Hare could be alive to answer them.

CHAPTER THIRTY-ONE

Netta lay back, relieved to place her right hand under the cool of the linen sheet. That nurse had been so gentle removing the cannula from the back of her hand, a wee round plaster now covering the bruised flesh. They were all right in here, busy of course, but once her curtains were pulled across and her different needs seen to, there was always a smile and a bit of chat, leaving the old lady comforted. If it wasn't for the incessant noises, Netta Gordon might have actually admitted to enjoying these past few days in the Queen Elizabeth hospital, or 'Sweaty Betty's' as the Glasgow folk now called it.

At least that auld biddy across the room had left, her continual shouts and cries during the night disturbing all the other ladies in this ward. Poor soul, Netta told herself. Dementia was an awfie thing, right enough, and she could only be thankful that, so far, she'd not fallen prey to that dreadful illness. Her memory was as sharp as ever, she'd assured the nice doctor who'd asked her all sorts of questions. Like what date it was and who was the prime minister? She'd answered politely enough though an inner mischievousness had made Netta want to give him a few daft replies instead. She and Daniel would chuckle about that at visiting time when she'd tell him how hard it had been to resist having some fun. Her face fell, remembering that her neighbour was on a later shift today, not finishing until midnight. Ah, well, he'd come in when he could, she consoled herself, pricking up her ears at a now familiar sound.

She hoped that rattle of a nearby trolley signalled the nice lady with her dinner and a cup of tea. *They did a brilliant apple pie and custard in here*, she'd confided to Daniel last time he'd been in.

Once we're in that new place I'll dae ye some grand crumbles, so I will, she'd promised him, remembering that bowl of Mrs Lorimer's own apples still sitting in her kitchen.

A couple more days and they'd maybe discharge her, that young doctor had said. *But no promises*, he'd added with a grin. Netta had smiled back but inwardly she had marvelled at someone who looked like they'd not long left school actually being in charge of people's health. They did say you were beginning to show your age when the polis looked like wee laddies but it had given Netta a start to find it also applied to doctors. Ach well, he must have passed all the exams right enough or he wouldn't know what he was on about.

'Cup of tea, Mrs Gordon?' The rattle of the trolley had stopped and Netta pulled herself up a bit more as the auxiliary appeared by the foot of her bed.

239

'Oh, aye, hen. That'd be smashing,' Netta replied and watched as the woman placed the teacup and saucer onto her tray. Not dinner time yet, then.

'And a couple of biscuits?'

Netta nodded. 'Thanks, pet.'

Minutes later Netta was savouring the last crumbs of her custard creams, a contented heaviness stealing over her. She'd just have a wee doss now. The old lady closed her eyes, images of that ground-floor flat appearing in her mind. A kitchen big enough to eat your dinner, she thought, the faintest of smiles playing around her lips as she dozed off again.

CHAPTER THIRTY-TWO

I t was no longer a good place to be, the woman told herself, shoving the last of her belongings into a suitcase.
That lassie across the hall had shaken her head when
Miranda mentioned the words social worker. *No*, the girl
had insisted. *Not that. One of the Colombians. Saw them
in the park.*

So, that's who the black guy was. One of Ncube's lot.
Another African who was part of the latest drug-dealing
gang, mainly Colombians. Funny how he had seemed so
nice at the time, not like the big guy all the girls dreaded.
Word had it that they'd made some sort of deal with
Frankie and were in the process of targeting the Eastern
European contingents. Before long a turf war could break
out in this part of the city, one of the Romanians had
warned them. No, this was no longer a safe place to be,
Miranda told herself.

And yet, it was strange, she thought, shoving the last of
her belongings into a bag, remembering the visit from the

man who'd turned down her offer to climb into bed with her. He wasn't a bit like any of the usual thugs who hung about with the dealers. Far from it. But maybe that just showed how cunning he was, slipping in quietly, pretending to care about the dead girl's child! Miranda fumed. He'd tricked her into believing he was a goddamned social worker when all along maybe he was trying to find out the link between her and the drugs she'd passed to Frankie. If they found out what she'd done . . . She shuddered. Wouldn't have been so bad if he'd been one of Angelika's punters. Nah, she'd have remembered a black man, nice-looking one an' all. But one of the Colombian gang? The gang who were picking off the dealers one by one.

She let a few choice expletives escape her lips as she shouldered her backpack, glancing round the room that had been her own space for . . . well, more than a year now. Would she miss it? Aye, mibbe. Funny how a room that seemed so wee and cramped yesterday now looked almost desirable. The last rays of the setting sun fell onto the curtains, turning them to deep rose pink. Why had she never seen it like this before?

She closed her mouth in a thin, determined line. There were other gaffs, other places she could hang out a while. And, if it all came crashing down? Ach, she'd think of that when it happened. The Romanians had been okay so long as you didnae take ony dodgy punters, keeping the rent on this place going, feeding the young ones and making sure they got regular health checks. After all, Miranda thought as she slipped out of the front door, human flesh was only a good commodity if you could keep it clean.

Outside, a bitter wind was blowing, the first hint of frost curling its fingers around her face, a threat rather than a caress, like some of the men who'd liked to hurt her. Miranda did not look back as she crossed the road, head bowed, feet taking her deeper into the city, away from all the questions about poor Angelika and her Irishman. Questions she was afraid to answer. They'd warned her, hadn't they? *Anyone asks about the Irishman, you know nothing*, they'd told her, a pair of hands around her slender throat, grinning faces that hid malicious intent. Yet what a fool she'd been, spilling the guy's name to that black man, thinking he was from social services, there to help the baby.

Miranda would never hear the wails of despair when her teenage flatmate finally opened the bedroom door to find her gone.

Nor would she see the man staring out of the chip shop, watching intently as she shifted the suitcase from one hand to the other, a thoughtful expression on his face.

Daniel sat quietly for a few minutes, listening as Netta described the most recent visit from her consultant.

'And what about you? Any mair news about that wee bairn?'

'I can't say very much,' he warned her, 'but Detective Superintendent Lorimer might be able to trace some of the baby's family.'

'Really?' Netta's eyes shone with excitement. 'They've found the lassie's parents?'

Daniel risked a quick glance towards the ward then back at his friend. Nobody was in earshot, he decided. 'It's not as simple as that, Netta,' he began. 'And there are some things that I shouldn't even be telling you. Hush-hush stuff.' He made a face.

'You know I'm good at keeping secrets,' she huffed. And that was true. Netta Gordon was someone that Daniel knew he would always trust.

'I know you won't tell anybody,' he assured her gently. 'It's to do with another case. You know the car bomb that happened?'

'Aye. They're no' sayin' it's IRA,' Netta retorted. 'But who else wid it be, eh? An MSP gets blown up. Sure, it's they Irish!'

'If I were to tell you that the body found in that car wasn't Truesdale . . . ?'

'Whit?' Netta's mouth opened wide.

'Shh, listen, you didn't hear that from me, okay?' Daniel looked around once more but there were no visitors surrounding the nearest bed, the patient sound asleep under her covers.

'Netta, wait till I tell you,' he whispered, leaning closer. 'The guy that was blown up was the baby's father.'

'Naw. You're kidding me,' she replied, shaking her head.

'Yes, it is,' Daniel insisted. 'DNA proves it. He was a regular visitor to Angelika's flat in Calder Street.' He bit his lip, considering how much more to tell her. 'I went there. On Lorimer's behalf.'

'On your own?'

He nodded. 'Before I started my shift,' he admitted. 'Left early and spoke to one of the girls. She took me for a social worker and I didn't disagree with her. You must never tell anyone about this, Netta. Seriously. I only told you to let you know the baby might have family somewhere.'

'I've suddenly gone quite deaf,' Netta told him, a slow smile curving on her lips. 'Auld age. Cannae hear a single word you've said, son.'

It was fine, he told himself. Netta was as steady as a rock.

'Any news about coming home?' Daniel asked, deliberately changing the subject.

'Naw, mibbe keep me in a wee while yet,' she replied. 'Now, ah'm dead tired, son. A' this excitement's fair worn me out.'

Daniel bent to kiss the old lady's forehead. 'I'll be back soon, Netta, dear,' he murmured, stepping back as he saw her eyelids begin to droop.

CHAPTER THIRTY-THREE

Questions for a dead man, Lorimer thought as he drove through the dark. But in truth he wanted to direct them to the man who ought to have been behind the wheel of that big car, wherever he was. Truesdale appeared to have vanished off the face of the earth, something that was actually rather difficult to do in this high-tech age. Either he was being held against his will or he had organised his life so carefully that he could remain hidden indefinitely. But why would he want to do that? He'd been vociferous about legalising drugs, making a nuisance of himself in parliament. Was that what was really behind the car bomb? But why put James O'Hare into his place? Had Truesdale known what was going to happen? The former addict seemed to have turned his life around, except for the liaison with Angelika Mahbed, the poor lass who'd succumbed to heroin. Had she been one of the addicts O'Hare had tried to help? And was that final lethal overdose simply a mistake? Or had someone wanted the Romanian girl dead?

Lorimer's mind buzzed with all these questions as he drove through the suburbs of Glasgow to reach his home. It was well after midnight and he had stayed far longer in the Govan office than he had intended. Several of his team had spent extra hours there, scrolling through page after online page of Glasgow City Mission, eager to glean any little bit of information that might help. For much of the time he had sat and pondered the strange case, trying to work out what motives each man had for being at the house in Strathblane. He had looked up a few of the other members of Glasgow City Mission, anxious to speak to others who had known O'Hare. Granger was a nice Christian man, but had he really known the former addict well enough to judge him? People often presented one face to those whom they wished to impress and a different one to folk who knew them better. At least the efforts of his team had borne fruit, several names and addresses to follow up tomorrow, including men and women from the Joint Drug Strategy who had seen O'Hare most recently.

A glimmer of moon passed behind a cloud, bare-branched trees stark against the pale light. It was tomorrow already, he realised, with a pang. A few hours to sleep, if his racing thoughts permitted, then back into the city before the dawn chorus began.

Across the city several people lay awake, staring into the dark.

Miranda huddled into the blanket she'd been given, watching the streaks of yellow reflected against the ceiling as cars passed by outside, their headlights guiding them to wherever they were going. She was glad enough to be on a sofa, all beds in this particular establishment taken up by the girls whose goodwill had allowed her in at all. Tomorrow she'd be earning her keep, standing on nearby corners to attract punters, the cash they'd give her handed over straight away as a mark of her gratitude. It would take time before she'd manage to find another room of her own but persistence always paid and already Miranda was planning on moving away from this city. It just took one well-heeled punter to set her up and sooner or later she'd find him and fleece him.

Had Angelika thought she had found her own sugar daddy? Paddy the Irishman had seemed the type to look after the lassie. Till that dreadful night when the cops came banging on the door, telling the other girls that she'd been found dead. There was lots she might have told the cops, but Miranda had learned early on how to keep her mouth shut and save her pretty face from a bruising. It had taken some guile on her part to slip away whenever the cops had come, desperate to avoid their questions.

Conscience doth make cowards of us all. Who had said that? Shakespeare? Yes, it sounded like Hamlet. Or Macbeth. Had he been that much of a coward? Was his fate to be like either of the characters from *Macbeth*, the wife driven to insanity, the once-lauded hero slain after his downward spiral to disgrace? Was he going mad asking himself too many questions when there was no way of finding any answers? As he lay on the soft bed, all was silent around him save for the creaks of old pipes somewhere in the heart of this building. It paid to stay put, they'd told him. Soon he'd

248

be moved but this was a nice place, make the most of it, why don't you? one of them had suggested, showing a glint of gold tooth as he'd smiled.

Tomorrow he would sit outside in the garden, watching the birds as he had done today, yesterday and every day since he had travelled here. Sometimes he'd close his eyes and pretend it was a holiday. But then memories of real holidays came flooding back, seaside boarding houses with greasy breakfasts and sand creasing all the damp towels. Why anybody thought that beaches were a pleasure was beyond him; 'life's a beach', surely one of the most risible clichés in the English language. Waiting. That was his life now that he'd made that fateful choice. Waiting and remembering.

Maggie woke with a start. Blinking, she turned to see the time on her bedside clock. Two-thirty. Enough time to regain her sleep, though she was reluctant to resume the dream she'd had of chasing a bearded man through the city streets only to have him turn around, a hypodermic needle brandished in his fist. O'Hare, Maggie thought, frowning. Dead and gone, now, perhaps basking in some spiritual hereafter, if Mark Granger were to be believed. She hoped so. Glancing fondly at her husband sleeping peacefully by her side, Maggie took a deep breath and closed her eyes once more, the words of a prayer in her head.

Make me a channel of Your peace, Where there is despair in life let me bring hope. Where there is darkness, only light . . .

In moments she was slumbering once more, all traces of anxiety wiped from her brow.

*

'Nooo!'

The scream in the dark was cut short, replaced by a gurgling sound as the blade slid along the man's throat. Then a single dull thud as his body hit the ground.

One after the other the victim's assailants lashed out, booted feet aiming blows at the dead man.

The sound of distant sirens made one of them stop suddenly. The stockiest of the trio jerked his head and then they all took off, running into the shadows.

High above the heap on the ground a crow gazed from his branch, curiosity and the scent of blood attracting the bird. Its beady eyes stared hard. There was no movement at all, no breath of life.

In one winged swoop the crow descended, claws grasping at the dark line between face and neck, beak ready to feast on its prize.

CHAPTER THIRTY-FOUR

He saw the other Alsatian bounding towards him across the park, Cody's tail beginning to wag as it drew nearer. There was no sign of the man, however.

'Here, boy,' Daniel called, noticing the leash that trailed from the dog's collar. 'Here, good lad,' he coaxed as the dog began its ritual sniffing around Cody.

It was easy enough to grasp the lead and to manoeuvre the dog in the direction it had come from, Cody trotting calmly by his side.

At first the park looked empty, an early morning mist rising from the wet grass, but then in the distance Daniel could discern a couple of figures, one of them possibly the dog's owner. As he walked downhill, he heard voices raised in argument, the taller of the two men gesticulating wildly. For a moment he stopped, wondering who the other fellow might be and if there was any chance of overhearing what was being said without them realising.

'Get out. Now!' the Zimbabwean was yelling as he moved

towards the other man, fists raised threateningly. 'And don't come back if you know what's good for you!'

Daniel frowned, peering more closely as the shorter man looked up and glared at the Zimbabwean who gave him such a hard push that he tumbled onto the grass.

He watched as the man scrambled to his feet and turned with a baleful look at the taller man before scurrying away towards the park gates, head bowed.

He would remember what this man looked like, Daniel knew, able to identify that face if he saw it on a police database.

He continued down the slope, the two dogs by his side.

At the sight of his master, the Alsatian began yelping furiously, straining on his lead.

The sound made the tall man turn to see them approaching.

'Hey, boy!' he called out, a grin now on his face.

'I found him up on the hill,' Daniel called out as they approached. 'Guess he must have scented his new friend.' He laughed, deliberately looking towards the man, pretending not to have seen the previous altercation. He let the lead slip from his hand and the big dog bounded towards his owner.

'Hey, Simba. Hey, boy.' The man grinned, then he looked up at Daniel. 'Thanks, man. I owe you one.'

Daniel smiled back and shrugged. 'Friends, eh?'

For a moment the man seemed nonplussed then his brow cleared as Daniel pointed to the two dogs.

'Yeah, these two have hit it off big time, I guess.'

'Well, be seeing you.' Daniel sketched a wave and

proceeded along the pathway, intent to put some distance between them both. Ingratiating himself too soon might raise the other man's suspicions.

'Yeah, hope so.' The man nodded, gazing at Daniel as he walked steadily away.

Ncube watched the other man intently, eyes narrowing. Zimbabwean, surely?

What was he doing over here? Had he scarpered from the law, as he had? Or was he some sort of academic type, the university close by? As he disappeared around the corner, Ncube found himself curious to know more about the man. Friend, he'd said, and for a second he had thought that referred to them both, a sudden flare of hope warming his cold heart. It had been a long time since he had called another man by that name. The memory of a laughing face came to him at that moment; rolling his eyes at every pretty girl they'd passed, grinning in excitement whenever they'd run away from trouble then collapsing in giggles once they'd outwitted the cops. Life had been one big adventure for that man. Jeremiah had been his friend for so long until . . . He shook his head, wanting to rid himself of the memories. Jaw clenched, he looked up at the early morning skies, pale and lucid in this cold northern land. Time to focus on the here and now, he told himself.

After this morning's dismissal of that Colombian idiot, he was one man down. This guy looked fit and strong as he strode along the path and he needed someone with muscle. It might pay to befriend him for that reason alone, see if he was the type to fit in with his operation. Maybe next time they met, he thought, turning his attention to the dog as it began to chase the pigeons, the birds taking flight and swooping overhead.

Mornings often brought a renewal of optimism, Lorimer told himself as he drove through quiet streets, the horizon fading from palest primrose yellow to eggshell blue. Today he would speak to an Irish woman across the water, the nearest family member of James O'Hare they'd been able to find. A sister, name of Breege McLaverty. One of those who had turned their backs on the errant brother when he'd sunk low, disgracing the family. He frowned, scolding himself. Who was he to judge why people became estranged from their siblings? Perhaps brother James had been of real concern, a bad influence on her kids, maybe? Already Lorimer was curious to know what the sister would make of this news, her brother dead after having shown his ability to change his former ways.

He pulled into the car park, noticing just a few other vehicles parked there. Govan police station housed the MIT whose officers worked only day shifts, often chalking up hours of overtime, unpaid in his own case, as well as the day-to-day police officers in uniform and CID whose shift patterns changed all the time. Like Daniel's, he thought, suddenly, wondering how his friend was coping with his new life across in Govanhill. That was another action he'd be handing out today, asking a couple of the team to visit the street woman calling herself Miranda. Daniel's visit had helped a lot and he was grateful for it, but it was important not to involve his Zimbabwean friend too much. He had his own work to carry out, after all, even though it had over-lapped with the Truesdale case.

Lorimer took the stairs two at a time, glad to feel no ache in any of his joints. It had been a while since he'd managed to climb a hill, Ben Mhor on Mull the last one he and Maggie had managed during their holiday at Leiter Cottage. Perhaps he and Daniel might try Ben Lomond before the first snows descended.

Thoughts of mountain tops vanished like morning mist as Lorimer reached his desk, eyeing the papers he'd left there hours before. Amongst them was a telephone number for Mrs Breege McLaverty of Athlone. Diligent enquiries had also been made about Frankie Fleming, the dealer who had used Lorenzo's for his handovers, but the dealer seemed to have gone to ground. Part of him wanted to jump on a plane and visit James O'Hare's sister for the tricky business of explaining her brother's death. Trouble was, while they were keeping the truth about Truesdale from the press, he could not justify meeting any of the dead man's family. It seemed so unfair, he realised, that little sick baby orphaned in its first weeks of life still being kept away from those who might find it in their hearts to care for him. Sooner or later the truth about the MSP would have to be revealed, but orders from the First Minister of Scotland were to keep that quiet for now. He'd felt bad keeping details from the manager at Glasgow City Mission but trusted the fellow to remain silent for now about O'Hare having died. Granger had seemed savvy enough to understand the need for discretion.

There was a knock on his door making Lorimer look up to see one of his detective constables.

'Sir, this has just come in,' the young man told him. 'It's Frankie Fleming. He's been found dead.'

Lorimer stood watching the scene of crime officers as they set about securing the scene. It was the back of a pub in Mount Florida, the premises closed and shuttered for now though the landlord had been alerted and was on his way, a uniformed officer had informed him.

Frankie Fleming's body was in a corner of the area, close by a row of metal barrels, hidden from plain view. He had seen the slashes across the man's face, the fatal wound across his throat, then looked around at the area where he'd been dumped. Metal fencing closed in the place on three sides, hard against a line of old trees, the yard littered with leaves and rubbish blown in by the wind. The gate into the back yard had swung open when the first responders had arrived, Lorimer had been advised, the chain fastening the padlock severed and lying on the ground. Someone had intended to break in here, all right. But had they brought Frankie with them, or had he come willingly?

'Any sign of a vehicle registered to the deceased?' he asked the DI from Govanhill.

'Aye, just along the road, there. That'll be their next job.' He jerked a thumb towards the SOCOs. 'And being Fleming's van, I bet there'll be more than just faint traces of drugs.'

Lorimer nodded. Fleming was well known in these parts as a dealer but recently there had been friction amongst the different gangs, as if some war was brewing here in Glasgow's Southside.

'One of Fleming's associates was hauled out of the River Cart,' the DI continued. 'Same sort of injuries,' he added, with a meaningful raise of his eyebrows.

A new contingent, said to be mainly Colombians, was on the up and up, Lorimer recalled. Could that be who was behind these killings?

'Was his van locked?' he asked, getting back to his original query.

'Yes, sir. We found the keys in his jacket pocket.' The DI gave Lorimer a quizzical look. *What is the head of the MIT doing here?* the officer's glance seemed to ask.

'Fleming was a person of interest to us in another matter,' Lorimer explained, registering the unspoken question. 'I'll be grateful for your report on this.'

Later, after the van arrived ready to transport Fleming's body to the city mortuary, Lorimer walked slowly around the area. A loud cawing made him look up to see a crow, its beady eyes looking down at him.

'What did you see, I wonder?' Lorimer asked the bird softly, then turned and made his way to where he had left his car. The DI would let him know what the pub landlord said once he'd interviewed him. It was time to let the detectives here do their job, he decided. Someone had wanted Frankie Fleming out of the way before the cops from the MIT could lay hands on him. Morrison. Had to be the owner of Lorenzo's who'd spread the word, he thought grimly, wondering if his next stop ought to be the fish bar in Calder Street.

CHAPTER THIRTY-FIVE

Victim of Car Bomb not MSP

The man killed in a car bomb explosion in the village of Strathblane has been identified as former drug addict, James O'Hare. Police investigation and forensic examination have shown that the deceased had been living in the MSP's home at the time of the tragedy. Robert Truesdale has so far failed to come forward to give any explanation about his disappearance and sources in Holyrood confirmed that the MSP had intended to resign prior to the incident. Death threats may have forced the man into hiding and, in the light of O'Hare's tragic death, kept Truesdale in a secret location to avoid any further attempts on his life. Police are anxious to trace anyone who was known to James O'Hare, a reformed addict and born-again Christian who had been helping with the rehabilitation of other drug users.

A blurry photograph of O'Hare and one of Truesdale sat neatly side by side, on the *Gazette*'s front page, similarity in the features of both men easy to see.

It was the work of moments for the caller to lift the phone and press a number.

'You've seen the news?'

There was a pause then a grunt that he took for affirmation.

'Don't waste any more time,' he commanded. 'Get rid of him now.'

'Well, what d'you make of that?'

Mark Granger passed the newspaper to his colleague as they sat together in the coffee room at Glasgow City Mission.

'I never knew there was any relation between them,' the woman remarked, giving her head a slight shake. 'Were they cousins or something? You'd think one of them would've said. James never did talk about his family,' she added sadly.

'Maybe. But the press would have found that out, don't you think?' Granger replied doubtfully.

'We might not have noticed how similar they looked when Mr Truesdale was at any of the meetings but, seeing it here, well ... do you think there's a family connection?'

'Truesdale? O'Hare? These aren't similar names. No,' he shook his head more firmly, 'I think it is just a coincidence.'

'Poor James. I can't believe he's dead. And in such a horrible way. Who would want to kill him?'

'It says the bomb was meant for the other man, that MSP.' Granger lowered his voice a little, glancing around the room where some of their clients were sitting sipping at mugs of soup.

'Do you remember speaking to either of them the day of the conference?'

'No,' Granger replied. 'It was such a busy day and the sponsors had wanted to meet me. But I did see them together.' He broke off with a frown. 'We were just taking a coffee break after Truesdale had delivered that speech. Think you'd gone somewhere but I was right behind them both in the queue ...' Granger tailed off thoughtfully, a faraway look in his eyes.

'They were together?' his colleague asked, leaning forward conspiratorially. 'You mean they knew one another?'

Granger shook his head. 'I hadn't thought so. Oh, why didn't I remember this when the police came to see me!'

'You already knew that James was dead?' the woman gasped, covering her mouth with her hand.

'Yes. Sorry.' He looked at her sadly. 'They swore me to secrecy. Anyway, let me tell you what I can remember. You see, I overheard them talking and Truesdale was asking James something ...' He stopped abruptly and sat up.

'What?'

'I remember, now. He was asking James to look after someone for him. You know how James was with his lame ducks.' Granger paused and scratched his chin as if trying to remember. 'Oh, what was that name ...?'

'Go on,' his colleague urged.

'It was Sally!' Granger exclaimed, snapping his fingers. 'Truesdale was asking James O'Hare to look after someone called Sally for him.'

'Mark, this might be important,' the woman insisted. 'Look. It says here ...' she pointed to the foot of the newspaper article, 'any information should be given to the police.' She looked up at the manager of the mission. 'There's the number. What're you going to do about it?'

Later that day a DC in the MIT received the message that Mr Granger from Glasgow City Mission had passed on something he considered to be important via the information hotline. The man had subsequently been interviewed and a statement taken.

Sally, the DC mused. Not a name that had come up in the investigation so far. Was that relevant? Did it add anything to what they already had? His fingers flew across the keyboard as he typed up the short report and pressed a key. Everyone would see this now and perhaps one of the team might make something of it.

Lorimer stared at the DC's report, frowning. Truesdale had not been married to anything but politics, by all accounts. Whoever Sally was, she was part of Truesdale's scene, and it sounded as if she might need looking after.

A small smile lit up his blue eyes and he reached for his phone.

'Mrs Jardine? Detective Superintendent Lorimer here. I wanted to run something past you.'

'Well, this might well be the reason O'Hare was staying in Strathblane. And it explains the load of groceries bought for the duration of a house-sitter's stay.' Lorimer paused

261

for a moment, knowing full well he had the attention of all the officers in front of him. 'Perhaps Truesdale genuinely expected to return to his new home.' His grin broadened as he faced the assembled members of his team. 'Home to Sally,' he paused for full effect, 'the cat.'

'The *cat's* called Sally?'

'Not a girlfriend, then?'

'That was what Granger overheard?'

Comments filled the room, officers surprised by this latest piece of news.

'Looks like it,' Lorimer agreed. 'Yet, the fact that O'Hare really did resemble Truesdale ought not to be taken out of the equation. Look at it this way. Truesdale offers money to the Irishman to house-sit and look after his cat. O'Hare is happy to agree, why wouldn't he? Respectable member of the Scottish Parliament, nothing suspicious about him. After all, he'd just heard the man give a speech about the rehabilitation of offenders. Perhaps O'Hare warmed to the man, felt that Truesdale was on their side?'

'And maybe he liked cats?' Molly chipped in.

'Yes, maybe he liked cats. One thing we ought to remember is the money Angelika had that Monday night before she overdosed. Where did she get it? My guess is that O'Hare gave it to Angelika. And, if I am correct, that was money James O'Hare was paid in advance for house-sitting.'

'You think he meant well, not realising she was going to blow a wad on the heroin that killed her?' Molly asked.

'Could be,' Lorimer answered. They would never know the answer to that question but a part of him hoped that

James O'Hare had envisioned better things for the woman and their child.

'But why ask a joker like Morrison to keep an eye on her?'

'Des Morrison is one of these plausible characters,' Lorimer replied. 'Genial wee guy in the local chippie. It's possible that O'Hare was completely unaware of the drug dealing going on there. After all, apart from the footage of Frankie Fleming passing drugs to the woman, we really have nothing on Morrison himself.'

'And now Fleming's dead,' Giles broke in. 'Very convenient for someone.'

Lorimer nodded. 'It does look a bit like that, but we have to remember there was a lot of in-fighting amongst the different factions in the city along with locals like Frankie Fleming ... all vying to be top dog.'

'A lot of them over in Govanhill,' someone remarked.

'And that new element as well. Colombians,' another officer put in.

'It's the second murder there in recent weeks,' Lorimer reminded them. 'One of Fleming's own men, Kenny Ritchie, was found in the River Cart. Govanhill CID are still investigating that but it looks very much like a drugs war has been brewing in that part of the city. And we have preliminary findings that Fleming's wounds resemble those of his henchman.'

'Someone's out to make trouble,' an officer remarked.

'What if O'Hare wasn't the squeaky-clean reformed addict he seemed, though?' Giles suggested. 'Maybe there's more to him cosying up to Morrison than meets the eye?'

Lorimer nodded slowly, acknowledging this.

'Yes, that's possible, as are so many theories. And there are other questions that have to be asked and followed up. Now that O'Hare's identity has been made public by our press office, it's essential that we find out more about the Irishman.' He gave his team a grin. 'We're going to be busy, not just here but across the Irish Sea too.'

A familiar ringtone made him reach for his mobile.

'Lorimer.'

'FM wants a word,' Caroline Flint's crisp voice told him. 'Can you get through here now?'

'Holyrood?'

'Yes.'

'Be there as soon as, ma'am,' Lorimer replied, rapidly calculating the time it would take to drive to the capital.

CHAPTER THIRTY-SIX

On another day it would have been a pleasant trip, but today Lorimer's mind was on the meeting ahead with two of the most powerful people in all of Scotland.

Calum McKenzie had been adamant that Lorimer met with him in his Holyrood office, other items in the man's busy agenda postponed for now. Whatever it was he needed had to be of the greatest importance, Lorimer felt. The journey along the M8 passed in a haze, fields and trees blurred with thickening mist as the motorway rose towards Shotts, the sky leaden with rain-filled clouds even as he drove past the West Lothian villages and towns towards the capital.

Edinburgh wasn't any brighter as he parked outside the Scottish Parliament building, a steady drizzle soaking him as soon as he stepped out of the car. In minutes he was past the security on the ground floor, a brief salute from the on-duty officer who recognised the detective superintendent's name. A tall man came down the stairs to meet him, his hand outstretched.

'Malcolm Hinchliffe,' he said. 'I'm ... rather I was Mr Truesdale's private secretary. Please come this way, Detective Superintendent. The First Minister is waiting for you.'

'Mr Hinchliffe.' Lorimer nodded as they shook hands. 'Good to meet you.'

'Sir, perhaps after this meeting you might find time for a chat?' Hinchliffe asked, his polished vowels suggesting to Lorimer a background that had included some expensive private education. He gave the man a keen look as they ascended the stairs. Smartly dressed in an understated sort of way, plain grey suit and a striped tie of muted blue hues as became his position within this building. Molly had mentioned that Hinchliffe was possibly the person who had known Truesdale best and he had been dumbfounded by the revelation that his boss had apparently been wearing that silver cross. Hopefully, Lorimer thought, once this meeting with the FM was over, he'd have time to see Truesdale's secretary. Hinchliffe's instinct had been spot-on: the body he had seen in the Glasgow City Mortuary was not Truesdale's at all.

Hinchliffe opened the wooden doors of the First Minister's office and waited until Lorimer had entered before retreating and closing them quietly as he left, leaving him to face the First Minister and the chief constable.

'Lorimer.' Calum McKenzie stood up from behind his desk and walked towards the detective superintendent. 'Thanks for coming. This dreadful business ...' He tailed

266

off and looked across at Caroline Flint. 'We've been discussing how best to proceed.' McKenzie waved Lorimer into a chair next to Flint's.

'There's coffee in a flask,' Caroline murmured, gesturing towards a tray on the FM's desk where a coffee cup and saucer lay ready for him.

'Thanks.' Lorimer leaned across and poured himself a cup, the fragrant smell of coffee welcome.

'Caroline and I . . .' McKenzie nodded towards the chief constable, 'we've been having a serious talk about the next stage of this business.' He folded his hands in front of him.

Caroline, that was progress, Lorimer thought, hearing her first name being used. The Englishwoman must have found favour in this man's sight. Or else he was seeking something from the head of Police Scotland.

'We need to know exactly what steps you are taking to find my missing MSP,' McKenzie said gravely, looking directly at Lorimer.

'Disappearing in the twenty-first century is far harder than at any time in history,' Lorimer told the First Minister, recalling a lecture he sometimes gave to new recruits. 'Given the footprint that almost everybody leaves from mobile phone usage, and media connections, not to mention passports, banking and official registration of births, marriages and domain, then when a man like Robert Truesdale vanishes the likelihood of finding him alive diminishes with every passing day.'

'I know all that,' McKenzie sighed irritably. 'But you haven't come up with his corpse, have you?'

Lorimer gritted his teeth. There were so many historical

accounts of men and women vanishing apparently into thin air, never to be found, and he could tell this man a few of them. Plus the exorbitant amounts of money spent by the police in hunting for each and every one of them. It wasn't his job to remind the First Minister of Scotland about the financial burden the police had to face; Chief Constable Flint was welcome to that particular task.

'As I said, it is very hard for him to have disappeared of his own volition. There has been absolutely no trace of him anywhere in the UK or overseas. Either his plan to get away was so carefully conceived that he has managed to give us the slip or he has in fact been killed by person or persons unknown.'

'And what do you think, Superintendent?'

Lorimer might have told this man that it was not his job to make up scenarios but rather to base everything on evidence. And, so far, it looked as if James O'Hare had been inveigled into a twisted plan to give Truesdale a fresh start somewhere else in the world, leaving those who had known the MSP thinking that the burned corpse in that car was really him.

'If he is alive,' Lorimer began, 'then he must surely know by now that O'Hare has been identified. That might make him do something rash like try to flee overseas or else he may be bunkered down in a place where he thinks we'll never find him.'

Calum McKenzie had the grace to nod, apparently acceding to this reply. 'We're all under pressure from different sources, Lorimer. Even I am answerable to His Majesty's security services,' he said with a slight shrug that made Lorimer realise that this man was also feeling the burden of responsibility that came with his position. 'So, what now? Keep hunting for Truesdale?'

'We are keeping an open mind about what he may have done, where he could have gone. So far there has been no movement on his bank cards or phone and I suspect he has squirrelled away his cash. However,' he took a deep breath, 'we cannot discount the possibility that the car bomb was intended for Truesdale and that a subsequent attempt on his life has succeeded.'

'Any leads at all?'

'Not yet,' Lorimer admitted. 'We have put feelers out in various sources amongst the drug gangs and there is one in particular that interests us.'

He went on to describe the new Colombian element that had entered the city, suspicion that the recent murders of Fleming and Ritchie were signs of an attempt to take over these existing gangs. 'I am also sending some of my team to Ireland to talk to O'Hare's family,' he added. 'We still cannot discount them.'

'The recent drugs seizures did show that Ireland was a stopping-off point en route to Scotland,' McKenzie agreed.

'It's a fairly tenuous link but we can't ignore it,' Lorimer assured him, though privately he thought the investigation into bombs and drugs relating to old IRA factions would be another waste of resources.

'Perhaps you ought to go there yourself,' McKenzie told him. 'Make it look as if we are pulling out all the stops. The public need assurance that Police Scotland is doing its job, you know.'

*

It had not been a suggestion to be chewed over by the detective superintendent but a direct order, Lorimer knew as he left the FM's office.

He was stepping down the staircase towards the reception hall when a voice stopped him.

'Superintendent Lorimer?'

He turned to see the rangy figure of Malcolm Hinchliffe standing on the top of the stairs, a raincoat slung over his shoulders.

'Are you in a terrific hurry, sir, or have you time for that coffee?'

Hinchliffe led Lorimer to a small out-of-the-way coffee shop in one of the many small side streets of Edinburgh's Old Town.

'Nicer to get out of the office, don't you think?' He smiled, his mouth curving in a suggestion of humour. It was evident that Truesdale's former secretary was keen to distance them from the parliament building and Lorimer was curious to know why.

Once ensconced at a corner table, two steaming cups of coffee between them, Hinchliffe gave the detective a sheepish grin.

'Sorry to waylay you like this, sir, but I thought it only right to have a quiet chat,' Hinchliffe began. 'You see, I think I know the real reason why Robert Truesdale sold his old house.'

'Not just a cost-cutting exercise? Downsizing?'

Hinchliffe shook his head solemnly. 'It began not long after his mother died.' He took a brief sip of his cappuccino.

'He had been inundated with all of these nasty online comments, even death threats, as you know. And he'd remarked about selling up and getting away from Glasgow.'

Lorimer listened intently, wondering what was coming next.

'At first, I assumed he was thinking of relocating here, to the capital. Maybe buying a nice flat in the New Town. Prices here are always on the high side,' he admitted, something Lorimer knew well from conversations with his counterparts in Lothian and Borders. 'But I think he wanted to leave Scotland altogether.'

'You have proof of this? Not just a memory of Truesdale's remarks?'

'I think so. You see, as his secretary I was responsible for keeping his diary up to date and I found several entries that made me think he was planning a getaway.'

'Go on.'

'At first, I assumed he was taking a much-needed holiday. Strange as it may seem, in all the time I worked here Robert never took what you and I would consider a proper break. Even when members were off for the usual scheduled intervals, he never seemed to go far from home. But then it looked as if all that was about to change.' Hinchliffe took another sip of his coffee then continued. 'He had a bundle of brochures in his desk drawer. I found them one day when I was looking for something else, don't remember what ... anyway, there was a pile of travel brochures wrapped in two sheets of printer paper with a rubber band around them.'

'And you looked to see what they were?'

'My curiosity got the better of me,' Hinchliffe admitted with a rueful grin. 'I unwrapped them and saw they were all brochures with different destinations, mainly South America, you know, rainforests and suchlike. I admit I was astounded. Robert had never expressed the slightest interest in travelling anywhere that wasn't to do with the job and had no interest that I knew of in wildlife or the natural world.'

'And it looked as if he wanted to hide these brochures from view? Wrapping them up like that?'

Malcolm Hinchliffe had the grace to look shame-faced. 'Probably. But it is, or rather was, my job to look after all of his secretarial needs and so, perhaps, one could say I was just tidying up?'

'Perhaps,' Lorimer agreed.

'Not long after that I saw they had all vanished. I thought he'd been browsing the idea of a getaway, a whim that hadn't lasted. MSPs do work terribly hard, you know, and their constituents are never slow to make demands on their time.'

'But that wasn't all you wanted to tell me?' Lorimer guessed.

'No,' Hinchliffe replied, looking steadily at the detective. 'It was the letter that clinched it for me. You see, just before he decided to sell up, Robert received a letter with an unusual stamp. I'm something of a birder and this was a rather nice stamp of a black-billed toucan. Bit odd these days to receive snail mail, you know, so I suppose once again my natural curiosity was aroused, especially mail from Colombia.' He gave a self-deprecating grin that made him look endearingly boyish.

'And?'

'Well. It's my job to log his mail and so, when I asked him about this particular letter, he became angry, shouted at me to mind my own effing business. I was taken aback, as you can imagine.'

'And this letter?'

'He stuffed it into his inside pocket and stormed out of the office in a terrible rage. I knew he could be a bit hasty, especially during debates, but he had never spoken to me like that in all the time we'd been together.'

'Why are you telling me this now?' Lorimer asked.

Hinchliffe looked around the café as if to ensure that nobody was watching or listening to him, a gesture that reminded the detective that a member of HM's security might be hovering somewhere nearby at this very moment and that Hinchliffe evidently had reason to be cautious.

'Because of this,' he said softly, taking a plain brown A4 envelope from his jacket pocket and sliding it across the table. 'You'll find the contents interesting, I believe. And to be honest, I think I'd rather it was you who saw this than anybody associated with Holyrood.'

He did not examine the contents until he was back in the car park, deciding that the café was too exposed to prying eyes. Hinchliffe had made his apologies, heading back to Holyrood, but assuring Lorimer of his fullest cooperation any time in the future. Slipping on a pair of rubber gloves, he opened the envelope.

There were several sheets of A4 paper, lines of figures that at first meant nothing to the detective superintendent.

273

Till he reached the final paragraph and saw Truesdale's signature in pen written on a dotted line. He flicked back and made sure that each page was in some sort of order then read the small print on that last page.

Could this really be right? Were these transactions undertaken by cartels in Colombia for enormous sums of money, each dated carefully in the margin, and signed off by the man who had disappeared? Hinchliffe's face had been sombre as he'd handed over the envelope.

'I had no idea Robert was involved with people like that,' he had said, shaking his head and staring at Lorimer as though to gauge his reaction.

This might be the missing piece of jigsaw in the puzzle that was Robert Truesdale. If this was right, and he'd make sure to have these documents vetted carefully, then it suggested that Truesdale, rather than being the spearhead for changing the law on drugs, had in fact been behind bringing them into the country. And not just in dribs and drabs, if these figures were to be believed, but in such quantities that he might well have wiped out the opposing drug gangs in the city once and for all, replacing them with . . .?

And it was here that Lorimer paused for thought. Had Truesdale run for the hills? Vanished into the depths of some South American country, perhaps? And left someone else in charge? Someone who had sufficient experience in this heinous trade to carry out his bidding? And it was then that his mind turned once more to the small man who ran a modest fish and chip shop in Govanhill.

Des Morrison had been part of Jack Gallagher's outfit back in the day when the Glasgow gangster had monopolised most of the organised crime in the city, finally put away by Lorimer and now under the closest possible security. Somehow, Morrison had bought Lorenzo's and ran it as an apparently legitimate business, always managing to stay one step ahead of the law, just as Gallagher had done for too many years. His boys had not fared so well, though, spending time at several of HM's establishments. Could Morrison have had anything to do with these transactions? So far, they had found no link between Truesdale and the owner of Lorenzo's, only the video tapes that had shown Angelika Mahbed, O'Hare and Frankie Fleming. Yes, they could do Morrison for his premises being used during a drugs transaction but the footage might have been anything at all, certainly not proof that could stand up in a court of law, no matter how much it looked as if the poor Romanian woman had actually handed over a wad of cash.

He stared past the windscreen, seeing nothing but wondering for the first time how Fleming had got hold of these powerful drugs. Had they been part of the heroin flooding in from overseas? Or was someone cutting them in a lab somewhere in the heart of the city, endangering lives in order to increase profits?

And was Truesdale the mastermind behind it all? He frowned. It didn't make sense. Why have such a high public profile in the run-up to the legislation of drugs debates? Unless he had fabricated his entire campaign, making it a useful smokescreen for his real activities? The bravado of such an idea took his breath away. But then so did the idea of a car bomb blowing an innocent man away in order to fake your own death.

He slid the pages back into the envelope and locked them in his glove compartment. These would go across to Gartcosh right away, Lorimer decided, fastening his seat belt, and setting off from the multistorey car park.

CHAPTER THIRTY-SEVEN

The sea never stays the same from day to day, or hour by hour, he had found. His had been a life of travelling from place to place, mainly between cities. But now he had time on his hands, time to sit and watch the tide rolling in, see the changes as sunshine flickered on the waves or the dying light cloaked the water with shadows. Night had become his favourite time to look out at the water, moonlight dancing on its surface, phosphorescence bubbling as if the very ocean had turned into a jacuzzi. Once, on a cold and frosty night, unable to sleep, he had come out to the wooden bench, a fleece blanket wrapped around his shoulders, and watched as the sky changed from emerald to magenta, the Northern Lights displaying a magic that took his breath away. Sitting, eyes wide, the man almost expected to hear the sound of music floating across those waves of colour. When the sky became dark once more, it was as if he'd been dreaming. Cold arms wrapped around him, he'd stumbled back indoors, taking the images with him.

He'd wait here in this place until the tides shifted and a boat arrived. And then? It did not take a night sitting on the chilly bench to make him shiver as much as the thought of what lay ahead. If it all went wrong.

CHAPTER THIRTY-EIGHT

Evan shivered as his teacher finished reading the passage from their book. *Fleshmarket* was scary, even though it had happened all those centuries ago. There were posters on the classroom wall, lurid depictions of life back then. And it brought the story even more to life, especially those two shady characters, Burke and Hare. Evan had decided from the beginning that he didn't like them one little bit. And the way Mrs Allan read made them come to life, the class sitting spellbound, listening to their teacher's words.

Now she was asking questions and Evan sat back, making himself as small as he could. It wasn't that he was less intelligent than the other twelve-year-olds whose hands had shot up, he was simply not one to draw attention to himself. But then the teacher's next question made him catch his breath.

'How does the writer manage to make you suspicious about a character?' Mrs Allan asked and Evan thought hard. Not about the villains in the story, but about what he had seen night after night before that bomb had shaken every home near his street.

Suddenly, he wanted to talk to someone, tell them about it. As if she had divined his thoughts, the teacher's eyes fell on Evan. Had she given him a slight nod? He took a deep breath and stared back. Then the moment was over and one of the girls was giving her opinion in a loud, excitable voice.

When the bell rang for lunch break, Evan sat in his place, bag clutched on his lap, the others pushing and shoving to leave the classroom, Mrs Allan on her feet, shepherding them into the corridor. Still, he sat at his desk, waiting.

'Evan?' Mrs Allan looked surprised to see him there. 'Everything okay?'

His feet felt leaden as he approached her desk, heavy backpack swinging in both hands.

'See what you said about being suspicious, Mrs Allan?' Evan swallowed, hearing his voice nervous, coming out like a wee kid's, high and piping.

'Yes,' she replied, sitting with folded hands, looking kindly at Evan as if she had all the time in the world to listen to him. 'Yes, Evan . . .?'

'It's like this,' he began, his mind whirling from the story. 'I saw something I think is really important. But my mum thinks it's just my imagination. I know what I saw, though, honest I do!'

'You want to tell me?' the teacher asked with an encouraging smile.

Evan nodded. 'It was a few nights before the bomb went off,' he began. There was no need for the teacher to ask which bomb. Everyone knew exactly what he meant since the incident was still the main topic of conversation. 'I saw something suspicious.' His voice was stronger now that he had her undivided attention.

'Go on.' Mrs Allan nodded.

Evan dropped his bag on the floor, needing both hands to express what he had seen. 'It was a big car. BMW.' He spread his arms wide. 'Seven Series, I reckon,' he said, with all the seriousness he could muster. 'I can tell by the shapes, even in the dark,' he insisted, as though fearful his words might be doubted. 'I saw it three nights in a row, as if it was looking for something, up and down, slowly, on the street and round to where the car blew up. Casing the joint, isn't that what they say on TV?'

Mrs Allan smiled and nodded again. 'Yes, that's right. What time was this, Evan?'

'Oh, late, miss, after I should have been in bed. About one o'clock in the morning.'

'And you saw it driving slowly around? Just before the bomb went off? Or was it a few days before that?'

'Exactly three days before, miss. Like, the third time was hours before it happened.' Evan's voice dropped to a whisper, his eyes widening at the thought.

'Do you live across the road from where the car bomb exploded? Is that how you saw this?'

'Not exactly,' Evan replied, feeling a warmth stealing into his cheeks. 'My bedroom is at the back and it looks right over to Strathmirren Gardens. Ours is a corner house a bit lower down from theirs and I can see the whole street in both directions,' he explained. 'I saw when it drove around and when it stopped.' He bit his lip, the memory blurring at the edges, as a dream often did. He knew what he had seen. But what happened afterwards just didn't make sense.

His teacher listened as Evan recounted the details of what he had seen.

'I think this might be important,' he said at last.

The teacher kept her eyes on him, nodding silently, then smiled.

'Evan, I agree with you,' Mrs Allan said slowly. 'I think you may well have seen something suspicious. In fact, I believe this is something you ought to share with the police who are investigating it.'

A thrill of something that wasn't fear shot through the boy's body. *She believed him!*

'What should I do, Mrs Allan?' he asked.

Melanie Allan was not one of her usual patients, Dr Williams thought, wondering what had brought the teacher from Balfron to the surgery that afternoon. She'd met the woman only once since Evan had begun attending Balfron high school and remembered her as a kindly person who had enthused about their son's talent for writing stories. *An overactive imagination*, she had replied, dismissing the praise, and wishing that Evan's science teachers were as complimentary as this woman.

She opened the door of her surgery and took a few steps out into the waiting room.

'Melanie Allan?'

She watched as the woman gathered up her bags and came towards her. There was no sign of a stoop in her carriage, nor did the patient seem at all pale or anxious. It was then that the GP remembered the surgery manager telling her that this visit was something personal.

'Mrs Allan, please come in.' She smiled warmly, ushering the teacher into her office and closing the door behind her. 'Take a seat,' she added, sitting behind her own desk, and looking at the new arrival with curiosity.

'It's a bit irregular, I know, but your receptionist said there was a slot, so I thought I'd just take a chance,' the teacher began.

'What seems to be the problem?' Dr Williams asked, her voice deliberately soothing.

Melanie Allan gave her a lopsided sort of smile. 'It's not really my problem, doctor,' she began. 'But I think it might be yours.'

Once Evan's teacher had gone, Harriet Williams sat still, the spasm of anger that she had felt dissolving in a wave of self-doubt. Yes, she'd admitted to this nice woman that she had dismissed Evan's story as so much make-believe. *But if it were true . . .?* Mrs Allan had let the question hang between them. She had listened carefully, something she did with every person who walked into her room, taking note of the teacher's insistence that Evan was afraid to upset his mother but also terrified that he'd be in trouble if he kept what he had seen to himself.

Tears smarted in her eyes as she considered how she had let him down, telling him to go upstairs, do his maths. When had they last sat down together and talked about . . . well, anything other than schoolwork?

There would be another visit from the police. That was to be expected. But this time, she would be the one doing the listening and not the talking.

CHAPTER THIRTY-NINE

'I'll go if you like,' Molly offered. She had no plans for this evening and her curiosity had been whetted by the news that a local lad had wanted to speak to them about something he had seen.

Lorimer looked as if he were considering her offer. Molly was good with kids, despite not having any of her own. The boss knew that and she was certain that the family liaison officer would be glad of her company.

'Okay. Let me know what the lad says as soon as you're back,' he agreed. 'I'm off home now but you can get me any time. We'll be at the Brightmans' for dinner later, as it happens.'

'Sure.' Molly gathered up her bag and coat then walked from the detective superintendent's room. They were all working long hours right now and she hazarded a guess that the dinner over at Kelvingrove would be more than a social occasion, the pathologist and her husband no doubt keen to know the latest update on this case.

*

Faith Thomson was a cheerful, rosy-cheeked woman in her late forties, more like a jolly grandmother in her appearance than a police officer. In truth, Faith had recently joined that group, her daughter Joy having presented the Thomson family with twin boys. All the way to Strathblane, Faith enthused about 'the wee lads', as she called them, revelling in her new role, and hinting that she might take early retirement once Joy's maternity leave was over. Molly listened, indulging the new granny, and asking all the right questions about birth weight, familial likeness, and her daughter's recovery. She was somewhat relieved to have heard that Joy had given birth to sons, speculation in the office about names for girls that included Hope and Charity. The Thomsons were all members of the Salvation Army, which explained their penchant for biblical-sounding names, and were well regarded amongst the officers in Govan.

'This boy, he's first year at Balfron. His mother's a GP out in Killearn,' the family liaison officer told her, waving a tube of extra strong mints in Molly's direction.

'That's right,' Molly said. 'Thanks, just take one out for me, please,' she added, glancing at the packet of mints then focusing on the winding road once more. It was ages since she had driven out here and Molly found herself enjoying the drive, her headlights dipped for now as the sky darkened to a deeper shade of cobalt. As she sucked the sweet, the detective sergeant felt a surge of optimism about the visit they were to make. A few things were falling into place like pieces of a jigsaw that had not seemed to fit before. The cat, for one, she thought, and began to relate that particular story to the FLO.

'Here we are already,' Faith announced chirpily as they

entered the village. 'Now let's see what this young fella has to tell us.'

Harriet Williams opened her front door to see the two women standing there, neither of them in uniform.

'Oh.' She took an involuntary step back as if they had barged in already, though neither Faith nor Molly had moved from the path below the two front doorsteps.

It was the tall blonde whose card the doctor spotted first.

'You had better come in, officers,' she said at last, having scrutinised Molly's warrant card through her half-moon spectacles. 'Sorry it's just me. My husband's away on business at present.' Then, opening the door wider, she motioned for the women to enter, standing aside, and calling upstairs, 'Evan! Come down, please!'

Molly listened to the GP's command, noting an edge of irritation in the woman's voice. Was that because she was nervous about the arrival of two police officers, or was her annoyance directed at the son? For a moment Molly experienced a pang of sympathy towards the boy that increased when she saw him hurry down the stairs, his face drawn and white, dark eyes staring at the strangers standing in the hallway. He was still just a kid, she realised, fresh-faced with that particular bloom of youth that preceded adolescence, childhood lingering on. Faith had already spoken to his teacher, Mrs Allan, who'd described Evan Williams as a nice kid, not one of the cool types that tried to come the big man in the playground, but quiet and thoughtful, the sort who could do really well as the years progressed, with the right encouragement.

*

They were both ladies, Evan saw, with a pang of disappointment. He'd expected a man and a woman, same as before,
but this pair weren't even in uniform.

'Hi, Evan, I'm Faith and this is Molly,' the cheery one
said, putting out a hand for him to shake. Evan took it,
hoping she didn't feel the sticky sweat on his palms, then
dropped it as fast as he could without being rude.

'Hello,' he replied, giving both women a careful look
before turning to his mother.

'We'll sit in here, shall we?' Harriet Williams said crisply,
ushering them all into a large room at the front where
venetian blinds were partly shut, obscuring them from any
prying eyes.

Evan trailed behind his mother, keeping his eyes fixed
on her, waiting for the instruction about where he should
sit. She'd made it very clear earlier that the police officers
would be arriving and would want Evan to speak to them.
Don't mumble, she'd reminded him, *and for goodness sake don't
embroider your story. They want to hear the truth.*

And nothing but the truth, Evan had wanted to add, feeling
stung as if he was already in a witness box being judged.

'Hi, Evan.' The tall woman bent forward a little as she
took her place on the three-seater settee. 'Here, why don't
you pull over that chair and sit where we can talk to you?'

Evan followed Molly's gaze then looked around to see
the spindly-legged chair in the corner of the room, an old
antique thing that Mum had inherited before he'd been
born. Nobody ever sat on it, the precious heirloom more
decorative than functional.

'It's okay, Evan, do what Detective Sergeant Newton

asks,' his mother told him, her tone a little softer now, the one he supposed she used with her patients when they were really ill or frightened of hearing bad news.

He carried the little chair across the room, surprised at how light it was, then placed it in front of the settee where the two women were seated, facing them as if expecting some kind of an interrogation.

'Here, make yourself more comfortable,' the smaller of the two women said, handing him one of his mum's velvet scatter cushions.

Evan took it and placed it carefully between his back and the ornate carved wooden frame of the ancient chair.

'That's better.' Faith kept smiling at him and Evan suddenly realised that this was a lady who might understand kids, the way that his English teacher did. She'd been introduced as a family liaison officer and whilst he was a bit hazy about what the word liaison meant it did sound like she was used to dealing with people his age.

'Your teacher, Mrs Allan, suggested you should call us, is that correct?' the FLO asked.

Evan swallowed hard and nodded, then glancing at his mum's tense expression, realised that he ought to have said something. A silent nod was maybe worse than a mumble.

'Yes, she did,' he said. Then, as if a hard lump of ice inside had melted away, he began to speak more freely, the whole story of the book, *Fleshmarket*, coming out and how he'd been spurred on by the idea of suspicious characters.

'It was the way he stopped that third time,' Evan continued, looking all the time at Faith, hardly giving a moment's thought to the other officer by her side. 'It was during the school holiday so I wasn't going to get into trouble for staying up late. The first two nights the car was just driving around, really slowly, but that third night it stopped right outside the house where . . .' he gave a gulp, and then went on, his voice lowered in a whisper, 'the bomb went off.'

'That was just a few hours later. Is that correct, Evan?' Faith asked, as if Evan himself was the important one in this story, the only one to verify this account.

'Yes. I was asleep by then,' he admitted. 'It's usually well after midnight before I can really get to sleep.' He felt his cheeks redden and looked down at his hands clasped on his lap.

'Good games, eh?' Faith chuckled. 'Hard to stop once you've begun. Just need to keep going till you reach a better score?'

Her laughter made Evan look up, eyes widening at the notion this adult actually knew what it was like playing his favourite games and yet not blaming him for how addictive they had become.

'Tell us about that third night, Evan.'

He looked up at the tall detective, comforted by her gentle tone. She was nice, too, he thought, wondering where his idea about police officers being stern and fierce had come from. These two ladies were nothing like the cops in books or games, ready to fight a battle, guns blazing. Real life, Evan Williams was discovering, was not like that after all.

'He stopped outside the house. I know it was a man because that was the only time he got out of the car. I could see it under the streetlight, a blue colour, and I am certain it was the 7 Series of BMW. I like cars,' he explained simply.

'Did you see the registration number?'

'No, it was too dark,' he replied at once.

'And then . . .?' Molly asked quietly.

'He got out, like I said, and then he opened the boot. I couldn't see much of the other car, the big one that was blown up, cos he had parked right across the drive. Just its rear end. But then he disappeared for a while and I couldn't see what he was doing.'

'Could you see the front door of the house. Mr Truesdale's house?'

Evan shook his head. 'It was pitch dark and from the angle of our house, well, from my window, I could only see his car and the back of the other one.'

'Okay.' Molly nodded. 'Go on.'

'Strathmirren Gardens is higher up the hill from where we live,' Evan explained. 'So, my bedroom doesn't look onto the same level. Not like the houses across the road from us.' He gestured, indicating the homes on the opposite side of their avenue.

'Can we take a wee look?' Molly asked. 'So you can show us exactly?'

Evan turned to see if that was all right with his mother and she nodded, then rose to her feet.

'I need you to come with us, Dr Williams,' he heard Molly telling his mum and for once it was gratifying to see her nodding obediently instead of being the one to give all the orders.

*

Molly walked across to join the boy at his bedroom window. She could see what he had meant about being downhill from Strathmirren Gardens. Their large villa was closer to the main road that ran through the village whereas the bungalow Truesdale had bought was on a hill that overlooked this avenue. Molly stood close to the window, peering out into the darkening night. Yep, there it was beneath a street-lamp, an empty space where the wooden garage had once stood. Molly turned to Evan's mother.

'May I ask a favour, Dr Williams?' she said. 'Any chance you might drive along the route your son has been telling us about and then stop outside that house?'

The GP looked a little unsure, casting a glance towards Evan.

'It's okay, we won't question Evan about anything new relating to the case while you are not here,' Molly assured her. 'But I would like DC Thomson beside me for corroboration as we all watch from this window.'

'Go on, Mum,' Evan urged. 'I'll be fine with these officers,' he added, giving his mother an encouraging smile.

'Oh, very well then, but how long do you want me to park there?' Harriet Williams asked.

'Five minutes max,' Molly replied. 'Okay, d'you think, Faith?'

'Aye, that's ample time. Thanks, Dr Williams.' The FLO beamed at Evan's mother.

As she heard the mother's footsteps descending the stairs, Molly reached out and gave the boy a pat on his shoulder.

'Right, so you see this blue BMW coming around the

corner then turning into Strathmirren Gardens,' Molly began, fact-checking the boy's story.

'I guess he came from the main road but I don't see it from my room,' Evan said.

'That's possible, Evan, but guesses aren't allowed in this particular story, okay?' Faith laughed. 'Molly and I have to follow all sorts of rules and stick to them.'

'That's why an eyewitness account is so very, very important,' Molly added seriously.

'Here she is!' Evan called out and all three turned their attention to Harriet Williams's white saloon slowly rounding the corner.

'She has to park on the wrong side,' Evan said anxiously. Then, 'Whew, she's done it,' as the white vehicle crossed the street and came to a halt outside the bungalow.

'Look, you can't see beyond Mum's car!' Evan pointed.

'There is no way to tell what would be going on behind a parked car,' Molly murmured.

'Maybe he was placing a bomb under Mr Truesdale's car?' Evan cried suddenly. 'Is that what you think happened?' He looked from one woman to the other, eyes wide, thrilled by this new possibility.

Faith Thomson smiled down at the boy. 'That's another thing we're not allowed to do, I'm afraid,' she told him, shaking her head sadly. 'Making assumptions is sort of frowned upon in our line of work.'

'You need evidence.' Evan nodded wisely. 'That's why you go about in pairs, isn't it? One to back up the other . . . corr . . . corr . . .'

'Corroboration,' Faith finished for him.

'She's on the move again.' Molly motioned them both to the sight of the white car slowly driving away.

'You, my lad, have been a star,' Faith told Evan, clapping him on the back.

Molly saw the boy's wide grin as he looked up at the FLO. This had been a success in more ways than one, she thought as they made their way back downstairs. After tonight, she doubted if Evan Williams would worry that an active imagination was something of which to be ashamed. And they would be able to report back that in all likelihood they were now looking for a blue 7 Series BMW.

'Please, miss . . .'

The two women turned to see Evan scurrying downstairs after them.

'Can I ask you something?'

'Of course.' Molly smiled, waiting at the foot of the stair.

'The new car, Mr Truesdale's. Why did its alarm not go off when the man opened its boot?'

'Evan Williams told us the man had opened the car boot and at first we thought he meant the BMW,' Molly told Lorimer. 'But he made the point that he could see the SUV's rear sticking out and it was *that* boot the driver opened.'

'So, why didn't the alarm go off?' Lorimer finished for her. He was standing in the Brightmans' kitchen, the others still sitting around the dining room table, aware that the detective superintendent was taking Molly's call.

'Exactly what the boy asked me,' Molly agreed. 'Either the car was unlocked or . . .'

'Or whoever was in that BMW had spare keys for

Truesdale's motor,' he said. 'Bombers who plant things like that always seem to find a way. I doubt if those who blew stuff up during the Troubles worried about finding the owner's car keys. But perhaps that was a question we should have asked ourselves from the beginning.'

'What now, sir?'

'I think we need to go back a bit. Find out where that car was purchased. Talk to the dealer, see what sort of arrangement Truesdale had made. A big car like that, it costs plenty, brand new. And that's another thing that bothers me about a man who was supposed to be thrifty.'

He finished the call and walked slowly back to join the others as the sound of laughter came from the room next door, wishing he could banish the dark thoughts crowding into his head. Had Robert Truesdale given one set of keys of his new CR-V to O'Hare and kept the other? And who was that driver in the blue BMW?

'Work?' Rosie asked, her eyes bright with expectation.

'Aye, DS Newton's been to visit a lad in Strathblane,' Lorimer replied, sitting back down with Maggie and his friends. He looked around and saw that they were all gazing at him.

'Well, tell us,' Maggie laughed. And so he did, giving what small details Molly had passed on over the phone.

It was Solly who spoke first, his tone grave. 'This does sound as though it was planned,' he sighed. 'Say Truesdale picked up a man who resembles him sufficiently to pass himself off as himself. Just think what that means if his motive was to vanish off the face of the earth, make everyone believe he'd died.'

'Could he have cold-bloodedly plotted the death of an innocent man?' Maggie suggested quietly.

'Is there another explanation?' Rosie asked. 'Did he so detest a man who had born-again Christian credentials that he felt he wasn't worth bothering about?'

'Oh, surely not!' Maggie exclaimed.

'Who else had the keys to that Honda? O'Hare must have been given one set, and there's no listing of them in the wreckage.'

'Or in the house?' Maggie continued.

'I'll double-check,' Lorimer replied, his jaw hardening. Someone ought to have done that as a matter of routine. But then, it had been believed from the outset that Truesdale was the victim, no need to scrutinise what might be missing from the bungalow.

'Can you conceive of anybody going to that sort of extreme?' Maggie asked, turning to Solly.

The psychologist regarded her thoughtfully for a moment then nodded. 'I'm afraid that I can, Maggie,' he replied sorrowfully. 'The evil that men do . . . if we dwelt on that then we'd never sleep at night.'

CHAPTER FORTY

S he wasn't there.

Daniel's eyes widened as he rolled onto his side. His hands were stretched out under the duvet as if to grasp at something. Someone.

It had been so real, that dream, the dregs of which were still lingering in his consciousness. He could almost feel her warmth, sense her soft breath against his cheek. Molly.

It had felt so right having her in his arms.

Was this just a dream? Or a premonition of what was to come? Somehow in this moment of awakening, it didn't matter. What it showed him was how he truly felt about this woman.

He was beginning to enjoy leading Cody on his early morning walk, Daniel realised, strolling along, the hood of his jacket partly obscuring his features. There was a smile on his face that no amount of rainfall could erase, the memory of the dream still there. Whatever happened tomorrow or the next day no longer seemed to matter, he thought, marvelling at the knowledge that he had found someone to love. And there was an inner hope that she felt the same. It was time to stop dreaming, a little voice told him; time to do something instead.

Perhaps his lightness of mood was being transferred to the long-haired Alsatian, for Cody turned to regard Daniel from time to time, almost as if the animal had sensed his joy.

'Hi, Cody!' a voice called out and at once Daniel looked up to see the other black man standing by the pond, his dog running eagerly to meet his new friends.

The day before, Daniel had paused long enough to exchange pleasantries, the dogs' names, and compliments about their breed. As at first, Daniel had not lingered, though he had sensed the other man was showing interest in him, but perhaps today he might allow the conversation to flow, the man evidently pleased to see them both.

'Hi, good to see you again.' The African grinned, showing a set of fine teeth, one of his molars capped in gold.

'Aye, you too.'

'Zimbabwean, right?' the man asked, giving Daniel a closer look.

'Once upon a time,' Daniel agreed. 'I've been in Glasgow a good while now.'

'Better money over here,' the man laughed, a question in his voice.

'That's for sure,' Daniel replied. 'And you? Are you here for work, too?'

'Oh, yes, brother. Good money to be had here when you know the right people.' He flashed another grin at Daniel. 'Big business man, me. Doin' all right for meself.'

Daniel nodded and smiled, taking in the heavy gold chain around the man's neck, the flash of a diamond earring and that expensive watch peeping from under the cuff of his raincoat. 'Good, good. Nice to see a fellow doing well,' he assured him.

'And you, bro? You and your dog.' The man pointed at Cody who was behaving impeccably beside the frisking Simba. 'Doin' all right?'

'We get by,' Daniel said. 'Keeping going.'

'Oh, but that's not enough, bro,' the man protested. 'Fellow like you can do much better. Make more money?'

'Maybe.' Daniel shrugged. 'Maybe one day I'll be lucky and find a better job, who knows? Cost of feeding this one, oh, my!' He laughed and pretended to look a little shame-faced.

'Y'know, maybe it is your lucky day,' the man said, his voice dropping to a whisper. 'Maybe you and I can have a drink some time, a few smokes? Talk some business?'

'That's kind of you,' Daniel replied with a modest laugh. 'Maybe we can.' He shrugged.

His diffidence seemed to arouse something in the other man. 'Bro, you got a name?'

'I'm Danny,' Daniel said, holding out his hand.

'Well, Danny, welcome to my world. Name's Augustus,' he declared, giving Daniel's hand a firm shake. 'See that place over there? Corner of Park Lane and Gibson Street?'

'Offshore?'

'Meet me there night after tomorrow at eight. I think you and I could have lots to talk about.'

Daniel waved his hand aloft as he continued around the pond, Cody trotting obediently at his heels. He'd take the safer route this time, catch a bus from Great Western Road and arrange to meet the dog handler further away from Kelvingrove Park. *Just in case*, as the DI had advised him. Just in case you are being watched or followed. And he would be sure to look out for anybody jumping on a bus straight after him.

His heart beat a little faster as he walked through the gates and crossed the road. He'd done it! The easy part had been making contact with this man. The hard part would be sustaining the man's interest and infiltrating the organisation that so interested his superiors in Police Scotland.

Ncube threw a ball across the park and watched as Simba galloped after it, leaping up and catching it in his jaws. Could he catch this fellow like that? Throw out some bait, see if he grasped it, then reel him in till he became one of his own? As Simba came thundering back with the ball in his mouth and laid it at his master's feet, it struck the man how much loyalty this animal had for him. Pity that people weren't like that. Most of them simply did what he said for what they got out of it. It was a rare man that came to obey him out of loyalty rather than fear.

Could this Danny, who reminded him so much of his old friend, Jeremiah, ever be like that?

He picked up the ball again and threw it even further.

CHAPTER FORTY-ONE

WE ARE OPEN, the sign outside the Honda dealership in Titwood Road proclaimed as the two detectives drove in and parked the following morning. The paperwork found in Truesdale's Holyrood office had shown that the SUV had not been an outright purchase. Instead, it looked as though the MSP had chosen to pay a substantial monthly amount. DS Giles glanced across at his companion, Detective Constable Archie Singh, the newest recruit to the Major Incident Team. Singh had been fast-tracked since gaining his university degree in criminology, something that Davie Giles envied, having established his police career via a less academic route. Still, the foot-plodding mattered, each tiny new piece of information gathered adding to the sum of what they were beginning to know about the missing MSP. Lorimer had taken the blame for overlooking the matter of access to the Honda's boot, something a twelve-year-old schoolboy had pointed out. Now they were here to ask questions and hopefully formulate some ideas about why Truesdale had wanted that big car in the first place.

The booths were separated by noise-baffling partitions, the man in the smart suit who faced them across the desk keen to assure them they would not be overheard by any of the customers wandering around the showroom. Coffee and biscuits had been offered and accepted, Giles deeming it a good idea to be on an easier footing with Derek Brodie, the young man who had appeared a tad nervous at the sight of their warrant cards. Perhaps Brodie remembered occasions when he'd been caught for speeding? Or was his simply an inborn antipathy towards the police? Whatever the sales-man's initial misgivings they seemed to have disappeared by the time the coffees were finished, Davie Giles's easy manner helping to relax him.

'I remember the day he came in,' Brodie explained. 'It was pretty much a done deal.' He looked from Giles to Singh, the latter taking notes on his phone. 'He seemed to know exactly what he wanted, not at all unusual. When you're spending that amount of money, you do your homework first, shop around on the internet till you find what you're looking for.'

'Was there any particular reason Mr Truesdale chose that particular model of car?' Giles enquired.

'He wanted to see all the specifications,' Brodie told them. 'Had me show him each and every wee bit of kit. Even wanted to know about the electrics, how they worked and everything.'

Giles resisted glancing across at his DC. That was some-thing Singh would be jotting down, he expected.

'When did he take delivery of the vehicle?'

'Oh, let me see . . .' Brodie concentrated on the laptop on his desk, tapping a few keys then scrolling down to the page he wanted. 'Right. Okay. He wasn't trading anything in. Don't know how he got here. Taxi, maybe?' He shrugged. 'I never asked. Here we are. Aye, it was a Monday. October eleventh, just at the start of the school half term break. We'd been really busy that previous week and it was a lot quieter that morning. Fewer folk in the showroom.'

'And you did all the paperwork?'

Brodie straightened up a little before replying. 'I'm a senior sales assistant here,' he told them. 'We carry out the entire procedure for a customer from the moment he comes in to look around till the day we hand over the keys.'

'Speaking of keys, I suppose there are two sets for the new owner?'

Brodie nodded. 'That's right. That particular vehicle locks remotely, like most modern models, and we always give two sets to our customer so they have a spare for an emergency.'

Giles had expected this but had needed confirmation all the same. 'You'll have a copy of all the paperwork on file?'

Brodie nodded. 'The same as what I emailed over to you,' he agreed. 'Insurance agreement and everything. There's nothing fishy about this, is there?' he asked, an anxious frown clouding his face.

'Nothing to worry about,' Giles reassured him. 'We just needed to check everything out. Routine, you know.' He smiled.

Brodie threw them a quizzical look. 'Any idea why he changed his mind?'

'What do you mean?' Giles asked.

'Well, deciding not to buy it after all. Just lease hired instead.'

Giles sat stunned for a moment. None of the paperwork from Holyrood had shown this, he realised.

'Perhaps you might print us off a copy of that particular arrangement,' he said, trying to sound far more diffident than he felt.

'Sure. It was a shame, really. Big commission lost, you know. Still, if it was what a customer wanted?' Brodie shrugged.

'Getting back to the day you first met Mr Truesdale. Can you remember why he chose that particular model of car?'

Brodie's face relaxed once more. 'Oh, yes. I thought at the time he was a bit of a petrolhead, all the technical questions he was asking. He was particularly interested in buying a car that had easy access from the rear seats into the boot. Guess he must've had to do some of his own repairs in the past. Seemed to know what he was talking about, anyway. Most customers don't really know the ins and outs of motors. But he certainly did.'

Giles exchanged a glance with Singh and nodded briefly.

'Could you confirm that this was the man who you met, sir?' Singh asked, taking a photograph of Robert Truesdale from his inside pocket.

Brodie frowned and shook his head.

'That isn't the man who came into the dealership,' he said, handing back the photograph.

'Can you describe him to us?'

'Oh, let me think,' Brodie replied, tapping a pencil

on the edge of his desk. 'Not sure if I'd remember him, frankly. Medium brown hair, maybe? Glasses, I think. Older than you and me, maybe in his forties? Sorry, I didn't pay that much attention at the time. Too busy doing the paperwork. And we do have an awful lot of people coming and going.'

'Any chance you might have that particular meeting on CCTV?' Giles asked.

'Sorry, anything that was there will have been wiped by now,' Brodie sighed.

It was a nasty thought but one that could not be avoided. What if the Honda CR-V that Truesdale had ordered had been chosen specifically for the purpose of being blown up? He'd not spent over thirty grand on the car's purchase price, instead arranging a personal lease agreement that cost him a few hundred pounds, with an arrangement to make a monthly payment. That had vanished, of course, when it had been assumed the MSP was dead, the dealership recouping their loss through the insurers. Added to that, he had sent someone else on his behalf. Had he been so paranoid by then about being seen in public? Or was there another explanation? For someone had been in that dealership, signed the paperwork in Robert Truesdale's name and given the MSP's bank details.

Lorimer sat staring out the window of his office but seeing nothing. Had Truesdale actually planned his own death as they had discussed at the Brightmans' last night? He felt chilled by the idea that the MSP might have selected James O'Hare to be the victim.

It was a thought that had to be discussed in more depth and so, picking up his phone, Lorimer dialled the number that he knew off by heart.

CHAPTER FORTY-TWO

'Means, motive and opportunity,' Solly reminded him with a smile. They were sitting in Lorimer's office, the psychologist having agreed to come in to talk about the Truesdale case. After Molly's call the previous evening it had been hard returning to the supper party and relating the ins and outs of the case but Solly had engaged them in one amusing story after the other, a deliberate ploy to make him relax, Lorimer guessed. And, of course, it had worked. That and a very nice bottle of Merlot that had accompanied Rosie's lasagne, Maggie insisting on driving. *Gives me a shot at the new Lexus*, she'd laughed.

'Opportunity? Well, he knew exactly where his own car was parked, didn't he? And, had he paid someone to plant that bomb for him?'

'And the method, sadly, was all too obvious.' Solly shook his head. 'Imagine the absolute carnage if there had been kids walking to school that morning.' He shuddered. 'Thank goodness it happened during the autumn break.'

'So, we're really left with the one thing that bugs me. Why? If we hypothesise that it was the MSP then we have to ask this: why did Truesdale set off a bomb under his own new car?'

'He intended to disappear?' Solly suggested.

'That's just giving rise to yet another why,' Lorimer replied. 'Why did he want to disappear when he was on the brink of helping to make history by overturning the laws on drugs?'

'There were the death threats,' Solly reminded him.

'Well, he moved house. Maybe that was his attempt at getting away from that sort of thing?'

'Could be,' Solly replied though the dark eyes behind his horn-rimmed glasses seemed doubtful. 'It does seem a most extreme sort of thing to do, though, don't you think? Maybe he just wanted money from the house sale?'

Lorimer glanced at his friend. Solomon Brightman had the air of a wise owl, he thought, as his friend gazed steadily at him. *Solomon, the wise*, he remembered Maggie murmuring once, recalling that famed king from scripture. And he was someone worth listening to, Lorimer had learned over the years. Once, he had been sceptical about the ways of criminal profiling, seeing it as a bit of tomfoolery, but that was before he had come to see just how Solly looked at things and, more importantly, at people.

'Extreme is right,' he agreed. 'Can you imagine deliberately setting up another man in your place in order to have him killed in a car bomb and burned so that he was unrecognisable? I still can't conceive of Truesdale being a cold-blooded killer like that.'

'Yes, it is cold-blooded. And one would have to have very few qualms about doing it. Mr O'Hare's death may simply have been expedient to the plan to disappear. If it was *Truesdale's* plan,' Solly added.

'You think Truesdale's been coerced into doing this?'

Solly gave him a sad smile. 'I don't really think anything,' he answered. 'But we have to consider lots of possibilities that tie in with a motive. Say Truesdale is under so much pressure that he wants to step off the roundabout of politics. Would he go to all that trouble to do it? Kill a man?'

'It does sound far-fetched,' Lorimer admitted, yawning.

Solly laughed. 'Sorry we kept you late last night.'

'That's all right. It was good to spend an evening with you both. And Rosie's dinner was great. Hope we thanked her properly.'

'Leaving an empty lasagne dish was the biggest compliment you could have paid her,' Solly told him.

'Getting back to Truesdale. It looked to me as if he'd got in a load of nice groceries from Waitrose for his guest then simply taken off. There's no sign of him having been there overnight. Just one person was there at breakfast time.'

'And, if he'd asked O'Hare to look after the cat, perhaps he'd said he was going away for a bit?'

'Oh, poor man,' Lorimer sighed. 'He was a pawn in somebody's game, that's for sure.'

'You don't think ...?' Solly broke off, fingers teasing through the curls in his beard, his gaze thoughtful.

Lorimer remained silent. Once he'd have expressed impatience, but now he knew that whatever was percolating in this man's brain was worth waiting for.

'He was known to be an aggressive opponent of religion, particularly Christianity,' Solly said at last.

'It was when his secretary saw that chain, the one with the cross, that he made remarks like that,' Lorimer agreed. 'He seems to have detested organised religion, anything to do with the church. Even refused to have her minister officiate at his mother's funeral.'

'Hm, that does seem a bit extreme,' Solly agreed. 'But to dispose of a man as if he were expendable ... no, I just cannot see that, no matter how much O'Hare's religious views differed from Truesdale's.'

'But why go to all the bother of leasing that car? And remember, someone was making sure there was easy access to the boot. The man he'd sent to pick the car up for him. Not putting out a lot of money to buy it in the first place. It's almost as if he knew what was going to happen.' He turned to his friend. 'We've seen evil in people before, Solly. The sorts of things people can do to one another are sometimes hard to digest, I know. But we cannot ignore the facts. And the facts are that Robert Truesdale asked James O'Hare to look after his cat and left him his home, his clothes and his car. Looks to me as if Truesdale knew exactly what he was doing. He wanted O'Hare to be a decoy, to stand in for him. However, proving that is another matter and we won't do that till we find him.'

The psychologist had helped crystallise his thoughts, Lorimer decided. The dark ideas about a man plotting the death of another simply for his own convenience hadn't sat well with either of them. But that was not to say that

Truesdale hadn't used the Irishman in some way for his own ends, nefarious or otherwise. Was he the sort of man who was used to making others do his bidding? Like Karen Douglas arranging the cleaner, and the unidentified man who had sat in the dealership signing Truesdale's name on various documents. O'Hare had intended going somewhere that fatal morning. And early, too. Why was that? And where had he been heading? More questions that could not be ignored but perhaps never answered.

He recalled that meeting in Holyrood with Malcolm Hinchliffe. It seemed now as though Robert Truesdale was not the man the public knew and Lorimer doubted very much that the people of Scotland would ever know him as any more than a wayward MSP whose car had been bombed, the mystery of his whereabouts currently being put down as a stress-related matter by the press. Very few of the newshounds had probed much further than Holyrood, their press office giving out the suggestion that the MSP had gone into hiding, fearful of those who had sought to kill him, possibly affected by some sort of depression. Lorimer had heard Calum McKenzie on the TV news, admiring the smooth way the First Minister spoke, his comments rather vague but nevertheless seeming to satisfy his BBC interviewer. A frown crossed Lorimer's brow. Apart from the drug dealers they appeared to have found in and around Scottish waters, had the security services dug deeper into Truesdale's activities as a Member of the Scottish Parliament? Lorimer wondered just how much Calum McKenzie had been told prior to the initial request to find the missing man. Was Hinchliffe right, and had Truesdale

311

been involved in a global crime mob? He remembered the sponsorship deal the MSP had obtained to help the drugs initiative. It had been announced at the same conference where Mark Granger had overheard Truesdale speaking to O'Hare. That was something worth a bit of scrutiny by the MIT.

Given that Truesdale could have made contacts within the major drug-dealing gangs, would he have had enough clout to commandeer some of the nastier thuggish elements to do his bidding? Like the mysterious man planting a bomb beneath his own car? The thought came back once more, leaving Lorimer with a sick feeling in his stomach. He remembered how Jack Gallagher had worked, playing different elements of the drug gangs off one another, often keeping the major players at arm's length. And yet, it was hard to think of Robert Truesdale being cut from the same sort of cloth as the former drugs baron.

Who, then, might have done Truesdale's bidding instead? He thought of Hinchliffe, the charming man who had escorted him into the First Minister's office and what he had subsequently revealed to him that day in Edinburgh. Had there been someone else in the capital working with Truesdale? Even within the Scottish Parliament? No, something told him that the answer to where Truesdale was hiding would be found right here in Glasgow, amongst the lowlifes whose poisonous drugs spread like the roots of a malevolent tree beneath the surface of the city streets. Eastern Europeans, Glasgow neds and now a new group of Colombians, all intent on making money from the despair of addicts.

He bit his lip, thinking about his recent conversation with the chief constable who had informed him about PC Daniel Kohi being currently undercover at the behest of CID Govanhill.

Were their paths fated once more to cross in this case?

CHAPTER FORTY-THREE

The sea that had been glassy bright and mirror calm at seven that morning was now flecked with foam, dark clouds gathering on the horizon. Distant grey-green hills showed the Hebridean island of Mull, the Firth of Lorn separating him from the place where he now stood gazing out to sea. For days there had been no sign of anything other than the normal ferries and fishing boats plying their trade in these occasionally stormy waters, even the summertime yachts appeared to have found safer havens in dry docks. A lonely gull wheeled overhead, its plaintive cry chilling his blood. But it was the raven, surely, that was the bird of ill omen?

The cottage was off the beaten track, the narrow road with a cattle grid leading from the main carriageway and ending at a securely locked gate. A stand of tall Scots pine trees cast their shadows across the entrance, obscuring the way into the curved drive that had been worn into a path of beaten earth, grass and wild plants growing in the middle like a dual carriageway in miniature. No postman brought mail even as far as the gate, nor had he heard any vehicle approaching since his arrival. The only sounds were of sheep as they clipped along the lane and the mournful wail of seabirds or noisy clamour of oystercatchers. Still, his ear was attuned to the sound of a diesel motor whenever it chose to come to shore and fetch him away.

No man knoweth the day nor the hour. Who had said that? It didn't sound Shakespearean. His brow furrowed as he pondered the saying that had come into his head.

Too much time spent alone, he decided, and all this waiting was beginning to get to him. He'd been warned, oh yes, they'd stressed that it might happen, this feeling of being in limbo, stranded out here on the fringe of the Atlantic. But he'd dismissed their concerns. Concerns? No, that was the wrong word. None of them had any concern for him other than the influence he still retained amongst the people who mattered. Warnings, that was a better word. Yes, they'd insinuated that time spent on this isolated place might not be much of a holiday, no telephone or internet lest his presence be discovered. *It would drive me mad*, one of them had laughed, just before they'd set off at night, the wake from their small craft silvering the midnight waters.

A hissing sound made him start but it was just the wind blowing through a patch of dry grasses, chilling the bare skin on his neck. He shivered then and began walking back towards the safety of the small stone building that had been his home this past while. Winter was around the corner and soon these waters would be far less safe to make the journeys back and forth from one outpost to another. A dark speck on the horizon caught his attention and, stopping, he raised the field glasses to his eyes. Adjusting the lens, he focused until the grey craft came into view.

It was a patrol boat making its way along the firth. On the lookout for the very same people that he was hoping to see, he guessed. *They mustn't find you here*, they'd told him. But now he wasn't sure of anything any more. Would it be so bad to be taken from this place?

He grabbed the yellow dishcloth, pegged on the washing line, and returned to the cottage, closing the door firmly and locking it behind him, breathing hard. He would wait until he was certain that the boat had gone. It was a mistake, putting out even a little bit of laundry, the yellow cloth a sign of life in this desolate place, should any eyes be there to see it.

He stood still, hidden by the heavy wooden door, though in truth nobody would notice him from so far out in the firth. It was simply the instinct to do what he'd been told, to keep out of sight, he told himself at last, unclenching his hands and risking a look out of the window. Were there other eyes trained on this very spot where he stood? Someone in uniform taking a long clear look at the apparently abandoned building nestled amongst the hills? Or had they already seen that yellow dishcloth and wondered?

He watched the passage of the boat until it disappeared from sight, no doubt heading towards the Sound of Mull or even across to Oban and the mainland. Only then did he lower the binoculars, cold hands fastened around them in a rigid grip.

CHAPTER FORTY-FOUR

Netta clutched the zimmer frame as she felt herself sway a little. Then, gritting her teeth, she moved forward, stepping over the threshold of her flat, determined not to show her companion any sign of weakness. The house smelt fresh, she thought, sniffing the air. Had Daniel been in? She wouldn't put it past her friend to have prepared the place for her homecoming.

'Let's get our coat off and we'll just sit over there,' the woman beside her said in her sing-song voice.

Netta bit back a retort. It's *my* coat and *I'll* sit where I darned well like, she fumed inwardly. But they had all been so nice to her, this new person included, that she hadn't the heart to cause a fuss. Besides, a sudden fatigue threatened to overwhelm the old lady and she was grateful when the care assistant helped her off with the heavy coat and took her arm.

'There now, we'll have a wee cup of tea, shall we?'

'Aye, help yourself,' Netta told her. 'I don't mind *you*

sitting with *me* for a cuppa,' she continued, the woman's use of the plural pronoun grating on her. It was the same as when they called her darling or sweetheart (unless it was that nice young male nurse, of course). It just made her feel so ancient, as if she was unable to take care of herself.

Well, Netta, old girl, you'll just have tae pit up wi' it, she thought.

The care assistant who had accompanied her back to the high flats was busying herself in Netta's tiny kitchen, no doubt quite used to ferreting around in a stranger's home. That was what she would have to put up with several times a day, the occupational therapist had told her, though not phrasing her words in such a negative manner. There would be someone coming in to make her meals, help her to dress (only if you need it, they'd assured her) and do a tuck-in at night. Netta had grumbled a bit but now that she was actually sitting here, she could see the sense in all the different parts of the care package that had been put in place for her.

'Here we are.' The woman beamed at her, handing Netta one of her favourite porcelain mugs and setting down a paper napkin with a finger of shortbread on top.

'I don't remember buying these,' Netta murmured, picking up the shop-bought shortbread. 'I bake my own, you know.'

'Oh, I think it was your neighbour who left them. Along with the bags of groceries. A policeman, I believe?'

Netta breathed a sigh of relief, relaxing into her chair as she thought of Daniel.

'Oh, he's more than just a neighbour,' she told the woman.

'He's . . .' She paused for a moment, considering how to describe the black refugee who had made such a difference in her life. 'He's my best pal,' she said at last, then bit off a piece of the shortbread biscuit, crunched it thoughtfully. Nice of the lad, she told herself, quality shortbread but still not on a par with her own.

'That's lovely, so it is,' the care assistant said, sitting opposite Netta in the chair she normally reserved for Daniel. 'Good neighbours being good friends, I mean. Wish we had more like that. I can tell you some tales about a few of my old dears. All on their own, no families coming to see how they are, never mind offering to do their shopping for them or that. And as for neighbours? Too many folk busy doing their own thing to ask and see if an auld buddy needs a message. So, Mrs Gordon, you're a lucky lady having your pal do all that for you.'

Netta nodded, her mouth full of the shortbread. She might have told this woman of Daniel's plans for the new flat across on the Southside of the city but right now she was too tired to continue the conversation.

'Would you like a wee lie down after your tea, dear? Maybe put your feet up for a while?' There was concern on the woman's kindly face as she bent forward to pat Netta's knee.

Netta nodded, content to take the care assistant's advice.

'I'll stay till you're settled and someone will be in later on to give you your dinner,' she heard the woman say as her eyelids threatened to close.

Netta was only half aware of being guided to her bedroom and helped onto the bed. She heard the swish of curtains being drawn shut and felt the warmth of the tartan rug over her body before sleep overtook her at last.

The care assistant stood for a moment at the open doorway, gazing at the old woman. A small smile crept over her face. Fancy her best pal being a policeman! Maybe next time she visited Mrs Gordon she could mention her own family, their youngest girl hoping to join Police Scotland when she left college. Poor old thing, she thought, tiptoeing out to the hallway and gathering up her own belongings. Well, at least Netta Gordon had a good neighbour, even if none of her children had bothered to visit her in the hospital.

He would have to explain his change of shift patterns to Netta, he realised. This was one particular area of his work that he could not share with the old lady. Detective Sergeant Miller had given no indication of what Daniel ought to say to those closest to him and he was thinking of how to approach this very subject when his phone rang.

'Hi, it's Molly here. That you home, then?'

'Yes, just arrived, as it happens. Where are you?'

Daniel heard a throaty chuckle then, 'Look over to your right, Daniel.'

He glanced across the car park where a familiar car was sitting, the blonde detective waving at him. For a moment he wondered if he were dreaming, but no, she really was there.

'Ah, okay. Have you been waiting for me?'

'Not for too long. I calculated your arrival time,' Molly replied and Daniel saw a faint smirk on her face.

'Good detective work, eh?' he laughed, his heart beginning to thump.

'Have you time for a coffee?'

Daniel paused for the briefest of moments. Minutes ago, he'd been tired and hungry and intending to look in to see if Netta was all right. But now, all these thoughts were vanishing like mist over the mountains.

'Or we could get a bite to eat?'

'Yes.' Daniel grinned. 'I'm starving as it happens,' he replied, hardly trusting his own voice.

'Your car or mine?'

If he was surprised to see her parking in a bay marked RESIDENTS ONLY, Daniel hadn't shown it, Molly realised. Lilybank Gardens overlooked the hill that sloped down towards Ashton Lane, a favourite haunt of students from nearby Glasgow University, its pavements bordered by well-established trees.

'It won't take long for me to rustle up some food,' Molly told him as they left her car. 'Thought it might be better for us to have a chat somewhere more private than a restaurant.'

Daniel cocked his head to one side, regarding her intently, evidently intrigued.

'Wanted to give you a few pointers about being undercover,' she said, raising her eyebrows and grinning mischievously. 'Come on, I'm just one floor up, but we still have a decent view over the gardens.'

Molly unlocked the entry door and led him upstairs. This wasn't quite the way she had imagined bringing this guy to her home for the first time but, well, it was work, wasn't it?

Still, her heart beat just a little faster as they stepped into the hallway, Daniel's hand brushing her own as he turned to close the front door.

'Through here,' she said and headed towards a spacious front lounge that overlooked the car park. Lights twinkled from the nearby lane, its bars and cafés plus the famous Ubiquitous Chip restaurant busy at this time in the evening.

'What a lovely room!' Daniel exclaimed, looking around. 'Your own place?'

Molly nodded. 'Got fed up paying rent to a landlord some time back. Having a mortgage actually worked out a darned sight cheaper. Plus, the rise in house prices has meant this place is worth a helluva lot more than what I paid for it.'

She saw Daniel nodding and looking down at his hands for a moment.

Molly bit her lip. Why had she said that? Now that the words were out it felt as though she had been showing off. Of course, she ought to have remembered that Daniel had owned a property back in Zimbabwe. The home that had been burned to the ground by evil men, his poor wife and child perishing in the flames. Idiot! Molly cursed herself. That was not the best way to begin their conversation, was it?

'I'm off to pastures new, as it happens,' Daniel said, as though to lighten the mood.

'Undercover? Permanently?' Molly asked.

'No, I mean I'm moving house,' he replied, smiling at her. 'Not a place of my own. Can't afford that just yet. It'll take years to save enough for a deposit even on a small flat. But we're going to rent a nice old flat over on the Southside.'

'Oh.' Molly felt deflated suddenly. 'We', he'd said. She hadn't seen Daniel on his own for quite some time and Lorimer had never mentioned a new woman in the handsome Zimbabwean's life. But now it seemed as if she had missed her chance.

'Yes, Netta has agreed to come and stay with me, keep house once she's fit again. Really, I wanted to look after her,' he admitted with a self-conscious laugh. 'She's been so good to me and . . . well, it's like having an aunty nearby. She was dead set against the idea at first, but of course things changed.'

Molly listened as Daniel outlined the story of the old woman's collapse on the stairs when the lifts were off and her subsequent stay in the Queen Elizabeth. By the time he had finished telling her all of the details, her spirits had risen once more, the notion of her friend off with some other woman banished from her mind.

'Right, make yourself at home,' Molly told him. 'Glass of something nice while I toss something together? There's a bottle of Pinot Grigio in the fridge,' she suggested. Then, turning to one side commanded, 'Alexa, play some trad jazz.'

Daniel sat back in the chair, gazing over the lights of the nearby streets. Down beyond these building lay Byres Road, a main artery running from Great Western Road and the Botanic Gardens to the junction of Dumbarton Road and Argyle Street, Kelvingrove Art Gallery and Museum close by. He had walked these streets often that first winter in Glasgow, seeking warmth in the huge glass houses of the Botanics as well as meandering around the museum, and all for free. That was something that Netta had told him with pride in her voice, Glasgow folk sharing their treasures at no extra cost.

'Well, now, some things have changed since my time undercover, but the main things are still the same, as you will no doubt have been told.' He saw Molly looking intently at his face. 'Some folk would notice a black face amongst them in Glasgow but not so much here in the West End. There are students from all parts of the world here, so you should fit right in.'

'I know this area well,' Daniel replied. 'Perhaps Lorimer told you . . . ?'

Molly grinned at him. 'Aye, not many people know about your little escapade amongst the terrorists but yes, he did mention that to me. Discreetly, of course.'

'And I've been advised that the West End is where this particular Zimbabwean is living. Not on the Southside where the gang's activities seem to be taking place,' Daniel continued.

'Good,' Molly said simply. 'You've not been in uniform long enough over in Aikenhead Road for many of Glasgow's lowlifes to have clocked you so perhaps you will be a new face here?'

'That's what they are hoping,' Daniel agreed.

'How do you intend to get closer to this gang?' Molly asked, shifting a little nearer to Daniel.

I want to get close to you, Daniel thought, the faint scent of Molly's perfume making him rest his arm across the back of the settee where they were sitting.

'I've already made contact with the main guy,' he replied

cautiously. 'It involves meeting him in the park when he walks his dog at the same time every morning. It's a German shepherd.' Daniel edged a little nearer.

Molly was gazing at him now, her eyes soft, her mouth so inviting.

It was like a sigh of relief, that first gentle kiss, Daniel's fingers caressing her hair, Molly pulling him closer.

Later, they would look back on this moment and smile, wondering why it had taken them so long.

CHAPTER FORTY-FIVE

The airport was smaller than Lorimer remembered and it was not long till he had followed the exit signs and felt the faint smirr of rain on his face. There was nobody to meet him, just a line of taxis waiting for their fare, a small queue already formed along the pavement.

Soon he was in the back of a Skoda, the driver chatting about the latest political crisis in the UK and asking, what did our friend from Scotland make of it all? The friend from Scotland was non-committal, content to let the man talk nineteen to the dozen, preferring to watch the road that eventually led them into lush green countryside. It had been a few years since Lorimer had crossed the Irish Sea and he had forgotten how spaced out the little villages were, some no bigger than hamlets, the occasional castle towering on a hillside above them.

Athlone was a market town where some Scots had settled the previous century, particularly those skilled in the weaving industry, its mills one of the biggest employers back in those days. The taxi driver, having exhausted his line in politicians who 'were in it for what they could get', turned his talk to the history of the place before asking Lorimer once again for the exact address and checking it on his satnav.

'You'll be wanting a car to take you back, no doubt?' the driver asked Lorimer as he paid the man and collected a receipt once they'd arrived. 'Here, an' take my card. Sure, am I not after going to see my aunty Josie while I'm here?' He winked, waving a hand, and giving Lorimer a cheery grin.

The detective pocketed the man's card, deciding that he may as well make use of his offer, given that his visit might be brief. The rain that had begun as a faint mist was now drumming down hard on the Skoda's roof and Lorimer turned up his coat collar against the deluge, walking swiftly towards his destination. Would he really find out any more about James O'Hare? Or was this simply a waste of time and police resources, an exercise to satisfy the Scottish First Minister?

Breege McLaverty's home was a modern villa set in a large rectangle of green turf, a few terracotta pots lined up against the brightly painted white walls. A quick glance at the street showed a variety of different styles and Lorimer guessed that each home had been built to its owner's taste after purchasing a plot of land, something that the EU had enabled for folk in this part of the world.

He knocked on the half-glazed door, glad of the shelter from the blustery weather, noting the welcome mat placed right in the middle of the porch, three pairs of small wellington boots standing to one side.

The door opened and a tall woman with streaked blonde hair stood looking at him, her dark eyes full of questions.

'Mrs McLaverty? Detective Superintendent Lorimer. We spoke on the phone,' he said, flicking open his warrant card.

'Aye, we've been expecting you,' she said, standing aside. 'Come in then. That rain'll soak you in a minute, so it will.'

He followed her into the house, taking off his raincoat and folding it so that the worst of the water would not drip all over the woman's immaculate cream carpets.

'Would you just come into our kitchen? The kettle's newly boiled and I'm gasping for a cup myself.'

'Thank you,' Lorimer replied, turning a corner and finding himself in a huge room that led to a large conservatory, double bifold glass doors giving even more light plus a view of the garden and a wooded area beyond. Outside he could see a pink Wendy house and a yellow children's slide, the garden evidently having priority as the kids' playground. He leaned against an island unit where six barstool-style chairs were tucked beneath the work surface, watching as Breege McLaverty busied herself with the kettle, wondering if the warm smell wafting from a large range oven indicated recent home baking. A large steel-coloured fridge freezer held several hand drawings, evidently done by the children and fixed by magnets. Yes, he decided, this was a real family home that Breege McLaverty and her husband had created, a sudden pang of envy for what he and Maggie had missed.

'Tea or coffee?'

'Coffee, if it's no trouble,' he replied. 'Black with no sugar, thanks.'

'Sit you over there,' Breege told him, pointing towards a long settee with several squashy cushions. 'Take the weight off, why don't you.' She gave him a smile. 'Though by the looks of you, there's not so much to take off. You'll have a couple of pancakes, fresh off the girdle. Yes?'

'Yes, thank you,' he said, wondering if such hospitality was shown to every stranger who entered Breege McLaverty's home or was she making a special effort because this was a representative of Police Scotland?

'Right, then,' she said at last, setting down a cafetière of coffee beside a tray of mugs and buttered pancakes that were already waiting on a low wooden table.

He watched as the woman poured his coffee and her own before catching her eye.

'May I just say how sorry I am for your loss,' he began.

'Oh, James was lost to us a long time ago,' she said stiffly, the smile fading from her face. 'We hadn't heard from him in years. Wouldn't even have known how to get in touch. Nor would he, for that matter. Not now we're in Athlone.'

'He had changed a lot since he left Ireland,' Lorimer said, picking up his mug and taking a sip. 'I think you might even have been proud of him.'

'Is that so? Well, I have to believe a policeman, I suppose.'

'Your brother was in thrall to drugs for part of his life but he overcame addiction and became a Christian.'

'Oh, aye? In the prison, no doubt? I've heard of them that get converted when they're inside.'

'No, not at all. James did not have a police record, Mrs McLaverty. In fact, he managed to stay out of trouble.'

'And yet someone hated him enough to blow him away,' she snapped, eyes flashing.

'That is something we are investigating,' he told her. 'There is a distinct possibility this was a case of mistaken identity. That your brother was simply in the wrong place at the wrong time.'

The woman put her hand to her mouth and shook her head. 'I didn't mean ... oh, the poor lad ...'

Lorimer fished a clean handkerchief from his jacket pocket and handed it quietly to her.

She nodded in thanks, then blew her nose noisily, evidently more upset than she had expected to be.

'Before his death, James had been working with a government agency to help with the rehabilitation of drug addicts,' Lorimer explained. 'And he was well thought of by the people in Glasgow City Mission who had helped in his own recovery.'

'Good people?'

'Good people,' Lorimer agreed.

'So, why ...? Why was he in a car that exploded?'

Lorimer hesitated for a moment, trying to think of the best words to choose to explain the strange situation.

'We think he may have been house-sitting for Mr Robert Truesdale, a gentleman whom he'd befriended. A member of our Scottish Parliament who had been targeted on social media by some extremists.'

'The bomb was meant for *him*? How could that be so? Was he away on holidays or what?'

'It is possible that James was under the impression that he was looking after Truesdale's house and his cat. Sadly, your brother is no longer here to answer such questions but we have some evidence that this may have been the case.'

'Oh.' The sigh was long and drawn out as O'Hare's sister took in the enormity of all Lorimer was telling her.

'Tell me more about your brother,' Lorimer asked eventually.

'Let me show you some old pictures,' she suggested, rising from her chair and walking over to a dresser with several low cupboards.

He watched as she pulled out some leather-bound photo albums then set them down on the table before sitting next to her visitor. The following hour passed quickly, Breege telling stories about their childhood and the scrapes her brother had initiated.

'He was always a bit of a tearaway,' she confessed. 'By the time he was seventeen, Mammy was heartsore with him and Dada eventually ordered him out of the house. Told him to make his own way in the world.'

'There was no involvement with any political faction?'

'You mean the IRA? No, no, we grew up long after the Troubles. Besides, James was more interested in staying out late and getting stoned. Stupid wee boy . . .' She broke off, staring at one particular photo of the brother and sister, aged about five or six, on a beach somewhere, their arms around one another and grinning at the person behind the camera.

'Your parents . . .'

'Oh, long gone. We never knew where James was by then. No way to ask him to attend a funeral.'

'Well, perhaps there will be a chance to make your peace with him when we release his remains for burial,' Lorimer said softly.

'Aye, maybe.' Breege looked at him through narrowed eyes. 'You said there was something else. Something that you wanted me to know about James but you didn't want to talk about on the telephone.'

'I did,' Lorimer sighed. 'I'm afraid the story of your brother's sudden death is even sadder. You see, shortly before he was killed, James became a father.'

'No! James? Oh, dear God in heaven, who did he marry?'

'It wasn't a conventional relationship that your brother had with the baby's mother,' he began. And then, as Breege McLaverty listened, dark eyes wide with astonishment, Lorimer related the story of Angelika Mahbed.

'So, you see, this little boy is still in hospital, recovering from the toxicity that was passed from his mother.'

'And he hasn't a soul in the world?' Breege shook her head in disbelief, tears now coursing freely down her cheeks.

'We were trying to find Angelika's family in Romania but so far have had no success,' he told her.

'Well, the baby will come here,' she said firmly. 'To his real family. Of course he will.' She threw him a defiant look as though expecting him to argue. 'And, tell me, does this wee mite have a name?'

It was not his decision to make, of course, but Lorimer did hope that social services on both sides might come

332

to an agreement about the McLaverty family taking in O'Hare's child. As he hastened down the path to the waiting Skoda, Lorimer turned to take one final look at the McLaverty home.

Perhaps, he thought, one day there might be a fourth small pair of wellington boots lined up by that doorway.

CHAPTER FORTY-SIX

The darkness pressed down on him, choking every breath that he tried to take. At each swell, the boat rose and fell again, the taste of vomit bitter in his mouth. How far . . . how far? He wanted to cry out, but it was impossible to make himself heard against the roar of the engines. Was this what it was like to die? Trapped in this narrow space, no one to hear his screams . . .?

Sitting up, he took a deep breath as though the stifling sensation he'd imagined was real.

In front of him the gauzy curtains fluttered a little as a draught of air crept through a crack in the window frame.

He really could not go on any longer. Everyone had their breaking point and this, he realised, was his.

Blinking against the daylight, he felt a sense of calm as if somehow the tortured dream from which he'd just awoken had crystallised something in his mind, assuring him that far from being an admission of failure, this was a decision that he would not regret. He would pack up what belongings he could carry and head for the ferry terminal, catch the next available boat and then ...

He chewed his bottom lip, no further ideas coming to mind as he swung his legs out of bed. Once on the mainland, would he be safe from those forces that were conspiring to kill him? Safer than going quietly crazy in this place, a small inner voice suggested.

It was the matter of a few minutes to wash himself (the water was cold again) dress and gather up what he might need for a journey. There were buses from Oban to Glasgow as well as the train service, but if he felt in any danger, it might be easier to hop off a bus and hunker down in another small out-of-the-way place. He ran a hand over his chin, feeling the growth of beard. A quick glance in the mirror was enough to show how much his appearance had changed over these past days. His hair had needed a cut before that hasty departure and now was positively scruffy, not a bad cover, he supposed. Nobody would be looking for a backpacker on the road, clad in jeans and stout hiking boots.

It was cool outside and a brisk wind was blowing, the smell of seaweed wafting up from the shore. Gulls wheeled and cried overhead as he closed the cottage door and pulled it fast, slipping the key beneath a large flat stone, exactly where he had found it ... how many days ago? He shook his head as if to clear it, glancing at his wristwatch to check the date, his only means of keeping any sort of track of time passing.

Grasping a stout stick that leaned against the door post,

he hitched his pack a little higher onto his shoulders and then set off along the driveway, towards the five-barred gate.

There was an ominous creak as he pushed it aside, as if the very fabric of the wood disapproved of his flight. Then, with a clang, the catch slid into place and he walked away, looking straight ahead at the narrow road that twisted amongst birches and bracken, not once looking back at the place where they had brought him.

CHAPTER FORTY-SEVEN

'Going somewhere, Mr Morrison?'

Des Morrison whirled around from the back of his van to see the two plainclothes detectives grinning down at him.

'You again,' he snarled. 'What is it this time?'

He slammed the door shut and glared at them, hands held against the van as though to conceal what was inside.

Davie Giles watched as the first beads of perspiration began to course down the man's fleshy brow. It was far from being a warm day, but Des Morrison looked as though a cold drink might be needed to freshen him up.

'We'd like another word, Des,' Molly told him brightly. 'But first, why not open the van and let us see what you're in such a hurry to hide. It wouldn't be anything illegal, now, would it?'

It was a sorry-looking man that was led into the interview room at Helen Street, cuffed wrists bunched across his stomach.

'Don't know how that got in there,' he had muttered, not

very convincingly, when Giles had uncovered the stash of boxes claiming to be filled with French Lavender Talcum. It had been a matter of minutes to reveal their true contents, a record haul of what they suspected might be the poorly cut heroin that had been circulating in the area.

After that, Morrison had come along meekly enough, head down, his refusal to say any more at odds with his usual inclination to talk his way out of a sticky situation.

Now, in the same room where he had faced Molly and Lorimer before, he shuffled towards a chair and slumped down with a defeated sigh.

'We've got him this time,' Giles whispered as he stood outside in the corridor waiting for Lorimer.

'Looks like the last of his nine lives are up, right enough,' Molly replied, smiling.

'Eh?'

'Macavity, the mystery cat,' Molly explained. 'The one who was never at the scene of the crime. Who always got away with it.'

She looked over her shoulder at the man sitting dejectedly in the interview room. 'Could almost feel sorry for him if he wasn't spreading such human misery,' she remarked.

'Nah, folk like him don't deserve any pity,' Giles told her. 'And I hope when this comes to court, they throw the book at him.'

'He's in here, sir,' Molly said as Lorimer loped along the corridor towards them. 'That tip-off we got turned out to be spot on.'

*

Des Morrison had been aware ever since the discovery of Frankie's body that someone was keeping a less than friendly eye on him. Like any cat with a sixth sense, Morrison had felt an unwanted presence at different times of the day. A shadow on the corner that vanished as he drew into his home in Cambuslang, or footsteps that fell silent as he locked up each night in Calder Street, no sign of life to be seen or heard when he turned to see who was there. But he knew, oh yes, he knew that someone was out to get him. One of the Colombians, maybe, though he'd greased their palms often enough lately to keep them away. Whoever his stalker had been, he'd drawn the polis right to the door of his lock-ups, a place he'd thought to have hidden from prying eyes.

Now the inevitable had happened and he looked up to see the piercing blue eyes of a certain detective superintendent bearing down on him.

There were different ways of playing this, Lorimer knew, and Morrison would be hoping to offer up as much as he could in the hope of a reduced sentence. He was no longer a young man and the years ahead in prison would no doubt take their toll on him. Nevertheless, that would be his destination, no matter what was said in this room in the next few hours.

'Time's up, Des,' Lorimer said quietly, sitting opposite the little man.

'Aye.' The word fell from the man's lips as a sigh.

Lorimer turned on the recording and began the usual formalities of date, time, and those present.

'Well, Des, or would you rather I call you Mr Morrison for the tape?'

'Ach, suit yourself, Superintendent. S'all wan tae me.' The man shrugged.

'Right, Des,' Lorimer nodded. 'Let's not begin with what was discovered in a van at your premises in Rutherglen.'

'*Not* . . .?' Morrison looked up, repeating Lorimer's word, his eyes suddenly wide with hope.

'No, let's begin with a young woman called Angelika Mahbed. You remember her, don't you, Des? This was, after all, the young woman who died from a drug overdose.' He leaned forward, staring hard at Morrison, daring him to look away.

'Nothing tae do wi' me . . .'

'Ah, not true, Des. Not true at all. In fact, I think it will be highly likely that when that heroin we found today is tested it will be shown as a perfect match for the heroin that was found at Angelika's post-mortem examination.'

'I . . .' Morrison swallowed but appeared incapable of finishing whatever protestation he had been about to make.

'Yes, you see we've been interested in quantities of this coming into Scotland for quite some time, Des. And I'm hoping you might be willing to help us find just how these drugs have infiltrated our lovely country. A truly patriotic gesture, one might say,' he said with a smile.

'You know I cannae grass . . .'

'Up to you, Des.' Lorimer sat back and folded his arms in an affectation of nonchalance. 'No skin off my nose how long you're sent down for, now, is it?'

'Look, what if I telt ye everything I know,' Morrison

pleaded. 'Would I still be safe inside? You know how these things work, Mr Lorimer. A beating in the showers, a wee razor blade hidden in the soap and then it's all over. Can ye no' see how I'm placed here?'

Lorimer tilted his head to one side thoughtfully. 'A man of your age, you wouldn't stand a chance, is that what you're saying?'

Morrison nodded miserably.

Lorimer looked across at the duty solicitor who was regarding him with interest.

'What if we could guarantee your client might serve any future sentence in a secure wing? One that is designed to house those poor souls who are intellectually challenged, shall we say?'

'Me? In wi' the numpties?' Des cried out, as though affronted at the very idea of being incarcerated with other men deemed too mentally frail to co-exist with the regular inmates.

'What's your alternative?' Lorimer reasoned.

The sigh that came from the man across the table became a moan of defeat.

'Shall we begin, then?' Lorimer asked, unfolding his arms and drawing his chair closer to the table between them. 'Let's start with a certain cartel with links to South America. Colombia, to be exact.'

CHAPTER FORTY-EIGHT

The sea breeze had chilled his hands so that they were stiff clutching the railing but still he did not move from his position near the stern of the boat. Was it wrong to look back, see where he had been for all this time, mesmerised by the white wake arrowing through the choppy waters of the firth? The journey to the island seemed such a long time ago now, his passage concealed beneath rugs in the back of a transit van deemed necessary for his safety.

He remembered the nightmare now, the suffocating feeling as he writhed to be free of the weight holding him down. It had been such a vivid dream and his awakening was as if he had finally shaken free from the bonds that had held him. Had he been sleepwalking through these past days? Or was it weeks? He shook his head as if any attempt to calculate was destined to fail.

So far, he had resisted the temptation to queue at the small shop inside the boat, though the idea of buying a newspaper made him tremble with a sort of feverish longing. No phone. No internet. No contact with the outside world. And had it really been for his own safety? Keeping the forces of evil at bay? Not even trusting those representatives of law and order he had been brought up to respect? He had kept his head down and collar up, shuffling along in the line of foot passengers as soon as he'd spotted two men in high visibility jackets standing on the pier. Were they looking for him? His paranoia was real, even if their intention was simply to see the ferry off on its latest voyage.

Once there were fewer folk in that small booth, he'd pick up one of the papers, find a quiet seat and catch up with all that was happening in the wider world.

Later, far out into the firth, he sat next to a window, poring over the news, amazed at how little the world had changed. In-fighting between politicians, howls of recrimination for the slightest misdeeds, atrocities in far-off lands that made him wince a little less than if they'd been happening here on soil that he knew. Was it not ever thus? He turned over the pages, scanning headlines about local and national politics, ignoring the double-page adverts paid for by multinationals, until he reached shorter features accompanied by coloured pictures. Dancers from an Eastern European troupe had been performing at the Edinburgh Festival theatre, the photograph of the principals performing a breathtaking lift; a film he'd hoped to see had not gone down well with the reviewer of this paper; a new TV series based on a Scottish novel was being shot in the Highlands. Life, it seemed, was continuing despite his absence, something that once would have provoked a small sense of outrage but was actually a relief.

The article was at the foot of a page devoted to several lurid crimes, its inclusion almost an afterthought.

As he read, the words became blurred and he had to start again at the beginning. This could not be true, could it? They had warned him that he might be sought by the wrong people. They had told him to sit tight, wait for the boat that would carry him to a safer place. But he had disobeyed them, and was this now his punishment?

He looked up, fearful of catching the eye of any passenger who might be staring at him, pointing a finger, and whispering to their neighbour. But nobody seemed to have the slightest interest in the scruffy figure dressed in jeans and wearing an old khaki waterproof jacket. A woman passed by, striding towards the ladies' toilets, ignoring him completely. Outside, the water streamed past slowly, reflections from the land casting dark green shadows. Once someone let out a cry and several passengers pressed against the glass to catch sight of a pair of porpoises. But nobody could see him, sitting there, as if he had become less visible than a momentary glimpse of these creatures.

Was he dead? The thought clutched at his chest, palpitations real enough. He swallowed hard, tasting the bitter saliva, feeling his tongue against his teeth.

He'd escaped from the threat of death, hadn't he? For a moment he wanted to stand up, demand that this boat be turned around, that he was making a huge mistake after all. But he remained exactly where he was, hands clutching the newspaper, eyes drawn back to the words that had stricken him. Were they true? Had the things they described really happened?

And, most terrifying of all, would he ever be safe again?

CHAPTER FORTY-NINE

Molly listened as Lorimer outlined the latest progress in the search for Robert Truesdale and the drug cartel to which his name had been linked. The Glasgow-based organised crime syndicate had not begun and ended with Des Morrison, it seemed. Frankie Fleming's murder and that of his associate, Ritchie, had been ordered by a Colombian-based gangster named Vallejo who had sought to eliminate what he saw as meddlers in competition for the distribution of heroin in the city, aiming to make his own cartels dominant. Morrison's confession was now being laid open to the team and Molly concentrated on Lorimer's words, even as she found her thoughts straying to Daniel and his covert operation.

'Morrison saw the position he was in,' Lorimer continued, 'and we now know a lot more about who has been behind this influx of heroin, the strain we believe was responsible for Angelika Mahbed's death. Fleming and the others were small fry compared to the Colombian contingent. We have another person of interest now to add to those that Morrison has given us: a Zimbabwean national. PC Kohi is meeting this man tonight, in fact,' he said, making Molly shiver involuntarily at the thought of Daniel putting himself in danger. There had been times during her own undercover ops when she had experienced some perilous moments, the last of these ending that part of her career for good. So, her fears for Daniel were justified, she knew, digging her thumbnails into her hands.

'It's a joint op now,' Lorimer declared. 'So, I want you there to help PC Kohi. Okay, DS Newton?'

'Yes, sir,' she replied at once, listening carefully as Lorimer continued.

'Morrison was working for the Colombians but swears he never knew that Robert Truesdale was associated with them. Didn't deny that Truesdale was behind it all, but said he was only told what he needed to know, which I found reasonably convincing.'

Molly nodded to herself. The main players in most big gangs liked to keep their identities hidden, like Jack Gallagher, preferring to make a big show of their legitimate businesses behind which lay money-laundering, drug- and people-trafficking. The purchase of Lorenzo's fish and chip shop had been funded by Morrison's paymasters, though it would take a few lawyers to untangle that particular web of lies and deceit.

'We are still anxious to find Truesdale, dead or alive,' Lorimer told them. 'And also, the woman named Miranda. Morrison has told us that he saw her heading off from the flat. Looked like she was doing a runner.'

'What is her involvement?' DS Giles asked.

'Morrison says that she was recruited by the Romanians to help with the trafficking of girls. She'd also been working with Fleming, passing him drugs she'd obtained from Morrison, getting a cut for herself. He thinks she got a fright when Angelika died from that overdose. We've spoken to one of the teenagers in the Calder Street flat. Once Miranda knew Kohi wasn't the social worker she'd assumed him to be, she scarpered.'

'You think the woman's got a conscience?' Molly asked, in a tone of disgust.

'Could be. She was certainly afraid of being found in that flat.'

'The girl said she'd told Miranda that she thought Kohi was with the Colombians,' Giles put in.

'And that would scare her plenty,' Lorimer agreed. 'Assuming he was part of the Colombian gang would really put the frighteners on her. Especially after these two machete deaths.'

'Do we have any leads about who was behind them?' Molly asked.

Lorimer looked straight at her, his blue eyes full of understanding as though he sensed what was behind her question.

'We do,' he answered slowly. 'Big Zimbabwean guy who works for Vallejo called Ncube. Augustus Ncube.'

Netta wanted to rise from her armchair, but the carer was at the door to answer the bell before she could even move.

'Oh, hello.' She heard a familiar voice. 'I've come to visit Netta.'

'Come in, Daniel,' Netta called out. 'I'm through here.' She chuckled. Where else would she be, unless bed bound, and hopefully that spell was over for good.

'Netta, how are you today?' Daniel was at her side, hunkering down, a bouquet of yellow roses in his hands.

'For me?' Netta smiled coyly.

'For you, dear lady,' Daniel replied, then, standing up, he handed them to the woman in the purple overall who was hovering in the doorway of the lounge. 'Could you find a vase for these, please?' he asked.

'Oh, such nice roses,' the carer cooed. 'I'll cut their stems, pop them in boiling water for five minutes then give them a big drink. That way they'll last longer.'

'Cuppa?' Netta asked.

'I'll fill the kettle right up, Mrs Gordon, and make a pot for you and your friend,' the woman assured her. 'Would you like a piece of that Hallowe'en cake I brought?'

'Thanks,' Daniel replied, then, turning back to his friend, he drew up a chair and sat closer to the old lady. 'I'd almost forgotten it is Hallowe'en tonight. Hope I don't have to sing you a song?'

'No, tell me all your news instead,' Netta demanded. 'Any gory tales to share?'

Daniel laughed out loud at Netta's eager expression. He was always amazed at the capacity older ladies seemed to have for tales of criminal activity – the more macabre, the better. Her penchant for TV crime dramas had given Netta the idea that her friend would be chasing baddies all over the city rather than the diverse and sometimes routine work required by a probationer cop. However, the reality of his present undercover operation was to remain a complete secret.

'All very boring at work,' he told her. 'However, I have something rather special to share with you.'

Netta listened eagerly as he began to tell her about the tall blonde police officer who was part of the Major Incident Team and how their friendship was beginning to blossom into something more.

'You need to bring her here. To meet me,' she said decisively. 'After all, if you and I are going to be flatmates, I need to get to know all your ... friends,' she said, giving him a wicked grin.

'I will, I promise. But she and I, well, we don't always have the same rest days, you know,' he told her. 'But I will bring her up to visit. You'll love her, Netta, I just know you will.'

Netta sipped her tea and regarded him thoughtfully over the rim of her cup. There was something different about Daniel today. He seemed to have far more energy than most other times, particularly when he'd just come off a shift. Love, she told herself. It was a magical time in anybody's life. But for Daniel, who had loved and lost, well, didn't he deserve a second chance at happiness? She gave a contented sigh as she leaned back in her chair. Perhaps she might slip something into her next letter to Daniel's mum, Jeanette, her penfriend. Both women had become adept at writing in a sort of code, never mentioning Daniel by name, referring occasionally to their 'brave lion', an idea associated with the Biblical story of Daniel in the lion's den. She gave a yawn and laid down the cup and saucer.

'I've overstayed my welcome,' Daniel whispered. 'Looks like you are ready for a nap.'

'Come back again soon,' Netta murmured sleepily. 'And thanks again for the flowers. Fair cheer me up, so they do.' She smiled, glancing at the vase of yellow roses the carer had placed on a shelf where she could see them.

Daniel gave a huge sigh of relief as he closed the door behind him. Netta had been entranced by his story about Molly, though he had missed out some of their more intimate moments, of course. She wasn't daft, though, and that twinkle in her eyes had told him how happy she was that he had found someone special at last.

A memory of Chipo's face came to mind, her dimpled cheeks, and the way she looked at him so lovingly. Those times would never die. The moments of shared joy with his beloved wife were no less wonderful for being in the past. And Chipo would have wanted him to find new happiness, her generous nature assuring Daniel of that. It was the loss of Johannes that troubled him more often, the little boy's life cut so short. He would never see him grow up and go to school, never take him out to play football, teach him how to swim or ride a bicycle.

Biting his lip, Daniel blinked back tears. He was alive and had so much for which to be thankful; a good job, friends who cared about him and now this new love. Where might that lead?

Thoughts of the coming evening made him remember Molly's words of advice. How to arrive at a rendezvous without making it seem he was trying to attract a tail. Practising a certain diffidence if the man offered him a chance to join his gang. Being too eager might make the man suspicious. Being natural was the key. Tonight, he would not have Cody at his side, the police dog safely in his kennels. Perhaps he might take a bag, visit the local library, and select a few books to pique the other man's interest. Props could be helpful, Molly had told him as she had suggested that very ploy. Hillhead library was open at just the right time, too, and he could walk up University Avenue then along Gibson Street to Offshore café.

His mind readied for the next stage of his covert operation, Daniel settled down to read the latest reports coming in from the MIT, wondering how Molly had responded to the news about the man he was going to meet that night.

CHAPTER FIFTY

Having to earn her keep was something the woman was used to. Back in Calder Street, things had been a lot easier, the girls bringing in punters on a regular basis, getting her own cut of their money for looking after them. And Angelika ... well, maybe it was best she didn't think too hard about the dead woman and her baby. Miranda chewed a fingernail, the thought of that night haunting her still.

As Angelika had left with her baby, a blanket wrapped around her shoulders, Miranda had watched from the upstairs window, frowning as the Romanian woman had staggered along the street to a waiting car. She had followed its progress until it had gone out of sight. Going with a punter and taking the kid with her was just so weird, she'd thought at the time, shaking her head. But then, most of the junkies would risk anything for a fix.

Yet Angelika had weaned herself off the drugs in the days before she'd given birth. Paddy had seen to that, oh yes. Miranda had worried that one day he'd simply take her off and they'd never see her again. Was that what had happened? But Angelika had overdosed, so it couldn't have been Paddy in that strange car, could it? Had it been Frankie? Or one of the Romanian guys? None of the girls back in Govanhill had ever scored from anyone else, so far as she knew. Miranda shivered, thankful that she at least was not in thrall to the heroin that ravaged so many of the street workers. She'd salted away the money she'd been paid to look after the younger women, enough to have given her a new start over here in Glasgow's West End.

Tonight she was dressing up for a party, black fishnets over a black and red corset and a tight skirt that hugged her figure. Miranda looked at herself in the mirror. Black velvet pussycat ears crowned her blonde wig, whiskers drawn across her cheeks with eyeliner, long black evening gloves with silver claws painted on each finger. She leaned forward and practised purring at her reflection, the throbbing sound in her throat making her smile. Just a furry tail to attach and she was ready. It was a short walk from Oakfield Avenue down to Gibson Street and there was no rain forecast. The other girls were giggling in the kitchen, the scent of cannabis wafting along the hall. She raised her nose and sniffed. Maybe later, she decided. Once she'd found a man with plenty of money who wanted to make her purr.

Daniel was glad to see the number of people out on the streets tonight. Being surrounded by different groups somehow made him feel less exposed. It was a clear night for Hallowe'en. He looked up, seeing a cloud scud across the face of the moon; it was as if the moon itself was travelling rapidly across the skies, playing hide and seek amongst the clouds. He passed a tenement close where a group of giggling kids watched as one of their number pressed every button on the security pad, demanding entry. It wasn't only children out for a good time, he realised as he walked down University Avenue. The Students' Union further up the hill had resounded to loud music, a Hallowe'en party well under way. Here and there he met dark-robed figures of witches and ghouls, some of them deliberately leering at him and cackling with laughter as he feigned surprise.

There was music spilling out from Offshore, the café open for a private function tonight, one to which it seemed he had been invited. The man he had met in the park had made no mention of a gathering, but perhaps it was better to be in a crowd. Daniel looked down at his clothes, aware that he may have been expected to arrive in costume, though his new friend, Augustus, had not mentioned that. He was wearing his best jeans and a navy pea jacket over a camel crew-neck sweater, nothing flashy but smart casual enough for a night out and thick enough to hide the wires Molly had helped him with earlier. He hesitated before nearing the door. If this all went wrong ...? No, he told himself, don't go there.

The noise as he entered was deafening, deep drum-beats reverberating from a bank of speakers at the back of the café. Daniel looked around, hoping to see another black face.

'Danny, you came!'

Daniel felt the firm hand on his shoulder and he turned to look up at Augustus, relieved to see he too had come in his ordinary clothes, the same black jacket he'd worn in the park.

'Augustus, thanks for inviting me. Didn't know it was a party here tonight.' Daniel grinned, placing a hand on the man's arm for a moment.

'What can I get you to drink, man?' Augustus did a small dance, white teeth bared as he began to move to the beat of the music.

Daniel looked at the taller man's eyes, sure he'd been indulging in some form of opiate before his arrival.

'Just a Coke for me, thanks. Can't take alcohol right now,' Daniel replied. 'Upsets my meds, y'know?' He made a face, thankful that Molly had come up with a back story about an imaginary health problem.

'Too bad, my man,' Augustus exclaimed, throwing his hands up. 'Sorry to hear that.'

'Thanks,' Daniel replied with an exaggerated sigh. 'There are different ways of having fun, though, eh?'

Augustus threw back his head and guffawed. 'Sure are, man.' Then, turning, he walked towards the bar, moving his body to the rhythm of the music, stopping once to wave towards a corner where three men sat, bottles of beer on their table.

There was a crush of people lined up to wait their turn to order, but as Daniel watched, Augustus simply mowed through them till he reached the front. Nobody yelled out a word of protest; on the contrary, those ahead in the queue had simply melted away as they caught sight of him coming their way. It was a sign to Daniel not only that this man was well known here but also that he commanded the sort of authority that he had seen in dangerous gang leaders back in his own country.

It was as he waited for Augustus to return with their drinks that he spotted her; the pussycat costume drawing several eyes to the blonde woman sauntering casually into the café.

Miranda smiled as she walked slowly into the big room of Offshore. This was where the action would be tonight, the other girls had informed her. And it looked as if they were right. Several women were already seated at small tables, their feather boas and fairy outfits bright spots of colour amongst so many witches and goblins. No one else had dressed as a cat, however, and Miranda felt the warmth of admiring eyes looking her way. It would be easy enough to find a man here with money, she decided, glancing towards the bar where a dark-haired fellow stood, head and shoulders above most of the other punters.

It was when he turned around and she saw his face that she faltered. That scar ... the heavy gold chain around his throat ...

'Here, pussy, come and sit on my lap!' a voice cried out and Miranda felt herself being pulled in a strong grasp. Her high heels skittered on the wooden floor and before she knew it, she'd been thrust in between two young men who were patting her hair, laughing, and making cat noises at her.

It was better to play along with them rather than make a fuss, she realised. Anything to avoid drawing too much attention to herself.

'Does pussy want a saucer of milk?' one of them asked, slinging an arm around her shoulder.

Miranda nodded, pasting a smile on her face. 'Miaow,' she purred, cupping her nose with one gloved hand. 'Bailey's Irish cream for pussycat.' She snuggled up to the man beside her. She'd be safer here in their company, her back to Ncube, Miranda decided. And, if they both wanted company later on . . . well, why not?

Daniel had watched the woman stop suddenly, her pretty, made-up face freezing for an instant as Augustus turned from the bar.

He recognised that expression of fear. What did Miranda know about this man? Why was she here and, worst of all, would she recognise him too?

He saw Augustus motion to a table near the door where a small party of men and women were laughing and chatting. Daniel moved towards them, frowning, since there was no empty seat.

It was as Augustus Ncube stood beside the table that Daniel suddenly saw why Miranda had appeared frightened. All laughter stopped as each of the men and women looked up.

Then, as if by some unspoken agreement, they rose from the table and made their way outside into the street, drinks in hand. To have that sort of power over people . . . Daniel suppressed a shudder. This man who had befriended him was ruthless, he could see, inspiring fear in those who might stand in his way.

'Thanks.' Daniel smiled, pretending to ignore the small

incident, as if the couples at the table had moved away under their own volition. 'Cheers,' he said, taking the Coke bottle from Augustus and clinking it against the beer in the man's other hand.

Augustus sat down next to Daniel and took a long swig then, with an exhalation of satisfaction, set his bottle on the table.

'Brilliant night for a party,' Daniel began. 'Lots of kids out in the streets.'

Augustus grinned at him. 'They like to enjoy trick or treat. And I'm always ready with a few treats,' he added with a laugh.

Daniel patted his pockets. 'Next round on me,' he said firmly.

'Sure, same again.' Augustus nodded, then tilted the bottle up, swallowing hard till it was empty. 'Then, maybe you and I can have a little talk about . . .' he looked across at Daniel with a faint smile on his face, 'this and that.' He nodded, as if his new friend would understand his meaning.

The crowd at the bar parted for Daniel the same way he had seen happen for the bigger man; evidently any friend of Augustus was accorded the same sort of respect.

'Two Cokes and two Buds, please,' he asked the woman behind the bar who was dressed all in black, her grey hair tinted with purple, a necklace of white bones her only adornment.

Daniel glanced around as he waited for the order. The cat woman was still with the men whom he assumed were her friends. She had her back to the other tables and Daniel wondered if it would be wise to catch her attention. Would she be able to tell him more about this man, Augustus? Or would she be wary of seeing him again now that he was evidently a friend of the man who had inspired that look of terror? As he walked back, two bottles grasped in each hand, he saw Augustus watching him. He passed the table where Miranda was being cuddled between the two young fellows, the decision made for him. No way was he going to draw attention to the girl he'd spoken to in Calder Street.

He took his seat at the far side of the table this time, stretching his legs out as if the choice of seat was more comfortable, rather than its real intention, to make Augustus turn away from the other people in the room, especially the woman dressed like a cat.

'Okay, Danny, let's talk about you,' Augustus began, drawing in his chair and leaning towards Daniel. 'Tell me all about yourself.'

Daniel gave a modest grin. 'Not much to tell, really.' He shrugged. 'Didn't do that well back home . . .' He affected a shame-faced expression from which he hoped the man would deduce some criminal past. 'Over here seemed the best way to go . . . make some money . . . you know.'

'Oh, I know, Danny, I know. Back there . . .' Augustus gave a snarl, his lip curling in distaste as if the very thought of Zimbabwe was abhorrent. 'Better to be in the UK. Know your way around, make some money. Yes, sure it was a good choice. For both of us,' he added, staring at Daniel intently.

'I . . . I don't earn that much as a security guard,' Daniel admitted. 'But at least I got Cody cheap enough.'

'He's a great animal,' Augustus agreed. 'So well behaved. You train him yourself?'

Daniel shook his head. 'He was trained properly before I got him,' he answered truthfully.

'Simba's nuts,' Augustus said, laughing and shaking his head. 'Supposed to be a guard dog but he's just a big softy.'

'Do you need a guard dog?' Daniel asked, pretending to look worried. 'I'm sorry, but if that's why you asked me here tonight, I have to tell you, Cody's not for sale.'

'Whoa, man, no way,' Augustus replied, leaning back in his seat. 'Just wanted to do a favour for my brother,' he continued, softening his tone.

'Yeah?'

'Yeah. See, I'm a businessman, Danny, and I need people around me I can trust. Truth is, I've taken a shine to you, bro; maybe you might want to hang with me a bit more, see the sort of business I can put your way?'

He was talking about drugs, of course he was, Daniel realised. And he would play along with him, as if he knew the full score from a dealer's viewpoint. Having been a cop for so long, Daniel was well versed in every aspect of drug dealing and so it would not be difficult to simulate some past experience on the wrong side of the law.

'Good business?' Daniel ventured.

'Oh, very good,' Augustus nodded. 'Quality products.'

Daniel looked again at the man's eyes, thinking again that one of those very products had been sampled before arriving at the café. Not heroin, though, not the stuff that had killed a woman as her tiny baby clung to her breast.

'I don't do them myself,' Daniel said quietly. 'My condition . . .' He hung his head as though ashamed to admit to some sort of weakness.

'Too bad, man. Never mind. We can maybe find us a couple of lady friends tonight, what do you say?'

There were only so many refusals he could offer this man and so Daniel nodded, his eyes bright as though he approved of the idea.

CHAPTER FIFTY-ONE

It was late as the bus drew into the terminus opposite Glasgow Royal Concert Hall, the hiss of brakes and that opening door both welcome sounds. He had chosen a seat at the back, hoping not to be stared at by his fellow passengers, but most had spent the journey from Oban sleeping or listening to something on their phones. Across the aisle a mother gathered her little girl into her arms, hoisting a tote bag onto one shoulder. For a moment, he hesitated, the natural instinct to offer help being pushed down.

He was last to leave the bus, the driver already alighted from his cab and assisting passengers with luggage that had been stowed for the journey. Across the concourse, several inter-city buses were parked, most empty at this hour. He stood, pondering the question he had asked himself ever since leaving the island. Where was he heading? Back home was out of the question. He'd given some thought to catching another bus and arriving in the capital during the wee small hours. And yet, hadn't he been warned about the dangers of appearing there?

Somehow his feet were taking him through familiar streets, offices shuttered against the night, uphill where several restaurants still flooded the pavements with light. A young couple emerged from a place he had frequented as a younger man, hand in hand, eyes only for each other, ignoring him completely. Life had passed him by, he thought with a surge of self-pity, turning to watch as they made their way down West Regent Street towards the heart of the city. He was tired, that was all, he told himself. Tired and out of answers.

Stopping on the corner of Blythswood Square Gardens, he hesitated, looking at the entrance to the big hotel where he had hosted several dignitaries over the years. No, he sighed, looking down at his soiled footwear, not tonight. Just over the hill was the Malmaison. Perhaps that might be a better option.

The night manager smiled as he approached the reception desk.

'I've just arrived in Glasgow,' he told the young man. 'I'd like to book in for tonight, perhaps for longer?'

'Certainly, sir,' the manager replied, the newcomer's travel-weary appearance at odds with his educated accent. And if he found it strange that the new arrival insisted on paying cash, peeling several twenty-pound notes from a roll retrieved from his inside pocket, the night manager was too well trained to say so.

It was a matter of minutes before he found himself

climbing a staircase and being shown a well-furnished single room then handed the key.

'Breakfast is from seven-thirty until nine-thirty,' the young man said, with a smile. 'Enjoy your stay.'

He fumbled in his jacket pocket, drawing out another twenty.

'Here,' he said, handing the tip to the fellow whose eyes widened a fraction.

'Thank you, sir. Sleep well.'

Once the door was closed, he sank down on top of the bed, feeling the soft satin cover slide under his hands. He closed his eyes and sighed. A warm shower then a long, restful sleep.

Outside he could hear shouts of revelry, voices singing as they made their way through the city. Hallowe'en, he realised, remembering the villages he had passed on his journey, carved pumpkins lit up at windows, folk dressed up for this special night. A faint smile crossed his lips as he remembered the dark nights when he'd gone out guising. That's what they'd called it back then, before the American trick or treat lay hold of tradition. He opened his eyes, noticing the telephone by his bedside for the first time.

In moments he had dialled for an outside line, then a number he knew off by heart.

It took a few minutes ringing out, as he guessed it might, until a rather cross voice answered.

'Karen? It's Robert here.'

CHAPTER FIFTY-TWO

They'd been joined by two other men, possibly Colombians, Daniel thought, as Augustus introduced them as Diego and Ezra. It was evident that both of them looked to the tall Zimbabwean as their boss. The subject of finding women was greeted by a cheer from Ezra, the smaller of the pair whose skin was pitted with acne. 'Get me a babe!' he giggled, swaying slightly, his eyes glazed from whatever he'd been taking earlier in the evening. Frequent trips to the men's room and returning with lazy smiles on their faces had made Daniel wonder if Augustus had brought lines of cocaine for his henchmen to enjoy. The three of them were there now, leaving Daniel at their table. Whatever these men were doing, it seemed Augustus intended that all four of them were up for a night of fun that included women. Now on his own, Daniel turned round to see if Miranda was still at the table with those two guys. The music had become more mellow now, perhaps a sign that the management were preparing to close the café. An old Beatles number, 'Michelle', was playing, the guitar accompaniment to Paul McCartney's words creating a warmer atmosphere. And, perhaps, a deliberate attempt to signal the winding down of this party.

Across the city Lorimer would be waiting. And, if everything went according to plan, he might even have a chance to report back to the detective superintendent before this night was over.

'What else do we know about Ncube?' Lorimer asked the man on the other end of the telephone line.

'Jailed in Harare a few years back but released well before the end of his sentence. Just why that happened is unclear, but it coincided with the time Kohi's home was set ablaze,' the man from the security services replied.

'Any chance he would recognise Daniel?'

'I doubt it. The authorities in Harare believe the entire family perished in that fire. There is even a gravestone with Kohi's name on it.'

Lorimer chewed his lower lip for a moment. That particular cover-up reminded him of another man who had disappeared, presumed dead, though the truth about his whereabouts was still to be revealed.

'And the main man in Colombia? Vallejo?'

'We have intelligence now that suggests he was in direct contact with someone in Edinburgh. Possibly even in the heart of the Scottish government.'

'That tallies with what Truesdale's secretary told me,' Lorimer confirmed. 'And so, are we looking at the possibility that Truesdale's been spirited away to South America?'

There was a pause during which Lorimer watched the lights from the nearby motorway, most people going about their lawful business, unaware of the deeper and darker elements that ran through this city.

'There is nothing that we can find to show he has left Scotland,' the man said slowly, as if measuring each word.

'But that doesn't mean he hasn't?' Lorimer asked.

'True, but our people have been extremely diligent in keeping watch in that part of the world. It is our belief that Robert Truesdale has either been hiding out in some remote part of the country or . . .'

'Or he's dead, is that what you think?'

He heard a sigh on the other end of the line. 'Hard to tell when a body hasn't turned up, wouldn't you say?'

'So, meantime we try to break into this gang, find the source of these drugs and put a stop to whatever Robert Truesdale was doing?' Lorimer asked. Yet he was not happy, his own words sounding less than convincing. 'It still doesn't equate with a man who was crusading to legalise drugs, though, does it?'

'Robert! What on earth are you doing calling me at this hour of the night!'

Karen Douglas sounded so affronted that, for the first time in many weeks, Robert Truesdale began to smile. He could imagine his neighbour standing by the phone in her hallway, clutching a dressing gown around her body, hair in curlers. He remembered seeing her once or twice when she had lifted milk bottles from her doorstep as he'd set off for an early train to Edinburgh.

'Karen,' he began. 'I need your help.'

'The police have been here, Robert,' Karen said, a frosty edge to her tone. 'What on earth have you got mixed up in?'

'It's a long story, my dear,' he sighed. 'But you see, Karen, you are the only person I can trust. Is it possible you could drive into the city and meet me?'

CHAPTER FIFTY-THREE

'Where are we going?' Daniel asked, forcing an eagerness into his tone.

'Club I know, bro.' Augustus grinned. 'No worries, we'll be made very welcome, yes, boys?' He turned to Ezra and Diego who were close behind them.

'Yeah, man, night's just beginning,' Ezra giggled, twirling on the pavement as if to demonstrate his dance moves.

'Is it far?'

'You're driving us, Danny,' Augustus told him, clapping a hand on Daniel's shoulder. 'Motor not far from here.'

So, was that to be his role tonight? Given his pretence of being on prescription drugs, was he their designated driver? That suited him fine, Daniel thought as they turned off a side street into a darkened area between the shadowy tenements. Perhaps at one time it had been a place to stable horses, the wide opening leading to a patch of flat ground where four lock-ups had been built side by side. He watched as Augustus took out a bunch of keys and inserted one into a heavy padlock. The door slid open smoothly and Daniel stepped forward.

There, inside the lock-up, was a blue BMW. And, as he drew closer. Daniel Kohi could see that the big car was a 7 Series.

It had to be the same one that the boy had seen from his bedroom window!

'Like my wheels, bro?' Augustus asked, watching Daniel's expression.

'Wow!' Daniel replied, feigning admiration. 'And I get to drive this beauty?' He turned to smile at the taller man who tossed him a smaller set of keys.

'Let's go,' Augustus told him.

Daniel drove slowly around the corner and back down towards Offshore, listening as Augustus described the location of the Bluegrass club.

They were a few yards past the café when he caught sight of Miranda near the bridge across the River Kelvin, arm in arm with one of the guys at her table, her kitten ears bobbing under the lamplight as she walked beside him.

'Stop!' Augustus yelled out and Daniel pulled into the side, the car jerking as he braked sharply.

'That woman. Get her!' he commanded, turning to the two Colombians.

'Leave it to me,' Daniel shouted eagerly, pushing out of the driver's seat before the others had time to unfasten their seat belts.

He began to sprint towards the pair who were only yards ahead.

'Hey, you, want to have a word! That's my girl you're with!' he yelled, making them both turn to see him.

The man gave Daniel a look of horror then looked back to see the other men emerging from the car. He dropped Miranda's hand swiftly and began to run, leaving her staring at Daniel.

In moments, she'd taken off her high heels then began to run as fast as she could, barefooted.

Her companion was well ahead, sprinting towards Woodlands Road, no thought of the girl he'd clearly abandoned.

Daniel made to follow Miranda but she suddenly disappeared to his left and vanished into the gloom. He skidded to a halt then saw the steep staircase leading to a dark tunnel.

He could hear the faint sound of her feet as the woman fled into the night, his own boots thudding against each step.

Miranda turned just once as she made her way across a patch of waste ground and Daniel could see the raw terror in her eyes as she saw how close he was. She let out a cry and he saw her stumble. Then he was by her side, catching her arm and gripping it tightly.

'You!' she gasped.

'Keep quiet. I won't hurt you,' Daniel whispered. 'Just do what I tell you and it'll be all right.'

'But you're with *him*,' Miranda said in a shocked voice, struggling in Daniel's grasp.

'Just play nice and I'll make sure you're not hurt, okay?' he said softly.

'Got myself a kitty cat!' he called out as the others drew closer.

He could see Augustus standing on the bridge above

them, arms folded, grinning as Daniel sought to march the woman back towards the stairs.

'Well, look what we have here.' He grinned, gazing down at the woman who had finally stopped struggling in Daniel's grip. 'Get her into the car. We're going for a little ride.'

Daniel's heart was pounding as he drove towards the city centre, Augustus murmuring directions. He repeated each one, glancing at the man in the passenger seat for confirmation. Could his words be heard? And were there listening ears plotting their route right now, preparing to intercept them whenever they had arrived at their destination?

Behind him Ezra and Diego were having a bit of fun with Miranda, teasing her verbally, though careful not to touch what they perceived as the boss's goods. The woman had kept silent till now, whether from pure fright or to minimise whatever torments lay ahead. But then Daniel could hear muffled sobs, a sound that wrenched his heart.

'He's driving through the centre of the city,' one of the officers said as he sat in front of the computer screen, plotting the BMW's course. 'Looks like they're heading for the motorway.'

'Alert all units,' Lorimer commanded. 'But keep a distance from them until I say otherwise.'

'Left lane, looks like the turn-off to Stirling and Kincardine,' the officer told those who were listening on their own lines. 'Yes, that's it, taking the filter now.'

Lorimer watched as the screen showed the tiny dot on the road, knowing that Daniel Kohi was driving the same car that had been seen by a schoolboy out in Strathblane, seated beside one of the most wanted drug dealers in Scotland. So far, their plan was working and perhaps Daniel was leading them to the very place where Ncube had stored the heroin that was coming in from Colombia.

'Not going clubbing after all?' Daniel asked, smiling at the man next to him.

'Keep driving,' Augustus ordered. 'Take the 806 at junction 3. Okay? Slow down when I tell you.'

That would be a *no* then, Daniel thought, guessing that bypassing the city centre was something to do with having taken the woman captive.

'She going to be our bit of fun?' Daniel chuckled.

'Wait and see, bro. Just wait and see,' Ncube replied, reaching out to turn on some music.

Daniel glanced as he drove, watching the man close his eyes, his head swaying to a sonorous beat. How far gone was he on the dope he'd taken earlier? And what plans did he have for the woman he no longer heard crying quietly in the back of the car?

'Quarry taking the road towards Chryston and Stepps,' the officer said. 'Slowing down now. It's a country road till it merges with the old motorway. Okay, here they go, heading past Crowwood House hotel. Taking a right now and over the hill.'

Lorimer peered over the man's shoulder. He'd taken that country road once or twice, heading towards Gartcosh and the Scottish Crime Campus.

'Slowing down now. Turning into . . .' he hesitated for just a fraction before adding, 'abandoned farm buildings.'

There was a collective silence as each officer held their breath until the man in charge of the traffic screen uttered, 'They've stopped.'

Lorimer stood up, his teeth clenched. They knew Morrison's stash out in Rutherglen was only a small part of what they hoped to find. So, was this where Ncube had stored the bulk of contaminated heroin that had killed Angelika Mahbed? And had the unexpected presence of her former flatmate diverted these men from their original intention of spending several hours clubbing in Glasgow? Sometimes, he thought to himself, a little bit of luck was all that was needed and, perhaps, as 1 November began, whatever spirits now ruled All Saints' Day might be on their side.

CHAPTER FIFTY-FOUR

Karen Douglas pulled to a halt by the side of Blythswood Square Gardens. She switched off the engine and killed the lights then undid her seat belt. Robert had said he would be waiting for her here but so far, she could discern no human presence.

A movement to her right made her jump, but it was only an urban fox, trotting across the grass between the leafless trees, apparently unconcerned by the arrival of a car. She watched its progress, marvelling at the creature's boldness. This was his territory, Karen told herself, and it was she who was the intruder, a part of the city claimed as the fox's nightly domain.

A knock on her window, then the passenger door was opened and there he was, sitting beside her. The sight of him, scruffy-bearded and wild-eyed, made her gasp.

'My God, Robert! What on earth! You look like some sort of tramp,' Karen told him, her hand to her mouth. 'Where have you been? Don't you know half the country's been looking for you?' she demanded in a querulous tone.

'I do now,' he replied quietly. 'And it's a long story. Can we drive somewhere, Karen? This is a bit too public, even at this time of the night.'

'Night? It's almost two in the morning!' Karen replied, in icy tones. Then, as if noticing something in his eyes for the first time, she placed her gloved hand on his. 'I'm sorry. Yes, you're right. We'll go somewhere safe,' she said. 'Then you can tell me everything.'

The spot where they had spent hours together as children had seemed the obvious place to go, the wooden shelter by the pond safe from any prying eyes. It was far enough from any main roads to avoid curiosity from a passer-by, should there be any at this hour of the night, and Karen had parked her car around a corner, tucked away from sight.

She put her hand out and clasped his fingers. It wasn't fair, she thought. Here was a man who had wanted to make a difference but had been hounded out by forces that had proved stronger than his own resolve. Whatever her own political beliefs – and she and Robert had argued many a time from opposing viewpoints – the man whom she had known since childhood was worthy of the greatest sympathy as a broken human being. In the end it had not been the nastiness of social media threats that had finished him but something altogether different.

'What will you do now?' she asked, taking his arm and drawing closer, her instinct to shelter her friend stronger than the dismay she felt on hearing his story.

'I don't know,' he whispered huskily. 'Sometimes when I was on that island I felt as if I wanted to fly away with the seabirds, follow them over the cliff and disappear into the water.'

Karen blinked back tears. To think that he had descended into such an abyss of despair, believing that his existence no longer mattered. Yet, he had left his place of refuge, come back home, to her. That was not something to be ignored, surely?

'Do you really believe all that they told you? Now that you know what happened to your house-sitter?'

She watched as he shook his head, the unfamiliar beard and longer hair making Robert Truesdale look like another person, not the capable politician who had enjoyed the cut and thrust of televised debate or fearlessly proclaimed his opinions in Holyrood. He had changed, something broken in his spirit.

'You've still got me, Robert,' she said quietly. 'And you know I'll stand by you, no matter what happens.'

'It's finished, Karen. I can't pretend these things haven't happened and that it was not my fault that another man died when it should have been me.'

'You won't return to politics?'

He was silent for a moment then shook his head. 'No. I think I meant what I said as I wrote my letter of resignation.'

'But,' she hesitated, recalling something she'd read in the *Gazette*, 'the First Minister claims he never received it.'

'I left it in my briefcase.' He turned to her, mouth open. 'Oh, dear God!' He covered his face with his hands. 'It was in the car . . . it . . .'

Karen felt his body shaking with sobs as she took him in her arms and shushed him as if he were that little boy

378

she had once played with, crying after falling on gravel and skinning his knees.

'It'll be all right, Robert, hush, dear. Let's get you home then we can decide what to do in the morning.'

CHAPTER FIFTY-FIVE

Lorimer needed to be there. It was no longer enough to sit and watch from the safety of the room where a computer screen had followed Daniel's tracking device, something he had secreted under his clothing. If he was correct, then there were already armed officers waiting for his call, not so very far behind the BMW's trail.

Daniel was unarmed, all his kit stowed in the locker back at Aikenhead Road, and he would need all his wits about him to maintain the façade he had so far managed to create.

Lorimer thought for a moment about Maggie, Molly and Netta Gordon, women who would be distraught should anything happen to their friend, and most of all Jeanette Kohi back in Zimbabwe. He had guessed that his DS's relationship with Daniel had moved on recently and fervently hoped that after tonight he would not be dashing the tall blonde woman's hopes. Sometimes he wished he could send up a prayer, as Maggie often did, asking for protection for those she cared about.

He was in the Lexus and drawing away from the police headquarters when he noticed the moon sliding out from behind a cloud. Then a star sparked overhead, blinking from light years away, almost like a promise that whatever was happening down below, there was a certainty somewhere in the heavens.

His lips moved in a silent prayer to whoever might be listening, his own doubts put aside for the moment.

'Get her out,' Ncube snarled as Daniel pulled up at the back of a cluster of deserted farm buildings. Did the man in the passenger seat mean to harm Miranda? Had he brought them there to use her for sex? The woman was a known street worker, but he doubted if she would want to be the victim of gang rape. And, if he refused to participate . . .? He swallowed down the bitter taste of phlegm at the thought of such consequences.

'In here,' Ncube commanded, pointing to the back of a barn. Daniel hesitated as the Colombians frogmarched the struggling woman towards a door that was bolted top and bottom as well as secured by a heavy padlock and chain.

Daniel held Miranda's arm, shooting her a warning glance as Ncube and the others forged ahead, pushing aside the door. Then, as he entered, Diego returned, closing it behind them, a dull sound shutting out the night.

A bright light overhead illuminated the area, boxes on either side packed to the rafters wrapped in dark green heavy plastic, brightly coloured labels their only sign of identification. A red tractor sat at the far end of the barn, an

381

innocent enough item for a farm building. If he was right, then Daniel knew he was looking at the main depot where hard drugs were stored after being brought into Scotland by boat. Someone would have had to unload the cargo and bring it here, possibly disguised as normal packages on the back of a trailer. Hidden in plain sight, he thought, imagining the tractor being driven through the country lanes to its destination, no one questioning what it was delivering to this isolated outpost.

'You first!'

Daniel heard Augustus call out and looked up to see the man grinning at him.

'Danny, a reward for your services,' Augustus laughed. 'Pity about your meds, but there are some things we can all enjoy!' he continued, motioning Daniel to bring Miranda forward, confirming Daniel's worst fears.

And it was not only the fact he had to somehow create a distraction, he also needed to avoid discovery of the wires beneath his jersey.

He grinned back, desperate to maintain the façade of helpful new friend and gave Miranda a shove.

'Think she needs to . . . er . . . is there a toilet . . .?' He put a hand to his nose, feigning disgust at an imaginary smell off the woman, who had suddenly stopped resisting. Had she twigged that he was playing for time?

'In there.' Augustus pointed to a small door beyond the tractor. 'Stay with her in case she does anything stupid, Danny. Then we can all have some pleasure with her.'

The Colombians gave a cheer, uttering some lewd remarks in Spanish. He did not need to have the translation, the men's jeering tone sufficient for Daniel to interpret their meaning.

He marched Miranda to the far end of the barn, taking quick glances at the walls of packages, noting the labels were also in Spanish. Colombian drugs, then, he thought.

'In here.' He shoved the woman into the tiny cubicle and shut the door behind him to more roars of laughter and ribaldry from the other men.

'Take your time,' Daniel whispered. 'I think there will be a team of police officers here very soon.'

Miranda sat on the lavatory eyes wide with astonishment. 'You ...?'

'Shh.' Daniel laid a finger to his lips. 'Nothing is ever what it seems. Remember that. I'll try my best to get us both out of here safely.'

He was asleep now. Karen gazed down on the man in her bed, a fond smile on her lips. She should have given him the guest bedroom, of course, but something had prompted her to usher her old friend in here instead. Had she dreamed of him sharing her bed? Perhaps, a long time ago, but that was when they had both been young and foolish, before taking their separate paths in life.

She thought over the story Robert had told her, his guilt over the death of an innocent man darkening his features. But was he really as guilty as he believed? Paranoid, certainly, and suffering some sort of breakdown that had been exacerbated by his isolation on that island. *I trust you*, Robert had said, holding her hand and gazing up at Karen as she'd folded the sheet up to his chin. But what sort of trust was that? Trust to conceal him from the world?

Or trust to do the right thing as she saw fit?

Karen sat on a chair at the far end of her bedroom, listening to Robert's breathing become deep and even. He would sleep for hours, now, she thought. Closing her eyes, she thought about another man, one with piercing blue eyes that had regarded her intently yet whose voice had given her reason to feel that this was a man who would also do whatever was right. A man of authority who had left his number, offering Karen Douglas a chance to reach out for help.

And, if ever she needed help, surely it was now?

Rising silently from her chair, Karen slipped out of the room and headed to the kitchen where her mobile phone had been plugged in for the night.

There was only so much time before the three men would haul the woman out of the cubicle, so Daniel motioned for Miranda to get up, once she really had used the toilet, pulling the flush to indicate to those waiting outside that she'd finished.

'Sorry,' Daniel said, his whisper drowned by the sound of water cascading round the bowl. Then, gripping both her arms, he forced her out again into the middle of the barn.

The three men gave a cheer, hallooing and ululating as Daniel forced Miranda onto her knees. He made to undo his trousers, but a hand on his shoulder stopped him. Looking up he saw Augustus smiling at him, a strange expression in his eyes. Was the man simply drugged up, or was he beginning to suspect that his new-found friend was not all that he seemed?

'Strip!' Augustus commanded and the others took up the chant, clapping their hands and repeating the word over and over.

Perhaps it was Daniel's momentary hesitation that did it, but suddenly he found himself being propelled across the room, Ncube's hands on his shoulders.

For a moment he gasped. Then, before he had time to struggle, in one swift motion Ncube had yanked off his jersey, revealing the wires attached to Daniel's dark skin.

Silence fell on them both for a moment. Then, with a roar, Augustus Ncube launched himself at Daniel.

At once, Daniel dodged out of the way, the taller man crashing against the plastic-covered packages. He saw Miranda scramble to her feet and head back towards the toilet, other means of escape closed to them both.

With a growl that seemed to come from an animal rather than a human throat, Ncube turned and faced Daniel once more.

He sensed the other two coming towards him, their pursuit of the woman forgotten.

Then everyone seemed to freeze in a tableau as the faint but unmistakable sound of a siren approached.

'Get him!' Ncube roared, rubbing his shoulders where he had fallen against the hard wall of packaging.

Daniel turned, seeing the two Colombians begin to circle, their bodies bent menacingly towards him, fists clenched.

There was only one way out and Daniel decided to take it, making a dash towards the barn door, and grabbing the chain. If he could yank it open even a fraction ...

The two-tone sounds were growing closer and soon there

385

would be back-up, he told himself, grasping the chain and hauling it sideways with all his might.

For a split second he thought nothing was happening, then, with a creak, it began to slide open.

He burst through the gap and began to run.

The night air was cold on his face, the smell of wet grass pungent in his nostrils.

A few more paces and he might make it to the road, the police siren louder than ever.

The shot, when it came, seemed to split the night with its loud, resonant boom.

Daniel stumbled, wondering for a moment why he was falling.

Then blackness took him to a place he would remember no more.

CHAPTER FIFTY-SIX

Questions for a man who was not dead, after all, Lorimer thought as he sat opposite Robert Truesdale for the first time.

In some ways, the fugitive appeared more like O'Hare before the Irishman's transformation, the beard and haggard look reminding Lorimer of the old photograph. He was sitting, head down, hands clasping and unclasping, evidently ill at ease to be faced with the authorities he had tried so hard to evade.

'Tell me about James O'Hare,' Lorimer began. 'How did you come to meet him?'

Was that a sigh or a deep intake of breath?

Truesdale looked up eventually, then, as if Lorimer's gaze blinded him, he averted his eyes. Or was that perhaps a sign of his inner guilt?

'I met James at the conference,' Truesdale began. 'It was when I had succeeded in obtaining sponsorship for the initiative he belonged to.'

'And when was that?'

Truesdale paused to think, drawing his dark brows together. 'Towards the end of September,' he said. 'It was the start of a new year in parliament and the sponsorship was to last for three years. A real coup. Or so we thought at the time,' he added bitterly.

'You are a major shareholder in that particular company. Didn't you see that as a conflict of interest?'

'Me?' Truesdale gasped. 'No, that's completely wrong,' he said. 'Who told you that?'

Lorimer shook his head for a moment, giving nothing away. But Truesdale was speaking again.

'When I heard the report about the drugs haul . . .' Robert Truesdale spread his hands wide as though to emphasise that he had no foreknowledge of that hiding place.

Was that really true? The news of last night's raid and the arrest of a Colombian drug gang had been the main head-line in every news desk in the country, Augustus Ncube's image splashed across the internet. Had Robert Truesdale known nothing of the business between the crime mob, its money-laundering and drug-dealing activities in Scotland bringing death and despair to these shores? The pharma-ceutical business had been a useful front for the Colombian cartel, its apparent benevolent sponsorship of good causes even bringing praise from Scottish Enterprise. The crash of that company was imminent and the fallout would reflect badly on the present administration in Holyrood.

'You are claiming to have had no knowledge that the company sponsoring this drugs rehabilitation initiative was actually part of a Colombian network, is that correct?'

Another pause, then a definite sigh as Truesdale ran a hand through his greying hair.

'I ... there was nothing to connect me to anything other than the pharmaceutical company. My only involvement was to persuade them to sponsor the programme,' he said. 'I knew sod all about any illicit drugs or a Colombian cartel. If that's what you think, then you've got the wrong end of the stick. As a long-standing supporter of drugs rehabilitation, I was the obvious person to approach for a company looking to sponsor this particular area. Don't you see?' he asked, his voice cracking under the strain. 'I've been made to look like a ... a ... as if I knew what was happening ... I didn't.'

'And yet you were waiting for a boat to take you off the island of Colonsay, manned by a Colombian crew, isn't that correct?'

Truesdale hung his head and nodded. 'I was told to wait for them. Yes. But I had no inkling that they were doing anything more than protecting me from what I'd been told ...' He shook his head as if in disbelief at his own credulity. 'A hitman, that's what they said. And not just one quick bullet in the back of the head,' he added, wincing visibly. 'I'm not a brave man, Lorimer. I can handle the cut and thrust of politics as easily as the next man or woman, take the media storm as part and parcel of what it means to stick your head above the parapet ...'

Lorimer listened, hearing the stock phrases issue from the former MSP's lips. Perhaps he was finding it hard to speak in anything other than clichés, words deserting him after the enforced solitude of the remote island. Did he trust him any more than he trusted any politician who par-roted a particular party line? There was something about this man, however, that made him think carefully. Things were never always what they seemed and he had a feeling that Truesdale may well have been a victim rather than a perpetrator of vice.

'Let's get back to O'Hare,' he said at last, leaning back thoughtfully. 'We have a witness who overheard you asking him to look after your cat. Tell me about that.'

'Is she all right?' Truesdale asked. 'Sally. My cat. Karen didn't seem to know.'

'Your cat is fine,' Lorimer told him. 'Tell us about James O'Hare and why he was in your home.'

'It was Malcolm who spotted the similarity,' Truesdale began. 'Said he could have been my long-lost brother. I never had any siblings. Karen and I were more like brother and sister when we were young.' He looked away then, his eyes glazing over.

Truesdale was going off at a tangent, Lorimer realised, possibly the effect of mental anguish and sheer exhaustion making it hard for him to concentrate.

'You asked him for a favour?'

Again, a nod.

'Please speak for the recording,' Lorimer reminded him.

'Yes, I asked James O'Hare a very big favour. I knew once I moved to the new house that I was going away for a while, how long exactly I hadn't been told. He agreed to house-sit for me and look after Sally. It was a bit of a joke that there was a physical resemblance but I honestly didn't think he would come to any harm. You must believe me!' he exclaimed, leaning towards Lorimer, earnest fists clenched on the table.

'I wanted a new start in the village, away from the city, away from the press. And then ... well ... as soon as the house move was completed, I was advised to leave straight away, not to let anyone see me.'

'You asked Karen Douglas to arrange for the cleaning lady, Mrs Jardine, to come?'

'Yes. She was meant to be there when James was out. I didn't want anyone to talk to him. They'd have twigged it wasn't me as soon as he opened his mouth.'

'So, your intention was to put another man in your place? Even though you had been warned about being a target for an assassination?'

'Nobody knew where I was,' Truesdale insisted. 'It even took your lot a while to figure that out. I was sure James would be all right. I was told he'd be taken care of ...' He bit his lip and looked down.

'Who gave you that assurance, Robert?' Lorimer asked.

The man raised his head and looked straight at the detective superintendent, his eyes filled with tears. 'I can't do that,' he whispered. 'And ... nobody would believe me.' He dropped his gaze again.

Was he hearing the truth, part of a truth, or a tissue of lies? Lorimer wondered. This man had had enough time to create a cover story whilst waiting to be whisked off the island by Colombian drug dealers. And yet, here he was, returning to Glasgow of his own volition, seeking out a friend he had known since childhood rather than the protection of his paymasters. Malcolm Hinchliffe had been fairly explicit about Truesdale's links with Colombians, he reminded himself. So, why had Truesdale not waited for that boat? Or sought out refuge with Ncube and his cohorts?

He's an innocent man, caught up in something that's too big for him, Karen Douglas had told him when she had called. Was she right? And, had Hinchliffe misinterpreted those letters and documents? He had only the secretary's word for the existence of that letter and the travel brochures secreted in his boss's desk, after all. Yet it had been Malcolm Hinchliffe who had drawn attention to the fact that the burned body with its silver chain and cross was a total discrepancy when he had been asked to identify the bomb victim.

'James was happy to stay,' Truesdale went on, his eyes staring into space. 'He liked cats. Said he wanted one of his own when he and his girlfriend found a place to stay. I gave him loads of cash, of course. They'd told me to take it all with me, all the money I had, in little rolls.' He looked across at Lorimer as if seeing him for the first time. 'It doesn't look an awful lot when they're all rolled up like that and stashed away in a rucksack. And to think it could all have been burned to a cinder if it had been me in that car. Never did have much use for a lot of money,' he added vaguely.

He was losing him now, Lorimer realised. Either Truesdale was experiencing some sort of breakdown, or his mind was disassociating itself from the reality of what had happened. It was time to end this conversation, make sure that Truesdale was taken to a place of safety where doctors could monitor his health and officers keep a close watch on him.

'Did he tell you he had a baby?' Truesdale turned to

Lorimer as they led him out of the room. 'Romanian girl, the mother was. She would have liked the bungalow, James said. I'd have given him more money if I'd known ...'

He didn't know anything until he read that newspaper, Karen Douglas had told him, and, watching the man stumble away from him, Lorimer began to wonder exactly who had filled Truesdale's mind with ideas about fleeing from certain death. If Robert Truesdale had been certain that the Irishman was not only safe in his village home but that he had been giving him a generous amount of money plus a taste of middle-class life, then it made sense that the shocking discovery of O'Hare's death had affected his sanity.

William Lorimer was experienced enough to tell truth from lies, most of the time. And, right now, as he watched the man being helped into a waiting ambulance, he felt that there had been a genuine conspiracy to get rid of the MSP. Had someone used Truesdale's close ties to the pharmaceutical sponsor to smear his name? After all, why would a man who had campaigned tirelessly to legalise drugs, the very thing that would be anathema to the cartels, emerge as their leader? Had his crusade been merely a front to disguise his real intentions? No, Lorimer decided, he'd met hard men before who had been gang bosses and Robert Truesdale simply did not fit the type. But was there really a type? Or had he been inured to gangsters like Jack Gallagher over the years?

He stood at the window of the room as the ambulance circled away, thinking of another man who had been taken away several hours before. Ncube and the others were in custody. They could wait a while longer before he sat and asked the sorts of questions that might lead him to the truth behind Robert Truesdale's disappearance and the bomb that might have been meant for him.

CHAPTER FIFTY-SEVEN

Daniel blinked then opened his eyes. All around him was blue, with light filtering from somewhere on his right. He was lying on his back, one arm stretched over a cool white sheet, a dull ache somewhere in the back of his head, a metallic taste in his mouth.

A draught of cold air came from beyond this blue tent he was lying in, then the unmistakable song of a bird outside. Lorimer would know what that was, Daniel Kohi told himself. And then the memories began to form shapes inside his head.

A woman screaming, fire raging, the smell of burning . . . No, he would not go there. It was important to focus on more recent memories, untangle them from the traumatic events back in Zimbabwe.

Instead, he tried to remember the blue car, the men who had taken him to that dark barn far from the city centre. There was a moment when he saw a flicker of something, the eyes of a man boring down on him . . . but then, nothing. Something had happened, though, to bring him to this place. A hospital, he decided, the blue transforming into drawn curtains around his bed, light from a window dappling against the ceiling. He tried to move but something stopped him, as if a heavy weight was pinning him to the bed.

Daniel looked at his right hand where a cannula dripped fluids from a tube, its origin out of his line of sight. There was a faint mechanical beat behind his head, monitors measuring whatever was going on inside his body. He heard the sound of a door opening beyond the blue curtain and then it parted and she was standing there, gazing down at him.

'Daniel, you're awake,' Molly whispered, drawing closer and laying a cool hand against his cheek.

'What happened?' Daniel asked, his voice husky as though something had been forced down his throat. 'I can't remember...'

He saw her smile then, her face radiant as she leaned towards him. 'Thank God you're all right,' she said. 'Maybe it's no bad thing your memory is failing you for a change.'

And then she told him.

Miranda felt clean for the first time in weeks, her body warm from the shower and the fresh clothes the woman officer had given her smelling of something floral and wholesome. She'd slept well, too, the bed in the hotel room comfortable, the police officer guarding her door allowing the young woman a feeling of security. Now she was in the back of a police car, heading for the police office in Helen Street where Detective Superintendent Lorimer was waiting for her.

'He's a decent bloke,' the woman beside her said. 'We all think highly of him and he's never one to prejudge anyone.'

'You mean he doesn't care I'm on the game?' Miranda asked cynically.

'That's right,' her companion agreed. 'And neither do we.' She nodded at the driver and the other officer in the front of the car. 'We're trained to have a duty of care for every single citizen,' she said firmly. 'Your rescuer knows all about that.'

'I guessed he was a cop. Eventually.'

She looked out of the window, seeing the streets where she had grown up, old tenements replaced by new houses and apartments, trees and shrubs softening the edges. The city had undergone a transformation since she'd first played here, an innocent wee girl until life had taken a bitter turn and she'd resorted to selling her body rather than have it used by those who should have cared for her. A duty of care? The phrase made Miranda's lip curl, thinking of the men in her family who had driven her to this way of life.

'Here we are.' The officer gave her a nudge as they slowed down and turned into a car park next to the police station, its blue and white chequered sign looming above. 'Just tell him the truth. He'll respect you all the more for that.'

Lorimer rose from behind his desk and came forward as the family liaison officer brought Miranda into his office.

'Hello, I'm Detective Superintendent Lorimer. How are you?' he asked, taking her hand and guiding her to a comfortable chair. 'This is my colleague, DS Giles.'

'Hi, Miranda.' Davie Giles's soft voice and friendly smile made the woman look at him with interest. How often had she been in the company of decent men who regarded her as a whole person, not merely a sex object? Lorimer wondered.

'Have you had breakfast? Or can we offer you some coffee?' Giles asked.

Lorimer saw her swallow and shake her head.

'I'm all right, thanks,' she replied, sitting gingerly on the edge of the chair.

'Miranda . . .?'

'Miranda Morrison,' she whispered, looking up at him fearfully.

'Any relation to . . .?'

'He's my uncle,' she shot back, looking from one man to the other. 'Didn't the wee bastard tell you that?'

Lorimer shook his head. That had not been one of the many things Morrison had let slip in their previous interviews and he wondered why. No love lost between this skinny young woman and the older man. And he could imagine a scenario where she had been exploited early on by the men in her family. That was a story for another day, a different officer.

'Last night wasn't the first time you had met Daniel?'

'The African cop with the Glasgow accent? Naw.' She chewed her lip. 'He came to Calder Street. Thought he wis from the social, so I did. Asking all about the baby. But he's one of yours?'

Lorimer nodded. 'Yes, he is. And you were lucky he was there when Ncube and his mates picked you up.'

'Aye,' she said softly. 'Been in a few jams in my time but I thought that wis it . . . know whit I mean?'

Lorimer watched as she crossed her legs, one foot jiggling nervously.

'I want you to tell us everything you know about Angelika Mahbed and what went on in that flat.'

'Where do I start?' Miranda gave a short laugh. 'I wis in charge of the younger ones. Romanian lassies that came tae find work and ended up on the game. You know whit goes on, right?' She glanced at Giles and Lorimer in turn.

Lorimer nodded. They both knew of such things from bitter past experience, rescuing young women and girls from what was no more than slavery in some cases.

'Angelika got hooked dead quickly. Needed her fixes and was on that cycle all the time I knew her until . . .' She broke off.

'Yes?'

'She met Paddy. The Irishman,' she began. 'Fell for each other, so they did. And then she got pregnant, silly cow. We could've helped her get rid of it but, oh no, Angelika was having none of it. Said she'd turned a corner, found a good fella who wis gonnae take care of her.'

'Did she come off the drugs?'

'Aye, she did,' Miranda admitted. 'Right up till she had the wean. And then, jist when I thought she might do a moonlight, move in with that Paddy, she goes off and . . . well . . .' Miranda looked across at Giles this time. 'She overdosed, didn't she?'

'I'm sorry, but that is exactly what the pathologist concluded from her post-mortem,' he replied.

'Tell me about that night, Miranda,' Lorimer continued. 'Can you remember any details? Who took her away from the flat? And do you know why she took the baby with her?'

There was a momentary silence, the woman hanging her head, her sleek dark hair falling in two curtains either side of her pale face. Then, a sigh dredged up from whatever depths she was fathoming.

'It wis Frankie Fleming gied her the drugs,' Miranda said at last. 'He said it wis something tae make her feel better. A new brand that wouldnae hurt her or the kid. Loada nonsense, of course. I couldnae say anything. Frankie would hae done me right there and then. It wis Frankie took her doon the stairs. I tried tae take him off her but she wouldnae let go of the bairn, no way. So I flung a blanket ower her shoulders. It wis a rotten night,' she whispered, closing her eyes as if to banish the memory. 'But I don't know who was waiting for them in that big blue car.'

Angelika was the last link to O'Hare, of course, and the reason the two men had lured her away, deliberately giving her a lethal dose. Fleming and Ncube had no doubt left her there to die with her child, Lorimer thought, recalling Daniel's description of finding the dead woman, the baby's cry alerting him to her body. Had one of those men covered them with that blanket? Or had Angelika drawn it over their faces as she breathed her last?

'Hey, Mr Lorimer. Can I have a fag?'

He smiled at her then and rose from his chair. 'Come on downstairs. There's no smoking allowed inside. But maybe we can all go for a walk?'

Later, he would tell Maggie about this young woman's plight and her despair at her friend's inability to stay off the heroin. The irony of James O'Hare giving his lover money to help her escape from her way of life was perhaps the saddest part of it all. Angelika had stayed clean for so many months then been destroyed by the drugs brought into Scotland by the Colombian gang. Just when O'Hare had seen the possibility of a new life for them all. No happy endings, he'd tell Maggie. Though the little boy might find safety with his aunty in Ireland, if all went to plan.

CHAPTER FIFTY-EIGHT

'I see Sir Henry Hinchliffe has died,' Davie Giles remarked as he walked beside Lorimer after they had seen Miranda Morrison safely on her way.

'Any relation to Malcolm Hinchliffe?' Lorimer asked.

'Yes, his father,' Giles replied. 'Malcolm's the only son and inherits the whole estate. It's near Peebles. A place called Woodend. It was in the news. Guess he'll be a rich man now, no need to work for his living at Holyrood, especially after the sensation about his boss.'

'That's interesting,' Lorimer said slowly. 'Perhaps we might pay Malcolm Hinchliffe a visit. There are things I'd like to ask him, things he maybe remembers about Truesdale that he hasn't mentioned.'

It was Malcolm who'd first noticed the resemblance, Truesdale had said. Was his refusal to name his so-called protectors anything to do with the parliamentary secretary himself? And was it Hinchliffe who had chosen that car from the Honda dealership?

Lorimer gritted his teeth. Had he been blindsided by the man's apparent willingness to divulge Truesdale's secret dealings with the Colombian cartel? And by his help with querying the identity of the burned body? What if someone had been planning all along to discredit the MSP, put him in the frame not only for killing an innocent man in the most horrible way but also naming him as the boss behind the crime group in Scotland that liaised with crime boss Vallejo, in Colombia?

' "The evil that men do . . ." ' he quoted softly.

'Julius Caesar,' Giles responded. ' "The evil that men do lives after them. The good is oft interred with their bones." We learned that in school.'

'Shakespeare had a lot to say about man's inhumanity to man,' Lorimer agreed. 'I wonder what he might have said about this particular case?'

The journey from Glasgow was shorter than he had anticipated, the ring road around Edinburgh quieter after the rush hour traffic. It reminded William Lorimer of previous trips when he had been investigating the murders of mainly retired police officers, his own former boss amongst them. This evening it was dry and the wind had dropped, November beginning to turn into winter. Soon there would be the first frosts as the nights drew in, each day shorter as the year turned to the darkest day of all.

'I'm curious about this estate near Peebles that you looked up,' Lorimer remarked. 'What else can you tell me about it?'

'Oh, it seems to be an old family home set in acres of land, farmed by several generations of Hinchliffes, its stewards passing on the precious artefacts that were said to abound in the Victorian mansion. You'll like it if it's full of artworks,' Giles grinned. 'The late incumbent was a keen racing man, the Borders courses, like Kelso, particular favourites. Rumour had it that he had inherited a gambling problem from Malcolm Hinchliffe's grandfather.'

'In that case, I wonder just how wealthy Hinchliffe might be after his father's estate is wound up.'

'Maybe he took that job in Holyrood knowing that he had to earn his own living?'

'Hm, maybe,' Lorimer mused as they drove on through the darkness. 'Perhaps he'll have a hard task to run the place if money's tight.'

Follow the money, Solly Brightman had said on more than one occasion, quoting a famous film, and that particular action was in progress even as Lorimer and Giles drove south, others in the Major Incident Team busy digging into Hinchliffe's financial activities. Never leave anything to chance, he had told his junior officers; small details are important and can sometimes be the key to solving a case. Would there be any details to be found here? he asked himself, leaving the dark country road behind and turning down a steep driveway.

The house, when he reached it, was an impressive neo-classical building, towers and turrets of the sort favoured by the Victorians, a few crow-stepped gables thrown into the mix as a nod towards its Scottish heritage. The car crunched across a gravel drive where three cars were currently parked, one of them a large black Mercedes, its bodywork gleaming under the moonlight.

'Someone's at home, then,' he said.

'Only natural for family and friends to gather together after a death,' Giles agreed as they made their way to the big house. 'But I'd be interested to know who these belong to,' he added, taking out his mobile. 'Give me a minute and I'll pass on their registration numbers.'

Although it was after ten o'clock, lights streamed out from several windows, much to Lorimer's relief. It had been his own decision not to call ahead, his desire to see Malcolm Hinchliffe face to face as he told him the latest news about Robert Truesdale, or as much of it that he wanted the man to hear. And DS Giles and he would be taking note of every little detail and nuance of Hinchliffe's behaviour.

There was a bell pull to one side that struck a sonorous note, reverberating through the night as Lorimer tugged it.

They did not have long to wait. He imagined the sound of footsteps and then the large doors opened and he saw Malcolm Hinchliffe standing there in a pool of light.

'Lorimer!' The man took a step forward, then stopped, mouth open in astonishment as Giles also emerged by his side. Then, as if remembering his manners, he beckoned them inside.

'DS David Giles. I don't believe you have met before,' Lorimer said, introducing his fellow officer.

'What brings you to Woodend House?' Malcolm Hinchliffe asked, his eyes narrowing as he looked at the tall detective and his younger colleague.

'My condolences,' Lorimer said, offering his hand to the other man. 'I heard about your father.'

'Yes, thank you. Difficult time, you know . . .' Hinchliffe

stared at them, frowning. 'It's rather late to come all this way to offer your condolences, Lorimer. So, I'm guessing there is another reason for your visit.'

'You are right,' Lorimer replied smoothly. 'Is there somewhere we can talk in private?'

The room Hinchliffe ushered them into was carpeted in a rich floral pattern, possibly dating from around the Arts and Crafts period, Lorimer thought, taking in a large walnut sideboard that sported several ornate and rather garish green and crimson vases. Oil paintings of landscapes hung on every wall and the delicately carved occasional chairs, with silken seat covers, were obviously from a bygone era. It was a room well worth studying and his first impression was that there might be a small fortune in the antiques and paintings right here, never mind the rest of the place. Lorimer had ditched his degree course in fine art to become a police officer, a decision he had rarely regretted, but he had never lost his eye for quality pieces like these.

'What is this all about?' Hinchliffe asked, a querulous note in his voice.

'I am sorry to disturb you at this hour,' Lorimer apologised, taking a seat at a circular table draped with a snow-white linen cover, and stretching out his long legs. 'We needed to talk to you about Robert Truesdale.'

'Well, it's jolly poor timing,' Hinchliffe objected, folding his arms and frowning at the two police officers. 'My wife and I have visitors right now. Father's death and everything . . .' He gave a slight shrug.

'Again, I apologise, but it is something that could not wait.'

'Very well, then. But I must inform the others of this unexpected interruption,' Hinchliffe insisted, backing out of the room. 'Can't allow my guests to ... well ...' He tailed off as he disappeared from the room.

'Any joy?' Lorimer whispered as Giles took out his mobile once more.

His detective sergeant nodded, eyes fixed on the small screen. 'Here, take a look at this.'

'Whew.' Lorimer gave a quiet whistle. 'What were the chances? Time to rally the troops, eh?'

By the time that Malcolm Hinchliffe returned, Lorimer had made the necessary calls, alerting every division in the area as well as his own team from the MIT. They would not be the only unexpected guests that the new owner of Woodend House would be receiving tonight, he thought, standing as the man re-entered the room.

'Right,' Hinchliffe said, drawing closer to the table. 'Can you make this quick, please?'

Lorimer gave him a smile, seeing the beads of perspiration on the man's forehead. He was right to be sweating, he thought, given just who was amongst his guests.

'It's about Robert Truesdale, of course,' Lorimer said. 'We spoke to him earlier today.'

'You what?' Hinchliffe's face paled. 'But how ...?'

'How did he get off the island of Colonsay when the boat wasn't due for another day?' Lorimer chuckled.

Hinchliffe fell silent, staring at the two men, his eyes darting from one to the other.

'Truesdale came home,' Lorimer explained. 'Got fed up

407

waiting, I guess, or became a bit mad all alone with no way of communicating with the outside world. Can't imagine what that could do to a politician who needs to know everything that is happening. Might very well make a man snap, don't you think?' He turned to ask Giles.

'Aye, that would do it for most folk,' Giles agreed. 'Especially if they're paranoid to begin with.'

'He told us all about his experiences,' Lorimer continued, watching Hinchliffe intently. 'So, we are here to ask you just what your own involvement is with a certain Colombian gentleman named Vallejo.'

There was a moment when Lorimer thought that Hinchliffe might simply collapse onto the floor, his face a ghastly shade of grey.

But then he turned and ran from the room, Giles and Lorimer in hot pursuit.

There was a shout from somewhere up above then Hinchliffe rushed out of the house, leaving the door wide open.

'Stop, Hinchliffe, it's all over!' Lorimer called out as he saw the man race across the gravel and head for a large expanse of lawn surrounded by trees.

In several quick strides he had caught up with the man, grabbing at his ankles, a perfect rugby tackle felling him.

Somewhere in the distance he could hear the sound of sirens, reinforcements on their way from the nearby town.

'Get Vallejo!' he shouted at Giles, who disappeared back into the house. 'Don't let him get away!'

He heard the man beneath him groan as he pulled his wrists back, clipping on the cuffs with a snap.

As he hauled the man to his feet, Lorimer looked towards the big house, its door flooded with light. A dark-haired woman in evening dress stood motionless, her handsome face regarding them dispassionately.

'Simone!' Hinchliffe cried out.

But the woman merely turned away and disappeared into the house.

'Not the best day you've had for a while, is it, Malcolm?' he ventured, hauling the man to his feet. 'And it's not over yet. There's an awful lot of explaining to do.'

CHAPTER FIFTY-NINE

Maggie Lorimer rolled onto her side, suddenly awake. She heard the familiar sound of his key in the door. The long sigh she breathed was one of relief after two nights spent alone without her husband. Bill had filled her in on the main parts of the arrests but Maggie was keen to hear the latest details.

She threw back the duvet as he entered the bedroom.

'Sorry, did I disturb you?' she heard him whisper.

'No,' Maggie replied. 'Come to bed, you must be freezing.'

In moments he'd stripped off his clothes and he was clasping her in his arms. She gave a yelp as his cold feet touched her legs.

'Sorry,' he laughed.

'Don't mind,' Maggie said, snuggling against him. 'Cuddle in and tell me all that's been going on.'

*

He was sound asleep as daylight began to break, Maggie drowsing by his side, thinking of the tale she had been told. A tale of such evil intent that it had taken her breath away. It had been a plot to incriminate Truesdale all along. She had gasped as Bill had related the extent to which Malcolm Hinchliffe had gone in order to create the false impression that his boss was in cahoots with a drug cartel and had been the instigator of the car bomb that had killed James O'Hare.

She remembered the pause in Bill's story as he recounted the moment he had pulled Malcolm Hinchliffe back from the ground. '"I look down towards his feet, but that's a fable."' He had quoted the lines referring to Iago, the arch villain of Shakespeare's *Othello*, so evil in his plotted downfall of his own boss that he seemed almost diabolic. It would be hard to teach that particular play now to her seniors without thinking of the man who had destroyed an innocent life and tried to ruin another's reputation.

Tomorrow Bill would be meeting the First Minister out at Tulliallan Castle in the company of Chief Constable Flint, and Maggie wondered just what those two leaders would make of the man who had helped solve this twisted case. Facing dangerous criminals came at a cost, as Daniel Kohi had learned, something that her own husband knew only too well. Perhaps, a little voice suggested, he might want to retire after this?

Tulliallan seemed like a strong fortress against the outside world, the trees now mostly bare, drifts of leaves sweeping across the pathways. He had passed the training college where Daniel had spent several weeks preparing for his new life in Police Scotland, a job that was already bringing the former inspector from Zimbabwe to the notice of many of his superiors. A commendation had been suggested and Lorimer would be happy to see that take place after his friend's contribution to uncovering the drugs haul.

He walked through the familiar corridors till he reached Caroline Flint's office. Straightening his tie, he knocked before entering the Chief Constable's domain.

'Lorimer, welcome.' Flint smiled up at him.

Calum McKenzie rose from his place by the window and crossed the room, taking Lorimer's hand in a firm clasp.

'I can't tell you how grateful we all are,' he began.

Lorimer resisted a cynical smile; the police press office had kept certain details from the media until such times as the trials began. Meantime, the public knew that there had been several major arrests, Vallejo and Hinchliffe's names to the fore, though the Zimbabwean and his cohorts had not escaped a mention in the news.

'Thank you. The members of my team will be pleased to hear that,' he said.

'And PC Kohi,' Flint put in. 'He is proving his worth in the short time he has been part of the force,' she added warmly.

'How did you guess that it was Hinchliffe behind it all and not Robert Truesdale?' McKenzie wanted to know.

Lorimer sat down next to the two senior figures, aware that it had been partly his own careful study of the case that had led him to this conclusion.

'Hinchliffe gave me verbal information but nothing that could be taken to a court in evidence,' he began. 'I thought it a trifle odd at the time that he mentioned a Colombian postage stamp that had the illustration of a bird. It was almost as if he were pandering to my own particular interest. Could have been a coincidence, of course.

'Then there was Truesdale himself. Why had he returned to Glasgow? Why seek out his old neighbour rather than find the same people who had assured him of their protection?'

'Hinchliffe's mob?'

Lorimer nodded. 'Hinchliffe was clever, though. He made sure never to be seen in the company of anyone other than Vallejo and even then, it was much closer to home, never in Edinburgh. We know from Des Morrison that Ncube was trying to take over several of the existing drug operations in the city. Frankie Fleming had been selling the Colombian product but was beginning to get too big for their liking. Take out the competition, that was what Ncube had been told. And meantime, Morrison kept an eye open on them all, passing information back to Malcolm Hinchliffe, even though he never knew the man by name.'

'He'll go down for a long time?' McKenzie asked and Lorimer nodded. Morrison had known better than to try and hide his own part in it all, the last forty-eight hours spent interrogating the men included time spent ferreting out the truth from Jack Gallagher's former henchman. Like most criminals who tried to put up a smokescreen of respectability, Morrison had only partially succeeded, his nefarious ways continuing behind the façade of a legitimate fish and chip shop business.

'As will the rest of them,' Flint assured him. 'Turns out that Hinchliffe's wife, Simone, is actually Colombian, not Venezuelan as her Wikipedia page asserts.'

413

Lorimer nodded, remembering the beautiful woman standing watching impassively as her husband and Vallejo were driven away in a police car. More digging might well reveal her part in all of this but that remained to be seen.

'Well, the Scottish Parliament is grateful for all that you and your people have done,' McKenzie told them. 'Robert never did manage to send that letter of resignation but I believe he still wishes to retire from politics.'

Lorimer thought about the broken man who had fled to the one woman he could trust, Karen Douglas. Neither had ever married. Had they been childhood sweethearts? Maggie had asked him the previous night. Perhaps, he'd replied, but that was something he might never know. Truesdale was currently undergoing some rehabilitation in a facility in Glasgow, Karen visiting him every day.

'The little boy,' Lorimer began. 'What is to happen to Angelika and James's child?'

'He's going home to Athlone soon,' Flint told him. 'Fostered at first, but hopefully adopted into the family in Ireland. These things take time but a year from now he may very well be with his aunt and cousins, never knowing they're not his own big sisters.'

That was one satisfactory ending, Lorimer thought, remembering the woman in Athlone and the large garden with its climbing frame.

'They're calling him James,' Flint added. 'Fitting, don't you think?'

Lorimer swallowed down a sudden lump in his throat. It had been a long few days and exhaustion was beginning to make him feel a little frayed around the edges.

'Time off for you, I think, Detective Superintendent,' Flint told him firmly.

'A holiday?' McKenzie asked.

Lorimer shook his head. 'Just a few days' rest,' he told them. 'I'm owed some leave.'

He planned to take time during these next days to see Daniel safely home from hospital. His injuries would heal in time, and he guessed that Netta was already fussing over him as they prepared to move into the new flat. That was also something he could help with, Lorimer thought. It would be a new start for the old lady and Daniel. And, with Molly now a large part of his life, he knew that his friend would recover, strengthened by his experiences.

As he walked back down to where he had parked the Lexus, Lorimer looked up, the cry of the oystercatchers alerting him to their flight. They were the symbol of the college here, the motto 'Be wise, be wise' in Gaelic mimicking their cry.

Others would come here to begin their training, following in his own footsteps, the path of law and order chosen by men and women intent on making a difference.

ACKNOWLEDGEMENTS

Oh, Police Scotland! What a lot I owe to so many of your officers. Firstly, to Chief Constable Sir Iain Livingstone for allowing me access to everything I seem to request! Thank you, so much. To Superintendent Rob Hay, huge thanks not only for allowing me access to a passing-out parade at Tulliallan and showing me around the college, but also for giving me precious insights into the weeks of training that go into making a man or woman ready to become a police officer here in Scotland. To Sandra Deslandes-Clark for her warmth and enthusiasm in helping me to understand the lives of officers from different ethnic minorities. Thanks to those officers at Jackton training college, particularly Jen Steven, Kirsty O'Hare, Danny and Alan for all the detailed information about how a police officer begins their journey as well as demonstrating elements of the necessary kit. Once again, I found the philosophy behind policing in Scotland is underpinned by a duty of care to all fellow citizens. Thanks to former DCI Bob Frew for always being

417

there to answer questions, especially about the MIT, and for former DS Mairi Milne, who is a great help with procedural details.

As always, I am very grateful for the guidance of my friend, consultant pathologist Dr Marjorie Turner.

To Magnus Linklater, for the informative article in *The Times* regarding how decades of cuts in other sectors seriously affect the fight against crime. Reading reports about real issues and cases really does make a difference in authenticating a story.

Thanks to grandson, Blake, for the character of Sally. That was very helpful. Thanks to daughter, Suzy, for suggesting my old friend Nicola Morgan's novel *Fleshmarket*. That fitted the bill nicely as a book for first years.

Huge thanks to former ballistics expert and friend Alistair Paton for the remark he made one lunchtime that unplugged a blockage in my plot. I am so grateful for your help, Alistair, and for always lending me books about interesting things like gunpowder. And for knowing so much more about bombs than I do.

As ever, my thanks to Dr Jenny Brown, best agent in the world and a dear friend who is always there to cheer me on. Thanks to the editorial team at Sphere, especially my brilliant editor Rosanna as well as Cath, Millie, Brionee, Emma, Rebecca, Liz, Ben, Jon, Suzy and Sean. May I make a mention of dear Thalia Proctor, whose untimely death has robbed us all of a fabulous copy editor and good friend. If there is a library in heaven, I hope you'll approve of this one, Thal.

Thanks to all my readers whose support and

encouragement keep me going. It has been marvellous catching up with so many of you as festivals and talks open up once more.

Last, but by no means least, thanks to Donnie, the world's best and most patient roadie. Bless you.

Alex Gray 2022